THE WORKS OF CHARLES DICKENS

HOUSEHOLD EDITION

OLIVER TWIST

NEW-YORK.
HARPER & BROTHERS
FRANKLIN SQUARE

CHARLES DICKENS.

THE ADVENTURES

OF

OLIVER TWIST.

BY

CHARLES DICKENS.

WITH TWENTY-EIGHT ILLUSTRATIONS BY J. MAHONEY.

NEW YORK:

HARPER & BROTHERS, PUBLISHERS,

FRANKLIN SQUARE.

1872.

PREFACE.

ONCE upon a time it was held to be a coarse and shocking circumstance, that some of the characters in these pages are chosen from the most criminal and degraded of London's population.

As I saw no reason, when I wrote this book, why the dregs of life (so long as their speech did not offend the ear) should not serve the purpose of a moral, as well as its froth and cream, I made bold to believe that this same Once upon a time would not prove to be All-time or even a long time. I saw many strong reasons for pursuing my course. I had read of thieves by scores; seductive fellows (amia ble for the most part), faultless in dress, plump in pocket, choice in horse-flesh, bold in bearing, fortunate in gallantry, great at a song, a bottle, pack of cards or dice-box, and fit companions for the bravest. But I had never met (except in HOGARTH) with the miserable reality. It appeared to me that to draw a knot of such associates in crime as really did exist; to paint them in all their deformity, in all their wretchedness, in all the squalid misery of their lives; to show them as they really were, forever skulking uneasily through the dirtiest paths of life, with the great black ghastly gallows closing up their prospect, turn them where they might; it appeared to me that to do this would be to attempt a something which was needed, and which would be a service to society. And I did it as I best could.

In every book I know, where such characters are treated of, allurements and fascinations are thrown around them. Even in the Beggars' Opera, the thieves are represented as leading a life which is rather to be envied than otherwise: while MACHEATH, with all the captivations of command, and the devotion of the most beautiful girl and only pure character in the piece, is as much to be admired and emulated by weak beholders, as any fine gentleman in a red coat who has purchased, as VOLTAIRE says, the right to command a couple of thousand men, or so, and to affront death at their head. Johnson's question, whether any man will turn thief because Macheath is reprieved, seems to me beside the matter. I ask myself, whether any man will be deterred from turning thief because of Macheath's being sentenced to death, and because of the existence of Peachum and Lockit; and remembering the captain's roaring life, great appearance, vast success, and strong advantages, I feel assured that nobody having a bent that way will take any warning from him, or will see any thing in the play but a flowery and pleasant road, con ducting an honorable ambition—in course of time—to Tyburn Tree.

In fact, Gay's witty satire on society had a general object, which made him quite regardless of example in this respect, and gave him other and wider aims. The same may be said of Sir Edward Bulwer's admirable and powerful novel of Paul Clifford, which can not be fairly considered as having, or as being intended to have, any bearing on this part of the subject, one way or other.

What manner of life is that which is described in these pages, as the every-day existence of a Thief? What charms has it for the young and ill-disposed, what allurements for the most jolter-headed of juve niles ? Here are no canterings on moonlit heaths, no merry-makings in the snuggest of all possible cav erns, none of the attractions of dress, no embroidery, no lace, no jack-boots, no crimson coats and ruffles, none of the dash and freedom with which " the road " has been time out of mind invested. The cold, wet, shelterless midnight streets of London; the foul and frowzy dens, where vice is closely packed and lacks the room to turn; the haunts of hunger and disease; the shabby rags that scarcely hold together; where are the attractions of these things ?

There are people, however, of so refined and delicate a nature, that they can not bear the contemplation of such horrors. Not that they turn instinctively from crime; but that criminal characters, to suit them, must be, like their meat, in delicate disguise. A Massaroni in green velvet is an enchanting creature;

but a Sikes in fustian is insupportable. A Mrs. Massaroni, being a lady in short petticoats and a fancy dress, is a thing to imitate in tableaux and have in lithograph on pretty songs ; but a Nancy, being a creature in a cotton gown and cheap shawl, is not to be thought of. It is wonderful how Virtue turns from dirty stockings; and how Vice, married to ribbons and a little gay attire, changes her name, as wedded ladies do, and becomes Romance.

But as the stern truth, even in the dress of this (in novels) much exalted race, was a part of the purpose of this book, I did not, for these readers, abate one hole in the Dodger's coat, or one scrap of curl-paper in Nancy's disheveled hair. I had no faith in the delicacy which could not bear to look upon them. I had no desire to make proselytes among such people. I had no respect for their opinion, good or bad; did not covet their approval; and did not write for their amusement.

It has been observed of Nancy that her devotion to the brutal house-breaker does not seem natural. And it has been objected to Sikes in the same breath—with some inconsistency, as I venture to think— that he is surely overdrawn, because in him there would appear to be none of those redeeming traits which are objected to as unnatural in his mistress. Of the latter objection I will merely remark, that I fear there are in the world some insensible and callous natures, that do become utterly and incurably bad. Whether this be so or not, of one thing I am certain: that there are such men as Sikes, who, being closely followed through the same space of time and through the same current of circumstances, would not give, by the action of a moment, the faintest indication of a better nature. Whether every gentler human feeling is dead within such bosoms, or the proper chord to strike has rusted and is hard to find, I do not pretend to know ; but that the fact is as I state it, I am sure.

It is useless to discuss whether the conduct and character of the girl seems natural or unnatural, prob able or improbable, right or wrong. IT is TRUE. Every man who has watched these melancholy shades of life, must know it to be so. From the first introduction of that poor wretch, to her laying her blood stained head upon the robber's breast, there is not a word exaggerated or overwrought. It is emphat ically God's truth, for it is the truth He leaves in such depraved and miserable breasts ; the hope yet lingering there ; the last fair drop of water at the bottom of the weed-choked well. It involves the best and worst shades of our nature; much of its ugliest hues, and something of its most beautiful ; it is a contradiction, an anomaly, an apparent impossibility; but it is a truth. I am glad to have had it doubt ed, for in that circumstance I should find a sufficient assurance (if I wanted any) that it needed to be told.

In the year one thousand eight hundred and fifty, it was publicly declared in London by an amazing Alderman, that Jacob's Island did not exist, and never had existed. Jacob's Island continues to exist (like an ill-bred place as it is) in the year one thousand eight hundred and sixty-seven, though improved and much changed.

OLIVER TWIST.

CHAPTER I.

TREATS OF THE PLACE WHERE OLIVER TWIST WAS BORN, AND OF THE CIRCUMSTANCES ATTENDING HIS BIRTH.

MONO other public buildings in a certain town, which for many reasons it will be prudent to refrain from mentioning, and to which I will assign no fictitious name, there is one anciently common to most towns, great or small: to wit, a work-house; and in this work-house was born—on a day and date which I need not trouble myself to repeat, inasmuch as it can be of no possible consequence .to the reader, in this stage of the business at all events the item of mortality whose name is prefixed to the head of this chapter.

For a long time after it was ushered into this world of sorrow and trouble, by the parish surgeon, it remained a matter of considerable doubt whether the child would survive to bear any name at all; in which case it is somewhat more than probable that these memoirs would never have appeared; or, if

they had, that being comprised within a couple of pages, they would have possessed the inestimable merit of being the most concise and faithful speci men of biography extant in the literature of any age or country.

Although I am not disposed to maintain that the being born in a work-house, is in itself the most for tunate and enviable circumstance that can possibly befall a human being, I do mean to say that in this particular instance, it was the best thing for Oliver Twist that could by possibility have occurred. The fact is, that there was considerable difficulty in inducing Oliver to take upon himself the office of respiration,a troublesome practice, but one which custom has rendered necessary to our easy existence; and for some time he lay gasping on a little flock mattress, rather unequally poised between this world and the next: the balance being decidedly in favor of the latter. Now, if, during this brief period, Oliver had been surrounded by careful grandmothers, anxious aunts, experienced nurses, and doctors of

OLIVER TWIST.

profound wisdom, he would most inevitably and in dubitably have been killed in no time. There being nobody by, however, but a pauper old woman, who was rendered rather misty by an unwonted allow ance of beer; and a parish surgeon who did such matters by contract; Oliver and Nature fought out the point between them. The result was, that, after a few struggles, Oliver breathed, sneezed, and pro ceeded to advertise to the inmates of the work-house the fact of a new burden having been imposed upon the parish, by setting up as loud a cry as could rea sonably have been expected from a male infant who had not been possessed of that very useful append age, a voice, for a much longer space of time than three minutes and a quarter.

As Oliver gave this first proof of the free and proper action of his lungs, the patchwork coverlet which was carelessly flung over the iron bedstead, rustled; the pale face of a young woman was raised feebly from the pillow; and a faint voice imperfect ly articulated the words, " Let me see the child, and die."

The surgeon had been sitting with his face turned toward the fire: giving the palms of his hands a warm and a rub alternately. As the young woman spoke, he rose, and advancing to the bed's head, said, with more kindness than might have been expected of him:

" Oh, you must not talk about dying yet."

"Lor bless her dear heart, no!" interposed the nurse, hastily depositing in her pocket a green glass bottle, the contents of which she had been tasting in a corner with evident satisfaction. " Lor bless her dear heart, when she has lived as long as I have, sir, and had thirteen children of her own, and all on 'em dead except two, and them in the wurkus with me, she'll know better than to take on in that way, bless her dear heart! Think what it is to be a mother, there's a dear young lamb, do."

Apparently this consolatory perspective of a moth er's prospects failed in producing its due effect. The patient shook her head, and stretched out her hand toward the child.

The surgeon deposited it in her arms. She im printed her cold white lips passionately on its fore head ; passed her hands over her face; gazed wild ly round; shuddered; fell back — and died. They chafed her breast, hands, and temples; but the blood had stopped forever. They talked of hope and com fort. They had been strangers too long.

" It's all over, Mrs. Thingummy!" said the surgeon at last.

" Ah, poor dear, so it is!" said the nurse, picking up the cork of the green bottle, which had fallen out on the pillow, as she stooped to take up the child. "Poor dear!"

" You needn't mind sending up to me, if the child cries, nurse," said the surgeon, putting on his gloves with great deliberation. " It's very likely it will be troublesome. Give it a little gruel if it is." He put on his hat, and, pausing by the bedside on his way to the door, added, " She was a good-looking girl, too; where did she come from ?"

" She was brought here last night," replied the old woman, "by the overseer's order. She was found lying in the street. She had walked some distance,

for her shoes were worn to pieces; but where she came from, or where she was going to, nobody knows."

The surgeon leaned over the body, and raised the left hand. " The old story," he said, shaking his head: " no wedding-ring, I see. Ah! Good-night!"

The medical gentleman walked away to dinner; and the nurse, having once more applied herself to the green bottle, sat down on a low chair before the fire, and proceeded to dress the infant.

What an excellent example of the power of dress, young Oliver Twist was! Wrapped in the blanket which had hitherto formed his only covering, he might have been the child of a nobleman or a beg gar; it would have been hard for the haughtiest stranger to have assigned him his proper station in society. But now that he was enveloped in the old calico robes which had grown yellow in the same service, he was badged and ticketed, and fell into his place at once a parish child the orphan of a work house the humble, half-starved drudge to be cuft-cd and buffeted through the world despised by all, and pitied by none.

Oliver cried lustily. If he could have known that ho ovns an orphan, left to the tender mercies of church wardens and overseers, perhaps he would have cried the louder.

CHAPTER II.

TREATS OF OLIVER TWIST'S GROWTH, EDUCATION, AND BOARD.

FOR the next eight or ten months, Oliver was the victim of a systematic course of treachery and deception. He was brought up by hand. The hun gry and destitute situation of the infant orphan was duly reported by the work-house authorities to the parish authorities. The parish authorities inquired with dignity of the work-house authorities whether there was no female then domiciled " in the house " who was in a situation to impart to Oliver Twist the consolation and nourishment of which he stood in need. The work-house authorities replied with hu mility, that there was not. Upon this, the parish au thorities magnanimously and humanely resolved that Oliver should be " farmed," or, in other words, that he should be dispatched to a branch work-house some three miles off, where twenty or thirty other juvenile offenders against the poor-laws, rolled about the floor all day, without the inconvenience of too much food or too much clothing, under the parental superin tendence of an elderly female, who received the cul prits at and for the consideration of sevenpence-half-penny per small head per week. Sevenpence-half-penny's worth per week is a good round diet for a child; a great deal may be got for sevenpence-half-penny, quite enough to overload its stomach, and make it uncomfortable. The elderly female was a woman of wisdom and experience; she knew what was good for children; and she had a very accurate perception of what was good for herself. So she ap propriated the greater part of the weekly stipend to her own use, and consigned the rising parochial gen eration to even a shorter allowance than was orig inally provided for them. Thereby finding in the

STARVATION OF THE HERO.

lowest depth a deeper still; and proving herself a very great experimental philosopher.

Every body knows the story of another experi mental philosopher who had a great theory about a horse being able to live without eating, and who demonstrated it so well, that he 'got his own horse down to a straw a day, and would unquestionably have rendered him a very spirited and rampacious animal on nothing at all, if he had not died, four-and-twenty hours before he was to have had his first comfortable bait of air. Unfortunately for the ex perimental philosophy of the female to whose pro tecting care Oliver Twist was delivered over, a sim ilar result usually attended the operation of her sys tem ; for at the very moment when a child had con trived to exist upon the smallest possible portion of the weakest possible food, it did perversely happen in eight and a half cases out of ten, either that it sickened from want or cold, or fell into the fire from neglect, or got half-smothered by accident; in any one of which cases, the miserable little being was usually summoned into another world, and there gathered to the fathers it had never known in this.

Occasionally, when there was some more than usually interesting inquest upon a parish child, who had been overlooked in turning up a bedstead, or in advertently scalded to death when there happened to be a washing   though the latter accident was very scarce, any thing approaching to a washing be ing of rare occurrence in the farm the jury would take it into their heads to ask troublesome ques tions, or the parishioners would rebelliously affix their signatures to a remonstrance. But these im pertinences were speedily checked by the evidence of the surgeon, and the testimony of the beadle; the former of whom had always opened the body and found nothing inside (which was very probable in deed), and the latter of whom invariably swore what ever the parish wanted; which was very self-devo tional. Besides, the board made periodical pilgrim ages to the farm, and always sent the beadle the day before, to say they were going. The children were neat and clean to behold when they went; and what more would the people have!

It can not be expected that this system of farming would produce any very extraordinary or luxuriant crop. Oliver Twist's ninth birthday found him a pale, thin child, somewhat diminutive in stature, and decidedly small in circumference. But nature or in heritance had implanted a good sturdy spirit in Oli ver's breast. It had had plenty room to expand, thanks to the spare diet of the establishment; and perhaps to this circumstance may be attributed his having any ninth birthday at all. Be this as it may, however, it was his ninth birthday; and he was keep ing it in the coal-cellar with a select party of two other young gentlemen, Avho, after participating with him in a sound thrashing, had been locked up for atrociously presuming to be hungry, when Mrs. Mann, the good lady of the house, was unexpectedly start led by the apparition of Mr. Bumble, the beadle, striving to undo the wicket of the garden-gate.

"Goodness gracious! Is that you, Mr. Bumble, sir ?" said Mrs. Mann, thrusting her head out of the window in well-affected ecstasies of joy. " (Susan, take Oliver and them two brats up stairs and wash

'em directly.) My heart alive! Mr. Bumble, how glad I am to see you, sure-ly!"

Now, Mr. Bumble was a fat man, and a choleric; so, instead of responding to this open-hearted salu tation in a kindred spirit, he gave the little wicket a tremendous shake, and then bestowed upon it a kick which could have emanated from no leg but a beadle's.

" Lor, only think," said Mrs. Mann, running out, for the three boys had been removed by this time,— " only think of that! That I should have forgotten that the gate was bolted on the inside, on account of them dear children! Walk in, sir; walk in pray, Mr. Bumble, do, sir."

Although this invitation was accompanied with a courtesy that might have softened the heart of a church-warden, it by no means mollified the beadle.

" Do you think this respectful or proper conduct, Mrs. Mann," inquired Mr. Bumble, grasping his cane, " to keep the parish officers a-waiting at your gar den-gate, when they come here upon porochial busi ness connected with the porochial orphans? Are you aweer, Mrs. Mann, that you are, as I may say, a porochial delegate, and a stipendiary ?"

" I'm sure, Mr. Bumble, that I was only a-telling one or two of the dear children as is so fond of you, that it was you a-coming," replied Mrs. Mann, with great humility.

Mr. Bumble had a great idea of his oratorical pow ers and his importance. He had displayed the one, and vindicated the other. He relaxed.

" Well, well, Mrs. Mann," he replied, in a calmer tone; " it may be as you say; it may be. Lead the way in, Mrs. Mann, for I come on business, and have something to say."

Mrs. Mann ushered the beadle into a small parlor with a brick floor; placed a seat for bim ; and offi ciously deposited his cocked hat and cane on the ta ble before him. Mr. Bumble wiped from his fore head the perspiration which his walk had engender ed, glanced complacently at the cocked hat, and smiled. Yes, he smiled. Beadles are but men: and Mr. Bumble smiled.

" Now don't you be offended at what I'm a-going to say," observed Mrs. Mann, with a captivating sweetness. " You've had a long walk, you know, or I wouldn't mention it. Now, will you take a little drop of somethink, Mr. Bumble."

" Not a drop. Not a drop," said Mr. Bumble, waving his right hand in a dignified, but placid manner.

" I think yon will," said Mrs. Mann, who had no ticed the tone of the refusal, and the gesture that had accompanied it. " Just a leetle drop, with a lit tle cold water, and a lump of sugar."

Mr. Bumble'coughed.

"Now, just a leetle drop," said Mrs. Mann, persua sively.

" What is it ?" inquired the beadle.

" Why, it's what I'm obliged to keep a little of in the house, to put into the blessed infants' Daffy, when they ain't well, Mr. Bumble," replied Mrs. Mann, as she opened a corner cupboard and took down a bot tle and glass. " It's gin. I'll not deceive you, Mr. B. It's gin."

" Do you give the children Daffy, Mrs. Mann ?" in-

OLIVER TWIST.

quired Bumble, following with his eyes the interest ing process of mixing.

" Ah, bless 'em, that I do, dear as it is," replied the nurse. "I couldn't see 'em suffer before my very eyes, you know, sir."

"No," said Mr. Bumble, approvingly; "no, you could not. You are a humane woman, Mrs. Mann." (Here she set down the glass.) "I shall take a early opportunity of mentioning it to the board, Mrs. Mann." (He drew it toward him.) "You feel as a mother, Mrs. Mann." (He stirred the gin-and-wa-ter.) " I—I drink your health with cheerfulness, Mrs. Maun;" and he swallowed half of it.

" And now about business," said the beadle, tak ing out a leathern pocket-book. "The child that was half-baptized Oliver Twist, is nine year old to day."

" Bless him!" interposed Mrs. Mann, inflaming her left eye with the corner of her apron.

"And notwithstanding a offered reward of ten pound, which was afterward increased to twenty pound. Notwithstanding the most superlative, and, I may say, supernat'ral exertions on the part of this parish," said Bumble, " we have never been able to discover who is his father, or what w r as his mother's settlemept, name, or con—dition."

Mrs. Mann raised her hands in astonishment; but added, after a moment's reflection, " How comes he to have any name at all, then ?"

The beadle drew himself up with great pride, and said, " I iuwented it."

" You, Mr. Bumble!"

" I, Mrs. Mann. We name our foundlings in al phabetical order. The last was a S— Swubble, I named him. This was a T — Twist, I named Mm. The next one as comes will be Unwin, and the next Vilkins. I have got names ready made to the end of the alphabet, and all the way through it again, when we come to Z."

" Why, you are quite a literary character, sir!" said Mrs. Mann.

"Well, well," said the beadle, evidently gratified with the compliment; " perhaps I may be. ferhaps I may be, Mrs. Mann." He finished the gin-and-wa-ter, and added, " Oliver being now too old to remain here, the board have determined to have him back into the house. I have come out myself to take him there. So let me see him at once."

" I'll fetch him directly," said Mrs. Mann, leaving the room for that purpose. Oliver, having had by this time as much of the outer coat of dirt which incrusted his face and hands, removed, as could be scrubbed off in one washing, was led into the room by his benevolent protectress.

" Make a bow to the gentleman, Oliver," said Mrs. Mann.

Oliver made a bow, which was divided between the beadle on the chair, and the cocked hat on the table.

" Will you go along with me, Oliver ?" said Mr. Bumble, in a majestic voice.

Oliver was about to say that he would go along with any body with great readiness, when, glancing upward, he caught sight of Mrs. Mann, who had got behind the beadle's chair, and was shaking her fist at him with a furious countenance. He took the hint at once, for the fist had been too often impress ed upon his body not to be deeply impressed upon his recollection.

" Will she go with me ?" inquired poor Oliver.

" No, she can't," replied Mr. Bumble. " But she'll come and see you sometimes."

This was no very great consolation to the child. Young as he was, however, he had sense enough to make a feint of feeling great regret at going away. It was no very difficult matter for the boy to call tears into his eyes. Hunger and recent ill-usage are great assistants if you want to cry; and Oliver cried very naturally indeed. Mrs. Mann gave him a thou sand embraces, and, what Oliver wanted a great deal more, a piece of bread-and-butter, lest he should si-cm too hungry when he got to the work-house. With the slice of bread in his hand, and the little brown-cloth parish cap on his head, Oliver was then led away by Mr. Bumble from the wretched home Avhcrr one kind word or look had never lighted the gloom of his infant years. And yet he burst into an agony of childish grief, as the cottage-gate closed after him. Wretched as were the little companions in misery he was leaving behind, they were the only friends he had ever known; and a sense of his loneliness in the great wide world, sank into the child's heart for the first time.

Mr. Bumble walked on with long strides; little Oliver, firmly grasping his gold - laced cuff, trotted beside him, inquiring at the end of every quarter of a mile whether they were " nearly there." To these interrogations Mr. Bumble returned very brief and snappish replies; for the temporary blandness which gin-and-water awakens in some bosoms had by this time evaporated; and he was once again a beadle.

Oliver had not been within the walls of the work house a quarter of an hour, and had scarcely com pleted the demolition of a second slice of bread, when Mr. Bumble, who had handed him over to the care of an old woman, returned; and, telling him it was a board night, informed him that the board had said he was to appear before it forthwith.

. Not having a very clearly defined notion of what a live board was, Oliver was rather astounded by this intelligence, and was not quite certain whether he ought to laugh or cry. He had no time to think about the matter, however; for Mr. Bumble gave him a tap on the head with his cane, to wake him up: and another oil the back to make him lively: and bidding him follow, conducted him into a large whitewashed room, where eight or ten fat gentlemen were sitting round a table. At the top of the table, seated in an arm-chair rather higher than the rest, was a particularly fat gentleman with a very round, red face.

" Bow to the board," said Bumble. Oliver brush ed away two or three tears that were lingering in his eyes; and seeing no board but the table, fortu nately bowed to that.

" What's your name, boy ?" said the gentleman in the high chair.

Oliver was frightened at the sight of so many gen tlemen, which made him tremble: and the beadle gave him another tap behind, which made him cry. These two causes made him answer in a very low and hesitating voice; whereupon a gentleman in a

BEFORE THE BOARD.

white waistcoat said he was a fool. Which was a capital way of raising his spirits, aud putting him quite at his case.

" Boy," said the gentleman in the high chair, " list en to me. You know you're an orphan, I suppose ?"

" What's that, sir?" inquired poor Oliver.

" The boy is a fool I thought he was," said the gentleman in the white waistcoat.

" Hush!" said the gentleman who had spoken first. " You know you've got no father or mother, and that you were brought up by the parish, don't you ?"

" Yes, sir," replied Oliver, weeping bitterly.

" What are you crying for ?" inquired the gentle man in the white waistcoat. And to be sure it was very extraordinary. What could the boy be crying for!

" I hope you say your prayers every night," said another gentleman, in a gruff voice; " and pray for the people who feed you and take care of you—like a Christian."

" Yes, sir," stammered the boy. The gentleman who spoke last was unconsciously right. It would have been very like a Christian, and a marvelously good Christian, too, if Oliver had prayed for the peo ple who fed and took care of Mm. But he hadn't, because nobody had taught him.

" Well! You have come here to be educated, and taught a useful trade," said the red-faced gentleman in the high chair.

" So you'll begin to pick oakum to-morrow morn ing at six o'clock," added the surly one in the white waistcoat.

For the combination of both these blessings in the one simple process of picking oakum, Oliver bowed low by the direction of the beadle, and was then hur ried away to a large ward: where, on a rough, hard bed, he sobbed himself to sleep. What a noble illus tration of the tender laws of England! They let the paupers go to sleep!

Poor Oliver! He little thought, as he lay sleeping in happy unconsciousness of all around him, that the board had that very day arrived at a decision which would exercise the most material influence over all his future fortunes. But they had. And this was it:

The members of this board were very sage, deep, philosophical men; and Avhen they came to turn their attention to the work-house, they found out at once, what ordinary folks would never have discov ered—the poor people liked it! It was a regular place of public entertainment for the poorer classes; a tavern where there was nothing to pay; a public breakfast, dinner, tea, and supper, all the year round; a brick and mortar elysium, where it was all play and no work. " Oho!" said the board, looking very knowing; " we are the fellows to set this to rights; we'll stop it all, in no time." So, they established the rule, that all poor people should have the alter native (for they would compel nobody, not they), of being starved by a gradual process in the house, or by a quick one out of it. With this view, they con tracted with the water-works to lay on an unlimited supply of water; and with a corn-factor to supply periodically small quantities of oatmeal; and issued three meals of thin gruel a day, with an onion twice a week, and half a roll on Sundays. They made a

great many other wise and humane regulations, hav ing reference to the ladies, which it is not necessary to repeat; kindly undertook to divorce poor married people, in consequence of the great expense of a suit in Doctors' Commons; and, instead of compelling a man to support his family, as they had theretofore done, took his family away from him, and made him a bachelor! There is no saying how many appli cants for relief, under these last two heads, might have started up in all classes of society, if it had not been coupled with the work-house; but the board were long - headed men, and had provided for this difficulty. The relief was inseparable from the work-house and the gruel; and that frightened peo ple.

For the first six months after Oliver Twist was removed, the system was in full operation. It was rather expensive at first, in consequence of the in crease in the undertaker's bill, and the necessity of taking in the clothes of all the paupers, which flut tered loosely on their wasted, shrunken forms, after a week or two's gruel. But the number of work house inmates got thin as well as the paupers; and the board were in ecstasies.

The room in which the boys were fed was a large stone hall, with a copper at one end ; out of which the master, dressed in an apron for the purpose, and assisted by one or two women, ladled the gruel at meal - times. Of this festive composition each boy had one porringer, and no more — except on occa sions of great public rejoicing, when he had two ounces and a quarter of bread besides. The bowls never wanted washing. The boys polished them with their spoons till they shone again; and when they had performed this operation (which never took very long, the spoons being nearly as large as the bowls), they would sit staring at the copper, with such eager eyes, as if they could have devoured the very bricks of which it was composed; employ ing themselves, meanwhile, in sucking their fingers most assiduously, with the view of catching up any stray splashes of gruel that might have been cast thereon. Boys have generally excellent appetites. Oliver Twist and his companions suffered the tor tures of slow starvation for three months: at last they got so voracious and wild with hunger, that one boy, who was tall for his age, and hadn't been used to that sort of thing (for his father had kept a small cook-shop), hinted darkly to his companions, that unless he had another basin of gruel per diem, he was afraid he might some night happen to eat the boy who slept next him, who happened to be a weakly youth of tender age. He had a wild, hungry eye; and they implicitly believed him. A council was held; lots were cast who should walk up to the master after supper that evening, and ask for more; and it fell to Oliver Twist.

The evening arrived; the boys took their places. The master, in his cook's uniform, stationed himself at the copper; his pauper assistants ranged them selves behind him; the gruel was served out; and a long grace was said over the short commons. The gruel disappeared; the boys whispered each other, and winked at Oliver; while his next neighbors nudged him. Child as he was, he was desperate I with hunger, and reckless with misery. He rose

OLIVER TWIST.

from the table; and advancing to the master, basin and spoon in hand, said, somewhat alarmed at his owu temerity:

" Please, sir, I want some more."

The master was a fat, healthy man ; but he turned very pale. He gazed in stupefied astonishment on the small rebel for some seconds, and then clung for support to the copper. The assistants were para lyzed with wonder; the boys with fear.

"What!" said the master at length, in a faint voice.

" Please, sir," replied Oliver, " I want some more."

The master aimed a blow at Oliver's head with the ladle; pinioned him in his arms; and shrieked aloud for the beadle.

The board were sitting in solemn conclave, when Mr. Bumble rushed into the room in great excite ment, and addressing the gentleman in the high chair, said,

"Mr. Limbkius, I beg your pardon, sir! Oliver Twist has asked for more."

There was a general start. Horror was depicted on every countenance.

" For more !" said Mr. Limbkins. " Compose your self, Bumble, and answer me distinctly. Do I under stand that he asked for more, after he had eaten the supper allotted by the dietary ?"

" He did, sir," replied Bumble.

" That boy will be hung," said the gentleman in the white waistcoat. "I know that boy will be hung."

Nobody controverted the prophetic gentleman's opinion. An animated discussion took place. Ol iver was ordered into instant confinement; and a bill was next morning pasted on the outside of the gate, offering a reward of five pounds to any body who would take Oliver Twist off the hands of the parish. In other words, five pounds and Oliver Twist were offered to any man or woman who want ed an apprentice to any trade, business, or calling.

" I never was more convinced of any thing in my life," said the gentleman in the white waistcoat, as he knocked at the gate and read the bill next morn ing : " I never was more convinced of any thing in my life, than I am that that boy will come to be hung."

As I purpose to show in the sequel whether the white-waistcoated gentleman was right or not, I should perhaps mar the interest of this narrative (supposing it to possess any at all), if I ventured to hint just yet, whether the life of Oliver Twist had this violent termination or no.

CHAPTER III.

RELATES HOW OLIVER TWIST WAS VERT NEAR GETTING A PLACE WHICH WOULD NOT HAVE BEEN A SINECURE.

FOR a week after the commission of the impious and profane offense of asking for more, Oliver remained a close prisoner in the dark and solitary room to which he had been consigned by the wis dom and mercy of the board. It appears, at first sight, not unreasonable to suppose that, if he had entertained a becoming feeling of respect for the

prediction of the gentleman in the white waistcoat, he would have established that sage individual's pro phetic character, once and forever, by tying one end of his pocket-handkerchief to a hook in the wall, and attaching himself to the other. To the performance of this feat, however, there was one obstacle; name ly, that pocket-handkerchiefs being decided articles of luxury, had been, for all future times and ages, removed from the noses of paupers by the express order of the board, in council assembled: solemnly given and pronounced under their hands and seals. There was a still greater obstacle in Oliver's youth and childishness. He only cried bitterly all day; and, when the long, dismal night came on, spread his little hands before bis eyes to shut out the darkness, and crouching in the corner, tried to sleep: ever and anon waking with a start and tremble, and drawing himself closer and closer to the wall, as if to feel even its cold hard surface were a protection in the gloom and loneliness which surrounded him.

Let it not be supposed by the enemies of "the system," that, during the period of his solitary in carceration, Oliver was denied the benefit of exer cise, the pleasure of society, or the advantages of re ligious consolation. As for exercise, it was nice cold weather, and he was allowed to perform his ablu tions every morning under the pump, in a stone yard, in the presence of Mr. Bumble, who prevented his catching cold, and caused a tingling sensation to pervade his frame, by repeated applications of the cane. As for society,he was carried every other day into the hall where the boys dined, and there socia bly flogged as a public warning and example. And so far from being denied the advantages of religious consolation, he was kicked into the same apartment every evening at prayer-time, and there permitted to listen to, and console his mind with, a general suppli cation of the boys, containing a special clause, there in inserted by authority of the board, in which they entreated to be made good, virtuous, contented, and obedient, and to be guarded from the sins and vices of Oliver Twist: whom the supplication distinctly set forth to be under the exclusive patronage and protection of the powers of wickedness, and an arti cle direct from the manufactory of the very Devil himself.

It chanced one morning, while Oliver's affairs were in this auspicious and comfortable state, that Mr. Gamfield, chimney-sweep, went his way down the High Street, deeply cogitating in his mind his ways and means of paying certain arrears of rent, for which his landlord had become rather pressing. Mr. Gamfield's most sanguine estimate of his finances could not raise them within full five pounds of the desired amount; and, in a species of arithmetical desperation, he was alternately cudgeling his brains and his donkey, when, passing the work-house, his eyes encountered the bill on the gate.

"Wo—o!" said Mr. Gamfield to the donkey.

The donkey was in a state of profound abstrac tion : wondering, probably, whether he was destined to be regaled with a cabbage-stalk or two when he had disposed of the two sacks of soot with which the little cart was laden; so, without noticing the word of command, he jogged onward.

Mr. Gamfield growled a fierce imprecation on the

ALMOST APPRENTICED.

donkey generally, but more particularly on his eyes; and, running after him, bestowed a blow on Ms head, which would inevitably have beaten in any skull but a donkey's. Then, catching hold of the bridle, he gave his jaw a sharp wrench, by way of gentle re minder that he was not his own master; and by these means turned him round. He then gave him another blow on the head, just to stun him till he came back again. Having completed these arrange ments, he walked up to the gate, to read the bill.

The gentleman with the white waistcoat was stand ing at the gate with his hands behind him, after hav ing delivered himself of some profound sentiments in the board-room. Having witnessed the little dispute between Mr. Gamfield and the donkey, he smiled joy ously when that person came up to read the bill, for he saw at once that Mr. Gamfield was exactly the sort of master Oliver Twist wanted. Mr. Gamfield smiled, too, as he perused the document; for five pounds was just the sum he had been wishing for; and, as to the boy with which it was incumbered, Mr. Gamfield, knowing Avhat the dietary of the work house was, well knew he would be a nice small pat tern, just the very thing for register stoves. So, he spelled the bill through again from beginning to end; and then, touching his fur cap in token of humility, accosted the gentleman in the white waistcoat.

" This here boy, sir, wot the parish wants to 'pren-tis," said Mr. Gamfield.

"Ay, my man," said the gentleman in the white waistcoat, with a condescending smile. " What of him ?"

" If the parish vould like him to learn a light pleas ant trade, in a good 'spectable chimbley-sweepiu' bis-ness," said Mr. Gamfield, " I wants a 'prentis, and I am ready to take him."

" Walk in," said the gentleman in the white waist coat, Mr. Gamfield having lingered behind, to give the donkey another blow on the head, and another wrench of the jaw, as a caution not to run away in his absence, followed the gentleman with the white waistcoat into the room where Oliver had first seen him.

" It's a nasty trade," said Mr. Limbkins, when Gamfield had again stated his wish.

"Young boys have been smothered in chimneys before now," said another gentleman.

" That's acause they damped the straw afore they lit it in the chimbley to make 'em come down agin," said Gamfield; " that's all smoke, and no blaze; vereas smoke ain't o' no use at all in making a boy come down, for it only siuds him to sleep, and that's wot he likes. Boys is wery obstiuit, and wery lazy, gen'lmen, and there's nothink like a good hot blaze to make 'em come down vith a run. It's humane too, gen'lmen, acause, even if they've stuck in the chimbley, roasting their feet makes 'em struggle to hextricate theirselves."

The gentleman in the white waistcoat appeared very much amused by this explanation; but his mirth was speedily checked by a look from Mr. Limbkins. The board then proceeded to converse among themselves for a few minutes, but in so low a tone, that the words " saving of expenditure," " look ed well in the accounts," " have a printed report pub lished," were alone audible. These only chanced to

be heard, indeed, on account of their being very fre quently repeated with great emphasis.

At length the whispering ceased; and the mem bers of the board, having resumed their seats and their solemnity, Mr. Limbkins said:

" We have considered your proposition, and we don't approve of it."

"Not at all," said the gentleman in the white waistcoat.

" Decidedly not," added the other members.

As Mr. Gamfield did happen to labor under the slight imputation of having bruised three or four boys to death already, it occurred to him that the board had, perhaps, in some unaccountable freak, taken it into their heads that this extraneous circum stance ought to influence their proceedings. It was very unlike their general mode of doing business, if they had; but still, as he had no particular wish to revive the rumor, he twisted his cap in his hands, and walked slowly from the table.

" So you won't let me have him, gen'lmen ?" said Mr. Gamfield, pausing near the door.

" No," replied Mr. Limbkins; " at least, as it's a nasty business, we think you ought to take some thing less than the premium we oifered."

Mr. Gamfield's countenance brightened, as, with a quick step, he returned to the table, and said,

" What'll you give, gen'lmen ? Come! Don't be too hard on a poor man. What'll you give ?"

" I should say three pound ten was plenty," said Mr. Limbkins.

" Ten shillings too much," said the gentleman in the white waistcoat.

" Come!" said Gamfield; " say four pound, gen'l men. Say four pound, and you've got rid on him for good and all. There!"

" Three pound ten," repeated Mr. Limbkins, firmly.

" Come! I'll split the difference, gen'lmen," urged Gamfield. " Three pound fifteen."

" Not a farthing more," was the firm reply of Mr. Limbkins.

" You're desperate hard upon me, gen'lmen," said Gamfield, wavering.

"Pooh! pooh! nonsense!" said the gentleman in the white waistcoat. " He'd be cheap with nothing at all, as a premium. Take him, you silly fellow! He's just the boy for you. He wants the stick, now and then : it'll do him good; and his board needn't come very expensive, for he hasn't been overfed since he was born. Ha! ha! ha!"

JMr. Gamfield gave an arch look at the faces round the table, and, observing a smile on all of them, grad ually broke into a smile himself. The bargain was made. Mr. Bumble was at once instructed that Oli ver Twist and his indentures were to be conveyed before the magistrate, for signature and approval, that very afternoon.

In pursuance of this determination, little Oliver, to his excessive astonishment, was released from bond age, and ordered to put himself into a clean shirt. He had hardly achieved this very unusual gymnas tic performance, when Mr. Bumble brought him, with his own hands, a basin of gruel, and the holiday al lowance of two ounces and a quarter of bread. At this tremendous sight, Oliver began to cry very pit-eously: thinking, not unnaturally, that the board

OLIVER TWIST.

must have determined to kill him for some useful purpose, or they never would have begun to fatten him up in that way.

" Don't make your eyes red, Oliver, but eat your food and be thankful," said Mr. Bumble, in a tone of impressive pomposity. " You're a going to be made a 'prentice of, Oliver."

"A 'prentice, sir!" said the child, trembling.

" Yes, Oliver," said Mr. Bumble. " The kind and blessed gentlemen which is so many parents to you, Oliver, when you had none of your own, are a going to 'prentice you, and to set you up in life, and make a man of you: although the expense to the parish is three pound ten!—three pound ten, Oliver!—seventy shillings—one hundred and forty sixpences!—and all for a naughty orphan which nobody can't love."

As Mr. Bumble paused to take breath, after deliv ering this address in an awful voice, the tears rolled down the poor child's face, and he sobbed bitterly.

" Come," said Mr. Bumble, somewhat less pompous ly, for it was gratifying to his feelings to observe the effect his eloquence had produced; " come, Oliver! Wipe your eyes with the cuffs of your jacket, and don't cry into your gruel; that's a very foolish ac tion, Oliver." It certainly was, for there was quite enough water in it already.

On their way to the magistrate, Mr. Bumble in structed Oliver that all he would have to do would be to look very happy, and say, when the gentleman asked him if he wanted to be apprenticed, that he should like it very much indeed; both of which in junctions Oliver promised to obey: the rather as Mr. Bumble threw in a gentle hint, that if he failed in either particular, there was no telling what would be done to him. When they arrived at the office, he was shut up in a little room by himself, and admon ished by Mr. Bumble to stay there, until he came back to fetch him.

There the boy remained, with a palpitating heart, for half an hour. At the expiration of which time Mr. Bumble thrust in his head, unadorned with the cocked hat, and said aloud:

" Now, Oliver, my dear, come to the gentleman." As Mr. Bumble said this, he put on a grim and threat ening look, and added, in a low voice, " Mind Avhat I told you, you young rascal!"

Oliver stared innocently in Mr. Bumble's face at this somewhat contradictory style of address; but that gentleman prevented his offering any remark thereupon, by leading him at once into an adjoin ing room: the door of which was open. It was. a large room, with a great window. Behind a desk sat two old gentlemen with powdered heads: one of whom was reading the newspaper; while the other was perusing, with the aid of a pair of tortoise-shell spectacles, a small piece of parchment which lay be fore him. Mr. Limbkins was standing in front of the desk on one side; and Mr. Gamfield, with a par tially washed face, on the other; while two or three bluff-looking men, in top-boots, were lounging about.

The old gentleman with the spectacles gradually dozed off, over the little bit of parchment; and there was a short pause, after Oliver had been stationed by Mr. Bumble in front of the desk.

" This is the boy, your worship," said Mr. Bumble.The old gentleman who was reading the newspa

per raised his head for a moment, and pulled the oth er old gentleman by the sleeve; whereupon the last-mentioned old gentleman woke up.

" Oh, is this the boy ?" said the old gentleman.

" This is him, sir," replied Mr. Bumble. " Bow to the magistrate, my dear."

Oliver roused himself, and made his best obeisance. He had been wondering, with his eyes fixed on the magistrates' powder, whether all boards were born with that white stuff on their heads, and were boards from thenceforth on that account.

"Well," said the old gentleman, "I suppose he's fond of chimney-sweeping ?"

" He dotes on it, your worship," replied Bumble; giving Oliver a sly pinch, to intimate that he had better not say he didn't.

" And he will be a sweep, will he ?" inquired the old gentleman.

" If we was to bind him to any other trade to-mor row, he'd run away simultaneous, your worship," re plied Bumble.

" And this man that's to be his master—you, sir— you'll treat him well, and feed him, and do all that sort of thing, will you ?" said the old gentleman.

" When I says I will, I means I will," replied Mr. Gamfield, doggedly.

" You're a rough speaker, my friend, but you look an honest, open-hearted man," said the old gentle man : turning his spectacles in the direction of the candidate for Oliver's premium, whose villainous countenance was a regular stamped receipt for cru elty. But the magistrate was half blind and half childish, so he couldn't reasonably be expected to discern what other people did.

" I hope I am, sir," said Mr. Gamfield, with an ugly leer.

" I have no doubt you are, my friend," replied the old gentleman, fixing his spectacles more firmly on his nose, and looking about him for the inkstand.

It was the critical moment of Oliver's fate. If the inkstand had been where the old gentleman thought it was, he would have dipped his pen into it, and signed the indentures, and Oliver would have been straightway hurried off. But, as it chanced to be immediately under his nose, it followed, as a matter of course, that he looked all over his desk for it, with out finding it; and happening in the course of his search to look straight before him, his gaze encoun tered the pale and terrified face of Oliver T\vist: who, despite all the admonitory looks and pinches of Bumble, was regarding the repulsive countenance of his future master, with a mingled expression of horror and fear, too palpable to be mistaken, even by a half-blind magistrate.

The old gentleman stopped, laid down his pen, and looked from Oliver to Mr. Limbkins; who attempted to take snuff with a cheerful and unconcerned aspect.

"My boy!" said the old gentleman, leaning over the desk. Oliver started at the sound. He might be excused for doing so: for the words were kindly said; and strange sounds frighten one. He trembled violently, and burst into tears.

" My boy!" said the old gentleman, " you look pale and alarmed. What is the matter ?"

" Stand a little away from him, Beadle," said the other magistrate: laying aside the paper, and lean-

ANOTHER PLACE OFFERS.

iug forward with aii expression of interest. " Now, boy, tell us what's the matter: don't be afraid."

Oliver fell on his knees, and clasping his hands to gether, prayed that they would order him back to the dark room—that they would starve him beat him kill him, if they pleased rather than send him away with that dreadful man.

" Well!" said Mr. Bumble, raising his hands and eyes with most impressive solemnity. " Well! of all the artful and designing orphans that ever I see, Oliver, you are one of the most barcfacedest."

" Hold your tongue, Beadle," said the second old gentleman, when Mr. Bumble had given vent to this compound adjective.

" I beg your worship's pardon," said Mr. Bumble, incredulous of his having heard aright. " Did your worship speak to me ?"

" Yes. Hold your tongue."

Mr. Bumble was stupefied with astonishment. A beadle ordered to hold his tongue! A moral revolu tion!The old gentleman in the tortoise-shell spectacles looked at his companion, he nodded significantly.

" We refuse to sanction these indentures," said the old gentleman: tossing aside the piece of parchment as he spoke.

" I hope," stammered Mr. Limbkins: " I hope the magistrates will not form the opinion that the au thorities have been guilty of any improper conduct, on the unsupported testimony of a mere child."

" The magistrates are not called upon to pronounce any opinion on the matter," said the second old gen tleman sharply. " Take the boy back to the work house, and treat him kindly. He seems to want it."

That same evening, the gentleman in the white waistcoat most positively and decidedly affirmed, not only that Oliver would be hung, but that he would be drawn and quartered into the bargain. Mr. Bumble shook his head with gloomy mystery, and said he wished he might come to good; where-unto Mr. Gamfield replied, that he wished he might come to him ; which, although he agreed with the beadle in most matters, would seem to be a wish of a totally opposite description.The next morning, the public were once more in formed that Oliver Twist was again To Let, and that five pounds would be paid to auy body who would take possession of him.

CHAPTER IV.

OLIVER, BEING OFFERED ANOTHER PLACE, MAKES HIS FIRST ENTRY INTO PUBLIC LIFE.

IN great families, when an advantageous place can not be obtained, either in possession, reversion, re mainder, or expectancy, for the young man who is growing up, it is a very general custom to send him to sea. The board, in imitation of so wise and salu tary an example, took counsel together on the expe diency of shipping off Oliver Twist in some small trailing vessel bound to a good unhealthy port. This suggested itself as the very best thing that could pos sibly be done with him ; the probability being that the skipper would flog him to death, in a playful B

mood, some day after dinner, or would knock his brains out with an iron bar; both pastimes being, as is pretty generally known, very favorite and common recreations among gentlemen of that class. The more the case presented itself to the board, in this point of view, the more manifold the advantages of the step appeared; so, they came to the conclusion that the only way of providing for Oliver effectually, was to send him to sea without delay.

Mr. Bumble had been dispatched to make various preliminary inquiries, Avith the view of finding out some captain or other who wanted a cabin-boy with out any friends; and was returning to the work house to communicate the result of his mission; when he encountered at the gate no less a person than Mr. Sowerberry, the parochial undertaker.

Mr. Sowerberry was a tall, gaunt, large -jointed man, attired in a suit of threadbare black, with darned cotton stockings of the same color, and shoes to an swer. His features were not naturally intended to wear a smiling aspect, but he was in general rather given to professional jocosity. His step was elastic, and his face betokened inward pleasantry, as he ad vanced to Mr. Bumble, and shook him cordially by the hand.

" I have taken the measure of the two women that died last night, Mr. Bumble," said the undertaker.

" You'll make your fortune, Mr. Sowerberry," said the beadle, as he thrust his thumb and forefinger into the proffered snuff-box of the undertaker: which was an ingenious little model of a patent coffin. " I say you'll make your fortune, Mr. Sowerberry," re peated Mr. Bumble, tapping the undertaker on the shoulder, in a friendly manner, with his cane.

" Think so f' said the undertaker, in a tone which half admitted and half disputed the probability of the event. "The prices allowed by the board are very small, Mr. Bumble."

" So are the coffins," replied the beadle: with pre cisely as near an approach to a laugh as a great offi cial ought to indulge in.

Mr. Sowerberry was much tickled at this: as of course he ought to be; and laughed a long time without cessation. "Well, well, Mr. Bumble," he said at length, " there's no denying that, since the new system of feeding has come in, the coffins are something narrower and more shallow than they used to be; but we must have some profit, Mr. Bum ble. Well-seasoned timber is an expensive article, sir; and all the iron handles come, by canal, from Birmingham."

" Well, well," said Mr. Bumble, " every trade has its drawbacks. A fair profit is, of course, allowable."

" Of course, of course," replied the undertaker; " and if I don't get a profit upon this or that particu lar article, why, I make it up in the long run, you see—he! he! he!"

" Just so," said Mr. Bumble.

" Though I must say," continued the undertaker, resuming the current of observations which the bea dle had interrupted: " though I must say, Mr. Bum ble, that I have to contend against one very great disadvantage: which is, that*all the stout people go off the quickest. The people who have been better off, and have paid rates for many years, arc the first to sink when they come into the house; and let me

OLIVER TWIST.

tell you, Mr. Bumble, that three or four inches over one's calculation makes a great hole in one's prof its : especially when one has a family to provide for, sir."

As Mr. Sowerberry said this, with the becoming in dignation of an ill-used man; and as Mr. Bumble felt that it rather tended to convey a reflection on the honor of the parish; the latter gentleman thought it advisable to change the subject. Oliver Twist being uppermost in his mind, he made him his theme.

" By-the-bye," said Mr. Bumble, " you don't know any body who wants a boy, do you ? A porochial 'prentis, who is at present a dead-weight; a mill stone, as I may say; round the porochial throat? Liberal terms, Mr. Sowerberry, liberal terms!" As

put it on, I remember, for the first time, to attend the inquest on that reduced tradesman, who died in a door-way at midnight."

"I recollect," said the undertaker. "The jury brought it in, ' Died from exposure to the cold, and want of the common necessaries of life,' didn't they ?"

Mr. Bumble nodded.

"And they made it a special verdict, I think," said the undertaker, " by adding some words to the effect that if the relieving officer had

" Tush! Foolery!" interposed the beadle. " If the board attended to all the nonsense that ignorant jurymen talk, they'd have enough to do."

"Very true," said the undertaker; "they would indeed."

" LIBERAL TERMS, MR. 8OWEHBERRY, LIBERAL TERMS 1"

Mr. Bumble spoke, he raised his cane to the bill above him, and gave three distinct raps upon the words " five pounds;" which were printed thereon in Eo-man capitals of gigantic size.

" Gadso!" said the undertaker, taking Mr. Bum ble by the gilt-edged lappel of his official coat; " that's just the very thing I wanted to speak to you about. You know—dear me, what a very elegant button this is, Mr. Bumble! I never noticed it be fore."

" Yes, I think it is rather pretty," said the beadle, glancing proudly downward at the large brass but tons which embellished his coat. "The die is the same as the porochial seal—the Good Samaritan heal ing the sick and bruised man. The board presented it to me on New-year's morning, Mr. Sowerberry. I

"Juries," said Mr. Bumble, grasping his cane tight ly, as was his wont when working into a passion: "juries is ineddicated, vulgar, groveling wretches."

" So they are," said the undertaker.

"They haven't no more philosophy nor political economy about 'em than that," said the beadle, snap ping his fingers contemptuously.

" No more they have," acquiesced the undertaker.

" I despise 'em," said the beadle, growing very red in the face.

" So do I," rejoined the undertaker.

"And I only wish we'd a jury of the independent sort in the house for a week or two," said the beadle; " the rules and regulations of the board would soon bring their spirit down for 'em."

" Let 'em alone for that," replied the undertaker.

ANOTHER PLACE OFFERS.

So saying, he smiled approvingly, to calm the rising wrath of the indignant parish officer.

Mr. Bumble lifted off his cocked hat; took a hand kerchief from the inside of the crown; wiped from his forehead the perspiration which his rage had en gendered ; fixed the cocked hat on again; and, turn ing to the undertaker, said, in a calmer voice:

" Well; what about the boy ?"

" Oh!" replied the undertaker; " why, you know, Mr. Bumble, I pay a good deal toward the poor's rates."

" Hem!" said Mr. Bumble. " Well ?"

"Well," replied the undertaker, "I was thinking that if I pay so much toward 'em, I've a right to get as much out of 'em as I can, Mr. Bumble ; and so— and so—I think I'll take the boy myself."

Mr. Bumble grasped the undertaker by the arm, and led him into the building. Mr. Sowerberry was closeted with the board for five minutes, and it was arranged that Oliver should go to him that evening " upon liking "—a phrase which means, in the case of a parish apprentice, that if the master find, upon a short trial, that he can get enough work out of a boy without putting too much food into him, he shall have him for a term of years, to do what he likes with.

When little Oliver was taken before " the gentle men " that evening; and informed that he was to go, that night, as general house-lad to a coffin-maker's; and that if he complained of his situation, or ever came back to the parish again, he would be sent to sea, there to be drowned, or knocked on the head, as the case might be, he evinced so little emotion, that they by common consent pronounced him a hardened young rascal, and ordered Mr. Bumble to remove him forthwith.

Now, although it was very natural that the board, of all people in the world, should feel in a great state of virtuous astonishment and horror at the smallest tokens of want of feeling on the part of any body, they were rather out, in this particular instance. The simple fact was, that Oliver, instead of possess ing too little feeling, possessed rather too much; and was in a fair way of being reduced, for life, to a state of brutal stupidity and sullenness by the ill-usage he had received. He heard the news of his destination in perfect silence; and, having had his luggage put into his hand—which was not very difficult to carry, inasmuch as it was all comprised within the limits of a brown paper parcel, about half a foot square by three inches deep—he pulled his cap over his eyes; and once more attaching himself to Mr. Bumble's coat cuff, was led away by that dignitary to a new scene of suffering.

For some time, Mr. Bumble drew Oliver along, without notice or remark; for the beadle carried his head very erect, as a beadle always should: and, it being a windy day, little Oliver was completely en shrouded by the skirts of Mr. Bumble's coat as they blew open, and disclosed to great advantage his flap ped waistcoat and drab plush knee-breeches. As they drew near to their destination, however, Mr. Bumble thought it expedient to look down, and see that the boy was in good order for inspection by his new master: which he accordingly did, with a tit and becoming air of gracious patronage.

" Oliver!" said Mr. Bumble.

" Yes, sir," replied Oliver, in a low, tremulous voice.

"Pull that cap off your eyes, and hold up your head, sir."

Although Oliver did as he was desired, at once, and passed the back of his unoccupied hand briskly across his eyes, he left a tear in them when he looked up at his conductor. As Mr. Bumble gazed sternly upon him, it rolled down his cheek. It was followed by another, and another. The child made a strong effort, but it was an unsuccessful one. Withdrawing his other hand from Mr. Bumble's, he covered his face with both; and wept until the tears sprung out from between his chin and bony fingers.

" Well!" exclaimed Mr. Bumble, stopping short, and darting at his little charge a look of intense malignity. " Well! Of all the ungratefullest, and worst - disposed boys as ever I see, Oliver, you are the—"

" No, no, sir," sobbed Oliver, clinging to the hand which held the well-known cane; " no, no, sir; I will be good indeed; indeed, indeed I will, sir! I am a very little boy, sir; and it is so— so— :

" So what ?" inquired Mr. Bumble, in amazement.

" So lonely, sir! So very lonely!" cried the child. " Every body hates me. Oh! sir, don't, don't, pray, be cross to me!" The child beat his hand upon his heart; and looked in his companion's face, with tears of real agony.

Mr. Bumble regarded Oliver's piteous and helpless look, with some astonishment, for a few seconds; hemmed three or four times in a husky manner; and after muttering something about " that troublesome cough," bade Oliver dry his eyes and be a good boy. Then once more taking his hand, he walked on with him in silence.

The undertaker, who had just put up the shutters of his shop, was making some entries in his day-book by the light of a most appropriate dismal candle, when Mr. Bumble entered.

"Aha!" said the undertaker: looking up from the book, and pausing in the middle of a word; " is that you, Bumble ?"

" No one else, Mr. Sowerberry," replied the beadle. * Here! I've brought the boy." Oliver made a bow.

" Oh! that's the boy, is it ?" said the undertaker, raising the candle above his head, to get a better view of Oliver. " Mrs. Sowerberry, will yon have the goodness to come here a moment, my dear ?"

Mrs. Sowerberry emerged from a little room be hind the shop, and presented the form of a short, thin, squeezed-up woman, with a A r ixeuish counte nance.

"My dear," said Mr. Sowerberry, deferentially, " this is the boy from the work-house that I told you of." Oliver bowed again.

" Dear me!" said the undertaker's wife, " he's very small."

" Why, he is rather small," replied Mr. Bumble: looking at Oliver as if it were his fault that he was no bigger; " he is small. There's no denying it. But he'll grow, Mrs. Sowerberry—he'll grow."

"Ah! I dare say he will," replied the lady pettish ly, " on our victuals and our drink. I see no saving in parish children, not I; for they always cost more to keep than they're worth. However, men always think they know best. There! Get down stairs, lit-

OLIVER TWIST.

tie bag o' bones." With this, the undertaker's wife opened a side door, and pushed Oliver down a steep flight of stairs into a stone cell, damp and dark: forming the ante-room to the coal-cellar, and de nominated "kitchen:" wherein sat a slatternly girl, in shoes down at heel, and blue worsted stockings very much out of repair.

" Here, Charlotte," said Mrs. Sowerberry, who had followed Oliver down, "give this boy some of the cold bits that were put by for Trip. He hasn't come home since the morning, so he may go without 'em. I dare say the boy isn't too dainty to eat 'em — are you, boy ?"

Oliver, whose eyea had glistened at the mention of meat, and who was trembling with eagerness to devour it, replied in the negative; and a plateful of coarse broken victuals was set before him.

I wish some well-fed philosopher, whose meat and drink turn to gall within him—whose blood is ice, whose heart is iron—could have seen Oliver Twist clutching at the dainty viands that the dog had neg lected. I wish he could have witnessed the horrible avidity with which Oliver tore the bits asunder with all the ferocity of famine. There is only one thing I should like better; and that would be to see the Philosopher making the same sort of meal himself, with the same relish.

" Well," said the undertaker's wife, when Oliver had finished his supper: which she had regarded in silent horror, and with fearful auguries of his future appetite: " have you done ?"

There being nothing eatable within his reach, Oli ver replied in the affirmative.

" Then come with me," said Mrs. Sowerberry: tak ing up a dim and dirty lamp, and leading the way up stairs; " your bed's under the counter. You don't mind sleeping among the coffins, I suppose ? But it doesn't much matter whether you do or don't, for you can't sleep anywhere else. Come, don't keep me here all night!"

Oliver lingered no longer, but meekly followed his new mistress.

CHAPTEE V. .

OLIVER MINGLES WITH NEW ASSOCIATES. GOING TO A FUNERAL FOR THE FIRST TIME, HE FORMS AN UNFA VORABLE NOTION OF HIS MASTER'S BUSINESS.

k LIVER, being left to himself in the undertaker's shop, set the lamp down on a workman's bench, and gazed timidly about him with a feeling of awe and dread, which many people a good deal older than he will be at no loss to understand. An unfinished coffin on black tressels, which stood in the middle of the shop, looked so gloomy and death-like that a cold tremble came over him every time his eyes wan dered in the direction of the dismal object: from which he almost expected to see some frightful form slowly rear its head, to drive him mad with terror. Against the wall were ranged, in regular array, a long row of elm boards cut into the same shape: looking in the dim light, like high-shouldered ghosts with their hands in their breeches-pockets. Coffin-plates, elm-chips, bright-headed nails, and shreds of black cloth, lay scattered on the floor; and the wall

behind the counter was ornamented with a lively representation of two mutes in very stiff neckcloths, on duty at a large private door, with a hearse drawn by four black steeds, approaching in the distance. The shop was close and hot. The atmosphere seemed tainted with the smell of coffins. The recess beneath the counter in which his flock mattress was thrust, looked like a grave.

Nor Avere these the only dismal feelings which de pressed Oliver. Ho was alone in a strange place; and we all know how chilled and desolate the best of us will sometimes feel in such a situation. The boy had no friends to care for, or to care for him. The regret of no recent separation was fresh in his mind; the absence of no loved and well-remembered face sank heavily into his heart. But his heart was heavy, notwithstanding ; and he wished, as he crept into his narrow bed, that that were his coffin, and that he could be lain in a calm and lasting sleep in the church-yard ground, with the tall grass waving gently above his head, and the sound of the old deep bell to soothe him in his sleep.

Oliver was awakened in the morning, by a loud kicking at the outside of the shop-door: which, be fore he could huddle on his clothes, was repeated, in an angry and impetuous manner, about twenty-five times. When he began to undo the chain, the legs desisted, and a voice began.

" Open the door, will yer ?" cried the voice which belonged to the legs which had kicked at the door.

" I will, directly, sir," replied Oliver, undoing the chain, and turning the key.

" I suppose yer the new boy, ain't yer ?" said the voice through the key-hole.

" Yes, sir," replied Oliver.

" How old are yer ?" inquired the voice.

" Ten, sir," replied Oliver.

" Then I'll whop yer when I get in," said the voice; " you just see if I don't, that's all, my work'us brat!" and having made this obliging promise, the voice began to whistle.

Oliver had been too often subjected to the proc ess to which the very expressive monosyllable just recorded bears reference, to entertain the smallest doubt that the owner of the voice, whoever he might be, would redeem his pledge, most honorably. He drew back the bolts with a trembling hand, and opened the door.

For a second or two, Oliver glanced up the street, and down the street, and over the way: impressed with the belief that the unknown, who had addressed him through the key-hole, had walked a few paces off, to warm himself; for nobody did he see but a big charity-boy, sitting on a post in front of the house, eating a slice of bread and butter: which he cut into wedges, the size of his mouth, with a clasp-knife, and then consumed with great dexterity.

" I beg your pardon, sir," said Oliver at length: seeing that no other visitor made his appearance; " did you knock f'

" I kicked," replied the charity-boy.

" Did you want a coffin, sir f' inquired Oliver, in nocently.

At this the charity-boy looked monstrous fierce; and said that Oliver would want one before long, if he cut jokes with his superiors in that way.

NEW IDEA IN THE UNDERTAKING WAY.

" Yer don't know who I am, I suppose, Work'us?" said the charity-boy, iii continuation : descending from the top of the post, meanwhile, with edifying-gravity.

" No, sir," rejoined Oliver.

" I'm Mister Noah Claypole," said the charity-boy, " and you're under me. Take down the shutters, yer idle young ruffian !" With this, Mr. Claypole admin istered a kick to Oliver, and entered the shop with a dignified air, which did him great credit. It is diffi cult for a large-headed, small-eyed yonth, of lumber ing make and heavy countenance, to look dignified under any circumstances; but it is more especially so, when superadded to these personal attractions are a red nose and yellow smalls.

Oliver, having taken down the shutters, and broken a pane of glass in his efforts to stagger away beneath the weight of the first one to a small court at the side of the house in which they were kept during the day, was graciously assisted by Noah: who having consoled him with the assurance that " he'd catch it," condescended to help him. Mr. Sowerberry came down soon after. Shortly afterward, Mrs. Sowerber ry appeared. Oliver having " caught it," in fulfill ment of Noah's prediction, followed that young gen tleman down the stairs to breakfast.

" Come near the fire, Noah," said Charlotte. " I saved a nice little bit of bacon for you from master's breakfast. Oliver, shut that door at Mister Noah's back, and take them bits that I've put out on the cover of the bread-pan. There's your tea; take it away to that box, and drink it there, and make haste, for they'll want you to mind the shop. D'ye hear ?"

" D'ye hear, Work'us ?" said Noah Claypole.

" Lor, Noah!" said Charlotte," what a rum creature you are! Why don't you let the boy alone ?"

" Let him alone!" said Noah. " Why every body lets him alone enough, for the matter of that. Nei ther his father nor his mother will ever interfere with him. All his relations let him have his own way pretty well. Eh, Charlotte ? He! he! he!"

" Oh, you queer soul!" said Charlotte, bursting into a hearty laugh, in which she was joined by Noah; after which they both looked scornfully at poor Oli ver Twist, as he sat shivering on the box in the cold est corner of the room, and ate the stale pieces which had been specially reserved for him.

Noah was a charity-boy, but not a work-house or phan. No chance child was he, for he could trace his genealogy all the way back to his parents, who lived hard by; his mother being a washer-woman, and his father a drunken soldier, discharged with a wooden leg, and a diurnal pension of twopence-half penny and an unstateable fraction. The shop-boys in the neighborhood had long been in the habit of branding Noah, in the public streets, with the igno minious epithets of " leathers," " charity," and the like ; and Noah had borne them without reply. But, now that fortune had cast in his way a nameless or phan, at whom even the meanest could point the fin ger of scorn, he retorted on him with interest. This affords charming food for contemplation. It shows us what a beautiful thing human nature may be made to be; and how impartially the same amiable quali ties are developed in the finest lord and the dirtiest charity-boy.

Oliver had been sojourning at the undertaker's some three weeks or a month. Mr. and Mrs. Sower-berry—the shop being shut up — were taking their supper in the little back-parlor, when Mr. Sowerber ry, after several deferential glances at his wife, said,

" My dear— : He was going to say more ; but, Mrs. Sowerberry looking up, with a peculiar unpro-pitious aspect, he stopped short.

"Well," said Mrs. Sowerberry, sharply.

" Nothing, my dear, nothing," said Mr. Sowerberry.

" Ugh, you brute !" 4 said Mrs. Sowerberry.

" Not at all, my dear," said Mr. Sowerberry, hum bly. " I thought you didn't want to hear, my dear. I was only going to say—

" Oh, don't tell me what you were going to say," interposed Mrs. Sowerberry. " I am nobody ; don't consult me, pray. / don't want to intrude upon your secrets." As Mrs. Sowerberry said this, she gave an hysterical laugh, which threatened violent conse quences.

" But, my dear," said Sowerberry, " I want to ask your advice."

" No, no, don't ask mine," replied Mrs. Sowerber ry, in an aifecting manner: " ask somebody else's." Here there was another hysterical laugh, which frightened Mr. Sowerberry very much. This is a very common and much-approved matrimonial course of treatment, which is often very effective. It at once reduced Mr. Sowerberry to begging, as a spe cial favor, to be allowed to say what Mrs. Sowerberry was most curious to hear. After a short altercation of less than three-quarters of an hour's duration, the permission was most graciously conceded.

" It's only about young Twist, my dear," said Mr. Sowerberry. "A very good-looking boy, that, my dear."

" He need be, for he eats enough," observed the lady.

" There's an expression of melancholy in his face, my dear," resumed Mr. Sowerberry, " which is very interesting. He would make a delightful mute, my love."

Mrs. Sowerberry looked up with an expression of considerable wonderment. Mr. Sowerberry remark ed it; and, without allowing time for any observa tion on the good lady's part, proceeded.

" I don't mean a regular mute to attend grown-up people, my dear, but only for children's practice. It would be very new to have a mute in proportion, my dear. You may depend upon it, it would have a su perb effect."

Mrs. Sowerberry, who had a good deal of taste in the undertaking way, was much struck by the nov elty of this idea; but, as it would have been com promising her dignity to have said so, under existing circumstances, she merely inquired, with much sharp ness, why such an obvious suggestion had not pre sented itself to her husband's mind before ? Mr. Sowerberry rightly construed this as an acquies cence in his proposition ; it was speedily determined, therefore, that Oliver should be at once initialr< I into the mysteries of the trade; and, with this view, that he should accompany his master on the very next occasion of his services being required.

The occasion was not long in coining. Half an hour after breakfast next morning, Mr. Bumble en-

OLIVES TWIST.

tered the shop; and supporting his cane against the counter, drew forth his large leathern pocket-book: from which he selected a small scrap of paper, which he handed over to

Sowerberry.

" Aha," said the undertaker, glancing over it with a lively countenance; " an order for a coffin, eh ?"

"For a coffin first, and a porochial funeral after ward," replied Mr. Bumble, fastening the strap of the leathern pocket-book, which, like himself, was very corpulent.

" Bayton," said the undertaker, looking from the scrap of paper to Mr. Bumble. " I never heard the name before."

Bumble shook his head, as he replied, " Obstinate people, Mr. Sowerberry; very obstinate. Proud, too, I'm afraid, sir."

" Proud, eh ?" exclaimed Mr. Sowerberry, with a sneer. " Come, that's too much."

"Oh, it's sickening," replied the beadle. "Anti-monial, Mr. Sowerberry!"

" So it is," acquiesced the undertaker.

"We only heard of the family the night before last," said the beadle; "and we shouldn't have known any thing about them, then, only a woman who lodges in the same house made an application to the porochial committee for them to send the po rochial surgeon to see a woman as was very bad. He had gone out to dinner; but his 'prentice (which is a very clever lad) sent 'em some medicine in a blacking-bottle, off-hand."

"Ah, there's promptness," said the undertaker.

" Promptness, indeed!" replied the beadle. " But what's the consequence; what's the ungrateful be havior of these rebels, sir ? Why, the husband sends back word that the medicine won't suit his wife's complaint, and so she sha'n't take it—says she sha'n't take it, sir. Good, strong, wholesome medicine, as was given with great success to two Irish laborers and a coal-heaver only a week before—sent 'em for nothing, with a blacking-bottle in — and he sends back word that she sha'n't take it, sir!"

As the atrocity presented itself to Mr. Bumble's mind in full force, he struck the counter sharply with his cane, and became flushed with indignation.

" Well," said the undertaker, " I ne—ver—-did—"

" Never did, sir!" ejaculated the beadle. " No, nor nobody never did; but, now she's dead, we've got to bury her; and that's the direction; and the sooner it's done, the better."

Thus saying, Mr. Bumble put on his cocked hat wrong side first, in a fever of parochial excitement; and flounced out of the shop.

" Why, he was so angry, Oliver, that he forgot even to ask after you!" said Mr. Sowerberry, looking after the beadle as he strode down the street.

" Yes, sir," replied Oliver, who had carefully kept himself out of sight during the interview; and who was shaking from head to foot at the mere recollec tion of the sound of Mr. Bumble's voice. He needn't have taken the trouble to shrink from Mr. Bumble's glance, however; for that functionary, on whom the prediction of the gentleman in the white waistcoat had made a very strong impression, thought that now the undertaker had got Oliver upon trial the subject was better avoided, until such time as he •should be firmly bound for seven years, and all dan ger of his being returned upon the hands of the par ish should be thus effectually and legally overcome.

"Well," said Mr. Sowerberry, taking up his hat, " the sooner this job is done, the better. Noah, look after the shop. Oliver, put on your cap and come with me." Oliver obeyed, and followed his master on his professional mission.

They walked on for some time through the most crowded and densely inhabited part of the town; and then, striking down a narrow street more dirty and miserable than any they had yet passed through, paused to look for the house which was the object of their search. The houses on either side were high and large, but very old, and tenanted by people of the poorest class: as their neglected appearance would have sufficiently denoted, without the concur rent testimony afforded by the squalid looks of the few men and women who, with folded arms and bod ies half doubled, occasionally skulked along. A great many of the tenements had shop-fronts; but these were fast closed, and mouldering away; only the upper rooms being inhabited. Some houses, which had become insecure from age and decay, were pre vented from falling into the street by huge beams of wood reared against the walls, and firmly plant ed in the road; but even these crazy dens seemed to have been selected as the nightly haunts of some houseless wretches, for many of the rough boards which supplied the place of door and window were wrenched from their positions, to afford an aperture wide enough for the passage of a human body. The kennel was stagnant and filthy. The very rats, which here and there lay putrefying in its rotten ness, were hideous with famine.

There was neither knocker nor bell-handle at the open door where Oliver and his master stopped ; so, groping his way cautiously through the dark pas sage, and bidding Oliver keep close to him and not be afraid, the undertaker mounted to the top of the first flight of stairs. Stumbling against a door on the landing, he rapped at it with his knuckles.

It was opened by a young girl of thirteen or four teen. The undertaker at once saw enough of what the room contained, to know it was the apartment to which he had been directed. He stepped in; Ol iver followed him.

There was no fire in the room; but a man was crouching, mechanically, over the empty stove. An old woman, too, had drawn a low stool to the cold hearth, and was sitting beside him. There were some ragged children in another corner; and in a small recess, opposite the door, there lay upon the ground something covered with an old blanket. Ol iver shuddered as he cast his eyes toward the place, and crept involuntarily closer to his master; for though it was covered up, the boy felt that it was a corpse.

The man's face was thin and very pale; his hair and beard were grizzly; his eyes were bloodshot. The old woman's face was wrinkled; her two remain ing teeth protruded over her under lip; and her eyes were bright and piercing. Oliver was afraid to look at either her or the man. They seemed so like the rats he had seen outside.

" Nobody shall go near her," said the man, start ing fiercely up, as the undertaker approached the re-

cess. "Keep back! Damn you, keep back, if you've a life to lose!"

"Nonsense, my good man," said the undertaker, who was pretty well used to misery in all its shapes. " Nonsense!"

" I tell you," said the man, clenching his hands, and stamping furiously on the floor—" I tell you I won't have her put into the ground. She couldn't rest there. The worms would worry her—not eat her—she is so worn away."

The undertaker offered no reply to this raving; but producing a tape from his pocket, knelt down for a moment by the side of the body.

"Ah!" said the man: bursting into tears, and sink ing on his knees at the feet of the dead woman; " kneel down, kneel down—kneel round her, every one of you, and mark my words! I say she was starved to death. I never knew how bad she was, till the fever came upon her; and then her bones were starting through the skin. There was neither fire nor candle; she died in the dark—in the dark! She couldn't even see her children's faces, though we heard her gasping out their names. I begged for her in the streets; and they sent me to prison. When I came back, she was dying; and all the blood in my heart has dried up, for they starved her to death. I swear it before the God that saw it! They starved her!" He twined his hands in his hair; and, with a loud scream, rolled groveling upon the floor: his eyes fixed, and the foam covering his lips.

The terrified children cried bitterly; but the old woman, who had hitherto remained as quiet as if she had been wholly deaf to all that passed, menaced them into silence. Having unloosed the cravat of the man who still remained extended on the ground, she tottered toward the undertaker.

" She was my daughter," said the old woman, nod ding her head in the direction of the corpse, and speaking with an idiotic leer, more ghastly than even the presence of death in snch a place. " Lord, Lord! Well, it is strange that I who gave birth to her, and was a woman then, should be alive and merry now, and she lying there: so cold and stiff! Lord, Lord! —to think of it; it's as good as a play—as good as a play!"

As the wretched creature mumbled and chuckled in her hideous merriment, the undertaker turned to go away.

" Stop, stop!" said the old woman in a loud whis per. " Will she be buried to-morrow, or next day, or to-night ? I laid her out; and I must walk, you know. Send me a large cloak: a good warm one: for it is bitter cold. We should have cake and wine, too, before we go! Never mind; send some bread— only a loaf of bread and a cup of water. Shall we have some bread, dear ?" she said eagerly, catching at the undertaker's coat, as he once more moved to ward the door.

" Yes, yes," said the undertaker, " of course. Any thing you like!" He disengaged himself from the old woman's grasp; and, drawing Oliver after him, hur ried away.

The next day (the family having been meanwhile relieved with a half-quartern loaf and a piece of cheese, left with them by Mr. Bumble himself), Oli ver and his master returned to the miserable abode;

where Mr. Bumble had already arrived, accompanied by four men from the work-house, who were to act as bearers. An old black cloak had been thrown over the rags of the old woman and the man; and the bare coffin having been screwed down, was hoisted on the shoulders of the bearers, and carried into the street.

" Now you must put your best leg foremost, old lady!" whispered Sowerberry in the old woman's ear; "w T e are rather late; and it won't do to keep the clergyman waiting. Move on, my men—as quick as you like!"

Thus directed, the bearers trotted on under their light burden; and the two mourners kept as near them as they could. Mr. Bumble and Sowerberry walked at a good smart pace in front; and Oliver, whose legs were not so long as his master's, ran by the side.

There was not so great a necessity for hurrying as Mr. Sowerberry had anticipated, however; for when they reached the obscure corner of the church-yard in which the nettles grew, and where the parish graves were made, the clergyman had not arrived; and the clerk, who was sitting by the vestry-room fire, seemed to think it by no means improbable that it might be an hour or so before he came. So they put the bier on the brink of the grave; and the two mourners waited patiently in the damp clay, with a cold rain drizzling down, while the ragged boys whom the spectacle had attracted into the church-yard played a noisy game at hide-and-seek among the tomb stones, or varied their amusements by jumping back ward and forward over the coffin. Mr. Sowerberry and Bumble, being personal friends of the clerk, sat by the fire with him, and read the paper.

At length, after a lapse of something more than an hour, Mr. Bumble, and Sowerberry, and the clerk, were seen running toward the grave. Immediately afterward, the clergyman appeared, putting on his surplice as he came along. Mr. Bumble then thrash ed a boy or two, to keep up appearances; and the reverend gentleman, having read as much of the bu rial service as could be compressed into four minutes, gave his surplice to the clerk, and walked away again.

" Now, Bill!" said Sowerberry to the grave-digger. "Fill up!"

It was no very difficult task; for the grave was so full, that the uppermost coffin was within a few feet of the surface. The grave-digger shoveled in the earth ; stamped it loosely down with his feet; shoul dered his spade; and walked off, followed by the boys, who murmured very loud complaints at the fun being over so soon.

" Come, my good fellow!" said Bumble, tapping the man on the back. " They want to shut up the yard."

The man, who had never once moved since he had taken his station by the grave-side, started, raised his head, stared at the person who had addressed him, walked forward for a few paces, and fell down in a swoon. The crazy old woman was too much oc cupied in bewailing the loss of her cloak (which the undertaker had taken off) to pay him any attention; so they threw a can of cold water over him; and when he came to, saw him safely out of the church yard, locked the gate, and departed on their different ways.

OLIVER TWIST.

" Well, Oliver," said Sowerberry, a.s they walked home, " how do you like it ?"

" Pretty well, thank you, sir," replied Oliver, with considerable hesitation. " Not very much, sir.'^

"Ah, you'll get used to it in time, Oliver," said Sowerberry. " Nothing when vou are used to it, my boy."

Oliver wondered, in his own mind, whether it had taken a very long time to get Mr. Sowerberry used to it. But he thought it better not to ask the ques tion ; and walked back to the shop, thinking over all he had seen and heard.

CHAPTER VI.

OLIVER, BEING GOADED BY THE TAUNTS OF NOAH, BOUSES INTO ACTION, AND RATHER ASTONISHES HIM.

TlHE month's trial over, Oliver was formally ap prenticed. It was a nice sickly season just at this time. In commercial phrase, coffins were look ing up; and, in the course of a few weeks, Oliver ac quired a great deal of experience. The success of Mr. Sowerberry's ingenious speculation exceeded even his most sanguine hopes. The oldest inhabitants recol lected no period at which measles had been so prev alent, or so fatal to infant existence; and many were the mournful processions which little Oliver headed, in a hat-band reaching down to his knees, to the in describable admiration and emotion of all the- moth ers in the town. As Oliver accompanied his master in most of his adult expeditious, too, in order that he might acquire that equanimity of demeanor and full command of nerve which are essential to a finished undertaker, he had many opportunities of observing the beautiful resignation and fortitude with which some strong-minded people bear their trials and losses.

For instance; when Sowerberry had an order for the burial of some rich old lady or gentleman, who was surrounded by a great number of nephews and nieces, who had been perfectly inconsolable during the previous illness, and whose grief had been wholly irrepressible even on the most public occasions, they would be as happy among themselves as need be— quite cheerful and contented—conversing together with as much freedom and gayety, as if nothing whatever had happened to disturb them. Husbands, too, bore the loss of their wives with the most heroic calmness. Wives, again, put on weeds for their hus bands, as if, so far from grieving in the garb of sor row, they had made up their minds to render it as becoming and attractive as possible. It was observ able, too, that ladies and gentlemen who were in pas sions of anguish during the ceremony of interment, recovered almost as soon as they reached home, and became quite composed before the tea-drinking was over. All this was very pleasant and improving to see; and Oliver beheld it with great admiration.

That Oliver Twist was moved to resignation by the example of these good people, I can not, although I am his biographer, undertake to affirm with any degree of confidence; but I can most distinctly say, ! that for many months he continued meekly to sub- ; mit to the domination and ill-treatment of Noah

Claypole: who used him far worse than before, now that his jealousy was roused by seeing the new boy promoted to the black stick and hat-band, while he, the old one, remained stationary in the muffin-cap and leathers. Charlotte treated him ill, because Noah did ; and Mrs. Sowerberry was his decided en emy, because Mr. Sowerberry was disposed to be his friend; so, between these three on one side, and a glut of funerals on the other, Oliver was not alto gether as comfortable as the hungry pig was when he was shut up, by mistake, in the grain department of a brewery.

And now I come to a very important passage in Oliver's history; for I have to record an act, slight and unimportant perhaps in appearance, but which indirectly produced a material change in all his fu ture prospects and proceedings.

One day, Oliver and Noah had descended into the kitchen at the usual dinner-hour, to banquet upon a small joint of mutton—a pound and a half of the worst end of the neck—when Charlotte being called out of the way, there ensued a brief interval of time, which Noah Claypole, being hungry and vicious, con sidered he could not possibly devote to a worthier purpose than aggravating and tantalizing young Ol iver Twist.

Intent upon this innocent amusement, Noah put his feet on the table-cloth ; and pulled Oliver's hair; and twitched his ears; and expressed his opinion that he was a " sneak;" and furthermore announced his intention of coming to see him hanged, whenever that desirable event should take place; and entered upon various other topics of petty annoyance, like a malicious and ill-conditioned charity-boy as he was. But, none of these taunts producing the desired ef fect of making Oliver cry, Noah attempted to be more facetious still; and in this attempt, did what many small wits, with far greater reputations than Noah, sometimes do to this day, when they want to be funny. He got rather personal.

" Work'us," said Noah, " how's your mother ?"

"She's dead," replied Oliver; "don't you say any thing about her to me!"

Oliver's color rose as he said this; he breathed quickly; and there was a curious working of the mouth and nostrils, which Mr. Claypole thought must be the immediate precursor of a violent fit of crying. Under this impression he returned to the charge.

" What did she die of, Work'us ?" said Noah.

"Of a broken heart, some of our old nurses told me," replied Oliver: more as if he were talking to himself than answering Noah. "I think I know what it must be to die of that!"

"Tol de rol lol lol, right fol lairy, Work'us," said Noah, as a tear rolled down Oliver's cheek. " What's set you a sniveling now ?"

"Not you" replied Oliver, hastily brushing the tear away. " Don't think it."

" Oh, not me, eh ?" sneered Noah.

" No, not you," replied Oliver, sharply. " There, that's enough. Don't say any thing more to me about her; you'd better not!"

"Better not!" exclaimed Noah. "Well! Better not! Work'us, don't be impudent. Your mother, too! She was a nice 'un, she was. Oh, Lor!" And

MURDER.

here Noah nodded his head expressively; and curled np as much of his small red nose as muscular action could collect together for the occasion.

" Yer know, Work'us," continued Noah, embolden ed by Oliver's silence, and speaking in a jeering tone of affected pity—of all tones the most annoying— " Yer know, Work'us, it can't be helped now; and of course yer couldn't help it then; and I'm very sorry for it; and I'm sure we all are, and pity yer very much. But yer must know, Work'us, yer mother was a regular right-down bad 'un."

" What did you say ?" inquired Oliver, looking up very quickly.

"A regular right-down bad 'un, Work'us," replied

His breast heaved; his attitude was erect; his eye bright and vivid; his whole person changed, as he stood glaring over the cowardly tormentor who now lay crouching at his feet; and defied him with an energy he had never known before.

" He'll murder me!" blubbered Noah. " Charlotte! missis! Here's the new boy a murdering of me! Help! help! • Oliver's gone mad! Char—lotte!"

Noah's shouts were responded to by a loud scream from Charlotte and a louder from Mrs. Sowerberry; the former of whom rushed into the kitchen by a side door, while the latter paused on the staircase till she was quite certain that it was consistent with the preservation of human life to come farther down.

OLIVER BATHES ASTONIbllBS NOA1I.

Noah, coolly. " And it's a great deal better, Work'us, that she died when she did, or else she'd have been hard laboring in Bridewell, or transported, or hung; which is more likely than either, isn't it ?"

Crimson with fury, Oliver started up; overthrew the chair and table; seized Noah by the throat; shook him, in the violence of his rage, till his teeth chattered in his head; and, collecting his whole force into one heavy blow, felled him to the ground.

A minute ago, the boy had looked the quiet, mild, dejected creature that harsh treatment had made him. But his spirit was roused at last; the cruel insult to his dead mother had set his blood on fire.

" Oh, yon little wretch!" screamed Charlotte, seiz ing Oliver with her utmost force, which was about equal to that of a moderately strong man in partic ularly good training. " Oh, you little un-grate-ful, mur-de-rous, hor-rid villain!" And between every syllable Charlotte gave Oliver a blow with all her might, accompanying it with a scream for the bene fit of society.

Charlotte's fist was by no means a light one ; but, lest it should not be effectual in calming Oliver's wrath, Mrs. Sowerberry plunged into the kitchen, and assisted to hold him with one hand, while she scratched his face with the other. In this favorable

OLIVER TWIST.

position of affairs, Noah rose from the ground, and pommeled him behind.

This was rather too violent exercise to last long. When they were all wearied out, and could tear and beat no longer, they dragged Oliver, struggling and shouting, but nothing daunted, into the dust-cellar, and there locked him up. This being done, Mrs. Sowerberry sunk into a chair, and burst into tears.

"Bless her, she's going off!" said Charlotte. "A glass of water, Noah, dear. Make haste!"

" Oh! Charlotte," said Mrs. Sowerberry: speaking as well as she could, through a deficiency of breath, and a sufficiency of cold water, which Noah had poured over her head and shoulders. "Oh! Char lotte, what a mercy we have not all been murdered in our beds!"

" Ah! mercy indeed, ma'am," was the reply. " I only hope this'll teach master not to have any more of these dreadful creaturs, that are born to be mur derers and robbers from their very cradle. Poor Noah! he was all but killed, ma'am, when I come in."

" Poor fellow!" said Mrs. Sowerberry, looking pit-eously on the charity-boy.

Noah, whose top waistcoat - button might have been somewhere on a level with the crown of Ol iver's head, rubbed his eyes with the inside of his wrists while this commiseration was bestowed upon him, and performed some affecting tears and sniffs.

" What's to be done!" exclaimed Mrs. Sowerberry. " Your master's not at home; there's not a man in the house, and he'll kick that door down in ten min utes." Oliver's vigorous plunges against the bit of timber in question rendered this occurrence highly probable.

" Dear, dear! I don't know, ma'am," said Charlotte, " unless we send for the police officers."

" Or the millingtary," suggested Mr. Claypole.

" No, no," said Mrs. Sowerberry: bethinking her self of Oliver's old friend. " Run to Mr. Bumble, Noah, and tell him to come here directly, and not to lose a minute; never mind your cap! Make haste! You can hold a knife to that black eye, as you run along. It'll keep the swelling down."

Noah stopped to make no reply, but started off at his fullest speed; and very much it astonished the people who were out walking, to see a charity-boy tearing through the streets pell-mell, with no cap on his head, and a clasp-knife at his eye.

CHAPTER VII.

OLIVER CONTINUES REFRACTORY.

"VfOAH CLAYPOLE ran along the streets at Ms ±\ swiftest pace, and paused not once for breath until he reached the work-house gate. Having rest ed here, for a minute or so, to collect a good burst of sobs and an imposing show of tears and terror, he knocked loudly at the wicket; and presented such a rueful face to the aged pauper who opened it, that even he, who saw nothing but rueful faces about him at the best of times, started back in astonish ment.

" Why, what's the matter with the boy!" said the old pauper.

" Mr. Bumble! Mr. Bumble!" cried Noah, with well-affected dismay: and in tones so loud and agitated, that they not only caught the ear of Mr. Bumble himself, who happened to be hard by, but alarmed him so much that he rushed into the yard without his cocked hat—which is a very curious and remark able circumstance: as showing that even a beadle, acted upon by a sudden and powerful impulse, may be afflicted with a momentary visitation of loss of self-possession, and forgetfuluess of personal dignity.

"Oh, Mr. Bumble, sir!" said Noah: " Oliver, sir— Oliver has—"

" What ? What ?" interposed Mr. Bumble, with a gleam of pleasure in his metallic eyes. "Not run away; he hasn't run away, has he, Noah ?"

" No, sir, no. Not run away, sir, but he's turned wicious," replied Noah. " He tried to murder me, sir; and then he tried to murder Charlotte; and then missis. Oh! what dreadful pain it is! Such agony, please, sir!" And here Noah writhed and twisted his body into an extensive variety of eel-like positions; thereby giving Mr. Bumble to under stand that, from the violent and sanguinary onset of Oli^r Twist, he had sustained severe internal in jury and damage, from which he was at that mo ment suffering the acutest torture.

When Noah saw that the intelligence he commu nicated perfectly paralyzed Mr. Bumble, he imparted additional effect thereunto, by bewailing his dread ful wounds ten times louder than before; and when he observed a gentleman in a white w r aistcoat cross ing the yard, he was more tragic in his lamentations than ever: rightly conceiving it highly expedient to attract the notice, and rouse the indignation, of the gentleman aforesaid.

The gentleman's notice was very soon attracted; for he had not walked three paces, when he turned angrily round, and inquired what that young cur was howling for, and why Mr. Bumble did not favor Mm with something which would render the series of vocular exclamations so designated an involun tary process ?

" It's a poor boy from the free-school, sir," replied Mr.Bumble, "who has been nearly murdered — all but murdered, sir—by young Twist."

" By Jove!" exclaimed the gentleman in the white waistcoat, stopping short. " I knew it! I felt a strange presentiment from the very first, that that audacious young savage would come to be hung!"

" He has likewise attempted, sir, to murder the fe male servant," said Mr. Bumble, with a face of ashy paleness.

" And his missis," interposed Mr. Claypole.

"And his master, too, I think you said, Noah?" added Mr. Bumble.

" No! he's out, or he would have murdered him," replied Noah. " He said he wanted to."

" Ah! Said he wanted to, did he, my boy ?" in quired the gentleman in the white waistcoat.

" Yes, sir," replied Noah. " And please, sir, missis wants to know whether Mr. Bumble can spare time to step up there, directly, and flog him—'cause mas ter's out."

" Certainly, my boy; certainly," said the gentle man in the white waistcoat: smiling benignly, and patting Noah's head, wMch was about three inches

higher than his own. " You're a good boy—a very good boy. Here's a penny for you. Bumble, just step up to Sowerberry's with your cane, and see what's best to be done. Don't spare him, Bumble."

" No, I will not, sir," replied the beadle: adjusting the wax-end which was twisted round the bottom of his cane, for purposes of parochial flagellation.

" Tell Sowerbeny not to spare him either. They'll never do any thing with him, without stripes and bruises," said the gentleman in the white waistcoat.

" I'll take care, sir," replied the beadle. And the cocked hat and cane having been, by this time, ad justed to their owner's satisfaction, Mr. Bumble and Noah Claypole betook themselves with all speed to the undertaker's shop.

Here the position of affairs had not at all improved. Sowerberry had not yet returned, and Oliver con tinued to kick, with undiminished vigor, at the cellar-door. The accounts of his ferocity, as related by Mrs. Sowerberry and Charlotte, were of so startling a na ture, that Mr. Bumble judged it prudent to parley, before opening the door. With this view he gave a kick at the outside, by way of prelude; and then, ap plying his mouth to the key-hole, said, in a deep and impressive tone:

"Oliver!"

" Come; you let me out!" replied Oliver, from the inside.

" Do you know this here voice, Oliver '?" said Mr. Bumble.

" Yes," replied Oliver.

" Ain't you afraid of it, sir ? Ain't you a-trembling while I speak, sir ?" said Mr. Bumble.

" No!" replied Oliver, boldly.

An answer so different from the one he had expect ed to elicit, and was in the habit of receiving, stag gered Mr. Bumble not a little. He stepped back from the key-hole, drew himself up to his full height, and looked from one to another of the three by-standers, in mute astonishment.

" Oh, you know, Mr. Bumble, he must be mad." .said Mrs. Sowerberry. " No boy in half his senses could.venture to speak so to you."

" It's not Madness, ma'am," replied Mr. Bumble, after a few moments of deep meditation. "It's Meat."

" What ?" exclaimed Mrs. Sowerberry.

" Meat, ma'am, meat," replied Bumble, with stern emphasis. " You've overfed him, ma'am. You've raised a artificial soul and spirit in him, ma'am, un becoming a person of his condition: as the board, Mrs. Sowerberry, who are practical philosophers, will tell you. What have paupers to do with soul or spirit ? It's quite enough that we let 'em have live bodies. If you had kept the boy on gruel, ma'am, this would never have happened."

" Dear, dear!" ejaculated Mrs. Sowerberry, piously raising her eyes to the kitchen ceiling; " this comes of being liberal!"

The liberality of Mrs. Sowerberry to Oliver had consisted in a profuse bestowal upon him of all the dirty odds and ends which nobody else would eat; so there was a great deal of meekness and self-devotion in he* voluntarily remaining under Mr. Bumble's heavy accusation. Of which, to do her justice, she was wholly innocent in thought, word, or deed.

"Ah!" said Mr. Bumble, when the lady brought her eyes down to earth again; " the only thing that can be done now, that I know of, is to leave him in the cellar for a day or so, till he's a little starved down; and then to take him out, and keep bim on gruel all through his apprenticeship. He comes of a bad family. Excitable natures, Airs. Sowerberry! Both the nurse and doctor said that that mother of his made her way here, against difficulties and pain that would have killed any well-disposed woman, weeks before."

At this point of Mr. Bumble's discourse, Oliver, just hearing enough to know that some new allu sion was being made to his mother, recommended kicking, with a violence that rendered every other sound inaudible. Sowerberry returned at this junct ure. . Oliver's offense having been explained to him, with such exaggerations as the ladies thought best calculated to rouse his ire, he unlocked the cellar-door in a twinkling, and dragged his rebellious ap prentice out by the collar.

Oliver's clothes had been torn in the beating he had received; his face was bruised and scratched; and his hair scattered over his forehead. The angry flush had not disappeared, however; and when he was pulled out of his prison, he scowled boldly on Noah, and looked quite undismayed.

" Now, you are a nice young fellow, ain't you ?" said Sowerberry; giving Oliver a shake, and a box on the ear.

" He called my mother names," replied Oliver.

" Well, and what if he did, you little ungrateful wretch ?" said Mrs. Sowerberry. " She deserved what he said, and worse."

" She didn't," said Oliver.

" She did," said Mrs. Sowerbeny.

" It's a lie!" said Oliver.

Mrs. Sowerberry burst into a flood of tears.

This flood of tears left Mr. Sowerberry no alterna tive. If he had hesitated for one instant to punish Oliver most severely, it must be quite clear to every experienced reader that he would have been, accord ing to all precedents in disputes of matrimony es tablished, a brute, an unnatural husband, an insult ing creature, a base imitation of a man, and various other agreeable characters too numerous for recital within the limits of this chapter. To do him justice, he was, as far as his power went—it was not very extensive — kindly disposed toward the boy; per haps, because it was his interest to be so; perhaps, because his wife disliked him. The flood of tears, however, left him no resource; so he at once gave him a drubbing, which satisfied even Mrs. Sowerber ry herself, and rendered Mr. Bumble's subsequent ap plication of the parochial cane rather unnecessary. For the rest of the day, he was shut up in the back kitchen, in company with a pump and a slice of bread; and, at night, Mrs. Sowerberry, after making various remarks outside the door, by no means com plimentary to the memory of his mother, looked into the room, and, amidst the jeers and pointings of Noah and Charlotte, ordered him up stairs to his dismal bed.

It was not until he was left alone in the silence and stillness of the gloomy workshop of the under taker, that Oliver gave way to the feelings which

the day's treatment may he supposed, likely to have awakened in a mere child. He had listened to their taunts with a look of contempt; he had borne the lash without a cry; for he felt that pride swelling in his heart which would have kept down a shriek to the last, though they had roasted him alive. But now, when there was none to see or hear him, he fell upon his knees on the floor; and, hiding his face in his hands, wept such tears as, God send for the cred it of our nature, few so young may ever have cause to pour out before him!

For a long time Oliver remained motionless in this attitude. The caudle was burning low in the socket when he rose to his feet. Having gazed cau tiously round him, and listened intently, he gently undid the fastenings of the door, and looked abroad.

It was a cold, dark night. The stars seemed, to the boy's eyes, farther from the earth than he had ever seen them before; there was no wind; and the sombre shadows thrown by the trees upon the ground, looked sepulchral and death-like, from being so still. He softly reclosed the door. Having availed himself of the expiring light of the candle to tie up in a handkerchief the few articles of wearing apparel he had, sat himself down upon a bench to wait for morning.

With the first ray of light that struggled through the crevices in the shutters, Oliver arose, and again unbarred the door. One timid look around—one moment's pause of hesitation he had closed it be hind him, and was in the open street.

He looked to the right and to the left, uncertain whither to fly. . He remembered to have seen the wagons, as they went out, toiling up the hill. He took the same route; and arriving at a foot-path across the fields, which he knew, after some dis tance, led out again into the road, struck into it, and walked quickly on.

Along this same foot-path, Oliver well remember ed he had trotted beside Mr. Bumble, when he first carried him to the work-house from the farm. His way lay directly in front of the cottage. His heart beat quickly when he bethought himself of this, and he half resolved to turn back. He had come a long way though, and should lose a great deal of time by doing so. Besides, it was so early that there was very little fear of his being seen; so he walked on.

He reached the house. There was no appearance of its inmates stirring at that early hour. Oliver stopped, and peeped into the garden. A child was weeding one of the little beds; as he stopped, he raised his pale face and disclosed the features of one of his former companions. Oliver felt glad to see him before he went; for, though younger than him self, he had been his little friend and playmate. They had been beaten, and starved, and shut up to gether many and many a time.

" Hush, Dick!" said Oliver, as the boy ran to the gate, and thrust his thin arm between the rails to greet him. " Is any one up ?"

" Nobody but me," replied the child.

" You mustn't say you saw me, Dick," said Oliver. " I am running away. They beat and ill-use me, Dick; and I am going to seek my fortune some long way off. I don't know where. How pale you are!"

" I heard the doctor tell them I was dying," re plied the child, with a faint smile. " I am very glad to see you, dear; but don't stop, don't stop!"

" Yes, yes, I will, to say good-bye to you," replied Oliver. " I shall see you again, Dick. I know I shall. You will be well and happy!"

" I hope so," replied the child. " After I am dead, but not before. I know the doctor must be right, Oliver, because I dream so much of Heaven, and An gels, and kind faces that I never see when I am awake. Kiss me," said the child, climbing up the low gate, and flinging his little arms round Oliver's neck: " Good-bye, dear! God bless you!"

The blessing was from a young child's lips, but it was the first that Oliver had ever heard invoked upon his head; and through the struggles and suf ferings, and troubles and changes, of his after-life, he never once forgot it.

CHAPTER VIII.

OLIVER WALKS TO LONDON. HE ENCOUNTERS ON THE ROAD A STRANGE SORT OF TOUNG GENTLEMAN.

OLIVER reached the stile at which the by-path terminated, and once more gained the high road. It was eight o'clock now. Though he was nearly five miles away from the town, he ran, and hid behind the hedges, by turns, till noon, fearing that he might be pursued and overtaken. Then he sat down to rest by the side of the mile-stone, and be gan to think, for the first time, where he had better go and try to live.

The stone by which he was seated bore, in large characters, an intimation that it was just seventy miles from that spot to London. The name awaken ed a new train of ideas in the boy's mind. London! —that great large place! — nobody — not even Mr. Bumble—could ever find him there! He had often heard the old men in the work-house, too, say that no lad of spirit need want in London; and that there were ways of living in that vast city which- those who had been bred up in country parts had no idea of. It was the very place for a homeless boy, who must die in the streets unless some one helped him. As these things passed through his thoughts, he jumped upon his feet and again walked forward.

He had diminished the distance between himself and London by full four miles more, before he recol lected how much he must undergo ere he could hope to reach his place of destination. As this considera tion forced itself upon him, he slackened his pace a little, and meditated upon his means of getting there. He had a crust of bread, a coarse shirt, and two pairs of stockings in his bundle. He had a penny too—a gift of Sowerberry's after some funeral in which he had acquitted himself more than ordinarily well—in his pocket. " A clean shirt," thought Oliver, " is a very comfortable thing; and so are two pairs of darned stockings; and so is a penny; but they are small helps to a sixty-five miles' walk in winter time." But Oliver's thoughts, like those of most other people, although they were extreme^ ready and active to point out his difficulties, were wholly at a loss to suggest any feasible mode of surmount-

THE YOUNG PILGRIM'S PROGRESS.

ing them; so, after a good deal of thinking to no particular purpose, he changed his little bundle over to the other shoulder, and trudged on,

Oliver walked twenty miles that day ; and all that time tasted nothing but the crust of dry bread, and a few draughts of water, which he begged at the cot tage-doors by the road-side. When the night came, he turned into a meadow; and, creeping close under a hay-rick, determined to lie there till morning. He felt frightened at first, for the wind moaned dismally over the empty fields; and he was cold and hungry, and more alone than he had ever felt before. Being very tired with his walk, however, he soon fell asleep and forgot his troubles.

He felt cold and stiff when he got up next morn ing, and so hungry that he was obliged to exchange the penny for a small loaf, in the very first village through which he passed. He had walked no more than twelve miles, when night closed in again. His feet were sore, and his legs so weak that they trem bled beneath him. Another night passed in the bleak, damp air, made him worse; when he set for ward on his journey next morning, he could hardly crawl along.

He waited at the bottom of a steep hill till a stage coach came up, and then begged of the outside pas sengers ; but there were very few who took any no tice of him; and even those told him to wait till they got to the top of the hill, and then let them see how far he could run for a halfpenny. Poor Oliver tried to keep up with the coach a little way, but was unable to do it, by reason of his fatigue and sore feet. When the outsides saw this, they put their half pence back into their pockets again, declaring that he was an idle young dog, and didn't deserve any thing; and the coach rattled away and left only a cloud of dust behind.

In some villages, large painted boards were fixed up, warning all persons who begged within the dis trict that they would be sent to jail. This fright ened Oliver very much, and made him glad to get out of those villages with all possible expedition. In others, he would stand about the inn-yards, and look mournfully at every one who passed: a proceeding which generally terminated in the landlady's order ing one of the post-boys who were lounging about to drive that strange boy out of the place, for she was sure he had come to steal something. If he begged at a farmer's house, ten to one but they threatened to set the dog on him; and when he showed his nose in a shop, they talked about the beadle—which brought Oliver's heart into his mouth —very often the only thing he had there for many hours together.

In fact, if it had not been for a good-hearted turn pike-man, and a benevolent old lady, Oliver's trou bles would have been shortened by the very same process which had put an end to his mother's; in other words, he would most assuredly have fallen dead upon the king's highway. But. the turnpike-niiin gave him a meal of bread and cheese; and the old lady, who had a shipwrecked grandson wander ing barefoot in some distant part of the earth, took pity upon the poor orphan, and gave him what little she coiild afford—and more—with such kind and gentle words, and such tears of sympathy and com

passion, that they sank deeper into Oliver's soul, than all the sufferings he had ever undergone.

Early on the seventh morning after he had left his native place, Oliver limped slowly into the little town of Bamet. The window-shutters w r ere closed; the street was empty; not a soul had awakened to the business of the day. The sun was rising in all its splendid beauty; but the light only served to show the boy his own lonesomeness and desolation, as he sat, with bleeding feet and covered with dust, upon a door-step.

By degrees the shutters were opened; the window-blinds were drawn up; and people began passing to and fro. Some few stopped to gaze at Oliver for a moment or two, or turned round to stare at him as they hurried by; but none relieved him, or troubled themselves to inquire how he came there. He had no heart to beg. And there he sat.

He had been crouching on the step for some time: wondering at the great number of public-houses (every other house in Baruet was a tavern, large or small), gazing listlessly at the coaches as they passed through, and thinking how strange it seemed that they could do, with ease, in a few hours, what it had taken him a whole week of courage and determina tion beyond his years to accomplish: when he was roused by observing that a boy, who had passed him carelessly some minutes before, had returned, and was now surveying him most earnestly from the op posite side of the way. He took little heed of this at first; but the boy remained in the same attitude of close observation so long, that Oliver raised his head, and returned his steady look. Upon this, the boy crossed over, and, walking close up to Oliver, said,

" Hullo, my covey! What's the row ?"

The boy who addressed this inquiry to the young wayfarer, was about his own age: but one of the queerest-looking boys that Oliver had ever seen. He was a snub-nosed, flat-browed, common-faced boy enough; and as dirty a juvenile as one would wish to see; but he had about him all the airs and man ners of a man. He was short of his age; with rath er bow legs, and little, sharp, ugly eyes. His hat was stuck on the top of his head so lightly, that it threat ened to fall off every moment—and would have done so, very often, if the wearer had not had a knack of every now and then giving his head a sudden twitch, which brought it back to its old place again. He wore a man's coat, which reached nearly to his heels. He had turned the cuffs back, half-way up his arm, to get his hands out of the sleeves: apparently with the ultimate view of thrusting them into the pockets of his corduroy trowsers; for there he kept them. He was, altogether, as roystering and swaggering a young gentleman as ever stood four feet six, or some thing less, in his bluchers. .

" Hullo, my covey! What's the row ?" said this strange young gentleman to Oliver.

" I am very hungry and tired," replied Oliver: the tears standing in his eyes as he spoke. " I have walked a long way. I have been walking these seven days."

" Walking for sivin days!" said the young gentle man. " Oh, I see. Beak's order, eh ? But," he add ed, noticing Oliver's look of surprise, " I suppose you don't know what a beak is, my flash com-pan-i-on."

OLIVER TWIST.

Oliver mildly replied, that he had always heard a bird's month described by the term in question.

" My eyes, how green!" exclaimed the young gen tleman. " Why, a beak's a madgst'rate; and when you walk by a beak's order, it's not straight forerd, but always a-going up, and nivir a-couiiug down agin. Was you never on the mill ?"

" What mill ?" inquired Oliver.

" What mill! Why, the mill—the mill as takes up so little room that it'll work inside a Stone Jug; and always goes better when the wind's low with people, than when it's high; acos then they can't get work men. But come," said the young gentleman; " you want grub, and you

shall have it. I'm at low-wa ter-mark myself—only one bob and a magpie; but,
which the strange boy eyed him from time to time with great attention.

" Going to London ?" said the strange boy, when Oliver had at length concluded.

" Yes."

" Got any lodgings ?"

"No."

"Money?"

"No."

The strange boy whistled, and put his arms into his pockets as far as the big coat sleeves would let them go.

" Do you live in London ?" inquired Oliver.

" Yes, I do, when I'm at home," replied the boy. " I suppose you want some place to sleep in to-night, don't you F

" HULLO, MY COVEY !

as far as it goes, I'll fork out and stump. Up with you on your pins. There! Now then! Morrice!"

Assisting Oliver to rise, the young gentleman took him to an adjacent chandler's shop, where he pur chased a sufficiency of ready-dressed ham and a half-quartern loaf, or, as he himself expressed it, " a four-penny bran!" the ham being kept clean and pre served from dust by the ingenious expedient of mak ing a hole in the loaf by pulling out a portion of the crumb, and'stuffing it therein. Taking the bread under his arm, the young gentleman turned into a small public-house, and led the way to a tap-room in the rear of the premises. Here a pot of beer was brought in by direction of the mysterious youth; and Oliver, falling to at his new friend's bidding, made a long and hearty meal, during the progress of

" I do, indeed," answered Oliver. " I have not slept under a roof since I left the country."

"Don't fret your eyelids on that score,"said tlir young gentleman. "I've got to be in London to night ; and I know a 'spectable old genelman as lives there, wot'll give you lodgings for nothink, and nev er ask for the change—that is, if any genelman he knows interduces you. And don't he know me f Oh, no ! not in the least! By no means. Certainly not!"

The young gentleman smiled, as if to intimate that the latter fragments of discourse were playfully iron ical ; and finished the beer as he did so.

This unexpected offer of shelter was too tempting to be resisted; especially as it was immediately fol lowed up, by the assurance that the old gentleman

THE ARTFUL DODGER.

referred to would doubtless provide Oliver with a comfortable place, without loss of time. This led te a more friendly and confidential dialogue; from which Oliver discovered that his friend's name was Jack Dawkins, and that he was a peculiar pet and protege of the elderly gentleman before mentioned.

Mr. Dawkins's appearance did not say a vast deal in favor of the comforts which his patron's interest obtained for those whom he took under his protec tion ; but, as he had a rather flighty and dissolute mode of conversing, and furthermore avowed that among his intimate friends he was better known by the sobriquet of " The artful Dodger," Oliver conclud ed that, being of a dissipated and careless turn, the moral precepts of his benefactor had hitherto been thrown away upon him. Under this impression, he secretly resolved to cultivate the good opinion of the old gentleman as quickly as possible; and, if he found the Dodger incorrigible, as he more than half suspected he should, to decline the honor of his fur ther acquaintance.

As John Dawkius objected to their entering Lon don before nightfall, it was nearly eleven o'clock when they reached the turnpike at Islington. They crossed from the Angel into St. John's road; struck down the small street which terminates at Sadler's Wells Theatre; through Exmouth Street and Cop pice Row; down the little court by the side of the work-house; across the classic ground which once bore the name of Hockley-iu-the-Hole; thence into Little Saffron Hill; and so into Saffron Hill the Great; along which the Dodger scudded at a rapid pace, directing Oliver to follow close at his heels.

Although Oliver had enough to occupy his atten tion in keeping sight of his leader, he could not help bestowing a few hasty glances on either side of the way, as he passed along. A dirtier or more wretch ed place he had never seen. The street was very narrow and muddy, and the air was impregnated with filthy odors. There were a good many small shops; but the only stock-in-trade appeared to be heaps of children, who, even at that time of night, were crawling in and out at the doors, or screaming from the inside. The sole places that seemed to prosper amidst the general blight of the j lace were the public-houses; and in them the lowest orders of Irish were wrangling with might and main. Cov ered ways and yards, which here and there diverged from the main street, disclosed little knots of houses, where drunken men and women were positively wal lowing in filth*; and from several of the door-ways, great ill-looking fellows were cautiously emerging, bound, to all appearance, on no very well-disposed or harmless errands.

Oliver was just considering whether he hadn't bet ter run away, when they reached the bottom of the hill. His conductor, catching him by the arm, push ed open the door of a house near Field Lane; and, drawing him into the passage, closed it behind them.

" Now, then!" cried a voice from below, in reply to a whistle from the Dodger.

" Plummy and slam!" was the reply.

This seemed to be some watch-word or signal that all was right; for the light of a feeble candle gleam ed on the wall at the remote end of the passage; and a man's face peeped out from where a balus trade of the old kitchen staircase had been broken away.

" There's two on you," said the man, thrusting the candle farther out, and shading his eyes with his hand. " Who's the t'other one f'

"A new pal," replied Jack Dawkins, pulling Oli ver forward.

" Where did he come from ?"

" Greenland. Is Fagin up stairs ?"

"Yes; he's a sortiif the wipes. Up with you!" The candle was drawn back, and the face disap peared.

Oliver, groping his way with one hand, and hav ing the other firmly grasped by his companion, as cended with much difficulty the dark and broken stairs; which his conductor mounted with an ease and expedition that showed he was well acquainted with them. He threw open the door of a back-room, and drew Oliver in after him.

The walls and ceiling of the room were perfectly black with age and dirt. There was a deal table be fore the fire: upon which were a candle stuck in a ginger-beer bottle, two or three pewter pots, a loaf and butter, and a plate. In a frying-pan, which was on tlie fire, and which was secured to*the mantel shelf by a string, some sausages were cooking; and standing over them, with a toasting-fork in his hand, was a very old, shriveled Jew, whose villainous-look ing and repulsive face was obscured by a quantity of matted red hair. He was dressed in a greasy flannel gown, with his throat bare; and seemed to be divid ing his attention between the frying-pan and a clothes-horse, over which a great number of silk handkerchiefs were hanging. Several rough beds, made of old sacks, were huddled side by side on the floor. Seated round the table were four or five boys, none older than the Dodger, smoking long clay pipes and drinking spirits, with the air of middle-aged men. These all crowded about their associates as he whispered a few words to the Jew; and then turned round and grinned at Oliver. So did the Jew tiimself, toasting-fork in hand.

"This is him, Fagin," said Jack Dawkins; "my friend Oliver Twist."

The Jew grinned; and, making a low obeisance to Oliver, took him by the hand, and hoped he should have the honor of his intimate acquaintance. Upon this, the young gentlemen with the pipes came round him, and shook both his hands very hard—especial ly the one in which he held his little bundle. One young gentleman was very anxious to hang up his cap for him; and another was so obliging as to put his hands in his pockets, in order that, as he was very tired, he might not have the trouble of emptying them himself when he went to bed. These civilities would probably have been extended much farther, but for a liberal exercise of the Jew's toasting-fork on the heads and shoulders of the affectionate youths who offered them.

" We are very glad to see you, Oliver, very," said the Jew. " Dodger, take off the sausages ; and draw a tub near the fire for Oliver. Ah, you're a-staring at the pocket-handkerchiefs! eh, my dear! There are a good many of 'em, ain't there? We've just looked 'em out, ready for the wash; that's all, Oli ver—that's all. Ha! ha! ha!"

OLIVER TWIST.

The latter part of this speech was hailed by a bois terous shout from all the hopeful pupils of the merry old gentleman; in the midst of which they went to supper.

Oliver ate his share, and the Jew then mixed him n glass of hot gin and water: telling him he must drink it off directly, because another gentleman wanted the tumbler. Oliver did as he was desired. Immediately afterward he felt himself gently lifted on to one of the sacks; and then he sunk into a deep sleep.

CHAPTER IX.

CONTAINING FARTHER PARTICULARS CONCERNING THE PLEASANT OLD GENTLEMAN AND HIS HOPEFUL PUPILS.

IT was late next morning when Oliver awoke, from a sound, long sleep. There was no other person in the room but the old Jew, who was boiling some coffee in a saucepan for breakfast, and whistling softly to himself as he stirred it round and round with an iron spoon. He would stop every now and then to listen when there was the least noise below; and when h« had satisfied himself, he would go on, whistling and stirring again, as before.

Although Oliver had roused himself from sleep, he was not thoroughly awake. There is a drowsy state, between sleeping and waking, when you dream more in five minutes with your eyes half open, and your self half conscious of every thing that is passing around you, than you would in five nights with your eyes fast closed, and your senses wrapped in perfect unconsciousness. At such times, a mortal knows just enough of what his mind is doing, to form some glimmering conception of its mighty powers, its bounding from earth and spurning time and space, when freed from the restraint of its corporeal asso ciate.

Oliver was precisely in this condition. He saw the Jew with his half-closed eyes; heard his low Avhistling; and recognized the sound of the spoou grating against the saucepan's sides; and yet the self-same senses were mentally engaged, at the same time, in busy action with almost every body he had ever known.

When the coffee was done, the Jew drew the sauce pan to the hob. Standing, then, in an irresolute at titude for a few minutes, as if he did not well know how to employ himself, he turned round and looked at Oliver, and called him by his name. He did not answer, and was to all appearance asleep.

After satisfying himself upon this head, the Jew stepped gently to the door: which he fastened. He then drew forth, as it seemed to Oliver, from some trap in the floor, a small box, which he placed care fully on the table. His eyes glistened as he raised the lid and looked in. Dragging an old chair to the table, he sat down ; and took from it a magnificent gold watch, sparkling with jewels.

"Aha!" said the Jew, shrugging up his shoulders, and distorting every feature with a hideous grin. •' Clever dogs! Clever do'gs! Staunch to the last! Never told the old parson where they were. Never peached upon old Fagin! And why should they ? It wouldn't have loosened the knot, or kept the drop

up, a minute longer. No, 110, no! Fine fellows! Fine fellows!"

With these, and other muttered reflections of the like nature, the Jew once more deposited the watch in its place of safety. At least half a dozen more were severally drawn forth from the same box, and surveyed with equal pleasure ; besides rings, brooch es, bracelets, and other articles of jewelry, of such magnificent materials, and costly workmanship, that Oliver had no idea even of their names.

Having replaced these trinkets, the Jew took out another, so small that it lay in the palm of his hand. There seemed to be some very minute inscription on it; for the Jew laid it flat upon the table, and, shad ing it with his hand, pored over it, long and earnest ly. At length he put it down, as if despairing of success, and, leaning back in his chair, muttered:

" What a fine thing capital punishment is !> Dead men never repent; dead men never bring awkward stories to light. Ah, it's a fine thing for the trade! Five of 'em strung up in a row, and none left to play booty, or turn white-livered!"

As the Jew uttered these words, his bright dark eyes, which had been staring vacantly before him, fell on Oliver's face ; the boy's eyes were fixed on his in mute curiosity; and although the recognition was only for an instant for the briefest space of time that can possibly be conceived—it was enough to show the old man that he had been observed. He closed the lid of the box with a loud crash ; and, lay ing his hand on a bread-knife which was on the ta ble, started furiously up. He trembled very much though ; for, even in his terror, Oliver could see that the knife quivered in the air.

"What's that?" said the Jew. "What do you watch me for ? Why are you awake ? What have you seen? Spe»k out, boy! Quick quick! for your life!"

" I wasn't able to sleep any longer, sir," replied Oliver, meekly. " I am very sorry if I have disturbed you, sir."

" You were not awake an hour ago ?" said the Jew, scowling fiercely on the boy.

" No! No, indeed!" replied Oliver.

" Are you sure ?" cried the Jew, with a still fiercer look than before, and a threatening attitude.

" Upon my word I was not, sir," replied Oliver, earnestly. " I was not, indeed, sir."

" Tush, tush, my dear!" said the Jew, abruptly re suming his old manner, and playhig with the knife a little, before he laid it down; as if to induce the belief that he had caught it up in mere sport. " Of course I know that, my dear. I only tried to frighten you. You're a brave boy. Ha! ha! you're a brave boy, Oliver!" The Jew rubbed his hands with a chuckle, but glanced uneasily at the box, notwith standing.

" Did you see any of these pretty things, my dear ?" said the Jew, laying his hand upon it after a short pause.

" Yes, sir," replied Oliver.

"Ah!" said the Jew, turning rather pale. "They —they're mine, Oliver; my little property. All I have to live upon, in my old age. The folks call me a miser, my dear. Only a miser ; that's all."

Oliver thought the old gentleman must be a de-

IN THE PLEASANT OLD GENTLEMAN'S HOUSE.

elded ruiser to live in snch a dirty place, with so many watches; but, thinking that perhaps his fond ness for the Dodger and the other boys cost him a good deal of money, he only cast a deferential look at the Jew, and asked if he might get up.

" Certainly, my dear, certainly," replied the old gentleman.' " Stay. There's a pitcher of water in the corner by the door. Bring it here; and I'll give you a basin to wash in, my dear."

Oliver got up; walked across the room; and stoop ed for an instant to raise the pitcher. When he turned his head, the box was gone.

He had scarcely washed himself, and made every thing tidy by emptying the basin out of the win dow, agreeably to the Jew's directions, when the Dodger returned, accompanied by a very sprightly young friend, whom Oliver had seen smoking on the previous night, and who was now formally intro duced to him as Charley Bates. The four sat down, to breakfast on the coffee, and some hot rolls and ham which the Dodger had brought home in the crown of Ms hat.

"Well," said the Jew, glancing slyly at Oliver, and addressing himself to the Dodger, "I hope you've been at work this morning, my dears ?"

" Hard," replied the Dodger.

"As Xails," added Charley Bates.

"Good boys, good boys!" said the Jew. "What have you got, Dodger ?"

"A cbuple of pocket-books," replied that young gentleman.

" Lined ?" inquired the Jew, with eagerness.

" Pretty well," replied the Dodger, producing two pocket-books; one green, and the other red.

Xot so heavy as they might be," said the Jew, after looking at the insides carefully; "but very neat and nicely made. Ingenious workman, ain't he, Oliver ?"

"Very, indeed, sir," said Oliver. At which Mr. Charles Bates laughed uproariously; very much to the amazement of Oliver, who saw nothing to laugh at in any thing that had passed.

" And what have you got, my dear ?" said Fagin to Charley Bates.

Wipes," replied Master Bates; at the same time producing four pocket-handkerchiefs.

"Well," said the Jew, inspecting them closely; " they're very good ones, very. YOTI haven't marked them well, though, Charley; so the marks shall be picked out with a needle, and we'll teach Oliver how to do it. Shall us, Oliver, eh ? Ha! ha! ha!"

" If you please, sir," said Oliver.

" You'd like to be able to make pocket - handker chiefs as easy as Charley Bates, wouldn't you, my den ?" said the Jew.

"Very much, indeed, if youll teach me, sir," replied Oliver.

Master Bates saw something so exquisitely ludi crous in this reply, that he burst into another laugh; which laugh, meeting the coffee he was drinking, and carrying it down some wrong channel, very near ly terminated in his premature suffocation.

" He is so jolly green!" said Charley when he re covered, as an apology to the company for his unpo-lite behavior.

The Dodger said nothing, but he smoothed Oliver's 0

hair over his eyes, and said he'd know better by-and-by; upon which the old gentleman, observing Oliver's color mounting, changed the subject by asking wheth er there had been much of a crowd at the execution that morning? This made him wonder more and more; for it was plain from the replies of the two boys that they had both been there; and Oliver nat urally wondered how they could possibly have found time to be so very industrious.

When the breakfast was cleared away, the merry old gentleman and the two boys played at a very curious and uncommon game, which was performed in this way: The merry old gentleman, placing a snuff-box in one pocket of his trowsers, a note-case in the other, and a watch in his waistcoat pocket, with a guard-chain round his neck, and sticking a mock - diamond pin in his shirt, buttoned his coat tight around him, and putting his spectacle-case and handkerchief in his pockets, trotted up and down the room with a stick, in imitation of the manner in which old gentlemen walk about the streets any hour in the day. Sometimes he stopped at the fire-place, and sometimes at the door, making believe that he was staring with all his might into shop - windows. At such times he would look constantly round him, for fear of thieves, and would keep slapping all his pockets in turn, to see that he hadn't lost any thing, in such a very funny and natural manner, that Oli ver laughed till the tears ran down his face. All this time the two boys followed him closely about, get ting out of his sight, so nimbly, every time he turned round, that it was impossible to follow their motions. At last, the Dodger trod upon his toes, or ran upon his boot accidentally, while Charley Bates stumbled up against him behind; and in that one moment they took from him, with the most extraordinary rapid ity, snuff-box, note-case, watch-guard, chain, shirt-pin, pocket-handkerchief, even the spectacle-case. If the old gentleman felt a hand in any one of his pockets, he cried out where it was; and then the game began all over again.

When this game had been played a great many times, a couple of young ladies called to see the young gentlemen ; one of whom was named Bet, and the other Nancy. They wore a good deal of hair, not very neatly turned up behind, and were rather untidy about the shoes and stockings. They were not exactly pretty, perhaps; but they had a great deal of color in their faces, and looked quite stout and hearty. Being remarkably free and agreeable in their manners, Oliver thought them very nice girls indeed. As there is no doubt they were.

These visitors stopped a long time. Spirits were produced, in consequence of one of the young ladies complaining of a coldness in her inside; and the con versation took a very convivial and improving turn. At length Charley Bates expressed his opinion that it was time to pad the hoof. This, it occurred to Oliver, must be French for going out; for, directly afterward, the Dodger, and Charley, and the two young ladies went away together, having been kind ly furnished by the amiable old Jew with money to spend.

" There, my dear," said Fagin. " That's a pleasant life, isn't it ? They have gone out for the day."

" Have they done work, sir I" inquired Oliver.

" Yes," said the Jew ; " that is, unless they should unexpectedly come across any when they are out; and they won't neglect it, if they do, my dear, de pend upon it. Make 'em your models, my dear. Make 'em your models," tapping the fire-shovel on the hearth to add force to his words: "do every thing they bid you, and take their advice in all mat ters—especially the Dodger's, my dear. He'll be a great man himself, and will make you one too, if you take pattern by him.—Is my handkerchief hanging out of my pocket, my dear ?" said the Jew, stopping short.

" Yes, sir," said Oliver.

" See if you can take it out, without my feeling it, as you saw them do when we were at play this morning."

Oliver held up the bottom of the pocket with one hand, as he had seen the Dodger hold it, and drew the handkerchief lightly out of it with the other.

" Is it gone ?" cried the Jew.

" Here it is, sir," said Oliver, showing it in his hand.

" You're a clever boy, my dear, 7 * said the playful old gentleman, patting Oliver on the head approv ingly. " I never saw a sharper lad. Here's a shil ling for you. If you go on in this way, you'll be the greatest man of the time. And now come here, and I'll show you how to take the marks out of the hand kerchiefs."

Oliver wondered what picking the old gentleman's pocket in play had to do with his chances of being a great man. But,, thinking that the Jew, being so much his senior^ must know best, he followed him quietly to the table, and was soon deeply involved in his new study.

CHAPTER X.

OLIVER BECOMES BETTER ACQUAINTED WITH THE CHAR ACTERS OF HIS NEW ASSOCIATES, AND PURCHASES EX PERIENCE AT A HIGH PRICE. BEING A SHORT BUT VERT IMPORTANT CHAPTER IN THIS HISTORY.

FOR many days Oliver remained in the Jew's room, picking the marks out of the pocket-hand kerchiefs, (of which a great number were brought home,) and sometimes taking part in the game al ready described, which the two boys and the Jew played, regularly, every morning. At length he be gan to languish for fresh air, and took many occa sions of earnestly entreating the old gentleman to allow him to go out to work, with his two com panions.

Oliver was rendered the more anxious to be act ively employed, by what he had seen of the stern morality of the old gentleman's character. When ever the Dodger or Charley Bates came home at night empty-handed, he would expatiate with great vehemence on the misery of idle and lazy habits ; and would enforce upon them the necessity of an active life, by sending them supperless to bed. On one oc casion, indeed, he even went so far as to knock them both down a flight of stairs ; but this was carrying out his virtuous precepts to an unusual extent.

At length, one morning, Oliver obtained the per mission he had so eagerly sought. There had been

no handkerchiefs to work upon for two or three days, and the dinners had been rather meagre. Per haps these were reasons for the old gentleman's giv ing his assent; but, whether they were or no, he told Oliver he might go, and placed him under the joint guardianship of Charley Bates and his Mend the Dodger.

The three boys sallied out; the Dodger Avith his coat-sleeves tucked up, and his hat cocked, as xisual; 'Master Bates sauntering along with his hands in his pockets; and Oliver between them, wondering where they were going, and what branch of manufacture he would be instructed in first.

The pace at which they went was such a very lazy, ill-looking saunter, that Oliver soon began to think his companions were going to deceive the old gentleman, by not going to work at all. The Dodger had a vicious propensity, too, of pulling the caps from the heads of small boys and tossing them down areas; while Charley Bates exhibited some very loose notions concerning the rights of property, by pilfering divers apples and onions from the stalls at the kennel sides, and thrusting them into pock ets which were so surprisingly capacious, that they seemed to undermine his whole suit of clothes in ev ery direction. These things looked so bad that Ol iver was on the point of declaring his intention of seeking his Avay back in the best way he could;

when his thoughts were suddenly directed into an other channel by a very mysterious change of be havior on the part of the Dodger.

They were just emerging from a narrow court not far from the open square in Clerkeuwell, which is yet called, by some strange perversion of terms, " The Green," when the Dodger made a sudden stop; and, laying his finger on his lip, drew his companions back again, with the greatest caution and circum spection.

"What's the matter?" demanded Oliver.

" Hush!" replied the Dodger. " Do you see that old cove at the book-stall ?"

" The old gentleman over the way ?" said Oliver. " Yes, I see him."

" He'll do," said the Dodger.

"A prime plant," observed Master Charley Bates.

Oliver looked from one to the other, with the greatest surprise; but he was not permitted to make any inquiries; for the two boys walked stealthily across the road, and slunk close behind the old gen tleman toward whom his attention had been direct ed. Oliver walked a few paces after them; and, not knowing whether to advance or retire, stood looking on in silent amazement.

The old gentleman was a very respectable-looking personage, with a powdered head and gold specta cles. He was dressed in a bottle-green coat with a black velvet collar; wore white trowsers; and car ried a smart bamboo cane under his arm. He had taken up a book from the stall, and there he stood, reading away as hard as if he were in his elbow-chair in his own study. It is very possible that he fancied himself there, indeed; for it was plain, from his abstraction, that he saw not the book-stall, nor the street, nor the boys, nor, in short, any thing but the book itself, which he was reading straight through, turning over the leaf when he got to the

OUT FOR A WALK.

bottom of a page, beginning at the top line of the next one, and going regularly on, with the greatest interest and eagerness.

What was Oliver's horror and alarm as he stood a few paces off, looking on with his eyelids as wide open as they would possibly go, to see the Dodger plunge his hand into the old gentleman's pocket, and draw from thence a handkerchief! To see him hand the same to Charley Bates; and finally to be hold them both running away round the corner at full speed!

In an instant the whole mystery of the handker chiefs, and the watches, and the jewels, and the Jew,

But the old gentleman was not the only person who raised the hue-aud-cry. The Dodger and Mas ter Bates, unwilling to attract public attention by running down the open street, had" merely retired into the very first door-way round the corner. They no sooner heard the cry, and saw Oliver running, than, guessing exactly how the matter stood, they issued forth with great promptitude; and, shouting " Stop thief!" too, joined in the pursuit like good cit izens.

Although Oliver had been brought Tip by philos ophers, he was not theoretically acquainted with the beautiful axiom that self-preservation is the first law

" STOP

rushed upon the boy's mind. He stood, for. a mo ment, with the blood so tingling through all his veins from terror, that he felt as if he were in a burning fire; then, confused and frightened, he took to his heels; and, not knowing what he did, made off as fast as he could lay his feet to the ground.

This was all done in a minute's space. In the very instant when Oliver began to run, the old gen tleman, putting his band to his pocket, and miss ing his handkerchief, turned sharp round. Seeing the boy scudding away at such a rapid pace, he very natiirally concluded him to be the depredator; and, shouting "Stop thief!" with all his might,made off after him, book in hand.

of nature. If he had been, perhaps he would have been prepared for this. Not being prepared, how ever, it alarmed him the more; so away he went like the wind, with the old gentleman and the two boys roaring and shouting behind him.

" Stop thief! Stop thief!" There is a magic in the sound. The tradesman leaves his counter, and the carman his wagon; the butcher throws down his tray; the baker his basket ;. the milkman his pail; the errand-boy his parcels; the school-boy his marbles; the pavior his pick-axe; the child his bat-tledoor. Away they run, pell-mell, helter-skelter, slap-dash: tearing, yelling, screaming, knocking down the passengers as they turn the corners, rous-

OLIVER TWIST.

ing up the dogs, and astonishing the fowls; and streets, squares, and courts, re-echo with the sound.

" Stop thief! Stop thief!" The cry is taken up by a hundred voices, and the crowd accumulate at every turning. Away they fly, splashing through the mud, and rattling along the pavements: up go the windows, out run the people, onward bear the mob—a whole audience desert Punch in the very thickest of the plot, and, joining the rushing throng, swell the shout, and lend fresh vigor to the cry," Stop thief! Stop thief!"

"Stop thief I" Stop thief!" There is a passion for hunting something deeply implanted in the human breast. One wretched breathless child, panting with exhaustion; terror in his looks; agony in his eyes; large drops of perspiration streaming down his face; strains every nerve to make head upon his pursuers; and as they follow on his track, and gain upon him every instant, they hail his decreasing strength with still louder shouts, and whoop and scream with joy. " Stop thief!" Ay, stop him, for God's sake, were it only in mercy!

Stopped at last! A clever blow. He is down upon the pavement; and the crowd eagerly gather • round him: each new-comer jostling and struggling with the others to catch a glimpse. " Stand aside!" "Give him a little air!" "Nonsense! he don't de serve it !" " Where's the gentleman f" " Here he is, coming down the street." " Make room there for the gentleman !" " Is this the boy, sir ?" " Yes."

Oliver lay, covered with mud and dust, and bleed ing from the mouth, looking wildly round upon the heap of faces that surrounded him, when the old gentleman was officiously dragged and pushed into the circle by the foremost of the pursuers.

" Yes," said the gentleman, " I am afraid it is the boy."

"Afraid!"murmured the crowd. "That's a good 'un!"

" Poor fellow!" said the gentleman, " he has hurt himself."

" did that, sir," said a great lubberly fellow, step ping forward; " and preciously I cut my knuckle agin' his mouth. I stopped him, sir."

The fellow touched his hat with a grin, expecting something for his pains; but the old gentleman, ey ing him with an expression of dislike, looked anx iously round, as if he contemplated running away himself: which it is very possible he might have at-.tempted to do, and thus have afforded another chase, had not a police officer (who is generally the last per son to arrive in such cases) at that moment made his way through the crowd, and seized Oliver by the collar.

" Come, get up," said the man, roughly.

" It wasn't me indeed, sir. Indeed, indeed, it was two other boys," said Oliver, clasping his hands pas sionately, and looking round. " They are here some where."

" Oh no, they ain't," said the officer. He meant this to be ironical, but it was true besides; for the Dodger and Charley Bates had filed off down the first convenient court they came to. " Come, get up!"

" Don't hurt him," said the old gentleman, compas sionately.

" Oh no, I won't hurt him," replied the officer,

tearing his jacket half off his back, in proof thereof. " Come, I kuow you; it won't do. Will you stand upon your legs, you young devil ?"

Oliver,'who could hardly stand, made a shift to raise himself on his feet, and was at once lugged along the streets by the jacket-collar at a rapid pace. The gentleman walked on with them by the officer's side ; and as many of the crowd as could achieve the feat got a little ahead, and stared back at Oliver from time to time. The boys shouted in triumph; and on they went.

CHAPTER XI.

TKEATS OF MR. FANG, THE POLICE MAGISTRATE ; AND FURNISHES A SLIGHT SPECIMEN OF HIS MODE OF AD MINISTERING JUSTICE.

THHE offense had been committed within the dis-JL trict, and indeed in the immediate neighborhood of, a very notorious metropolitan police office. The crowd had only the satisfaction of accompanying Ol iver through two or three streets, and down a place called Mutton Hill, when he was led beneath a low archway, and up a dirty court, into this dispensary of summary justice, by the back way. It was a small paved yard into which they turned; and here they encountered a stout man with a bunch of whiskers on his face, and a bunch of keys in his hand.

"What's the matter now?" said the man carelessly.

"A young fogle-hunter," replied the man w r ho had Oliver in charge.

"Are you the party that's been robbed, sir?" in quired the man with the keys.

" Yes, I am," replied the old gentleman; " but I am not sure that this boy actually took the hand kerchief. I would rather not press the case."

" Must go before the magistrate now, sir," replied the man. " His worship will be disengaged in half a minute. Now, young gallows!"

This was an invitation for Oliver to enter through a door which he unlocked as he spoke, and which led into a stone cell. Here he was searched, and, nothing being found upon him, locked up.

This cell was in shape and size something like an area cellar, only not so light. It was most intolera bly dirty ; for it was Monday morning ; and it had been tenanted by six drunken people, who had been locked up, elsewhere, since Saturday night. But this is little. In our station-houses, men and women are every night confined on the most trivial charges — the word is worth noting—in dungeons, compared with which, those in Newgate, occupied by the most atrocious felons, tried, found guilty, and under sen tence of death, are palaces. Let any one who doubts this compare the two.

The old gentleman looked almost as rueful as Oli ver when the key grated in the lock. He turned with a sigh to the book, which had been the innocent cause of all this disturbance.

" There is something in that boy's face," said the old gentleman to himself as he walked slowly away, tapping his chin with the cover of the book, in a thoughtful manner; "something that touches and interests me. Can he be innocent ? He looked like.

—By-tlie-bye," exclaimed the old gentleman, halting very abruptly, and staring up into the sky, " Bless my soul! Where have I seen something like that look before ?"

After musing for some minutes, the old gentleman walked, with the same meditative face, into a back anteroom opening from the yard; and there, retir ing into a corner, called up before his mind's eye a vast amphitheatre of faces over which a dusky cur tain had hung for many years. " No," said the old gentleman, shaking his head; " it must be imagina tion."

He wandered over them again. He had called them into view, and it was not easy to replace the shroud that had so long concealed them. There were the faces of friends, and foes, and of many that had been almost strangers peering intrusively from the crowd; there were the faces of young and blooming girls that were now old women; there were faces that the grave had changed and closed upon, but which the mind, superior to its power, still dressed in their old freshness and beauty, calling back the lustre of the eyes, the brightness of the smile, the beaming of the soul through its mask of clay, and whispering of beauty beyond the tomb, changed but to be heightened, and taken from earth only to be set up as a light, to shed a soft and gentle glow upon the path to heaven.

But the old gentleman could recall no one counte nance of which Oliver's features bore a trace. So, he heaved a sigh over the recollections he had awak ened ; and being, happily for himself, an absent old gentleman, buried them again in the pages of the musty book.

He was roused by a touch on the shoulder, and a request from the man with the keys to follow him into the office. He closed his book hastily, and was at once ushered into the imposing presence of the renowned Mr. Fang.

The office was a front parlor, with a paneled wall. Mr. Fang sat behind a bar, at the upper end; and on one side the door was a sort of wooden pen in which poor little Oliver was already deposited; trembling very much at the awfulness of the scene.

Mr. Fang was a lean, long-backed, stiff-necked, middle-sized man, with no great quantity of hair, and what he had, growing on the back and sides of his head. His face was stern, and much flushed. If he were really not in the habit of drinking rather more than was exactly good for him, he might have brought an action against his countenance for libel, and have recovered heavy damages.

The old gentleman bowed respectfully; and ad vancing to the magistrate's desk, said, suiting the action to the word, " That is my name and address, sir." He then withdrew a pace or two; and, with another polite and gentlemanly inclination of the head, waited to be questioned.

Now, it so happened that Mr. Fang was at that moment perusing a leading article in a newspaper of the morning, adverting to some recent decision of his, and commending him, for the three hundred and fiftieth time, to the special and particular notice of the Secretary of State for the Home Department. He was out of temper; and he looked up with an angry scowl.

"Who are you ?" said Mr. Fang.

The old gentleman pointed, with some surprise, to his card.

"Officer!" said Mr. Fang, tossing the card con temptuously away with the newspaper. "Who is this fellow ?'

" My name, sir," said the old gentleman, speaking like a gentleman, " my name, sir, is Brownlow. Per mit me to inquire the name of the magistrate who offers a gratuitous and unprovoked insult to a re spectable person, under the protection of the bench." Saying this, Mr. Brownlow looked round the office as if in search of some person who would afford him the required information.

" Officer!" said Mr. Fang, throwing the paper on one side, " what's this fellow charged with ?"

" He's not charged at all, your worship," replied the officer. " He appears against the boy, your wor ship."

His worship knew this perfectly well; but it was a good annoyance, and a safe one.

"Appears against the boy, does he?" said Fang, surveying Mr. Brownlow contemptuously from head to foot. " Swear him!"

" Before I am sworn, I must beg to say one word," said Mr. Brownlow: " and that is, that I really nev er, without actual experience, could have believed— :

" Hold your tongue, sir," said Mr. Fang, peremp torily.

" I will not, sir!" replied the old gentleman.

" Hold your tongue this instant, or I'll have you turned out of the office!" said Mr. Fang. " You're an insolent, impertinent fellow. How dare you bully a magistrate ?"

"What!" exclaimed the old gentleman, redden-jng.

" Swear this person," said Fang to the clerk. " I'll not hear another word. Swear him."

Mr. Browulow's indignation was greatly roused; but reflecting, perhaps, that he might only injure the boy by giving vent to it, he suppressed his feelings and submitted to be sworn at once.

"Now," said Fang, "what's the charge against this boy ? What have you got to say, Sir ?"

" I was standing at a book-stall—" Mr. Brownlow began.

" Hold your tongue, sir," said Mr. Fang. " Police man ! Where's the policeman ? Here, swear this policeman. Now, policeman, what is this ?"

The policeman, with becoming humility, related how he had taken the charge; how he had searched Oliver, and found nothing on his person; and how that was all he knew about it.

" Are there any witnesses ?" inquired Mr. Fang.

" None, your worship," replied the policeman.

Mr. Fang sat silent for some minutes, and then, turning round to the prosecutor, said in a towering passion,

" Do you mean to state what your complaint against this boy is, man, or do yon not ? You have been sworn. Now, if you stand there, refusing to give evidence, I'll punish you for disrespect to the bench ; I will, by—"

By what, or by whom, nobody knows, for the clerk and jailer coughed very loud, just at the right mo ment ; and the former dropped a heavy book upon

OLIVER TWIST.

the floor, thus preventing the word from being heard—accidentally, of course.

With many interruptions, and repeated insults, Mr. Brownlow contrived to state his case ; observing that, in the surprise of the moment, he had run after the boy because he saw him running away ; and ex pressing his hope that, if the magistrate should be lieve him, although not actually the thief, to be con nected with thieves, he would deal as leniently with him as justice would allow.

" He has been hurt already," said the old gentle man, in conclusion. "And I fear," he added, with great energy, looking toward the bar, " I really fear that he is ill."

" Oh! yes, I dare say !" said Mr. Fang, with a sneer. " Come, none of your tricks here, you young vaga bond ; they won't do. What's your name ?"

Oliver tried to reply, but his tongue failed him. He was deadly pale ; and the whole place seemed turning round and round.

" What's your name, you hardened scoundrel ?" de manded Mr. Fang. " Officer, what's his name ?"

This was addressed to a bluff old fellow in a striped •waistcoat, who was standing by the bar. He bent over Oliver, and repeated the inquiry ; but finding him really incapable of understanding the question, and knowing that his not replying would only in furiate the magistrate the more, and add to the se verity of his sentence, he hazarded a guess.

" He says his name's Tom White, your worship," said this kind-hearted thief-taker.

"Oh, he won't speak out, won't he ?" said Fang. " Very well, very well. Where does he live ?"

" Where he can, your worship," replied the officer; again pretending to receive Oliver's answer.

" Has he any parents ?" inquired Mr. Fang. ,

" He says they died in his infancy, your worship," replied the officer, hazarding the usual reply.

At this point of the inquiry, Oliver raised his head ; and, looking round with imploring eyes, murmured a feeble prayer for a draught of water.

" Stuff and nonsense!" said Mr. Fang : " don't try to make a fool of me."

" I think he really is ill, your worship," remon strated the officer.

" I know better," said Mr. Fang.

" Take care of him, officer," said the old gentle man, raising his hands instinctively; "he'll fall down."

" Stand away, officer," cried Fang; " let him, if he likes."

Oliver availed himself of the kind permission, and fell to the floor in a fainting fit. The men in the of fice looked at each other, but no one dared to stir.

" I knew he was shamming," said Fang, as if this were incontestable proof of the fact. " Let him lie there ; he'll soon be tired of that."

" How do you propose to deal with the case, sir ?" inquired the clerk in a low voice.

" Summarily," replied Mr. Fang. " He stands com mitted for three months — hard labor, of course. Clear the office."

The door was opened for this purpose, and a cou ple of men were preparing to carry the insensible boy to his cell; when an elderly man of decent but poor appearance, clad in an old suit of black, rushed

hastily into the office, and advanced toward the bench.

" Stop, stop ! Don't take him away! For Heav en's sake stop a moment!" cried the new-comer, breathless with haste.

Although the presiding Genii in such an office as this exercise a summary and arbitrary power over the liberties, the good name, the character, almost the lives, of Her Majesty's subjects, especially of the poorer class ; and although, within such walls, enough fantastic tricks are daily played to make the angels blind Avith weeping; they are closed to the public, save through the medium of the daily press.* Mr. Fang was consequently not a little indignant to see an unbidden guest enter in such irreverent dis order.

" What is this ? Who is this ? Turn this man out. Clear the office !" cried Mr. Fang.

" I will speak," cried the man; " I will not be turned out. I saw it all. I keep the book-stall. I demand to be sworn. I will not be put down. Mr. Fang, you must hear me. You must not refuse, sir."

The man was right. His manner was determined; and the matter was growing rather too serious to be hushed up.

" Swear the man," growled Mr. Fang, with a very ill grace. " Now, man, what have you got to say ?"

"This," said the man: "I saw three boys—two others and the prisoner here—loitering on the oppo site side of the way, when this gentleman was read ing. The robbery was committed by another boy. I saw it done; and I saw that this boy was perfect ly amazed and stupefied by it." Having by this time recovered a little breath, the worthy book-stall keeper proceeded to relate, in a more coherent man ner, the exact circumstances of the robbery.

" Why didn't you come here before ?" said Fang, after a pause.

"I hadn't a soul to mind the shop," replied the man. " Every body who could have helped me had joined in the pursuit. I could get nobody till five minutes ago ; and I have run here all the way."

" The prosecutor was reading, was he ?" inquired Fang, after another pause.

" Yes," replied the man. " The very book he has in his hand."

" Oh, that book, eh ?" said Fang. " Is it paid for ?"

" No, it is not," replied the man, with a smile.

" Dear me, I forgot all about it !" exclaimed the absent old gentleman, innocently.

" A nice person to prefer a charge against a poor boy!" said Fang, with a comical effort to look mi-. mane. " I consider, sir, that you have obtained pos session of that book under very suspicious and dis reputable circumstances ; and you may think your self very fortunate that the owTier of the property declines to prosecute. Let this be a lesson to you, my man, or the law will overtake you yet. The boy is discharged. Clear the office."

" D—n me !" cried the old gentleman, bursting out with the rage he had kept down so long, " d—n me! I'll"

" Clear the office !" said the magistrate. " Officers, do you hear ? Clear the office !"

* Or were virtually, then.

GETTING BETTER.

The maudate was obeyed ; and the indignant Mr. Brownlow was conveyed out, with the book in one hand and the bamboo cane in the other, in a per fect frenzy of rage and defiance. He reached the yard; and his passion vanished in a moment. Little Oliver Twist lay on his back on the pavement, with his shirt unbuttoned, and his temples bathed with water ; his face a deadly white ; and a cold tremble convulsing his whole frame.

" Poor boy! poor boy !" said Mr. Brownlow, bend ing over him. " Call a coach, somebody, pray. Di rectly!"

A coach was obtained, and Oliver, having been carefully laid on one seat, the old gentleman got in and sat himself on the other.

" May I accompany you I" said the book-stall keep er, looking in.

" Bless me, yes, my dear sir," said Mr. Brownlow quickly. "I forgot you. Dear, dear! I have this unhappy book still! Jump in. Poor fellow! There's no time to lose."

The book-stall keeper got into the coach; and away they drove.

CHAPTER XII.

IN WHICH OLIVER IS TAKEN BETTER CARE OF THAN HE EVER WAS BEFORE. AND IN WHICH THE NARRATIVE REVERTS TO THE MEBKY OLD GENTLEMAN AND HIS YOUTHFUL FRIENDS.

THE coach rattled away, over nearly the same ground as that which Oliver had traversed when he first entered London in company with the Dodger; and, turning a different way when it reached the Angel at Islington, stopped at length before a neat house, in a quiet shady street near Pentonville. Here a bed was prepared, without loss of time, in which Mr. Brownlow saw his young charge carefully and comfortably deposited ; and here he was tended with a kindness and solicitude that knew no bounds.

But, for many days, Oliver remained insensible to all the goodness of his new friends. The sun rose and sank, and rose and sank again, and many times after that; and still the boy lay stretched on his un easy bed, dwindling away beneath the dry and wast ing heat of fever. The worm does not his work more surely on the dead body, than does this slow creeping fire upon the living frame.

Weak, and thin, and pallid, he awoke at last from what seemed to have been a long and troubled dream. Feebly raising hinvelf in the bed, with his head rest ing on his trembling arm, he looked anxiously around.

" What room is this ? Where have I been brought to ?" said Oliver. " This is not the place I went to sleep in."

He uttered these words in a feeble voice, being very faint and weak; but they were overheard at once. The curtain at the bed's head was hastily drawn back, and a motherly old lady, very neatly and precisely dressed, rose, as she undrew it, from an arm-chair close by, in which she had been sitting at needle-work.

" Hush, my dear," said the old lady, softly. " Yon must be very quiet, or you will be ill again; and you

have been very bad—as bad as bad could be, pretty nigh. Lie down again; there's a dear!" With those words, the old lady very gently placed Oliver's head upon the pillow; and, smoothing back his hair from his forehead, looked so kind and lovingly in his face, that he could not help placing his little withered hand in hers, and drawing it round his neck.

" Save us!" said the old lady, with tears in her eyes, " What a grateful little dear it is! Pretty creetur! What would his mother feel if she had sat by him as I have, and could see him now!"

" Perhaps she does see me," whispered Oliver, fold ing his hands together; "perhaps she has sat by me. I almost feel as if she had."

" That was the fever, my dear," said the old lady, mildly.

" I suppose it was," replied Oliver, " because heav en is a long way off; and they are too happy there, to come down to the bedside of a poor boy. But if she knew I was ill, she must have pitied me, even there; for she was very ill herself before she died. She can't know any thing about me, though," added Oliver, after a moment's silence. " If she had seen me hurt, it would have made her sorrowful; and her face has always looked sweet and happy, when I have dreamed of her."

The old lady made no reply to this; but wiping her tears first, and her spectacles, which lay on the counterpane, afterward, as if they were part and parcel of those features, brought some cool stuff 1 for Oliver to drink; and then, patting him on the cheek, told him he must lie very quiet, or he would be ill again.

So Oliver kept very still; partly because he was anxious to obey the kind old lady in all things; and partly, to tell the truth, because he was completely exhausted with what he had already said. He soon fell into a gentle doze, from which he was awakened by the light of a candle; which, being brought near the bed, showed him a gentleman with a very large and loud-ticking gold watch in his hand, who felt his pulse, and said he was a great deal better.

" You are a great deal better, are you not, my dear ?" said the gentleman.

" Yes, thank you, sir," replied Oliver.

" Yes, I know you are," said the gentleman. " You're hungry too, ain't you ?"

" No, sir," answered Oliver.

" Hem!" said the gentleman. " No, I know you're not. He is not hungry, Mrs. Bed win," said the gen tleman, looking very wise.

The old lady made a respectful inclination of the head, which seemed to say that she thought the doc tor was a very clever man. The doctor appeared much of the same opinion himself.

" You feel sleepy, don't you, my dear ?" said the doctor.

" No, sir," replied Oliver.

"No," said the doctor, with a very shrewd and satisfied look. "You are not sleepy. Nor thirsty. Are you ?"

" Yes, sir, rather thirsty," answered Oliver.

" Just as I expected, Mrs. Bedwin," said the doc tor. " It's very natural that he should be thirsty. You may give him a little tea, ma'am, and some dry toast without any butter. Don't keep him too warm,

OLIVER TWIST.

ina'am; but be careful that you don't let Mm be too coltl; will you have the goodness ?"

The old lady dropped a courtesy. The doctor, af ter tasting the cool stuff, and expressing a qualified approval of it, hurried away, his boots creaking in a very important and wealthy manner as he went down stairs.

Oliver dozed off again soon after this; when he awoke, it was nearly twelve o'clock. The old lady tenderly bade him good-night shortly afterward, and left him in charge of a fat old woman who had just come; bringing with her, in a little bundle, a small Prayer-book and a large night-cap. Putting the lat ter on her head and the former on the table, the old woman, after telling Oliver that she had come to sit up with him, drew her chair close to the fire and went off into a series of short naps, checkered at fre quent intervals with sundry tumblings forward, and divers moans and chokiugs. These, however, had no w r orse effect than causing her to rub her nose very hard, and then fall asleep again.

And thus the night crept slowly on. Oliver lay awake for some time, counting the little circles of light which the reflection of the rush-light shade threw upon the ceiling, or tracing with his languid eyes the intricate pattern of the paper on the wall. The darkness and the deep stillness of the room were very solemn: as they brought into the boy's mind the thought that death had been hovering there, for many days and nights, and might yet fill it with the gloom and dread of his awful presence, he turn ed his face upon the pillow, and fervently prayed to Heaven.

Gradually he fell into that deep tranquil sleep which ease from recent suffering alone imparts; that calm and peaceful rest which it is pain to wake from. Who, if this were death, would be roused again to all the struggles and turmoils of life; to all its cares for the present, its anxieties for the future; more than all, its weary recollections of the past!

It had been bright day for hours, when Oliver opened his eyes; he felt cheerful and happy. The crisis of the disease was safely past. He belonged to the world again.

In three days' time he was able to sit in an easy-chair, well propped up with pillows; and, as he was still too weak to walk, Mrs. Bedwin had him carried down stairs into the little housekeeper's room, which belonged to her. Having him set here, by the fire side, the good old lady sat herself down too; and, being in a state of considerable delight at seeing him so much better, forthwith began to cry most violently.

" Never mind me, my dear," said the old lady. "I'm only having a regular good cry. There; it's all over now; and I'm quite comfortable."

" You're very, very kind to me, ma'am," said Oliver.

""Well, never you mind that, my dear," said the old lady ; " that's got nothing to do with your broth; and it's full time you had it; for the doctor says Mr. Brownlow may come in to see you this morning, and Ave must get up our best looks, because the better we look the more he'll be pleased." And with this, the old lady applied herself to warming up, in a little saucepan, a basinful of broth, strong enough, Oliver thought, to furnish an ample dinner, when reduced to the regulation strength, for three hundred and fifty paupers, at the lowest computation.

"Are you fond of pictures, dear?" inquired the old lady, seeing that Oliver had fixed his eyes, most intently, on a portrait which hung against the wall, just opposite his chair.

" I don't quite know, ma'am," said Oliver, without taking his eyes from the canvas; " I have seen so few that I hardly know. What a beautiful, mild face that lady's is!"

" All!" said the old lady, " painters always make ladies out prettier than they are, or they wouldn't get any custom, child. The man that invented the machine for taking likenesses might have known that would never succeed; it's a deal too honest. A deal," said the old lady, laughing very heartily at her own acuteuess.

" Is—is that a likeness, ma'am ?" said Oliver.

" Yes," said the old lady, looking up for a moment from the broth; " that's a portrait."

" Whose, ma'am ?" asked Oliver.

" Why, really, my dear, I don't know," answered the old lady, in a good-humored manner. " It's not a likeness of any body that you or I know, I expect. It seems to strike your fancy, dear."

" It is so very pretty," replied Oliver.

" Why, sure you're not afraid of it ?" said the old lady; observing, in great surprise, the look of awe with which the child regarded the painting.

" Oh, no, no!" returned Oliver, quickly; " but the eyes look so sorrowful; and where I sit, they seem fixed upon me. It makes my heart beat," added Oliver in a low voice, " as if it was alive, and wanted to speak to me, but couldn't."

"Lord save us!" exclaimed the old lady, start ing ; " don't talk in that way, child, You're weak and nervous after your illness. Let me wheel your chair round to the other side; and then you won't see it. There!" said the old lady, suiting the action to the word; " you don't see it now, at all events."

Oliver did see it in his mind's eye as distinctly as if he had not altered his position; but he thought it better not to worry the kind old lady; so he smiled gently when she looked at him; and

Mrs. Bedwin, satisfied that he felt more comfortable, salted and broke bits of toasted bread into the broth, with all the bustle befitting so solemn a preparation. Oliver got through it with extraordinary expedition. He had scarcely swallowed the last spoonful, when there came a soft rap at the door. " Come in," said the old lady; and in walked Mr. Brownlow.

Now, the old gentleman came in as brisk as need be; but he had no sooner raised his spectacles on his forehead, and thrust his hands behind the skirts of his dressing-gown to take a good long look at Oliver, than his countenance underwent a very great variety of odd contortions. Oliver looked very worn and shadowy from sickness, and made an ineffectual at tempt to stand up, out of respect to his benefactor, which terminated in his sinking back into the chair again; and the fact is, if the truth must be told, that Mr. Browulow's heart, being large enough for any six ordinary old gentlemen of humane disposition, forced a supply of tears into his eyes, by some hydraulic process which we are not sufficiently philosophical to be in a condition to explain.

BETTER AND BETTER.

" Poor boy! poor boy!" said Sir. Brownlow, clear ing his throat. " I'm rather hoarse this morning, Mrs. Bedwiii. I'm afraid I have caught cold."

" I hope riot, sir," said Sirs. Bedwin. " Every thing you have had has been well aired, sir."

" I don't know, Bedwin. I don't know," said Mr. Brownlow; " I rather think I had a damp napkin at dinner-time yesterday; but never mind that. How do you feel, my dear f'

"Very happy, sir," replied Oliver. "And very grateful indeed, sir, for your goodness to me."

" Good boy," said Sir. Browulow, stoutly. " Have you given him any nourishment, Bedwiu ? Any slops, eh?"

" He has just had a basin of beautiful strong broth, sir," replied Sirs. Bedwiu; drawing herself up slight ly, and laying a strong emphasis on the last word, to intimate that between slops and broth well com pounded there existed no affinity or connection what soever.

" Ugh!" said Sir. Brownlow, with a slight shud der ; " a couple of glasses of port-wine would have done him a great deal more good. Wouldn't they, Tom White, <-h .'"

" Sly name is Oliver, sir," replied the little invalid: with a look of great astonishment.

" Oliver," said Sir. Brownlow; " Oliver what ? Ol iver White, eh ?"

"No, sir; Twist—Oliver Twist."

" Queer name!" said the old gentleman. " What made you tell the magistrate your name was White ?"

"I never told him so, sir," returned Oliver, in amazement.

This sounded so like a falsehood, that the old gen tleman looked somewhat sternly in Oliver's face. It was impossible to doubt him; there was truth in ev ery one of its thin and sharpened lineaments.

" Some mistake," said Sir. Brownlow. But, al though his motive for looking steadily at Oliver no longer existed, the old idea of the resemblance be tween his features and some familiar face came upon him so strongly, that he could not withdraw his gaze.

" I hope you are not angry with me, sir ?" said Ol iver, raising his eyes beseechingly.

"No, no," replied the old gentleman. "Why! what's this ? Bedwin, look there!"

As he spoke, he pointed hastily to the picture above Oliver's head, and then to the boy's face. There was its living copy. The eyes, the head, the mouth—every feature was the same. The expres sion was, for the instant, so precisely alike, that the minutest line seemed copied with startling accuracy!

Oliver knew not the cause of this sudden excla mation ; for, not being strong enough to bear the start it gave him, he fainted away. A weakness on his part, which affords the narrative an opportunity of relieving the reader from suspense, in behalf of the two young pupils of the Slerry Old Gentleman; and of recording—

That when the Dodger, and his accomplished friend Slastcr Bates, joined in the hue-and-cry which was raised at Oliver's heels, in consequence of their exe cuting an illegal conveyance of Sir. Brownlow's per sonal property, as has been already described, they were actuated by a very laudable and becoming re

gard for themselves; and forasmuch as the freedom of the subject and the liberty of the individual are among the first and proudest boasts of a true-hearted Englishman, so, I need hardly beg the reader to ob serve, that this action should tend to exalt them in the opinion of all public and patriotic men, in almost as great a degree as this strong proof of their anxi ety for their own preservation and safety goes to corroborate and confirm the little code of laws which certain profound and sound-judging philosophers have laid down as the mainsprings of all Nature's deeds and actions; the said philosophers very wisely reducing the good lady's proceedings to matters of maxim and theory, and, by a very neat and pretty compliment to her exalted wisdom and understand ing, putting entirely out of sight any considerations of heart, or generous impulse and feeling. For these are matters totally beneath a female who is acknowl edged by universal admission to be far above the nu merous little foibles and weaknesses of her sex.

If I wanted any further proof of the strictly phil osophical nature of the conduct of these young gen tlemen in their very delicate predicament, I should at once find it in the fact (also recorded in a forego ing part of this narrative), of their quitting the pur suit, when the general attention was fixed upon Oli ver ; and making immediately for their home by the shortest possible cut. Although I do not mean to assert that it is usually the practice of renowned and learned sages to shorten the road to any great con clusion (their course, indeed, being rather to length en the distance, by various circumlocutions and dis cursive staggerings, like unto those in which drunk en men under the pressure of a too mighty flow of ideas, are prone to indulge); still, I do mean to say, and do say distinctly, that it is the invariable prac tice of many mighty philosophers, in carrying out their theories, to evince great wisdom and foresight in pro viding against every possible contingency which can be supposed at all likely to affect themselves. Thus, to do a great right, you may do a little wrong; and you may take any means which the end to be at tained will justify; the amount of the right, or the amount of the wrong, or, indeed, the distinction be tween the two, being left entirely to the philosopher concerned, to be settled and determined by his clear, comprehensive, and impartial view of his own par ticular case.

It was not until the two boys had scoured, with great rapidity, through a most intricate maze of nar row streets and courts, that they ventured to halt beneath a low and dark archway. Having remain ed silent here, just long enough to recover breath to speak, Master Bates uttered an exclamation of amusement and delight; and, bursting into an un controllable fit of laughter, flung himself upon a door step, and rolled thereon in a transport of mirth.

" What's the matter ?" inquired the Dodger.

" Ha! ha! ha!" roared Charley Bates.

" Hold your noise," remonstrated the Dodger, look ing cautiously round. " Do you want to be grabbed, stupid?"

" I can't help it," said Charley, " I can't help it! To see him splitting away at that pace, and cutting round the corners, and knocking up again the posts, and starting on again as if he was made of iron as

OLIVER TWIST.

well as them, and me with the wipe in my pocket, singing out arter him—oh, my eye!"
The vivid im agination of Master Bates presented the scene before him in too strong colors. As he

arrived at this apos trophe, he again rolled upon the door-step, and laugh ed louder than before.

" What'll Fagin say ?" inquired the Dodger; tak ing advantage of the next interval of breathlessness on the part of his friend to propound the question.

"What ?" repeated Charley Bates.

" Ah, what ?" said the Dodger.

" Why, what should he say ?" inquired Charley, stopping rather suddenly in his merriment; for the Dodger's manner was impressive. " What should he say ?"

Mr. Dawkins whistled for a couple of minutes;

The noise of footsteps on the creaking stairs, a few minutes after the occurrence of this conversation, roused the merry old gentleman as he sat over the fire with a saveloy and a small loaf in his left hand; a pocket-knife in his right; and a pewter pot on the trivet. There was a rascally smile on his white face as he turned round, and, looking sharply out from under his thick red eyebrows, bent his ear toward the door, and listened.

"Why, how's this?" muttered the Jew, changing countenance; " only two of 'em ? Where's the third I They can't have got into trouble. Hark!"

The footsteps approached nearer; they reached the landing. The door was slowly opened; and the Dodger and Charley Bates entered, closing it behind them.

WHAT'S BECOME OF THE BOY ?"

then, taking off his hat, scratched his head, and nod ded thrice.

" What do you mean ?" said Charley.

" Toor ml lol loo, gammon and spinnage, the frog he wouldn't, and high cockolornm," said the Dodger, with a slight sneer on his intellectual countenance.This was explanatory, but not satisfactory. Mas ter Bates felt it so; and again said, " What do you mean ?"

The Dodger made no reply; but putting his hat on again, and gathering the skirts of his long-tailed coat under his arm, thrust his tongue into his cheek, slapped the bridge of his nose some half-dozen times in a familiar but expressive manner, and, turning on his heel, slunk down the court. Master Bates fol lowed with a thoughtful countenance.

CHAPTER XIII.

SOME NEW ACQUAINTANCES ABE INTRODUCED TO THE INTELLIGENT READER, CONNECTED WITH WHOM VARI OUS PLEASANT MATTERS ARE

" TTTHERE'S Oliver ?" said the Jew, rising with a VV menacing look. " Where's the boy ?" The young thieves eyed their preceptor as if they were alarmed at his violence; and looked uneasily at each other. But they made no reply.

" What's become of the boy ?" said the Jew, seiz ing the Dodger tightly by the collar, and threaten ing him with horrid imprecations. " Speak out, or I'll throttle you!"

Mr. Fagiu looked so very much in earnest, that

A NEW ACQUAINTANCE.

Charley Bates, -who deemed it prudent in all cases to be on the safe side, and who conceived it hy no means improbable that it might be his turn to be throttled second, dropped upon his knees, and raised a loud, well-sustained, and continuous roar—some thing between a mad bull and a speaking-trumpet.

" Will you speak ?" thundered the Jew: shaking the Dodger so much that his keeping in the big coat at all seemed perfectly miraculous.

" Why, the traps have got him, and that's all about it," said the Dodger, sullenly. " Come, let go o' me, will yon!" And, swinging himself, at one jerk, clean out of the big coat, which he left in the Jew's hands, the Dodger snatched up the toasting-fork and made a pass at the merry old gentleman's waistcoat; which, if it had taken effect, would have let a little more merriment out than could have been easily replaced.

The Jew stepped back in this emergency, with more agility than could have been anticipated in a man of his apparent decrepitude; and, seizing up the pot, prepared to hurl it at his assailant's head. But Charley Bates, at this moment, calling his attention by a perfectly terrific howl, he suddenly altered its destination, and flung it full at that young gentle man.

" Why, what the blazes is in the wind now ?" growled a deep voice. "W T ho pitched that 'ere at me ? It's well it's the beer, and not the pot, as hit me, or I'd have settled somebody. I might have know'd, as nobody but an infernal, rich, plundering, thundering old Jew could afford to throw away any drink but water—and not that, unless he done the River Company every quarter. Wot's it all about, Fagin ? D— me, if my neck-handkercher an't lined with beer! Come in, you sneaking warmint! wot are you stopping outside for, as if you was ashamed of your master! Come in!"

The man who growled out these words was a stoutly-built fellow of about five-and-thirty, in a black velveteen coat, very soiled drab breeches, lace-up half boots, and gray cotton stockings, which in closed a bulky pair of legs, with large swelling calves — the kind of legs, which in such costume, always look in an unfinished and incomplete state without a set of fetters to garnish them. He had a brown hat on his head, and a dirty belcher handker chief round his neck, with the long frayed ends of which he smeared the beer from his face as he spoke. He disclosed, Vhen he had done so, a broad heavy countenance with a beard of three days' growth, and two scowling eyes; one of which displayed vari ous party-colored symptoms of having been recently damaged by a blow.

" Come in, d'ye hear ?" growled this engaging ruf fian.

A white shaggy dog, with his face scratched and torn in twenty different places, skulked into the room.

" Why didn't you come in afore ?" said the man. " You're getting too proud to own me afore company, are you ? Lie down !"

This command was accompanied with a kick, which sent the animal to the other end of the room. He appeared well used to it, however; for he coiled himself up in a corner very quietly, without utter ing a sound, and, winking his very ill-looking eyes twenty times in a minute, appeared to occupy him self in taking a survey of the apartment.

" What are you up to ? Ill-treating the boys, you covetous, avaricious, in-sa-ti-a-ble old fence ?" said the man, seating himself deliberately. " I wonder they don't murder you! / would if I was them. If I'd been your 'prentice, I'd have done it long ago, and — no, I couldn't have sold you afterward, for you're fit for nothing but keeping as a curiosity of ugliness in a glass bottle, and I suppose they don't blow glass bottles large enough."

" Hush! hush! Mr. Sikes," said the Jew, trembling; " don't speak so loud."

" None of your mistering," replied the ruffian; "you always mean mischief when you come that. You know my name: out with it! I sha'u't disgrace it when the time comes."

" Well, well, then—Bill Sikes," said the Jew, with abject humility. " You seem out of humor, Bill."

"Perhaps I am,"replied Sikes; "I should think you, was rather out of sorts too, unless you mean as little harm when you throw pewter pots about, as you do when you blab and— :

" Are you mad ?" said the Jew, catching the man by the sleeve, and pointing toward the boys.

Mr. Sikes contented himself with tying an imagi nary knot under his left ear, and jerking his head over on the right shoulder; a piece of dumb show which the Jew appeared to understand perfectly. He then, in cant terms, with which his whole conversation was plentifully besprinkled, but which would be quite unintelligible if they were recorded here, de manded a glass of liquor.

" And mind you don't poison it," said Mr. Sikes, laying his hat upon the table.

This was said in jest; but if the speaker could have seen the evil leer with which the Jew bit his pale lip as he turned round to the cupboard, he might have thought the caution not wholly unnecessary, or the wish (at all events) to improve upon the dis tiller's ingenuity not very far from the old gentle man's merry heart.

After swallowing two or three glasses of spirits, Mr. Sikes condescended to take some notice of the young gentlemen; which gracious act led to a con versation, in which the cause and manner of Oliver's capture were circumstantially detailed, with such alterations and improvements on the truth as to the Dodger appeared most advisable under the cir cumstances.

" Fm afraid," said the Jew," that he may say some thing which will get us into trouble."

" That's very likely," returned Sikes, with a mali cious grin. " You're blowed upon, Fagin."

" And I'm afraid, you see," added the Jew, speak ing as if he had not noticed the interruption; and regarding the other closely as he did so—" I'm afraid that, if the game was up with us, it might be up with a good many more, and that it would come out rath er worse for you than it would for me, my dear."

The man started, and turned round upon the Jew. But the old gentleman's shoulders were shrugged up to his ears; and his eyes were vacantly staring on the opposite wall.

There was a long pause. Every member of the respectable coterie appeared plunged in his own re-

OLIVER TWIST.

flections; not excepting the dog, who by a certain malicious licking of his lips seemed to be meditating an attack upon the legs of the first gentleman or lady he might encounter in the streets when he went out.

" Somebody must find out wot's been done at the office," said Mr. Sikes, in a much lower tone than he had taken since he came in.

The Jew nodded assent.

"If he hasn't peached, and is committed, there's no fear till he comes out again," said Mr.

Sikes, " and then he must be taken care on. You must get hold of him somehow."

Again the Jew nodded.

The prudence of this line of action, indeed, was ob vious ; but, unfortunately, there was one very strong objection to its being adopted. This was, that the Dodger, and Charley Bates, and Fagin, and Mr. Wil liam Sikes, happened, one and all, to entertain a vio lent and deeply-rooted antipathy to going near a po lice-office on any ground or pretext whatever.

How long they might have sat and looked at each other, in a state of uncertainty not the most pleasant of its kind, it is difficult to guess. It is not necessa ry to make any guesses on the subject, however; for the sudden entrance of the two young ladies whom Oliver had seen on a former occasion, caused the con versation to flow afresh.

" The very thing!" said the Jew. " Bet will go; won't you, my dear I"

" Wheres ?" inquired the young lady.

" Only just up to the office, my dear," said the Jew, coaxingly.

It is due to the young lady to say that she did not positively affirm that she would not, but that she merely expressed an emphatic and earnest desire to be " blessed " if she would; a polite and delicate eva sion of the request, which shows the young lady to have been possessed of that natural good-breeding which can not bear to inflict upon a fellow-creature the pain of a direct and pointed refusal.

The Jew's countenance fell. He turned from this young lady, who was gayly, not to say gorgeously attired, in a red gown, green boots, and yellow curl papers, to the other female.

" Nancy, my dear," said the Jew in a soothing man ner, " what do you say ?"

" That it won't do; so it's no use a-trying it on, Fagin," replied Nancy.

" What do you mean by that ?" said Mr. Sikes, lookiug up in a surly manner.

" What I say, Bill," replied the lady, collectedly.

" Why, you're just the very person for it," reason ed Mr. Sikes: "nobody about here knows any thing of you."

"And as I don't want 'em to, neither," replied Nan cy, in the same composed manner, " it's rather more no than yes with me, Bill."

" She'll go, Fagin," said Sikes.

" No, she won't, Fagin," said Nancy.

" Yes, she will, Fagin," said Sikes.

And Mr. Sikes was right. By dint of alternate threats, promises, and bribes, the lady in question was ultimately prevailed upon to undertake the commission. She was not, indeed, withheld by the same considerations as her agreeable friend; for, hav

ing recently removed into the neighborhood of Field Lane from the remote but genteel suburb of Ratcliffe, she was not .under the same apprehension of being recognized by any of her numerous acquaintance.

Accordingly, with a clean white apron tied over her gown, and her curl-papers tucked up under a straw bonnet—both articles of dress being provided from the Jew's inexhaustible stock — Miss Nancy prepared to issue forth on her errand.

" Stop a minute, my dear," said the Jew, producing a little covered basket. " Carry that in one hand. It looks more respectable, my dear."

" Give her a door-key to carry in her t'other one, Fagiu," said Sikes; " it looks real and geniviue like."

" Yes, yes, my dear, so it does," said the Jew, hang ing a large street-door key on the forefinger of the young lady's right hand. " There ; very good! Very good, indeed, my dear!" said the Jew, rubbing his hands.

" Oh, my brother! My poor, dear, sweet, innocent little brother!" exclaimed Nancy, bursting into tears, and wringing the little basket and the street-door key in an agony of distress. " What has become of him! Where have they taken him to! Oh, do have pity, and tell me what's been done with the dear boy, gentlemen; do, gentlemen, if you please, gentle men !"

Having uttered these words in a most lamentable and heart-broken tone—to the immeasurable delight of her hearers—Miss Nancy paused, winked to the company, nodded smilingly round, and disappeared.

"Ah! she's a clever girl, my dears," said the Jew, turning round to his young friends, and shaking his head gravely, as if in mute admonition to them to follow the bright example they had just beheld.

" She's a honor to her sex," said Mr. Sikes, filling his glass, and smiting the table with his enormous fist. " Here's her health, and wishing they was all like her!"

While these and many other encomiums were be ing passed on the accomplished Nancy, that young lady made the best of her way to the police-office; whither, notwithstanding a little natural timidity consequent upon walking through the streets alone and unprotected, she arrived in perfect safety short ly afterward.

Entering by the back way, she tapped softly with the key at one of the cell-doors, and listened. There was no sound within; so she coughed and listened again. Still there was no reply: so she spoke.

" Nolly, dear ?" murmured Nancy, in a gentle voice, "Nolly?"

There was nobody inside but a miserable shoeless criminal, who had been taken up for playing the flute, and who, the offense against society having been clearly proved, had been very properly commit ted by Mr. Fang to the House of Correction for one month; with the appropriate and amusing remark that since he had so much breath to spare, it would be more wholesomely expended on the tread - mill than in a nmsical instrument. He made no answer; being occupied in mentally bewailing the loss of the flute, which had been confiscated for the use of the county; so Nancy passed on to the next cell, and knocked there.

" Well!" cried a faint and feeble voice.

NANCY—THE PICTURE.

45

" Is there a little boy here ?" inquired Nancy, with a preliminary sob.

'• No," replied the voice; " God forbid!"

This was a vagrant of sixty-five, who was going to prison for not playing the flute; or, in other words, for begging in the streets, and doing nothing for his livelihood. In the next cell was another man, who was going to the same prison for hawking tin sauce pans without a license; thereby doing something for his living, in defiance of the Stamp-office.

But, as neither of these criminals answered to the name of Oliver, or knew any thing about him, Nancy made straight up to the bluff' officer in the striped waistcoat; and with the most piteous waitings and lamentations, rendered more piteous by a prompt and efficient use of the street-door key and the little bas ket, demanded her own dear brother.

"7 haven't got him, my dear," said the old man.

" Where is he ?" screamed Nancy, in a distracted manner.

" Why, the gentleman's got him," replied the of ficer.

" What gentleman ? Oh, gracious heavens! What gentleman f' exclaimed Nancy.

In reply to this incoherent questioning, the old man informed the deeply-affected sister that Oliver had been taken ill in the office, and discharged in consequence of a witness having proved the robbery to have been committed by another boy not in cus tody ; and that the prosecutor had carried him away, in an insensible condition, to his own residence; of and concerning which, all the informant knew was, that it was somewhere at Pentonville, he having heard that word mentioned in the directions to the coachman.

In a dreadful state of doubt and uncertainty, the agonized young woman staggered to the gate, and then, exchanging her faltering walk for a swift run, returned, by the most devious and complicated route she could think of, to the domicile of the Jew.

Mr. Bill Sikes no sooner heard the account of the expedition delivered, than he very hastily called upon the white dog, and, putting on his hat, expeditiously departed ; without devoting any time to the formal ity of wishing the company good-morning.

" We must know where he is, my dears; he must be found," said the Jew, greatly excited. " Charley, do nothing but skulk about till you bring home some news of him! Nancy, my dear, I must have him found. I trust to you, my dear—to you and the Art ful, for every thing! Stay, stay," added the Jew, unlocking a drawer with a shaking hand; "there's money, my dears. I shall shut up this shop to-night. You'll know Avhere to find me! Don't stop here a minute. Not an instant, my dears!"

With these words, he pushed them from the room; and carefully double-locking and barring the door behind them, drew from its place of concealment the box which he had unintentionally disclosed to Oliver. Then he hastily proceeded to dispose the watches and jewelry beneath his clothing.

A rap at the door startled him in this occupation. " Who's there f" he cried in a shrill tone.

" Me!" replied the voice of the Dodger, through the key-hole.

" What now ?" cried the Jew, impatiently.

"Is he to be kidnapped to the other ken, Nancy says ?" inquired the Dodger.

" Yes," replied the Jew,"" wherever she lays hands on him. Find him, find him out, that's all! I shall know what to do next; never fear:"

The boy murmured a reply of intelligence, and hurried down stairs after his companions.

" He has not peached, so far," said the Jew, as he pursued his occupation. "If he means to blab us among his new friends, we may stop his mouth yet."

CHAPTER XIV.

COMPRISING FURTHER PARTICULARS OF OLIVER'S STAY AT MR. BROWNLOW'S, WITH THE REMARKABLE PREDICTION WHICH ONE MR. GRIMWIG UTTERED CONCERNING HIM, WHEN HE WENT OUT ON AN ERRAND.

OLIVER soon recovering from the fainting-fit into which Mr. Brownlow's abrupt exclamation had thrown him, the subject of the picture was carefully avoided, both by the old gentleman and Mrs. Bed win, in the conversation that ensued; which indeed bore no reference to Oliver's history or prospects, but was confined to such topics as might amuse without ex citing him. He was still too weak to get up to breakfast; but, when he came down into the house keeper's room next day, his first act was to cast an eager glance at the wall, in the hope of again look ing on the face of the beautiful lady. His expecta tions were disappointed, however, for the picture had been removed.

"Ah!" said the housekeeper, watching the direc tion of Oliver's eyes. " It is gone, you see."

" I see it is, ma'am," replied Oliver. " Why have they taken it away I"

" It has been taken down, child, because Mr. Brown-low said that as it seemed to worry you, perhaps it might prevent your getting well, you know," rejoined the old lady.

" Oh, no, indeed. It didn't worry me, ma'am," said Oliver. " I liked to see it. I quite loved it."

" Well, well!" said the old lady, good-humoredly; " you get well as fast as ever you can, dear, and it shall be hung up again. There! I promise you that! Now, let us talk about Something else."

This was all the information Oliver could obtain about the picture at that time. As the old lady had been so kind to him in his illness, he endeavored to think no more of the subject just then; so he list ened attentively to a great many stories she told him, about an amiable and handsome daughter of hers, who was married to an amiable and handsome man, and lived in the country ; and about a son, who was clerk to a merchant in the West Indies; and who was, also, such a good young man, and wrote such dutiful letters home four times a year, that it brought the tears into her eyes to talk about them. When the old lady had expatiated, a long time, on the excellences of her children, and the merits of her kind good husband besides, who had been dead and gone, poor dear soul! just six-and-twenty years, it was time to have tea. After tea she began to teach Oliver cribbage, which he learned as quickly as she could teach, and at which game they played, with

OLIVER TWIST.

great interest and gravity, until it was time for the invalid to have some warm wine and water, with a slice of dry toast, and then to go cozily to bed.

They were happy days, those of Oliver's recovery. Every thing was so quiet, and neat, and orderly; every body was kind and gentle; that after the noise and turbulence in the midst of which he had always lived, it seemed like heaven itself. He was uo sooner strong enough to put his clothes on prop erly, than Mr. Browulow caused a complete new suit, and a new cap, and a new pair of shoes, to be pro vided for him. As Oliver was told that he might do what he liked with the old clothes, he gave them to a servant who had been very kind to him, and asked her to sell them to a Jew, and keep the money for her self. This she very readily did; and, as Oliver look ed out of the parlor window, and saw the Jew roll them up in his bag and walk away, he felt quite de lighted to think that they were safely gone, and that there was now no possible danger of his ever being sMe to wear them again. They were sad rags, to tell the truth; and Oliver had never had a new suit before.

One evening, about a week after the affair of the picture, as he was sitting talking to Mrs. Bedwin, there came a message down from Mr. Brownlow, that if Oliver Twist felt pretty well, he should like to see him in his study, and talk to him a little while.

" Bless us, and save us! Wash your hands, and let me part your hair nicely for you, child," said Mrs. Bedwiii. " Dear heart alive! If we had known he would have asked for you, we would have put you a clean collar on, and made you as smart as six pence !"

Oliver did as the old lady bade him; and, although she lamented grievously, meanwhile, that there was not even time to crimp the little frill that bordered his shirt-collar; he looked so delicate and handsome, despite that important personal advantage, that she went so far as to say, looking at him with great com placency from head to foot, that she really didn't think it would have been possible, on the longest notice, to have made much difference in him for the better.

Thus encouraged, Oliver tapped at the study door. On Mr. Browulow calling to him to come in, he found himself in a little backroom quite full of books, with a window, looking into some pleasant little gardens. There was a table drawn up before the window, at which Mr. Brownlow was seated reading. When he saw Oliver, he pushed the book away from him, and told him to come near the table, and sit down. Oli ver complied; marveling where the people could be found to read such a great number of books as seem ed to be written to make the world wiser. Which is still a marvel to more experienced people than Ol iver Twist, every day of their lives.

" There are a good many books, are there not, my boy ?" said Mr. Brownlow, observing the curiosity with which Oliver surveyed the shelves that reach ed from the floor«to the ceiling.

" A great number, sir," replied Oliver. " I never saw so many."

" You shall read them, if you behave well," said the old gentleman kindly ; " and you will like that bet ter than looking at the outsides—that is, in some

cases; because there are books of which the backs and covers are by far the best parts."

" I suppose they are those heavy ones, sir," said Oliver, pointing to some large qxiartos, with a good deal of gilding about the binding.

" Not always those," said the old gentleman, pat ting Oliver on the head, and smiling as he did so; " there are other equally heavy ones, though of a much smaller size. How should you like to grow up a clever man, and write books, eh ?"

" I think I would rather read tiiern, sir," replied Oliver.

" What! wouldn't you like to be a book-writer ?" said the old gentleman.

Oliver considered a little while; and at last said, he should think it would be a much better thing to be a book-seller; upon which the old gentleman laugh ed heartily, and declared he had said a very good thing. Which Oliver felt glad to have done, though he by no means knew what it was.

" Well, \vell," said the old gentleman, composing his features. "Don't be afraid! We won't make an author of you, while there's an honest trade to be learned, or brick-making to turn to."

" Thank you, sir," said Oliver. At the earnest manner of his reply, the old gentleman laughed again; and said something about a curious instinct, which Oliver, not understanding, paid no very great attention to.

" Now," said Mr. Brownlow, speaking if possible in a kinder, but at the same time in a much more seri ous manner, than Oliver had ever known him assume yet; " I want you to pay great attention, my boy, to what I am going to say. I shall talk to you with out any reserve; because I am sure you are as well able to understand me as many older persons would be."

" Oh, don't tell me you are going to send me away, sir, pray!" exclaimed Oliver, alarmed at the serious tone of the old gentleman's commencement. " Don't turn me out-of-doors to wander in the streets again. Let me stay here, and be a servant. Don't send me back to the wretched place I came from. Have mercy upon a poor boy, sir!"

" My dear child," said the old gentleman, moved by the warmth of Oliver's sudden appeal; " you need not be afraid of my deserting you, unless you give me cause."

" I never, never will, sir," interposed Oliver.

" I hope not," rejoined the old gentleman. " I do not think you ever will. I have been deceived be fore, in the objects whom I have endeavored to ben efit ; but I feel strongly disposed to trust you, never theless; and I am more interested in your behalf than I can well account for, even to myself. The persons on whom I have bestowed my dearest love lie deep in their graves; but, although the happi ness and delight of my life lie buried there too, I have not made a coffin of my heart, and sealed it up forever on my best affections. Deep affliction has but strengthened and refined them."

As the old gentleman said this in a low voice— more to himself than to his companion— and as he remained silent for a short time afterward, Oliver sat quite still.

" Well, well!" said the old gentleman at length, in

MR. GRIM WIG.

47

a more cheerful tone, " I only say this because you have a young heart; and knowing that I have suf fered great pain and sorrow, you will be more care ful, perhaps, not to wound me again. You say you are an orphan, without a friend in the world; all the inquiries I have been able to make confirm this statement. Let me hear ' your story; where you come from ; who brought you up; and how you got into the company in which I found you. Speak the truth, and you shall not be friendless while I live."

Oliver's sobs checked his utterance for some min utes ; when he was on the point of beginning to re late how he had been brought up at the farm, and carried to the work-house by Mr. Bumble, a peculiar ly impatient little double-knock was heard at the street-door; and the servant, running up stairs, an nounced Mr. Grimwig.

" Is he coming up ?" inquired Mr. Brownlow.

" Yes, sir," replied the servant. " He asked if there were any muffins in the house; and, when I told him yes, he said he had come to tea."

Mr. Brownlow smiled ; and, turning to Oliver, said that Mr. Grimwig was an old friend of his, and he must not mind his being a little rough in his man ners ; for he was a worthy creature at bottom, as he had reason to know.

" Shall I go down stairs, sir ?" inquired Oliver.

" No," replied Mr. Brownlow, " I would rather you remained here."

At this moment there walked into the room, sup porting himself by a thick stick, a stout old gentle man, rather lame in one leg, who was dressed in a blue coat, striped waistcoat, nankeen breeches and gaiters, and a broad-brimmed white hat, with the sides turned up with green. A very small-plaited shirt frill stuck out from his waistcoat; and a very long steel watch-chain, with nothing but a key at the end, dangled loosely below it. The ends of his white neckerchief were twisted into a ball about the size of an orange; the variety of shapes into which his countenance was twisted defy description. He had a manner of screwing his head on one side when he spoke, and of looking out of the corners of his eyes at the same time, which irresistibly reminded the beholder of a parrot. In this attitude he fixed himself, the moment he made his appearance; and, holding out a small piece of orange-peel at arm's length, exclaimed, in a growling, discontented voice,

'•Look here! do you see this! Isn't it a most wonderful and extraordinary thing that I can't call at a man's house but I find a piece of this poor surgeon's-friend on the staircase ? I've been lamed witli orange-peel once, and I know orange-peel will he niy death at last. It will, sir: orange-peel will be my death, or I'll be content to eat my own head, sir!"

This was the handsome offer with which Mr. Grim-wig backed and confirmed nearly every assertion he made ; and it was the more singular in his case, be cause, even admitting, for the sake of argument, the possibility of scientific improvements being ever brought to that pass which will enable a gentleman to eat his own head in the event of his being so dis posed, Mr. Grimwig's head was such a particularly large one, that the most sanguine man alive could hardly entertain a hope of being able to get through

it at a sitting—to put entirely out of the question a very thick coating of powder.

"I'll eat my head, sir," repeated Mr. Grimwig, striking his stick upon the ground. "Halloo! what's that?" looking at Oliver, and retreating a pace or two.

" This is young Oliver Twist, whom we were speaking about," said Mr. Brownlow.
Oliver bowed.

" You don't mean to say that's the boy who had the fever, I hope ?" said Mr. Grimwig, recoiling a lit tle taore. " Wait a minute! Don't speak! Stop—" continued Mr. Grimwig, abruptly, losing all dread of the fever in his triiunph at the discovery; " that's the boy w T ho had the orange! If that's not the boy, sir, who had the orange, and threw this bit of peel upon the staircase, I'll eat my head, and his too."

" No, no, he has not had one," said Mr. Browulow, laughing. " Come! Put down your hat; and speak to my young friend."

" I feel strongly on this subject, sir," said the irritable old gentleman, drawing off his gloves. " There's always more or less orange-peel on the pavement in our street; and I know it's put there by the surgeon's boy at the corner. A young woman stumbled over a bit last night, and fell against my garden-railings; directly she got up I saw her look toward his infernal red lamp with the pantomime-light. ' Don't go to him,' I called out of the win dow, ' he's an assassin! A man-trap!' So he is. If he is not— ' Here the irascible old gentleman gave a great knock on the ground with his stick; which was always understood by his friends to imply the customary offer, whenever it was not expressed in words. Then, still keeping his stick in his hand, he sat down; and, opening a double eye-glass, which he wore attached to a broad black ribbon, took a view of Oliver; who, seeing that he was the object of in spection, colored, and bowed again.

" That's the boy, is it ?" said Mr. Grimwig, at length.

" That is the boy," replied Mr. Brownlow.

" How are you, boy," said Mr. Grimwig.

"A great deal better, thank you, sir," replied Oli ver.

Mr. Browiilow, seeming to apprehend that his sin gular friend was about to say something disagreea ble, asked Oliver to step down stairs and tell Mrs. Bed win they were ready for tea; which, as he did not half like the visitor's manner, he was very happy to do.

"He is a nice-looking boy, is he not?" inquired Mr. Brownlow.

" I don't know," replied Mr. Grimwig, pettishly.

" Don't know ?"

"No. I don't know. I never see any difference in boys. I only know two sorts of boys. Mealy boys, and beef-faced boys."

"And which is Oliver?"

"Mealy. I know a friend who has a beef-faced boy—a fine boy, they call him; with -a round head, and fed cheeks, and glaring eyes; a horrid boy; with a body and limbs that appear to be swelling out of the seams of his blue clothes; with the voice of a pi lot, and the appetite of a wolf. I know him! The wretch!"

OLIVER TWIST.

" Come," said Mr. Brownlow, " these are not the characteristics of young Oliver Twist; so he needn't excite your wrath."

" They are not," replied Mr. Grimwig. " He may have worse."

Here Mr. Brownlow coughed impatiently; which appeared to afford Mr. Grimwig the most exquisite delight.

" He may have worse, I say," repeated Mr. Grim-wig. "Where does he come from? Who is he? What is he ? He has had a fever. What of that ? Fevers are not peculiar to good people; are they ? Bad people have fevers sometimes; haven't they, eh ? I knew a man who was hung in Jamaica for mur dering his master. He had had a fever six times; he wasn't recommended to mercy on that account. Pooh! nonsense!"

Now, the fact was that, in the inmost recesses of his own heart, Mr. Grimwig was strongly disposed to admit that Oliver's appearance and manner were un usually prepossessing; but he had a strong appetite for contradiction, sharpened on this occasion by the finding of the orange-peel; and, inwardly determin ing that no man should dictate to him whether a boy was well-looking or not, he had resolved, from the first, to oppose his friend. When Mr. Brownlow admitted that on no one point of inquiry could he yet return a satisfactory answer; and that he had postponed any investigation into Oliver's previous history until he thought the boy was strong enough to bear it; Mr. Grimwig chuckled maliciously. And he demanded, with a sneer, whether the housekeep er was in the habit of counting the plate at night; because, if she didn't find a table-spoon or two miss ing some sunshiny morning, why, he would be con tent to—and so forth.

All this, Mr. Brownlow, although himself some what of an impetuous gentleman, knowing his friend's peculiarities, bore with great good-humor. As Mr. Grimwig, at tea, was graciously pleased to express his entire approval of the muffins, matters went on very smoothly; and Oliver, who made one of the party, began to feel more at his ease than he had yet done in the fierce old gentleman's presence.

"And when are you going to hear a full, true, and particular account of the life and adventures of Oli ver Twist f' asked Grimwig of Mr. Brownlow, at the conclusion of the meal: looking sideways at Oliver, as he resumed the subject.

" To-morrow morning," replied Mr. Brownlow. " I would rather he was alone with me at the time. Come up to me to-morrow morning at ten o'clock, my dear."

" Yes, sir," replied Oliver. He answered with some hesitation, because he was confused by Mr. Grimwig's looking so hard at him.

" 111 tell you what," whispered that gentleman to Mr. Brownlow; " he won't come up to you to-morrow morning. I saw him hesitate. He is deceiving you, my good friend."

"I'll swear he is not," replied Mr. Brownlow, warmly.

" If he is not," said Mr. Grimwig," I'll—" and down went the stick.

"I'll answer for that boy's truth with my life!" said Mr. Browulow, knocking the table.

"And I for his falsehood with my head!" rejoined Mr. Grimwig, knocking the table also.

"We shall see," said Mr. Brownlow, checking his rising anger.

"We will," replied Mr. Grimwig, with a provoking smile; "we will."

As fate would have it, Mrs. Bedwin chanced to bring in, at this moment, a small parcel of books, which Mr. Brownlow had that morning purchased of the identical book-stall keeper, who has already figured in this history; having laid them on the ta ble, she prepared to leave the room.

" Stop the boy, Mrs. Bedwiu!" .said Mr. Brownlow ; " there is something to go back."

" He has gone, sir," replied Mrs. Bedwin.

" Call after him," said Mr. Browulow; " it's par ticular. He is a poor man, and they are not paid for. There are some books to be taken back, too."

The street-door was opened. Oliver ran one way, and the girl ran another: and Mrs. Bedwiu stood on the step and screamed for the boy ; but there was no boy in sight. Oliver and the girl returned, in a breathless state, to report that there were no tidings of him.

" Dear me, I am very sorry for that!" exclaimed Mr. Brownlow; " I particularly wished those books to be returned to-night."

" Send Oliver with them," said Mr. Grimwig, with an ironical smile; " he will be sure to deliver them safely, you know."

" Yes ; do let me take them, if you please, sir," said Oliver. " I'll run all the way, sir."

The old gentleman was just going to say that Oli ver should not go out on any account, when a most malicious cough from Mr. Grimwig determined him that he should ; and that, by his prompt discharge of the commission, he should prove to him the injus tice of his suspicious, on this head at least, at once.

" You shall go, my dear," said the old gentleman. " The books are on a chair by my table. Fetch them down."

Oliver, delighted to be of use, brought down the books under his arm in a great bustle; and waited, cap in hand, to hear what message he was to take.

" You are to say," said Mr. Brownlow, glancing steadily at Grimwig ; " you are to say that you have brought those books back; and that you have come to pay the four pound ten I owe him. This is a five-pound note, so you will have to bring me back ten shillings change."

" I won't be ten minutes, sir," replied Oliver, ea gerly. Having buttoned up the bank-note in his jacket pocket, and placed the books carefully under his arm, he made a respectful bow, and left the room. Mrs. Bedwin followed him to the street-door, giving him many directions about the nearest way, and the name of the book-seller, and the name of the street, all of which Oliver said he clearly understood. Hav ing superadded many injunctions to be sure and not take cold, the old lady at length permitted him to depart.

" Bless his sweet face !" said the old lady, looking after him. " I can't bear, somehow, to let him go out of my sight."

At this moment Oliver looked gayly round, and nodded before he turned the coiner. The old lady

smilingly returned his salutation, and, closing the door, went back to her own room.

" Let ine see; he'll be back in twenty minutes, at the longest," said Mr. Brownlow, pulling out his watch and placing it on the table. " It will be dark by that time."

" Oh! you really expect him to come back, do you f' inquired Mr. Griuiwig.

" Don't you ?" asked Mr. Brownlow, smiling.

The spirit of contradiction was strong in Mr. Grim-wig's breast at the moment; and it was rendered stronger by his friend's confident smile.

" No," he said, smiting the table with his fist, " I do not. The boy has a new suit of clothes on his back, a set of valuable books under his arm, and a five-pound note in his pocket. He'll join his old friends the thieves, and laugh at you. If ever that boy returns to this house, sir, I'll eat my head."

With these words he drew his chair closer to the table; and there the two friends sat, in silent ex pectation, with the watch between them.

It is worthy of remark, as illustrating the impor tance we attach to our own judgments, and the pride with which we put forth our most rash and hasty conclusions, that, although Mr. Grimwig was not by any means a bad-hearted man, and though he would have been unfeiguedly sorry to see his respected friend duped and deceived, he really did most ear nestly and strongly hope at that moment that Oli ver Twist might not come back.

It grew so dark, that the figures on the dial-plate were scarcely discernible; but there the two old gen tlemen continued to sit, in silence, with the watch between them.

CHAPTEE XV.

SHOWING HOW VERT FOND OF OLIVER TWIST THE MERBT OLD JEW AND MISS NANCY WERE.

IN the obscure parlor of a low public-house, in the filthiest part of Little Saffron Hill—a dark and gloomy den, where a flaring gas-light burned all day in the winter-time, and where no ray of sun ever shone in the summer—there sat, brooding over a lit tle pewter measure and a small glass, strongly im pregnated with the smell of liquor, a man in a vel veteen coat, drab shorts, half-boots, and stockings, whom even by that dim light no experienced agent of police would have hesitated to recognize as Mr. William Sikes. At his feet sat a white-coated, red-eyed dog; who occupied himself, alternately, in wink ing at his master with both eyes at the same time, and in licking a large, fresh cut on one side of his mouth, which appeared to be the result of some re cent conflict.

" Keep quiet, you warmint! Keep quiet!" said Mr. Sikes, suddenly breaking silence. Whether his meditations were 'so intense as to be disturbed by the dog's winking, or whether his feelings were so wrought upon by his reflections that they required all the relief derivable from kicking an unoffending animal to allay them, is matter for argument and consideration. Whatever was the cause, the effect was a kick and a curse, bestowed upon the dog si multaneously.

Dogs are not generally apt to revenge injuries in flicted upon them by their masters; but Mr. Sikes's dog, having faults of temper in common with his owner, and laboring, perhaps, at this moment, under a powerful sense of injury, made no more ado but at once fixed his teeth in one of the half-boots. Hav ing given it a hearty shake, he retired, growling, un der a form; just escaping the. pewter measure which Mr. Sikes leveled at his head.

" You would, would you ?'•' said Sikes, seizing the poker in one hand, and deliberately opening with the other a large clasp-knife, which he drew from his pocket. " Come here, you born devil! Come here! D'ye hear ?"

The dog no doubt heard, because Mr. Sikes spoke in the very harshest key of a very harsh voice; but, appearing to entertain some unaccountable objection to having his throat cut, he remained where he was, and growled more fiercely than before: at the same time grasping the end of the poker between his teeth, and biting at it like a wild beast.

This resistance only infuriated Mr. Sikes the more; who, dropping on his knees, began to assail the ani mal most furiously. The dog jumped from right to left, and from left to right: snapping, growling, and barking; the man thrust and swore, and struck and blasphemed; and the struggle was reaching a most critical point for one or other; when, the door sud denly opening, the dog darted out, leaving Bill Sikes with the poker and clasp-knife in his hands.

There must always be two parties to a quarrel, says the old adage. Mr. Sikes, being disappointed of the dog's participation, at once transferred his share in the quarrel to the new-comer.

"What the devil do you come in between me and my dog for ?" said Sikes, with a fierce gesture..

" I didn't know, my dear, I didn't know," replied Fagin, humbly; for the Jew was the new-comer.

" Didn't know, you white-livered thief!" growled Sikes. " Couldn't you hear the noise ?"

" Not a sound of it, as I'm a living man, Bill," re plied the Jew.

" Oh no! You hear nothing, you don't," retorted Sikes with a fierce sneer. " Sneaking in and out, so as nobody hears how you come or go! I wish you had been the dog, Fagin, half a minute ago."

"Why ?" inquired the Jew, with a forced smile.

" 'Cause the Government, as cares for the lives of such' men as you, as haven't half the pluck of curs, let's a man kill a dog how he likes," replied Sikes, shutting up the knife with a very expressive look ; " that's why."

The Jew nibbed his hands; and, sitting down at the table, affected to laugh at the pleasantry of his friend. He was obviously very ill at ease, how ever.

" Grin away," said Sikes, replacing the poker, and surveying him with savage contempt; " grin away. You'll never have the laugh at me, though, unless it's behind a night-cap. I've got the upper hand over you, Fa^in; and, d— me, I'll keep it. There! If I go, you \'7b.\'7bO; so take care of me."

" Well, well, my dear," said the Jew, " I know all that; we——we—have a mutual interest, Bill—a mu tual interest."

" Humph!" said Sikes, as if he thought the inter-
OLIVER TWIST.
est lay rather more on the Jew's side than on his. "Well, what have you got to say to me ?"

" It's all passed safe through the melting-pot," re plied Fagin, "and this is your share. It's rather more than it ought to be, my dear; but as I know you'll do me a good turn another time, and—"

" Stow that gammon!" interposed the robber, im patiently. " Where is it ? Hand over!"

" Yes, yes, Bill; give me time, give me time," re plied the Jew, soothingly. " Here it is! All safe!" As he spoke, he drew forth an old cotton handker chief from his breast; and untying a large knot in one corner, produced a small brown-paper packet. Sikes, snatching it from him, hastily opened it, and proceeded to count the sovereigns it contained.

" This is all, is it ?" inquired Sikes.

"All," replied the Jew.

"You haven't opened the parcel and swallowed one or two as you come along, have you ?" inquired Sikes, suspiciously. " Don't put on an injured look at the question: you've done it many a time. Jerk the tinkler."

These words, in plain English, conveyed an injunc tion to ring the bell. It was answered by another Jew, younger than Fagin, but nearly as vile and re pulsive in appearance.

Bill Sikes merely pointed to the empty measure. The Jew, perfectly understanding the hint, retired to fill it; previously exchanging a remarkable look with Fagin, who raised his eyes for an instant, as if in expectation of it, and shook his head in reply; so slightly that the action would have been almost im perceptible to an observant third person. It was lost upon Sikes, who was stooping at the moment to tie the boot-lace which the dog had torn. Possibly, if he had observed the brief interchange of signals, he might have thought that it boded no good to him.

" Is any body here, Barney ?" inquired Fagin; speaking, now that Sikes was looking on, without raising his eyes from the ground.

" Dot a shoul," replied Barney; whose words, whether they came from the heart or not, made their way through the nose.

" Nobody ?" inquired Fagin, in a tone of surprise; which perhaps might mean that Barney was at lib erty to tell the truth.

" Dobody but Biss Dadsy," replied Barney.

" Nancy !" exclaimed Sikes. " Where ? Strike me blind, if I don't honor that 'ere girl, for her native talents."

" She's bid havid a plate of boiled beef id the bar," replied Barney.

" Send her here," said Sikes, pouring out a glass of liquor. " Send her here."

Barney looked timidly at Fagin, as if for permis sion : the Jew remaining silent, and not lifting his eyes from the ground, he retired; and presently re turned, ushering in Nancy; who was decorated with the bonnet, apron, basket, and street-door key, com plete.

" You are on the scent, are you, Nancy ?" inquired Sikes, proffering the glass.

" Yes, I am, Bill," replied the young lady, dispos ing of its contents; " and tired enough of it I am, too. The young brat's been ill and confined to the crib; and—"

" Ah, Nancy, dear!" said Fagin, looking up.

Now, whether a peculiar contraction of the Jew's red eyebrows, and a half-closing of his deeply-set eyes, warned Miss Nancy that she was disposed to be too communicative, is not a matter of much impor tance. The fact is all we need care for here; and the fact is, that she suddenly checked herself, and with several gracious smiles upon Mr. Sikes, turned the conversation to other matters. In about ten min utes' time, Mr. Fagin was seized with a fit of cough ing ; upon which Nancy pulled her shawl over her shoulders, and declared it was time to go. Mr. Sikes, finding that he was walking a short part of her way himself, expressed his intention of accompanying her; they went away together, followed, at a little distance, by the dog, who slunk out of a back-yard soon as his master was out of sight.

The Jew thrust his head out of the room door when Sikes had left it; looked after him as he walked up the dark passage; shook his clenched fist; muttered a deep curse; and then, with a horrible grin, re-seat ed himself at the table; where he was soon deeply absorbed in the interesting pages of the Hue-and-Cry.

Meanwhile, Oliver Twist, little dreaming that he was within so very short a distance of the merry old gentleman, was on his way to the book-stall. When he got into Clerkenwell, he accidentally turned down a by-street which was not exactly in his way; but not discovering his mistake until he had got half way down it, and knowing it must lead in the right direction, he did not think it worth while to turn back; and so marched on, as quickly as he could, with the books under his arm.

He was walking along, thinking how happy and contented he ought to feel; and how much he would give for only one look at poor little Dick, who, starved and beaten, might be weeping bitterly at that very moment; when he was startled by a young woman screaming out very loud, " Oh, my dear broth er!" And he had hardly looked up, to see what the matter was, when he was stopped by having a pair of arms thrown tight round his neck.

" Don't!" cried Oliver, struggling. " Let go of me! Who is it ? What are you stopping me for ?"

The only reply to this was a great number of loud lamentations from the young woman Avho had em braced him; and who had a little basket and a street-door key in her hand.

" Oh my gracious!" said the young woman, " I've found him! Oh! Oliver! Oliver! Oh you naughty boy, to make me suffer sich distress on your account! Come home, dear, come. Oh, I've found him! Thank gracious goodness heavins, I've found him!" With these incoherent exclamations, the young woman burst into another fit of crying, and got so dreadful ly hysterical, that a couple of women who came up at the moment asked a butcher's boy with a shiny head of hair anointed with suet, who was also look ing on, whether he didn't think he had better run for the doctor. To which, the butcher's boy, who ap peared of a lounging, not to say indolent disposition, replied that he thought not.

" Oh, no, no, never mind," said the young woman, grasping Oliver's hand; " I'm better now. Come home directly, you cruel boy! Come!"

HIS RECAPTURE.

"What's the matter, ma'am ?" inquired, one of the women.

" Oh, ma'am," replied the young woman, " he ran away, near a month ago, from his parents, who are hard-working and respectable people ; and went and joined a set of thieves and bad characters ; and al most broke his mother's heart."

" Young wretch !" said one woman.

" Go home, do, you little brute !" said the other.

" I am not," replied Oliver, greatly alarmed. " I don't -know her. I haven't any sister, or father and mother either. I'm an orphan; I live at Penton-ville."

Help! help!" cried Oliver, struggling in the man's powerful grasp.

" Help !" repeated the man. " Yes; I'll help you, you young rascal! What books are these ? You've been a -stealing 'em, have you? Give 'em here." With these words, the man tore the volumes from his grasp, and struck him on the head.

" That's right!" cried a looker-on, from a garret-window. " That's the only way of bringing him to his senses!"

"To be sure !" cried a sleepy-faced carpenter, cast ing an approving look at the garret-window.

" It'll do him good!" said the two women.

YOU AKE ON TUB SCENT, ARE YOU, NAMOY ?"

" Only hear him, how he braves it out!" cried the young woman.

" Why, it's Nancy!" exclaimed Oliver; who now saw her face for the first time; and started back in irrepressible astonishment.

" You see he knows me!" cried Nancy, appealing to the by-standers. " He can't help himself. Make him come home, there's good people, or he'll kill his dear mother and father, and break my heart!"

"What the devil's this?" said a man, bursting out of a beer-shop, with a white dog at his heels; " young Oliver! Come home to your poor mother, you young dog! Come home directly."

"I don't belong to them. I don't know them.

"And he shall have it, too!" rejoined the man, ad ministering another blow, and seizing Oliver by the collar. " Come on, you young villain! Here, Bull's-eye, mind him, boy! Mind him!"

Weak with recent illness; stupefied by the blows and the suddenness of the attack; terrified by the fierce growling of the dog, and the brutality of the man; overpowered by the conviction of the by-stand ers that he really was the hardened little wretch he was described to be; what could one poor child do! Darkness had set in; it was a low neighborhood; no help was near; resistance was useless. In another moment he was dragged into & labyrinth of dark narrow courts, and was forced along them at a pace

OLIVER TWIST.

which rendered the few cries he dared to give utter ance to, unintelligible. It was of little moment, in deed, whether they were intelligible or no; for there was nobody to care for them, had they been ever so plain.

The gas-lamps were lighted; Mrs. Bedwin was waiting anxiously at the open door; the servant had run up the street twenty times to see if there were any traces of Oliver; and still the two old gentlemen sat, perseveringly, in the dark parlor, with the watch between them.

CHAPTER XVI.

RELATES WHAT BECAME OF OLIVER TWIST AFTER HE HAD BEEN CLAIMED BY NANCY.

THE narrow streets and courts at length termina ted in a large open space, scattered about which were pens for beasts, and other indications of a cat tle-market. Sikes slackened his pace when they reached this spot, the girl being quite unable to slip-port any longer the rapid rate at which they had hitherto walked. Turning to Oliver, he roughly commanded him to take hold of Nancy's hand.

"Do you hear?" growled Sikes, as Oliver hesita ted, and looked round.

They were in a dark corner, quite out of the track of passengers. Oliver saw but too plainly that re sistance would be of no avail. He held out his hand, which Nancy clasped tight in hers.

" Give me the other," said Sikes, seizing Oliver's unoccupied hand. " Here, Bull's-eye!" The dog looked up and growled. " See here, boy!" said Sikes, putting his other hand to Oliver's throat; " if he speaks ever so soft a word, hold him! D'ye mind!"

The dog growled again; and licking his lips, eyed Oliver as if he were anxious to attach himself to his windpipe without delay.

" He's as willing as a Christian, strike me blind if he isn't!" said Sikes, regarding the animal with a kind of grim and ferocious approval. "Now you know what you've got to expect, master, so call away as quick as you like; the dog will soon stop that game. Get on, young 'un!"

Bull's-eye wagged his tail in acknowledgment of this unusually endearing form of speech; and, giving vent to another admonitory growl for the benefit of Oliver, led the way onward.

It was Smithfield that they were crossing, al though it might have been Grosvenor Square for any thing Oliver knew to the contrary. The night was dark and foggy. The lights in the shops could scarcely struggle through the heavy mist, which thickened every moment and shrouded the streets and houses in gloom; rendering the strange place still stranger in Oliver's eyes; and making his un certainty the more dismal and depressing.

They had hurried on a few paces, when a deep church-bell struck the hour. With its first stroke his two conductors stopped, and turned their heads in the direction whence the sound proceeded.

" Eight o'clock, Bill," said Nancy, when the bell ceased.

" What's the good of telling me that; I can hear it, can't I ?" replied Sikes.

" I wonder whether they can hear it," said Nancy.

" Of course they can," replied Sikes. " It was Bar-tlemy time when I was shopped; and there waru't a penny trumpet in the fair as I couldn't hear the squeaking on. Arter I was locked up for the night, the row and din outside made the thundering old jail so silent, that I could almost have beat my brains out against the iron plates of the door."

" Poor fellows!" said Nancy, who still had her face turned toward the quarter in which the bell had sounded. " Oh, Bill, such fine young chaps as them!"

" Yes; that's all you women think of," answered Sikes. " Fine young chaps! Well, they're as good as dead, so it don't much matter."

With this consolation Mr. Sikes appeared to re press a rising tendency to jealousy, and, clasping Oliver's wrist more firmly, told him to step out again.

" Wait a minute!" said the girl, " I wouldn't hurry by if it was you that was coming out to be hung the next time eight o'clock struck, Bill. I'd walk round and round the place till I dropped, if the snow was on the ground, and I hadn't a shawl to cover me."

"And what good would that do?" inquired the unsentimental Mr. Sikes. " Unless you could pitch over a file and twenty yards of good stout rope, you might as well be walking fifty mile off, or not walk ing at all, for all the good it would do me. Come on, and don't stand preaching there.".

The girl burst into a laugh, drew her shawl more closely around her, and they walked away. But Oliver felt her hand tremble, and, looking up in her face as they passed a gas-lamp, saw that it had turned a deadly white.

They walked on by little-frequented and dirty ways, for a full half hour, meeting very few people, and those appearing from their looks to hold much the same position in society as Mr. Sikes himself. At' length they turned into a very filthy, narrow street, nearly full of old-clothes shops; the dog running forward, as if conscious that there was no further occasion for his keeping on guard, stopped before the door of a shop that was closed and apparently un-tenanted; the house was in a ruinous condition, and on the door was nailed a board, intimating that it was to let; which looked as if it had hung there for many years.

"All right," cried Sikes, glancing cautiously about.

Nancy stooped below the shutters, and Oliver heard the sound of a bell. They crossed to the opposite side of the street, and stood for a few moments under a lamp. A noise, as if a sash-window were gently raised, was heard; and soon afterward the door softly opened. Mr. Sikes then seized the terrified boy by the collar with very little ceremony, and all three were quickly inside the house.

The passage was perfectly dark. They waited, while the person who had let them in chained and barred the door.

"Any body here?" inquired Sikes.

"No," replied a voice, which Oliver thought he had heard before.

" Is the old 'un here ?" asked the robber.

" Yes," replied the voice; " and precious down in

RESTORED TO PLEASANT COMPANY.

the month he has been. Won't he be glad to see you? Oh, no!"

The style of this reply, as well as the voice which delivered it, seemed familiar to Oliver's ears; but it was impossible to distinguish even the form of the speaker in the darkness.

" Let's have a glim," said Sikes, " or we shall go breaking our necks, or treading on the dog. Look after your legs if you do!"

" Stand still a moment, and I'll get you one," re plied the voice. The receding footsteps of the speaker were heard; and, in another minute, the form of Mr. John Dawkius, otherwise the artful Dodger, ap peared. He bore in his right hand a tallow candle stuck in the end of a cleft stick.

The young gentleman did not stop to bestow any other mark of recognition upon Oliver than a humorous grin; but, turning away, beckoned the visitors to follow him down a flight of stairs. They crossed an empty kitchen; and, opening the door of a low, earthy-smelling room, which seemed to have been built in a small back-yard, were received with a shout of laughter.

" Oh, my wig, my wig!" cried Master Charles Bates, from whose lungs the laughter had proceed ed; "here he is! oh, cry, here he is! Oh, Fagin, look at him! Fagin, do look at him! I can't bear it; it is such a jolly game, I can't bear it. Hold me, somebody, while I laugh it out."

With this irrepressible ebullition of mirth, Master Bates laid himself flat on the floor, and kicked con vulsively for five minutes, in an ecstasy of facetious joy. Then jumping to his feet, he snatched the cleft stick from the Dodger; and, advancing to Oliver, viewed him round and round; while the Jew, tak ing off' his night-cap, made a great number of low bows to the bewildered boy. The Artful, meantime, who Avas of a rather saturnine disposition, and sel dom gave way to merriment when it interfered with business, rifled Oliver's pockets with steady assi duity.

" Look at his togs, Fagin!" said Charley, putting the light so close to his new jacket as nearly to set him on fire. "Look at his togs! Superfine cloth, and the heavy swell cut! Oh, my eye, what a game! And his books, too! Nothing but a gentleman, Fa-gin !"

" Delighted to see you looking so well, my dear," said the Jew, bowing with mock humility. " The Artful shall give you another suit, my dear, for fear you should spoil that Sunday one. Why didn't you write, my dear, and say you were coming ? We'd have got something warm for supper."

At this Master Bates roared again, so loud that Fagin himself relaxed, and even the Dodger smiled; but as the Artful drew forth the five-pound note at that instant, it is doubtful whether the sally or the discovery awakened his merriment.

" Halloo! what's that ?" inquired Sikes, stepping forward as the Jew seized the note. " That's mine, Fagin."

"No, no, my dear," said the Jew. "Mine, Bill, mine. You shall have the books."

" If that ain't mine," said Bill Sikes, putting on his hat with a determined air—" mine and Nancy's, that is—I'll take the boy back again."

The Jew started. Oliver started too, though from a very different cause; for he hoped that the dispute might really end in his being taken back.

" Come! Hand over, will you ?" said Sikes.

" This is hardly fair, Bill; hardly fair, is it, Nan cy ?" inquired the Jew.

" Fair or not fair," retorted Sikes, " hand over, I tell you! Do you think Nancy and me has got noth ing else to do with our precious time but to spend it in scouting arter, and kidnapping, every young boy as gets grabbed through you? Give it here, you avaricious old skeleton—give it here!"

With this gentle remonstrance, Mr. Sikes plucked the note from between the Jew's finger and thumb; and looking the old man coolly in the face, folded it up small, and tied it in his neckerchief.

" That's for our share of the trouble," said Sikes; " and not half enough, neither. You may keep the books, if you're fond of reading. If you ain't, sell 'em."

" They're very pretty," said Charley Bates, who, with sundry grimaces, had been affecting to read one of the volumes in question : " beautiful writing, isn't it, Oliver ?" At sight of the dismayed look with which Oliver regarded his tormentors, Master Bates, who was blessed with a lively sense of the ludicrous, fell into another ecstasy, more boisterous than the first.

" They belong to the old gentleman," said Oliver, wringing his hands; " to the good, kind old gentle man who took me into his house, and had me nursed, when I was near dying of the fever. Oh, pray send them back; send him back the books and money. Keep me here all my life long; but pray, pray send them back. He'll think I stole them; the old lady— all of them who were so kind to me—will think I stole them. Oh, do have mercy upon me, and send them back!"

With those words, which were uttered with all the energy of passionate grief, Oliver fell upon his knees at the Jew's feet, and beat his hands together in perfect desperation.

" The boy's right," remarked Fagin, looking cov ertly round, and knitting his shaggy eyebrows into a hard knot. " You're right, Oliver, you're right; they icill think you have stolen 'em. Ha! ha!" chuckled the Jew, rubbing his hands; " it couldn't have happened better if we had chosen our time!"

" Of course it couldn't," replied Sikes; " I kuow'd that, directly I see him coming through Clerkenwell, with the books under his arm. It's all right enough. They're soft-hearted psalm-singers, or they wouldn't have taken him in at all; and they'll ask no ques tions after him, fear they should be obliged to prose cute, and so get him lagged. He's safe enough."

Oliver had looked from one to the other, while these words were being spoken, as if he were bewil dered, and could scarcely understand what passed; but when Bill Sikes concluded, he jumped suddenly to his feet, and tore wildly from the room, uttering shrieks for help, which made the bare old house echo to the roof.

" Keep back the dog, Bill!" cried Nancy, springing before the door, and closing it, as the Jew and his two pupils darted out iu pursuit. " Keep back the dog; he'll tear the boy to pieces!"

" Serve him right!" cried Sikes, struggling to dis engage himself from the girl's grasp. " Stand off from me, or I'll split your head against the Avail!"

" I don't care for that, Bill, I don't care for that," screamed the girl, struggling violently with the man: " the child sha'n't be torn down by the dog, unless you kill me first."

"Sha'n't he!" said Sikes, setting his teeth. "I'll soon do that, if you don't keep off."

The housebreaker flung the girl from him to the farther end of the room, just as the Jew and the two boys returned, dragging Oliver among them.

"What's the matter here?" said Fagin, looking round.

" The girl's gone mad, I think," replied Sikes, sav agely.

" No, she hasn't," said Nancy, pale and breathless from the scuffle; " no, she hasn't, Fagiu; don't think it."

" Then keep quiet, will you ?" said the Jew, with a threatening look.

"No, I won't do that, neither," replied Nancy, speaking very loud. " Come! What do you think of that?"

Mr. Fagin was sufficiently well acquainted with the manners and customs of that particular species of humanity to which Nancy belonged to feel toler ably certain that it would be rather unsafe to pro long any conversation with her at present. With the view of diverting the attention of the company, he turned to Oliver.

" So you wanted to get away, my dear, did you ?" said the Jew, taking up a jagged and knotted club which lay in a corner of the fire-place; " eh ?"

Oliver made no reply. But he watched the Jew's motions, and breathed quickly.

*" Wanted to get assistance; called for the police, did you ?" sneered the Jew, catching the boy by the arm. " We'll cure you of that, my young master."

The Jew inflicted a smart blow on Oliver's shoul ders with the club; and was raising it for a second, when the girl, rushing forward, wrested it from his hand. She flung it into the fire, with a force that brought some of the glowing coals whirling out into the room.

" I won't stand by and see it done, Fagin," cried the girl. " You've got the boy, and what more would you have ? Let him be—let him be—or I shall put that mark on some of you, that will bring me to the gallows before my time."

The girl stamped her foot violently on the floor as she vented this tlireat; and with her lips compress ed, and her hands clenched, looked alternately at the Jew and the other robber: her face quite colorless from the passion of rage into which she had gradu ally worked herself.

" Why, Nancy," said the Jew, in a soothing tone; after a pause, during which he and Mr. Sikes had stared at one another in a disconcerted manner; " you—you're more clever than ever to-night. Ha! ha! my dear, you are acting beautifully."

" Am I ?" said the girl. " Take care I don't overdo it. You will be the worse for it, Fagin, if I do; and so I tell you in good time to keep clear of me."

There is something about a roused woman: espe cially if she add to all her other strong passions the

fierce impulses of recklessness and despair: which few men like to provoke. The Jew saw that it would be hopeless to affect any further mistake re garding the reality of Miss Nancy's rage; and, shrink ing involuntarily back a few paces, cast a glance, half imploring and half cowardly, at

Sikes: as if to hint that he was the fittest person to pursue the dia logue.

Mr. Sikes, thus mutely appealed to; and possibly feeling his personal pride and influence interested in the immediate reduction of Miss Nancy to reason; gave utterance to about a couple of score of curses and threats, the rapid production of which reflected great credit on the fertility of his invention. As they produced no visible effect on the object against whom they were discharged, however, he resorted to more tangible arguments.

" What do you mean by this ?" said Sikes ; back ing the inquiry with a very common imprecation concerning the most beautiful of human features; which, if it were heard aboA'e, only once out of ev ery fifty thousand times that it is uttered below, would render blindness as common a disorder as measles: " what do you mean by it ? Burn my body! Do you know who you are, and what you are ?"

" Oh, yes, I know all about it," replied the girl, laughing hysterically, and shaking her head from side to side with a poor assumption of indifference.

"Well, then, keep quiet," rejoined Sikes, with a growl like that he was accustomed to use when ad dressing his dog, " or I'll quiet you for a good long time to come."

The girl laughed again, even less composedly than before ; and, darting a hasty look at Sikes, turned her face aside, and bit her lip till the blood came.

" You're a nice one," added Sikes, as he surveyed her with a contemptuous air, "to take up the hu mane and gen-teel side! A pretty subject for the child, as you call him, to make a friend of!"

" God Almighty help me, I am !" cried the girl pas sionately ; " and I wish I had been struck dead in the street, or changed places with them we passed so near to-night, before I had lent a hand in bringing him here. He's a thief, a liar, a devil, all that's bad, from this night forth. Isn't that enough for the old Avretch, without blows ?"

" Come, come, Sikes," said the Jew, appealing to him in a reinonstratory tone, and motioning toward the boys, who were eagerly attentive to all that passed ; " we must have civil words—civil words, Bill."

" Civil words!" cried the girl, whose passion was frightful to see. "Civil words, you villain! Yes, you deserve 'em from me. I thieved for you when I was a child not half as old as this !" pointing to Oli ver. " I have been in the same trade, and in the same service, for twelve years since. Don't you kuow it ? Speak out! Don't you know it ?"

" Well, well," replied the Jew, with an attempt at pacification; " and, if you have, it's your living."

"Ay, it is!" returned the girl; not speaking, but pouring out the words in one continuous and vehe ment scream. " It is my living, and the cold, wet, dirty streets are my home; and you're the wretch that drove me to them long ago, and that'll keep me there, day and night, day and night, till I die!"

MR. BUMBLE, THE BEADLE.

55

" I shall do you a mischief!" interposed the Jew, goaded by these reproaches ; " a mischief worse than that, if you say much more!"

The girl said nothing more; but tearing her hair and dress in a transport of passion, made such a rush at the Jew as would probably have left signal marks of her revenge upon him, had not her wrists been seized by Sikes at the right moment; upon which she made a few ineffectual struggles, and fainted.

" She's all right now," said Sikes, laying her down in a corner. " She's uncommon strong in the arms, when she's up in this way."

The Jew wiped his forehead, and smiled, as if it were a relief to have the disturbance over; but nei ther he, nor Sikes, nor the dog, nor the boys, seemed to consider it in any other light than a common oc currence incidental to business.

" It's the worst of having to do with women," said the Jew, replacing his club; " but they're clever, and we can't get on, in our line, without 'em. Charley, show Oliver to bed."

" I suppose he'd better not wear his best clothes to-morrow, Fagin, had he ?" inquired Charley Bates.

" Certainly not," replied the Jew, reciprocating the grin with which Charley put the question.

Master Bates, apparently much delighted with his commission, took the cleft stick, and led Oliver into an adjacent kitchen, where there were two or three of the beds on which he had slept before; and here, with many uncontrollable bursts of laughter, he pro duced the identical old suit of clothes which Oliver had so much congratulated himself upon leaving off at Mr. Browulow's; and the accidental display of which, to Fagin, by the Jew who purchased them, had been the very first clue received of his where about.

" Pull off the smart ones," said Charley, " and I'll give 'em to Fagin, to take care of. What fun it is!"

Poor Oliver unwillingly complied. Master Bates rolling up the new clothes under his arm, departed from the room, leaving ©liver in the dark, and lock ing the door behind him.

The noise of Charley's laughter, and the voice of Miss Betsy, who opportunely arrived to throw water over her friend, and perform other feminine offices for the promotion of her recovery, might have kept many people awake under more happy circumstances than those in which Oliver was placed. But ho was sick and weary; and ho soon fell sound asleep.

CHAPTER XVII.

OLIVER'S DESTINY CONTINUING UNPROPITIOUS, BRINGS A GREAT MAN TO LONDON TO INJURE HIS REPUTATION.

IT is the custom on the stage, in all good murder ous melodramas, to present the tragic and the comic scenes, in as regular alternation, as the layers of red and white in a side of streaky bacon. The hero sinks upon his straw bed, weighed down by fetters and misfortunes ; in the next scene, his faith ful but unconscious squire regales the audience with a comic song. We behold, with throbbing bosoms, the heroine in the grasp of a proud and ruthless baron, her virtue and her life alike in danger, draw

ing forth her dagger to preserve the one at the cost of the other; and just as our expectations are wrought up to the highest pitch, a whistle is heard, and we are straightway transported to the great hall of the castle ; where a gray-headed seneschal sings a funny chorus with a funnier body of vassals, who are free of all sorts of places, from church vaults to palaces, and roam about in company, carolling perpetually.

Such changes appear absurd; but they are not so unnatural as they would seem at first sight. The transitions in real life from well-spread boards to death-beds, and from mourning weeds to holiday garments, are not a whit less startling; only there we are busy actors, instead of passive lookers-on, which makes a vast difference. The actors in the mimic, life of the theatre are blind to violent transi tions and abrupt impulses of passion or feeling, which, presented before the eyes of mere spectators, are at once condemned as outrageous and prepos terous.

As'sudden shiftings of the scene, and rapid changes of time and place, are not only sanctioned in books by long usage, but are by many considered as the great art of authorship—an author's skill in his craft, being, by such critics, chiefly estimated with rela tion to the dilemmas in which he leaves his charac ters at the end of every chapter—this brief introduc tion to the present one may perhaps be deemed un necessary. If so, let it be considered a delicate inti mation on the part of the historian that he is going back to the town in which Oliver Twist was born; the reader taking it for granted that there are good and substantial reasons for making the journey, or he would not be invited to proceed upon such an ex pedition.

Mr. Bumble emerged at early morning from the work-house gate, and walked with portly carriage and commanding steps up the High Street. He was in the full bloom and pride of beadlehood; his cocked hat and coat were dazzling in the morning sim; he clutched his cane with the vigorous tenacity of health and power. Mr. Bumble always carried his head high; but this morning it was higher than usual. There was an abstraction in his eye, an ele vation in his air, which might have warned an ob servant stranger that thoughts were passing in the beadle's mind too great for utterance.

Mr. Bumble stopped not to converse with the small shop-keepers and others who spoke to him deferentially, as he passed along. He merely re turned their salutations with a wave of his hand, and relaxed not in his dignified pace until he reach ed the farm where Mrs. Mann tended the infant pau pers with parochial care.

" Drat that beadle!" said Mrs. Maun, hearing the well-known shaking at the garden-gate. " If it isn't him at this time in the morning! Lauk, Mr. Bum ble, only think of its being you! Well, dear me, it is a pleasure, this is! Come into the parlor, sir, please."

The first sentence was addressed to Susan; and the exclamations of delight were uttered to Mr. Bum ble, as the good lady unlocked the garden-gate, and showed him, with great attention and respect, into the house.

" Mrs. Maun," said Mr. Bumble—not sitting upon,

OLIVER TWIST.

or dropping himself into a seat, as any common jack anapes would, but letting himself gradually and slowly down into a chair—" Mrs. Mann, ma'am, good-morning."

" Well, and good-morning to you, sir," replied Mrs. Mann, with many smiles; " and hoping you find yourself well, sir."

" So-so, Mrs. Mann," replied the beadle. "A poro-chial life is not a bed of roses, Mrs. Mann."

"Ah, that it isn't indeed, Mr. Bumble," rejoined the lady. And all the infant paupers might have chorused the rejoinder with great propriety, if they had heard it.

"A porochial life, ma'am," continued Mr. Bumble, striking the table with his cane, " is a life of worrit, and vexation, and hardihood; but all public charac ters, as I may say, must suffer prosecution."

Mrs. Mann, not very well knowing what the beadle meant, raised her hands with a look of sympathy, and sighed.

"Ah! You may well sigh, Mrs. Mann!" said the beadle.

Finding she had done right, Mrs. Mann sighed again: evidently to the satisfaction of the public character, who, repressing a complacent smile by looking sternly at his cocked hat, said,

" Mrs. Mann, I'm a-going to London."

"Lauk, Mr. Bumble!" cried Mrs. Mann, starting back.

" To London, ma'am," resumed the inflexible bea dle, " by coach. I and two paupers, Mrs. Mann! A legal action is a-coming on about a settlement; and the board has appointed me — me, Mrs. Mann — to depose to the matter before the Quarter-sessions at Clerkinwell. And I very much question," added Mr. Bumble, drawing himself up, "'whether the Clerkin well Sessions will not find themselves in the wrong box before they have done with me."

" Oh! you mustn't be too hard upon them, sir," said Mrs. Mann, coaxiugly.

"The Clerkinwell Sessions have brought it upon themselves, ma'am," replied Mr. Bumble; " and if the Clerkinwell Sessions find that they come olf rather worse than they expected, the Clerkinwell Sessions have only themselves to thank."

There was so much determination and depth of purpose about the menacing manner in which Mr. Bumble delivered himself of these words, that Mrs. Mann appeared quite awed by them. At length she said,

" You're going by coach, sir ? I thought it was always usual to send them paupers in carts."

" That's when they're ill, Mrs. Mann." said the bea dle. " We put the sick paupers into open carts in the rainy weather, to prevent their taking cold."

"Oh!" said Mrs.Mann.

"The opposition coach contracts for these two, and takes them cheap," said Mr. Bumble. "They are both in a very low state, and we find it would come two pound cheaper to move 'em than to bury r em—that is, if we can throw 'em upon another par ish, which I think we shall be able to do, if they don't die upon the road to spite us. Ha! ha! ha!"

When Mr. Bumble had laughed a little while, his eyes again encountered the cocked hat, and he be came grave.

" We are forgetting business, ma'am," said the bea dle ; " here is your porochial stipend for the month."

Mr. Bumble produced some silver money rolled up in a paper from his pocket-book, and requested a re ceipt ; which Mrs. Mann wrote.

" It's very much blotted, sir," said the farmer of infants; " but it's formal enough, I dare say. Thank you, Mr. Bumble, sir, I am very much obliged to you, I'm sure."

Mr. Bumble nodded blandly, in acknowledgment of Mrs. Mann's courtesy; and inquired how the chil dren were.

" Bless their dear little hearts!" said Mrs. Mann, with emotion, " they're as well as can be, the dears! Of course, except the two that died last week. And little Dick."

" Isn't that boy no better ?" inquired Mr. Bumble.

Mrs. Mann shook her head.

" He's a ill-conditioned, wicious, bad-disposed po rochial child that," said Mr. Bumble angrily. " Where is he ?"

" I'll bring him to you in one minute, sir," replied Mrs. Mann. " Here, you Dick!"

After some calling, Dick was discovered. Having had his face put under the pump, and dried upon Mrs. Mann's gown, he was led into the awful pres ence of Mr. Bumble, the beadle.

The child was pale and thin; his cheeks were sunk en : and his eyes large and bright. The scanty par ish dress, the livery of his misery, hung loosely on his feeble body; and his young limbs had wasted away like those of an old man.

Such was the little being who stood trembling be neath Mr. Bumble's glance; not daring to lift his eyes from the floor; and dreading even to hear the beadle's voice.

" Can't you look at the gentleman, you obstinate boy ?" said Mrs. Mann.

The child meekly raised his eyes, and encountered those of Mr. Bumble.

" What's the matter with you, porochial Dick t" inquired Mr. Bumble, with well-timed jocularity.

" Nothing, sir," replied the child, faintly.

" I should think not," said Mrs. Mann, who had, of course, laughed very much at Mr. Bumble's humor. " You want for nothing, I'm sure."

" I should like—" faltered the child.

" Heyday!" interposed Mrs. Mann," I suppose you're going to say that you do want for something, now ? Why, you little wretch—"

"Stop, Mrs. Mann, stop!" said the beadle, raising his hand with a show of authority. "Like what, sir, eh?"

" I should like," faltered the child, " if somebody that can write would put a few words down for me on a piece of paper, and fold it up and seal it, and keep it for me, after I am laid in the ground."

" Why, what does the boy mean ?" exclaimed Mr. Bumble, on whom the earnest manner and wan as pect of the child had made some impression, accus tomed as he was to such things. "What do you mean, sir ?"

" I should like," said the child, " to leave my dear love to poor Oliver Twist; and to let him know how often I have sat by myself and cried to think of his wandering about in the dark nights with nobody to

BUMBLE AFTER THE GUINEAS.

help him. Aud I should like to tell him," said the child, pressing his small hands together, and speak ing with great fervor, " that I was glad to die when I was very young; for, perhaps, if I had lived to be a man, and had grown old, my little sister, who is in heaven, might forget me, or be unlike me; and it would be so much happier if we were both children there together."

Mr. Bumble surveyed the little speaker from head to foot with indescribable astonishment; and, turn ing to his companion, said, " They're all in one story, Mrs. Mann. That out-dacious Oliver has demogal-ized them all!"

" I couldn't have believed it, sir!" said Mrs. Mann, holding up her hands, and looking malignantly at Dick. " I never see such a hardened little wretch!"

" Take him away, ma'am!" said Mr. Bumble, impe riously. " This must be stated to the board, Mrs. Maim."

" I hope the gentlemen will understand that it isn't my fault, sir ?" said Mrs. Mann, whimpering pathet ically.

" They shall understand that, ma'am; they shall be acquainted with the true state of the case," said Mr. Bumble. " There; take him away; I can't bear the sight on him."

Dick was immediately taken away and locked up in the coal-cellar. Mr. Bumble shortly afterward took himself off, to prepare for his journey.

At six o'clock next morning, Mr. Bumble—having exchanged his cocked hat for a round one, and in cased his person in a blue great-coat with a cape to it—took his place on the outside of the coach, accom panied by the criminals whose settlement was dis puted ; with whom, in due course of time, he arrived in London. He experienced no other crosses on the way than those which originated in the perverse be havior of the two paupers, who persisted in shiver ing and complaining of the cold, in a manner which, Mr. Bumble declared, caused his teeth to chatter in his head, and made him feel quite uncomfortable, al-thougn ne had a great-coat on.

Having disposed of these evil-minded persons for the night, Mr. Bumble sat himself down in the house at which the coach stopped; and took a temperate dinner of steaks, oyster-sauce, and porter. Putting a glass of hot gin-and-water on the chimney-piece, he drew his chair to the fire; and, with sundry moral reflections on the too-prevalent sin of discontent and complaining, composed himself to read the paper.

The very first paragraph upon which Mr. Bumble's eye rested was the following advertisement:

"FIVE GUINEAS REWARD.

" Whereas a young boy, named Oliver Twist, absconded, or was enticed, on Thursday evening last, from his home, at Pen-tonville, and has not since been heard of. The above reward will be paid to any person who will give such information as will lead to the discovery of the said Oliver Twist, or tend to throw any light upon his previous history, in which the adver tiser is, for many reasons, warmly interested."

And then followed a full description of Oliver's dn-ss, person, appearance, and disappearance; with the name and address of Mr. Brownlow at full length.

Mr. Bumble opened his eyes; read the advertise ment, slowly and carefully, three several times; and

in something more than five minutes was on his way to Pentouville; having actually, in his excitement, left the glass of hot gin-and-water nutasted.

" Is Mr. Brownlow at home ?" inquired Mr. Bumble of the girl who opened the door.

To this inquiry* the girl returned the not uncom mon, but rather evasive reply of, " I don't know; where do you come from ?"

Mr. Bumble no sooner uttered Oliver's name, in ex planation of his errand, than Mrs. Bedwin, who had been listening at the parlor-door, hastened into the passage in a breathless state.

" Come in, come in," said the old lady: " I knew we should hear of him. Poor dear! I knew we should. I was certain of it. Bless his heart! I said so, all along."

Having said this, the worthy old lady hurried back into the parlor again; and seating herself on a sofa, burst into tears. The girl, who was not quite so sus ceptible, had run up stairs meanwhile; and now re turned with a request that Mr. Bumble would follow her immediately; which he did.

He was shown into the little back study, where sat Mr. Brownlow and his friend Mr. Grimwig, with de canters and glasses before them. The latter gentle man at once burst into the exclamation:

"A beadle! A parish beadle, or I'll eat my head!"

"Pray don't interrupt just now," said Mr. Brown-low. " Take a seat, will you ?"

Mr. Bumble sat himself down, quite confounded by the oddity of Mr. Grimwig's manner. Mr. Brownlow moved the lamp, so as to obtain an uninterrupted view of the beadle's countenance; and said, with a little impatience,

" Now, sir, you come in consequence of having seen the advertisement ?"

" Yes, sir," said Mr. Bumble.

"And you are a beadle, are you not ?" inquired Mr. Grimwig.

" I am a porochial beadle, gentlemen," rejoined Mr. Bumble, proudly.

" Of course," observed Mr. Grimwig, aside, to his friend. "I knew he was. A beadle all over!"

Mr. Brownlow gently shook his head to impose si lence on his friend, and resumed:

" Do you know where this poor boy is now ?"

" No more than nobody," replied Mr. Bumble.

" Well, what do you know of him ?" inquired the old gentleman. " Speak out, my friend, if you have any thing to say. What do you know of him f'

" You don't happen to know any good of him, do you ?" said Mr. Grimwig, caustically; after an atten tive perusal of Mr. Bumble's features.

Mr. Bumble, catching at the inquiry very quickly, shook his head with portentous solemnity.

" You see ?" said Mr. Grimwig, looking triumph antly at Mr. Brownlow.

Mr. Brownlow looked apprehensively at Mr. Bum ble's pursed-up countenance; and requested him to communicate what he knew regarding Oliver, in as few words as possible.

Mr. Bumble put down his hat; unbuttoned his coat; folded his arms; inclined his head in a retro spective manner; and after a few moments' reflec tion, commenced his story.

It would be tedious if given in the beadle's words,

OLIVER TWIST.

occupying, as it did, some twenty minutes in the tell ing ; but the sum and substance of it was, That Ol iver was a foundling, born of low and vicious par ents. That he had, from his birth, displayed no better qualities than treachery, ingratitude, and mal ice. That he had terminated his brief career in the place of his birth, by making a sanguinary and cow ardly attack on an unoffending lad, and running away in the night-time from his master's house. In proof of his really being the person he represented himself, Mr. Bumble laid upon the table the papers he had brought to town. Folding his arms again, he then awaited Mr. Brownlow's observations.

" I fear it is all too true," said the old gentleman sorrowfully, after looking over the papers. " This is

" It can't be, sir. It can not be," said the old lady, energetically.

"I tell you he is," retorted the old gentleman. "What do you mean by can't bef We have just heard a full account of him from his birth; and he has been a thorough-paced little villain all his life."

" I never will believe it, sir," replied the old lady, firmly. " Never !"

" You old women never believe any thing but quack doctors and lying story-books," growled Mr. Grimwig. " I knew it all along. Why didn't you take my advice in the beginning; you would, if he hadn't had a fever, I suppose, eh ? He was interest ing, wasn't he ? Interesting! Bah!" And Mr. Grim-wig poked the fire with a flourish.

"A BEADLE! A PABISU BEADLE, OE I'LL EAT MY HEAD."

not mucn for your intelligence ; but I would gladly have given you treble the money, if it had been fa vorable to the boy."

. It is not improbable that if Mr. Bumble had been possessed of this information at an earlier period of the interview, he might have imparted a very differ ent coloring to his little history. It was too late to do it now, however; so he shook his head gravely, and, pocketing the five guineas, withdrew.

Mr. Brownlow paced the room to and fro for some minutes ; evidently so' much disturbed by the bea dle's tale, that even Mr. Grimwig forbore to vex him further.

At length he stopped, and rang the bell violently.

" Mrs. Bed win," said Mr. Brownlow, when the house keeper appeared; "that boy, Oliver, is an impostor."

" He was a dear, grateful, gentle child, sir," retort ed Mrs. Bedwiu, indignantly. " I know what chil dren are, sir, and have done these forty years; and people who can't say the same, shouldn't say auy thing about them. That's my opinion!"

This was a hard hit at Mr. Grimwig, Avho was a bachelor. As it extorted nothing from that gentle man but a smile, the old lady tossed her head, and smoothed down her apron preparatory to another speech, when she was stopped by Mr. Brownlow.

" Silence!" said the old gentleman, feigning an anger he was far from feeling. " Never let me hear the boy's name again. I rang to tell you that. Never. Never, on any pretense, mind ! You may leave the room, Mrs. Bedwiu. Remember! I am iu earnest."

A LONELY PLACE TO LIFE

There were sad hearts at Mr. Brownlow's that night.

Oliver's heart sank within him, when he thought of his good kind friends ; it was well for him that he could not know what they had heard, or it might have broken outright.

CHAPTER XVIII.

HOW OLIVER PASSED HIS TIME IN THE IMPROVING SO CIETY OF HIS REPUTABLE FRIENDS.

ABOUT noon next day, when the Dodger and Master Bates had gone out to pursue their cus tomary avocations, Mr. Fagiu took the opportunity of reading Oliver a long lecture on the crying sin of ingratitude: of which he clearly demonstrated he had been guilty, to no ordinary extent, in willfully absenting himself from the society of his anxious friends; and, still more, in endeavoring to escape from them after so much trouble and expense had been incurred in his recovery. Mr. Fagin laid great stress on the fact of his having taken Oliver in, and cherished him, when, without his timely aid, he might have perished with hunger; and he related the dis mal and affecting history of a young lad whom, in his philanthropy, he had succored under parallel cir cumstances, but who, proving unworthy of his confi dence and evincing a desire to communicate with the police, had unfortunately come to be hanged at the Old Bailey one morning. Mr. Fagin did not seek to conceal his share in the catastrophe, but lamented with tears in his eyes that the wrong-headed and treacherous behavior of the young person in ques tion had rendered it necessary that he should become the victim of certain evidence for the crown: which, if it were not precisely true, was indispensably nec essary for the safety of him (Mr. Fagin) and a few select friends. Mr. Fagin concluded by drawing a rather disagreeable picture of the discomforts of hanging ; and, with great friendliness and politeness of manner, expressed his anxious hopes that he might never be obliged to submit Oliver Twist to that un pleasant operation.

Little Oliver's blood ran cold, as he listened to the Jew's words, and imperfectly comprehended the dark threats conveyed in them. That it was possible even for justice itself to confound the innocent with the guilty when they were in accidental companionship, he knew already; and that deeply-laid plans for the destruction of inconveniently knowing or over-com municative persons, had been really devised and car ried out by the old Jew on more occasions than one, he thought by no means unlikely, when he recol lected the general nature of the altercations between that gentleman and Mr. Sikes, which seemed to bear reference to some foregone conspiracy of the kind. As he glanced timidly up, and met the Jew's search ing look, he felt that his pale face and trembling limbs were neither unnoticed nor unrelished by that wary old gentleman.

The Jew, smiling hideously, patted Oliver on the head, and said, that if he kept himself quiet, and ap plied himself to business, he saw they would be very good friends yet. Then, taking his hat, and covering

himself with an old patched great-coat, he went out, and locked the room-door behind him.

And so Oliver remained all that day, and for the greater part of many subsequent days, seeing no body between early morning and midnight, and left during the long hours to commune with his own thoughts; which, never failing to revert to his kind friends, and the opinion they must long ago have formed of him, were sad indeed.

After the lapse of a week or so, the Jew left the room-door unlocked; and he was at liberty to wan der about the house.

It was a very dirty place. The rooms up stairs had great high wooden chimney-pieces and large doors, with paneled walls and cornices to the ceil ings ; which, although they were black with neglect and dust, were ornamented in various ways. From all of these tokens Oliver concluded that a long time ago, before the old Jew was born, it had belonged to better people, and had perhaps been quite gay and handsome: dismal and dreary as it looked now.

Spiders had built their webs in the angles of the walls and ceilings; and sometimes, when Oliver walked softly into a room, the mice would scamper across the floor and run back terrified to their holes. With these exceptions, there was neither sight nor sound of any living thing; and often, when it grew dark, and he was tired of wandering from room to room, he would crouch in the comer of the passage by the street-door, to be as near living people as he could; and would remain there, listening and count ing the hours, until the Jew or the boys returned.

In all the rooms the mouldering shutters were fast closed: the bars which held them were screwed tight into the wood; the only light which was admitted stealing its Way through round holes at the top; which made the rooms more gloomy, and filled them with strange shadows. There was a back-garret window with rusty bars outside, which had no shut ter ; and out of this Oliver often gazed with a mel ancholy face for hours together; but nothing was to be descried from it but a confused and crowded mass of house-tops, blackened chimneys, and gable-ends. Sometimes, indeed, a grizzly head might be seen peering over the parapet-wall of a distant house: but it was quickly withdrawn again; and as the window of Oliver's observatory was nailed down, and dimmed with the rain and smoke of years, it was as much as he could do to make out the forms of the different objects beyond, without making any at tempt to be seen or heWd—which he had as much chance of being, as if he had lived inside the ball of St. Paul's Cathedral.

One afternoon, the Dodger and Master Bates being engaged out that evening, the first-named young gentleman took it into his head to evince some anx iety regarding the decoration of his person (to do him justice, this was by no means an habitual weak ness with him) ; and, with this end and aim, he con descendingly commanded Oliver to assist him in his toilet straightway.

Oliver was but too glad to make himself useful— too happy to have some faces, however bad, to look upon—too desirous to "conciliate those about him when he could honestly do so— to throw any objec tion in the way of this proposal. So he at once ex-

OLIVER TWIST.

pressed his readiness; and, kneeling on the floor, while the Dodger sat upon the table so that he could take his foot in his lap, he applied himself to a proc ess which Mr. Daw kins designated as "japanning his trotter-cases." The phrase, rendered into plain English, siguifieth, cleaning his boots.

Whether it was the sense of freedom and inde pendence which a rational animal may be supposed to feel when he sits on a table in an easy attitude smoking a pipe, swinging one leg carelessly to and fro, and having his boots cleaned all the time, with out even the past trouble of having taken them off, or the prospective misery of putting them on, to dis turb his reflections; or whether it was the goodness of the tobacco that soothed the feelings of the Dodg er, or the mildness of the beer that mollified his thoughts ; he was evidently tinctured, for the nonce, with a spice of romance and enthusiasm, foreign to his general nature. He looked down on Oliver, with a thoughtful countenance, for a brief space; and then, raising his head, and heaving a gentle sigh, said, half in abstraction, and half to Master Bates:

" What a pity it is he isn't a prig !"

"Ah!" said Master Charles Bates, "he don't know what's good for him."

The Dodger sighed again, and resumed his pipe, as did Charley Bates. They both smoked, for some seconds, in silence.

" I suppose you don't even know what a prig is ?" said the Dodger, mournfully.

" I think I know that," replied Oliver, looking up. " It's a th—; you're one, are you not ?" inquired Oli ver, checking himself.

" I am," replied the Dodger. " I'd scorn to be any thing else." Mr. Dawkins gave his hat a fero cious cock, after delivering this sentiment, and look ed at Master Bates, as if to denote that he would feel obliged by his saying any thing to the con trary.

" I am," repeated the Dodger. " So's Charley. So's Fagin. So's Sikes. So's Nancy. So's Bet. So we all are, down to the dog. And he's the downiest one of the lot!"

"And the least given to peaching," added Charley Bates.

" He wouldn't so much as bark in a witness-box, for fear of committing himself; no, not if you tied him up in one, and left him there without wittles for a fortnight," said the Dodger.

" Not a bit of it," observed Charley.

"He's a rum dog. Don't he look fierce at any strange cove that laughs or sings when he's in com pany !" pursued the Dodger. "Won't he growl at all, when he hears a fiddle playing! And don't he hate other dogs as ain't of his breed! Oh, no!"

" He's an out-and-out Christian," said Charley.

This was merely intended as a tribute to the ani mal's abilities, but it was an appropriate remark in another sense, if Master Bates had only known it; for there are a good many ladies and gentlemen, claiming to be out-and-out Christians, between whom and Mr. Sikes's dog there exist strong and singular points of resemblance.

"Well, well," said the Dodger, recurring to the point from which they had strayed; with that mind-fulness of his profession which influenced all his pro

ceedings. "This hasn't got any thing to do with young Green here."

"No more it has," said Charley. "Why don't you put yourself under Fagiu, Oliver ?"

"And make your fortim' out of hand?" added the Dodger, with a grin.

"And so be able to retire on your property, and do the gen-teel, as I mean to, in the very next leap-year but four that ever comes, and the forty-second Tues day in Trinity-week," said Charles Bates.

" I don't like it," rejoined Oliver, timidly ; " I wish they would let me go. I would rather go."

" And Fagiu would rathw not !" rejoined Charley.

Oliver knew this too well; but thinking it might be dangerous to express his feelings more openly, he only sighed, and went on with his boot-cleaning.

" Go !" exclaimed the Dodger. " Why, where's your spirit ? Don't you take any pride out of your self? Would you go and be dependent on your friends ?"

" Oh, blow that !" said Master Bates, drawing two or three silk handkerchiefs from his pocket, and tossing them into a cupboard, " that's too mean, that is."

" couldn't do it," said the Dodger, with an air of haughty disgust.

" You can leave your friends, though," said Oliver, with a half smile ; " and let them be punished for Avhat you did."

" That," rejoined the Dodger, with a wave of his pipe " that was all out of consideration for Fagiu, 'cause the traps know that we work together, and he might have got into trouble if we hadn't made our lucky; that was the move, wasn't it, Charley

Master Bates nodded assent, and would have spoken, but the recollection of Oliver's flight came so suddenly upon him, that the smoke he was inhal ing got entangled with a laugh, and went up into his head, and down into his throat ; and brought on a fit of coughing and stamping, about five minutes long.

" Look here !" said the Dodger, drawing forth a handful of shillings and halfpence. " Here's a jolly life! What's the odds where it comes from I Here, catch hold; there's plenty more where they were took from. You won't, won't you ? Oh, you pre cious flat!"

" It's naughty, ain't it, Oliver ?" inquired Charley Bates. " He'll come to be scragged, won't he f'

" I don't know what that means," replied Oliver.

" Something in this way, old feller," said Charley. As he said it, Master Bates caught up an end of his neckerchief, and, holding it erect in the air, dropped his head on his shoulder, and jerked a curious sound through his teeth ; thereby indicating, by a lively pantomimic representation, that scragging and hang ing were one and the same thing.

" That's what it means," said Charley. " Look how he stares, Jack! I never did see such prime compa ny as that 'ere boy ; he'll be the death of me, I know he will." Master Charles Bates, having laughed heartily again, resumed his pipe with tears in his eyes.

" You've been brought up bad," said the Dodger, surveying his boots with much satisfaction when Ol iver had polished them. " Fagin will make some-

IMPROVING ADVICE.

thing of you, though, or you'll be the first he ever ' had that turned out unprofitable. You'd better be gin at once; for you'll come to the trade long before you think of it; and you're only losing time, Oliver."

Master Bates backed this advice with sundry mor al admonitions of his own: which, being exhausted, he and his friend Mr. Dawkins launched into a glow ing description of the numerous pleasures incidental to the life they led, interspersed with a variety of hints to Oliver that the best thing he could do would be to secure Fagin's favor without more de lay, by the means which they themselves had em ployed to gain it.

"And always put this in your pipe, Nolly," said the Dodger, as the Jew was heard unlocking the door above, " if you don't take fogies and tickers— :

" What's the good of talking in that way ?" inter posed Master Bates: " he don't know what you mean."

" If you don't take pocket - handkechers and watches," said the Dodger, reducing his conversation to the level of Oliver's capacity, "some other cove will; so that the coves that lose 'em will be all the worse, and you'll be all the worse too, and nobody half a ha'p'orth the better, except the chaps wot gets them—and you've just as good a right to them as they have."

" To be sura, to be sure!" said the Jew, who had entered, unseen by Oliver. " It all lies in a nutshell, my dear—in a nutshell, take the Dodger's word for it. Ha! ha! ha! He understands the catechism of his trade."

The old man rubbed his hands gleefully together, as he corroborated the Dodger's reasoning in these terms; and chuckled with delight at his pupil's pro-ticiency.

The conversation proceeded no further at this time, for the Jew had returned home accompanied by Miss Betsy, and a gentleman whom Oliver had never seen before, but who was accosted by the Dodger as Tom Chitling; and who having lingered on the stairs to exchange a few gallantries with the lady, now made his appearance.

Mr. Chitling was older in years than the Dodger; having perhaps numbered eighteen winters; but there was a degree of deference in his deportment toward that young gentleman which seemed to in dicate that he felt himself conscious of a slight in feriority in point of genius and professional acquire ments. He had small twinkling eyes, and a pock marked face; wore a fur cap, a dark corduroy jacket, greasy fustian trowsers, and an apron. His ward robe was, in truth, rather out of repair; but he ex cused himself to the company by stating that his " time " was only out an hour before; and that, in consequence of having worn the regimentals for six weeks past, he had not been able to bestow any at tention on his private clothes. Mr. Chitling added, with strong marks of irritation, that the new way of fumigating clothes up yonder was infernal unconsti tutional, for it burned holes in them, and there was no remedy against the county. The same remark he considered to apply to the regulation mode of cut ting the hair, which he held to be decidedly unlaw ful. Mr. Chitling wound up his observations by stat ing that he had not touched a drop of any thing for forty-two mortal long hard-working days; and that

he " wished he might be busted if he warn't as dry as a lime-basket."

"Where do you think the gentleman has come from, Oliver f" inquired the Jew, with a grin, as the other boys put a bottle of spirits on the table.

" I—I—don't know, sir," replied Oliver.

" Who's that ?" inquired Tom Chitliug, casting a contemptuous look at Oliver.

"A young friend of mine, my dear," replied the Jew.

" He's in luck, then," said the young man, with a meaning look at Fagin. " Never mind where I came from, young 'un; you'll find your way there soon enough, I'll bet a crown!"

At this sally the boys laughed. After some more jokes on the same subject, they exchanged a few short whispers with Fagiu, and withdrew.

After some words apart between the last comer and Fagin, they drew their chairs toward the fire; and the Jew, telling Oliver to come and sit by him, led the conversation to the topics most calculated to interest his hearers. These were, the great advan tages of the trade, the proficiency of the Dodger, the amiability of Charley Bates, and the liberality of the Jew himself. At length these subjects displayed signs of being thoroughly exhausted; and Mr. Chit-ling did the same; for the house of correction be comes fatiguing after a week or two. Miss Betsy accordingly withdrew; and left the party to their repose.

From this day, Oliver was seldom left alone; but was placed in almost constant communication with the two boys, who played the old game with the Jew every day; whether for their own improvement or Oliver's, Mr. Fagin best knew. At other times the old man would tell them stories of robberies ho had committed in his younger days; mixed up with so much that was droll and curious, that Oliver could not help laughing heartily, and showing that he was amused, in spite of all his better feelings.

In short, the wily old Jew had the boy in his toils. Having prepared his mind, by solitude and gloom, to prefer any society to the companionship of his own sad thoughts in such a dreary place, he was now slowly instilling into his soul the poison which he hoped would blacken it, and change its hue forever.

CHAPTER XIX.

IN WHICH A NOTABLE PLAN* IS DISCUSSED AND DETER MINED ON.

IT was a chill, damp, windy night, when the Jew, buttoning his great-coat tight rdund his shriveled body, and pulling the collar up over his ears so as completely to obscnre the lower part of his face, emerged from his den. He paused on the step as the door was locked and chained behind him ; and having listened while the boys made all secure, and until their retreating footsteps were no longer audi ble, slunk down the street as quickly as he could.

The house to which Oliver had been conveyed was in the neighborhood of Whitechapel. The Jew stopped for an instant at the corner of the street;

and, glancing suspiciously round, crossed the road, and strnck off in the direction of Spitalfields.

The mnd lay thick .upon the stones, and a black mist hung over the streets; the rain fell sluggishly down, and every thing felt cold and clammy to the touch. It seemed just the night when it befitted such a being as the Jew to be abroad. As he glided stealthily along, creeping beneath the shelter of the walls and door-ways, the hideous old man seemed like some loathsome reptile, engendered in the slime and darkness through which he moved; crawling forth, by night, in search of some rich offal for a meal.

He kept on his course, through many winding and narrow ways, until he reached Bethnal Green; then, turning suddenly off to the left, he soon became in volved in a maze of the mean and dirty streets Avhich abound in that close and densely-populated quarter.

The Jew was evidently too familiar with the ground he traversed to be at all bewildered, either by the darkness of the night, or the intricacies of the way. He hurried through several alleys and streets, and at length turned into one, lighted only by a single lamp at the farther end. At the door of a house in this street he knocked; having ex changed a few muttered words with the person who opened it, he walked up stairs.

A dog growled as he touched the handle of a room-door ; and a man's voice demanded who was there.

" Only me, Bill; only me, my dear," said the Jew, looking in.

"Bring in your body, then," said Sikes. "Lie down, you stupid brute! Don't you know the devil when he's got a great-coat on ?"

Apparently, the dog had been somewhat deceived by Mr. Fagin's outer garment; for as the Jew unbut toned it, and threw it over the back of a chair, he retired to the corner from which he had risen; wag ging his tail as he went, to show that he was as well satisfied as it was in his nature to be.

"Well!"said Sikes.

"Well, my dear," replied the Jew.—"Ah! Nancy."

The latter recognition was uttered with just enough of embarrassment to imply a doubt of its reception; for Mr. Fagin and his young friend had not met since she had interfered in behalf of Oliver. All doubts upon the subject, if he had any, were speedily re moved by the young lady's behavior. She took her feet off the fender, pushed back her chair, and bade Fagin draw up his, without saying more about it: for it was a cold night, and no mistake.

" It is cold, Nancy dear," said the Jew, as he warm ed his skinny hands over the fire. " It seems to go ri^-ht through one," aided the old man, touching his side.

" It must be a piercer, if it finds its way through your heart," said Mr. Sikes. " Give him something to drink, Nancy. Burn my body, make haste! It's enough to turn a man ill, to see his lean old carcass shivering in that way, like a ugly ghost just rose from the grave."

Nancy quickly brought a bottle from a cupboard, in which there were many: which, to judge from the diversity of their appearance, were filled with several kinds of liquids. Sikes, pouring out a glass of bran dy, bade the Jew drink it off.

" Quite enough, quite, thankye, Bill," replied the Jew, putting down the glass after just setting his lips to it.

" What! You're afraid of our getting the better of you, are you f" inquired Sikes, fixing his eyes on the Jew. " Ugh!"

With a hoarse grunt of contempt, Mr. Sikes seized the glass, and threw the remainder of its contents into the ashes, as a preparatory ceremony to filling it again for himself, which he did at once.

The Jew glanced round the room as his compan ion tossed down the second glassful; not in curiosity, for he had seen it often before; but in a restless and suspicious manner habitual to him. It was a meanly furnished apartment, with nothing but the contents of the closet to induce the belief that its occupier was any thing but a working-man; and with no more suspicious articles displayed to view than two or three heavy bludgeons which stood in a corner, and a " life-preserver " that himg over the chimney-piece.

" There," said Sikes, smacking his lips. " Now I'm ready."

" For business ?" inquired the Jew.

" For business," replied Sikes; " so say what you've got to say."

"About the crib at Chertsey, Bill?" said the Jew, drawing his chair forward, and speaking in a very low voice.

" Yes. Wot about it ?" inquired Sikes.

"Ah! you know what I mean, my dear," said the Jew. " He knows what I mean, Nancy; don't he ?"

"No, he don't," sneered Mr. Sikes. " Or he won't, and that's the same thing. Speak out, and call things by their right names ; don't sit there winking and blinking, and talking to me in hints, as if you warn't the very first that thought about the robbery. Wot d'ye mean?"

" Hush, Bill, hush!" said the Jew, who had in vain attempted to stop this burst of indignation; " some body will hear us, my dear — somebody will hear us.' ;

" Let 'eui hear!" said Sikes; " I don't care." But as Mr. Sikes did care, on reflection, he dropped his voice as he said the words, and grew calmer.

" There, there," said the Jew, coaxingly. " It was only my caution, nothing more. Now, my dear, about that crib at Chertsey; when is it to be done, Bill, eh ? When is it to be done ? Such plate, my dear, such plate!" said the Jew; nibbing his hands, and elevating his eyebrows in a rapture of antici pation.

" Not at all," replied Sikes, coldly.

" Not to be done at all!" echoed the Jew, leaning back in his chair.

" No, not at all," rejoined Sikes. "At least it can't be a put-up job, as we expected."

" Then it hasn't been properly gone about," said the Jew, turning pale with anger. " Don't tell me !"

"But I will tell you," retorted Sikes. "Who are you that's not to be told? I tell yoti that Toby Crackit has been hanging about the place for a fort night, and he can't get one of the servants into a line."

" Do you mean to tell me, Bill," said the Jew, soft ening as the other grew heated, " that neither of the two men in the house can be got over ?"

BUSINESS AFOOT.

"Yes, I do mean to tell you so replied Sikes. " The old lady has had 'em these twenty year; and if you were to give 'em five hundred pound, they wouldn't be in it."

" But do you mean to say, my dear," remonstrated the Jew, " that the vomeu can't be got over ?"

" Not a bit of it," replied Sikes.

" Not by flash Toby Crackit ?" said the Jew, in credulously. " Think what women are, Bill."

"No; not even by flash Toby Crackit," replied Sikes. "He says he's worn sham whiskers, and a canary waistcoat, the whole blessed time he's been loitering down there, and it's all of no use."

"He should have tried mustaches and a pair of military trowsers, my dear," said the Jew.

" So he did," rejoined Sikes, " and they waru't of no more use than the other plant."

The Jew looked blank at this information. After ruminating for some minutes with his chin sunk on his breast, he raised his head and said, with a deep sigh, that if flash Toby Crackit reported aright, he feared the game was up.

"And yet," said the old man, dropping his hands on his knees, " it's a sad thing, my dear, to lose so much when we had set our hearts upon it."

" So it is," said Mr. Sikes. " Worse luck!"

A long silence ensued ; during which the Jew was plunged in deep thought, with his face wrinkled into an expression of villainy perfectly demoniacal. Sikes eyed him furtively from time to time. Nancy, apparently fearful of irritating the house-breaker, sat with her eyes fixed upon the fire, as if she had been deaf to all that passed.

" Fagin," said Sikes, abruptly breaking the still ness that prevailed; " is it worth fifty shiners extra, if it's safely done from the outside ?"

" Yes," said the Jew, as suddenly rousing himself.

" Is it a bargain ?" inquired Sikes.

"Yes, my dear, yes," rejoined the Jew; his eyes glistening, and every muscle in his face working with the excitement that the inquiry had awakened.

"Then," said Sikes, thrusting aside the Jew's hand, with some disdain, " let it come off as soon as you like. Toby and me vere over the garden-wall the night afore last, sounding the panels of the door and shutters. The crib's barred up at night like a jail; but there's one part we can crack safe and softly."

"Which is that, Bill ?" asked the Jew, eagerly.

" Why," whispered Sikes," as you cross the lawn—"

" Yes," said the Jew, bending his head forward, with his eyes almost starting out of it.

" Umph!" cried Sikes, stopping short, as the girl, scarcely moving her head, looked suddenly round, and pointed for an instant to the Jew's face. " Nev er mind which part it is. You can't do it without me, I know; but it's best to be on the safe side when one deals with you."

"As you like, my dear, as yon like," replied the Jew. "Is there no help wanted but yours and Toby's r

"None," said Sikes. "'Cept a centre-bit and a boy. The first we've both got; the second you must find us."

"A boy!" exclaimed the Jew. "Oh! then it's a panel, eh ?"

" Never mind wot it is!" replied Sikes. " I want a boy, and he musu't be a big un. Lord!" said Mr. Sikes, reflectively, " if I'd only got that young boy of Ned, the chimbley-sweeper's! He kept" him small on purpose, and let him out by the job. But the fa ther gets lagged; and then the Juvenile Delinquent Society comes and takes the boy away from a trade where he was arniug money, teaches him to read and write, and in time makes a 'prentice of him. And so they go on," said Mr. Sikes, his wrath rising with the recollection of his wrongs, " so they go on; and, if they'd got money enough (which it's a Providence they haven't), wo shouldn't have half a dozen boys left in the whole trade, in a year or two."

"No more we should," acquiesced the Jew, who had been considering during this speech, and had only caiight the last sentence. "Bill!"

"What now ?" inquired Sikes.

The Jew nodded his head toward Nancy, who was still gazing at the lire; and intimated by a sign that he would have told her to leave the room. Sikes shrugged his shoulders impatiently, as if he thought the precaution unnecessary; but complied, neverthe less, by requesting Miss Nancy to fetch him a jug of beer.

" You don't want any beer," said Nancy, folding her arms, and retaining her seat very composedly.

" I tell you I do," replied Sikes.

" Nonsense!" rejoined the girl, coolly. " Go on, Fa-gin. I know what he's going to say, Bill; he needn't mind me."

The Jew still hesitated. Sikes looked from one to the other in some surprise.

"Why, you don't mind the old girl, do you, Fa-gin '?" he asked at length. " You've known her long enough to trust her, or the Devil's in it. She ain't one to blab. Are you, Nancy ?"

"should think not!" replied the young lady: drawing her chair up to the table, and putting her elbows upon it.

" No, no, my dear, I know you're not," said the Jew; " but—" and again the old man paused.

" But wot ?" inquired Sikes.

" I didn't know whether she mightn't pYaps be out of sorts, you know, my dear, as she was the other night," replied the Jew.

At this confession Miss Nancy burst into a loud laugh; and, swallowing a glass of brandy, shook her head with an air of defiance, and burst into sundry exclamations of " Keep the game a-going!" " Never say die!" and the like. These seemed to have the effect of reassuring both gentlemen; for the Jew nodded his head with a satisfied air, and resumed his seat: as did Mr. Sikes likewise.

" Now, Fagin," said Nancy, with a laugh, " tell Bill at once about Oliver!"

" Ha! you're a clever one, my dear; the sharpest girl I ever saw!" said the Jew, patting her on the neck. " It was about Oliver I was going to speak, sure enough. Ha! ha! ha!"

"What about him?" demanded Sikes-

"He's the boy for you, my dear," replied the Jew, in a hoarse whisper, laying his finger on the side of his nose, and grinning frightfully.

" He!" exclaimed Sikes.

" Have him, Bill!" said Nancy. " I would, if I was

OLIVER TWIST.

in your place. He mayn't be so much up as any of the others; but that's not what you want, if he's only to open a door for you. Depend upon it he's a safe one, Bill."

"I know he is," rejoined Fagin. "He's been in good training these last few weeks, and it's time he began to Avork for his bread. Besides, the others are all too big."

" Well, he is just the size I want," said Mr. Sikes, ruminating.

"And will do every thing you want, Bill, my dear," interposed the Jew; " he can't help himself. That is, if you frighten him enough."

" Frighten him!" echoed Sikes. " It'll be no sham

" Ours!" said Sikes. " Yours, you mean."

" Perhaps I do, my dear," said the Jew with a shrill chuckle. " Mine, if you like, Bill."

"And wot," said Sikes, scowling fiercely on his agreeable friend, "wot makes you take so much pains about one chalk-faced kid, when you know there are fifty boys snoozing about Common Garden every night, as you might pick and choose from ?"

" Because they're of no use to me, my dear," re plied the Jew, with some confusion, " not worth the taking. Their looks convict 'em when they get into trouble, and I lose 'em all. With this boy, properly managed, my dears, I could do what I couldn't with twenty of them. Besides," said the Jew, recovering

THE BOY WAS LYING, FAST ASLEEP, ON A RUDE BED UPON TUB FLOOR.

frightening, mind you. If there's any thing queer about him when we once get into the work; in for a penny, in for a pound. You won't see him alive again, Fagin. Think of that before you send him. Mark my words!" said the robber, poising a crow bar, which he had drawn from under the bedstead.

" I've thought of it all," said the Jew, with energy. " I've—I've had my eye upon him, my dears, close— close. Once- let him feel that he is one of us—once fill his mind with the idea that he has been a thief— and he's ours! Ours for his life. Oho! It couldn't have come about better!"

The old man crossed his arms upon his breast, and, drawing his head and shoul ders into a heap, literally hugged himself for joy.

his self-possession, " he has us now if he could only give us leg-bail again; and he must be in the same boat with us. Never mind how he came there ; it's quite enough for my power over him that he was in a robbery ; that's all I want. Now, how much bet ter this is than being obliged to put the poor leetle boy out of the way—which would be dangerous, and we should lose by it besides."

" When is it to be done ?" asked Nancy, stopping some turbulent exclamation on the part of Mr. Sikes, expressive of the disgust with which he received Fa-gin's affectation of humanity.

"Ah, to be sure," said the Jew; "when is it to be done, Bill T"

THE VERT EOT FOR THE PURPOSE.

" I planned with Toby, the night arter to-morrow," rejoined Sikes in a surly voice, " if he heerd nothing from me to the contrairy."

" Good," said the Jew; " there's no moon."

"No,"rejoined Sikes.

" It's all arranged about bringing off the swag, is it ?" asked the Jew.

Sikes nodded.

"And about—"

" Oh, ah, it's all planned," rejoined Sikes, inter rupting him. " Never mind particulars. You'd bet ter bring the boy here to-morrow night. I shall get off the stones an hour arter daybreak. Then you hold your tongue, and keep the melting-pot ready, and that's all you'll have to do."

After some discussion, in which all three took an active part, it was decided that Nancy should repair to the Jew's next evening when the night had set in, and bring Oliver away with her; Fagin craftily observing that, if he evinced any disinclination to the task, he would be more willing to accompany the girl who had so recently interfered in his behalf, than any body else. It was also solemnly arranged that poor Oliver should, for the purposes of the con templated expedition, be unreservedly consigned to the care and custody of Mr. William Sikes; and fur ther, that the said Sikes should deal with him as he thought fit; and should not be held responsible by the Jew for any mischance or evil that might befall him, or any punishment w r ith which it might be nec essary to visit him: it being understood that, to ren der the compact in this respect binding, any repre sentations made by Mr. Sikes on his return should be required to be confirmed and corroborated, in all important particulars, by the testimony of flash Toby Crackit.

These preliminaries adjusted, Mr. Sikes proceeded to drink brandy at a furious rate, and to flourish the crowbar in an alarming manner; yelling forth, at the same time, most unmusical snatches of song, min gled with wild execrations. At length, in a fit of professional enthusiasm, he insisted upon producing his box of house-breaking tools: which he had no sooner stumbled in with, and opened for the purpose of explaining the nature and properties of the vari ous implements it contained, and the peculiar beau ties of their construction, than he fell over the box upon the floor, and went to sleep where he fell.

" Good-night, Nancy," said the Jew, muffling him self up as before.

" Good-night."

Their eyes met, and the Jew scrutinized her nar rowly. There was no flinching about the girl. She was as true and earnest in the matter as Toby Crack-it himself could be.

The Jew again bade her good-night, and, bestow ing a sly kick upon the prostrate form of Mr. Sikes while her back was turned, groped down stairs.

"Always the way," muttered the Jew to himself as he turned homeward. " The worst of these wom en is, that a very little thing serves to call up some long-forgotten feeling; and the best of them is, that it nev-r lasts. Ha! ha! The man against the child, for a bag of gold!"

Beguiling the time with these pleasant reflections, Mr. Fagin wended his way, through mud and mire,

to his gloomy abode: where the Dodger was sitting up, impatiently awaiting his return.

" Is Oliver abed ? I want to speak to him," was his first remark as they descended the stairs.

" Hours ago," replied the Dodger, throwing open a door. " Here he is."

The boy was lying, fast asleep, on a rude bed upon the floor; so pale with anxiety, and sadness, and the closeness of his prison, that he looked like death; not death as it shows iu shroud and coffin, but in the guise it wears when life has just departed; when a young and gentle spirit has, but an instant, fled to Heaven, and the gross air of the world has not had time to breathe upon the changing dust it hallowed.

"Not now," said the Jew, turning softly away. " To-morrow. To-morrow."

CHAPTER XX.

WHEREIN OLIVER IS DELIVERED OVER TO MR. WILLIAM SIKES.

WHEN Oliver awoke in the morning, he was a good deal surprised to find that a new pair of shoes, with strong thick soles, had been placed at his bedside, and that his old shoes had been removed. At first he was pleased with the discovery, hoping it might be the forerunner of his release; but such thoughts were quickly dispelled, on his sitting down to breakfast along with the Jew, who told him, in a tone and manner which increased his alarm, that he was to be taken to the residence of Bill Sikes that night.

"To—to—stop there, sir?" asked Oliver, anxiously.

" No, no, my dear. Not to stop there," replied the Jew. "We shouldn't like to lose you. Don't be afraid, Oliver, you shall come back to us again. Ha! ha! ha! We won't be so cruel as to send you away, my dear. Oh no, no!"

The old man, who was stooping over the fire toast ing a piece of bread, looked round as he bantered Oliver thus; and chuckled as if to show that he knew he would still be very glad to get away if he could.

" I suppose," said the Jew, fixing his eyes on Oli ver, " you want to know what you're going to Bill's for—eh, my dear ?"

Oliver colored, involuntarily, to find that the old thief had been reading his thoughts; but boldly said, Yes, he did want to know.

" Why, do you think ?'? inquired Fagin, parrying the question.

" Indeed I don't know, sir," replied Oliver.

" Bah!" said the Jew, turning away v.-ith a disap pointed countenance from a close perusal of the boy's face. " Wait till Bill tells you, then."

The Jew seemed much vexed by Oliver's not ex pressing any greater curiosity on the subject; but the truth is, that although Oliver felt very anxious, he was too much confused by the earnest cunning of Fagin's looks, and his own speculations, to make any further inquiries just then. He had no other opportunity, for the Jew remained very surly aud .si lent till night; when he prepared to go abroad.

" You may bum a candle," said the Jew, putting

OLIVES TWIST.

one upon the table. "And here's a book for you to read, till they come to fetch you. Good-night!"

" Good-night!" replied Oliver, softly.

The Jew walked to the door, looking over his shoulder at the boy as he went. Suddenly stopping, he called him by his name.

Oliver looked up; the Jew, pointing to the candle, motioned him to light it. He did so; and, as he placed the candlestick upon the table, saw that the Jew was gazing fixedly at him, with lowering and contracted brows, from, the dark end of the room.

"Take heed, Oliver! take heed!" said the old man, shaking his right hand before him in a warning manner. "He's a rough man, and thinks nothing of blood when his own is up. Whatever falls out, say nothing; and do what he bids you. Mind!" Placing a strong emphasis on the last word, he suf fered his features gradually to resolve themselves into a ghastly grin, and, nodding his head, left the room.

Oliver leaned his head upon his hand when the old man disappeared, and pondered, with a trembling heart, on the words he had just heard. The more he thought of the Jew's admonition, the more he was at a loss to divine its real purpose and meaning. He could think of no bad object to be attained by send ing him to Sikes which would not be equally well answered by his •
remaining with Fagin; and after meditating for a long time, concluded that he had been selected to perform some ordinary menial of fices for the house-breaker, until another boy, better suited for his purpose, could be engaged. He was too well accustomed to suffering, and had suffered too much where he was, to bewail the prospect of change very severely. He remained lost in thought for some minutes; and then, with a heavy sigh, snuff ed the candle, and, taking up the book which the Jew had left with him, began to read.

He turned over the leaves. Carelessly at first; but lighting on a passage which attracted his atten tion, he soon became intent upon the volume. It was a history of the lives and trials of great crimi nals, and the pages were soiled and thumbed with use. Here he read of dreadful crimes that made the blood run cold; of secret murders that had been committed by the lonely wayside; of bodies hidden from the eye of man in deep pits and wells, which would not keep them down, deep as they were, but had yielded them up at last after many years, and so maddened the murderers with the sight, that in their horror they had confessed their guilt, and yell ed for the gibbet to end their agony. Here, too, he read of men Avho, lying in their beds at dead of night, had been tempted (so they said) and led on, by their own bad thoughts, to such dreadful bloodshed as it made the flesh creep and the limbs quail to think of. The terrible descriptions were so real and vivid, that the sallow pages seemed to turn red with gore, and the words upon them to be sounded in his ears as if they were whispered, in hollow murmurs, by the spirits of the dead.

In a paroxysm of fear, the boy closed the book and thrust it from him. Then, falling upon his knees, he prayed Heaven to spare him from such deeds; and rather to will that he should die at once, than be reserved for crimes so fearful and appalling.

By degrees he grew more calm, and besought, in a low and broken voice, that he might be rescued from his present dangers; and that if any aid were to be raised up for a poor outcast boy who had never known the love of friends or kindred, it might come to him now, when, desolate and deserted, he stood alone in the midst of wickedness and guilt.

He had concluded his prayer, but still remained with his head buried in his hands, when a rustling noise aroused him.

" What's that !" he cried, starting up, and catch ing sight of a figure standing by the door. " Who's there ?"

" Me. Only me," replied a tremulous voice.

Oliver raised the candle above his head, and look ed toward the door. It was Nancy.

" Put down the light," said the girl, turning away her head. " It hurts my eyes."

Oliver saw that she was very pale, and gently in quired if she were ill. The girl threw herself into a chair with her back toward him, and wrung her hands, but made no reply.

"God forgive me!" she cried, after a while, "I never thought of this."

" Has any thing happened ?" asked Oliver. " Can I help you ? I will if I can. I will, indeed."

She rocked herself to and fro, caught her throat, and, uttering a gurgling sound, gasped for breath.

" Nancy!" cried Oliver, " what is it ?"

The girl beat her hands upon her knees, and her feet upon the ground; and, suddenly stopping, drew her shawl close round her, and shivered with cold.

Oliver stirred the fire. Drawing her chair close to it, she sat there for a little time, without speak ing ; but at length she raised her head, and looked round.

"I don't know what comes over me sometimes," said she, affecting to busy herself in arranging her dress; " it's this damp, dirty room, I think. Now, Nolly, dear, are you ready ?"

"Am I to go with you?" asked Oliver.

"Yes, I have come from Bill," replied the girl. " You are to go with me."

" What for ?" asked Oliver, recoiling.

"What for f" echoed the girl, raking her eyes, and averting them again the moment they encountered the boy's face. " Oh! - For no harm."

" I don't believe it," said Oliver, who had watched her closely.

" Have it your own way," rejoined the girl, affect ing to laugh. " For no good, then."

Oliver could see that he had some power over the girl's better feelings, and, for an instant, thought of appealing to her compassion for his helpless state. But then the thought darted across his mind that it was barely eleven o'clock, and that many people were still in the streets, of whom surely some might be found to give credence to his tale. As the reflec tion occurred to him, he stepped forward, and said, somewhat hastily, that lie was ready.

Neither his brief consideration nor its purport was lost on his companion. She eyed him narrowly while he spoke, and cast upon him a look of intelli gence which sufficiently showed that she guessed what had been passing in his thoughts.

"Hush!" said the girl, stooping over him, and

MB. SIKES READS OLIVER A LECTURE.

pointing to the door as she looked cautiously round. " You can't help yourself. I have tried hard for you, but all to 110 purpose. You are hedged round and round. If ever you are to get loose from here, this is not the time."

Struck by the energy of her manner, Oliver looked up in her face with great surprise. She seemed to speak the truth; her countenance was white and ag itated, and she trembled with very earnestness.

" I have saved you from being ill-used once, and I will again, and I do now," continued the girl, aloud; " for those who would have fetched you, if I had not, would have been far more rough than me. I have promised for your being quiet and silent; if you are not, you will only do harm to yourself and me too, and perhaps be my death. See here! I have borne all this for you already, as true as God sees me show it."

She pointed hastily to some livid bruises on her neck and arms, and continued, with great rapidity:

" Remember this! And don't let me suffer more for you. just now. If I could help you, I would; but I have not the power. They don't mean to harm you; whatever they make you do is no fault of yours. Hush! Every word from you is a blow for me. Give me your hand. Make haste! Your hand!"

She caught the hand which Oliver instinctively placed in hers, and, blowing out the light, drew him after her up the stairs. The door was opened quick ly by some one shrouded in the darkness, and was as quickly closed when they had passed out. A hack ney-cabriolet was in waiting; with the same vehe mence which she had exhibited in addressing Oli ver, the girl pulled him in with her, and drew the cur tains close. The driver wanted no directions, but lashed his horse into full speed without the delay of an instant.

The girl still held Oliver fast by the hand, and continued to pour into his ear the warnings and as surances she had already imparted. All was so quick and hurried, that he had scarcely time to rec ollect where he was, or how he came there, when the carriage stopped at the house to which the Jew's steps had been directed on the previous evening.

For one brief moment, Oliver cast a hurried glance along the empty street, and a cry for help hung upon his lips. But the girl's voice was in his ear, beseech ing him, in such tones of agony to remember her, that he had not the heart to utter it. While he hes itated the opportunity was gone; he was already in the house, and the door was shut.

" This way," said the girl, releasing her hold for the first time. "Bill!"

" Halloo!" replied Sikes, appearing at the head of the stairs, with a candle. " Oh! That's the time of day! Come on!"

This was a very strong expression of approbation, an uncommonly hearty welcome, from a person of Mr. Sikes's temperament. Nancy, appearing much gratified thereby, saluted him cordially.

"Bull's-eye's gone home with Tom," observed Sikes, as he lighted them up. " He'd have been in the w.'iy."

" That's right," rejoined Nancy.

" So you've got the kid," said Sikes, when they had all reached the room, closing the door as he spoke.

" Yes, here he is," replied Nancy.

" Did he come quiet ?" inquired Sikes.

" Like a lamb," rejoined Nancy.

" I'm glad to hear it," said Sikes, looking grimly at Oliver; " for the sake of his young carcass: as would otherways have suffered for it. Come here, young 'un; and let me read you a lectur', which is as well got over at once."

Thus addressing his new pupil, Mr. Sikes pulled off Oliver's cap and threw it into a corner; and then, taking him by the shoulder, sat himself down by the table, and stood the boy in front of him.

" Now, first: do you know wot this is ?" inquired Sikes, taking up a pocket-pistol which lay on the table.

Oliver replied in the affirmative.

"Well, then, look here," continued Sikes. "This is powder; that 'ere's a bullet; and this is a little bit of a old hat for waddin'."

Oliver murmured his comprehension of the differ ent bodies referred to; and Mr. Sikes proceeded to load the pistol, with great nicety and deliberation.

" Now it's loaded," said Mr. Sikes, when he had finished.

" Yes, I see it is, sir," replied Oh'ver.

"Well," said the robber, grasping Oliver's wrist, and putting the barrel so close to his temple that they touched; at which moment the boy could not repress a start; " if you speak a word when you're out o' doors with me, except when I speak to you, that loading will be in your head without notice. So, if you do make up your mind to speak without leave, say your prayers first."

Having bestowed a scowl upon the object of this warning, to increase its effect, Mr. Sikes continued.

"As near as I know, there isn't any body as would be asking very partickler arter you, if you was dis posed of; so I needn't take this devil-and-all of trouble to explain matters to you, if it warn't for your own good. D'ye hear me ?"

" The short and the long of what you mean," said Nancy—speaking very emphatically, and slightly frowning at Oliver^as if to bespeak his serious atten tion to her words—" is, that if you're crossed by him in this job you have on hand, you'll prevent his ever telling tales afterward by shooting him through the head, and will take your chance of swinging for it,, as you do for a great many other things in the way of business, every month of your life."

" That's it!" observed Mr. Sikes, approvingly; "women can always put things in fewest words.— Except when it's blowing up, and then they length ens it out. And now that he's thoroughly up to it, let's have some supper, and get a snooze before start ing."

In pursuance of this request, Nancy quickly laid the cloth; disappearing for a few minutes, she pres ently returned with a pot of porter and a dish of sheep's heads; which gave occasion to several pleas ant witticisms on the part of Mr. Sikes, founded upon the singular coincidence of "jemmies " being a cant name common to them, and also to an ingenious im plement much used in his profession. Indeed, the worthy gentleman, stimulated perhaps by the imme diate prospect of being on active service, was in great spirits anr good-humor; in proof whereof, it may be

OLIVER TWIST.

here remarked, that he humorously drank all the beer at a draught, and did not utter, on a rough calculation, more than four-score oaths during the whole progress of the meal.

Supper being ended—it may easily be conceived that Oliver had no great appetite for it — Mr. Sikes disposed of a couple of glasses of spirits-and-water, and threw himself on' the bed ; ordering Nancy, with many imprecations in case of failure, to call him at five precisely. Oliver stretched himself in his clothes, by command of the same authority, on a mattress upon the floor ; and the girl, mending the fire, sat before it, in readiness to arouse them at the appointed time.

For a long time Oliver lay awake, thinking it not impossible that Nancy might seek that opportunity of whispering some further advice; but the girl sat brooding over the fire, without moving, save now and then to trim the light. Weary with watching and anxiety, he at length fell asleep.

When he awoke, the table was covered with tea-things, and Sikes was thrusting various articles into the pockets of his great-coat, which hung over the back of a chair. Nancy was busily engaged in pre paring breakfast. It was not yet daylight; for the candle was still burning, and it was quite dark out side. A sharp rain, too, was beating against the win dow-panes ; and the sky looked black and cloudy.

" Now, then !" growled Sikes, as Oliver started up; " half-past five ! Look sharp, or you'll get no break fast ; for it's late as it is."

Oliver was not long in making his toilet ; having taken some breakfast, he replied to a surly inquiry from Sikes, by saying that he was quite ready.

Nancy scarcely looking at the boy, threw him a handkerchief to tie round his throat ; Sikes gave him a large rough cape to button over his shoulders. Thus attired, he gave his hand to the robber, who, merely pausing to show him with a menacing ges ture that he had that same pistol in a side-pocket of his great-coat, clasped it firmly in his, and, exchang ing a farewell with Nancy, led him away.

Oliver turned, for an instant, ^fhen they reached the door, in the hope of meeting a look from the girl. But she had resumed her old seat in front of the fire, and sat perfectly motionless before it.

IT was a cheerless morning when they got into the street; blowing and raining hard, and the clouds looking dull and stormy. The night had been very wet: large pools of water had collected in the road, and the kennels 'were overflowing. There was a faint glimmering of the coming day in the sky ; but it rather aggravated than relieved the gloom of the scene: the sombre light only serving to pale that which the street lamps afforded, without shedding any warmer or brighter tints upon the wet house-tops and dreary streets. There appeared to be nobody stirring in that quarter of the town; the windows of the houses were all closely shut; and ^hc streets through v.'hich they passed were noiseless and empty.

By the time they had turned into the Bethnal Green Road, the day had fairly begun to break. Many of the lamps were already extinguished; a few country wagons were slowly toiling on toward London; now and then a stage-coach, covered with mud, rattled briskly by: the driver bestowing, as he passed, an admonitory lash upon the heavy wagoner who, by keeping on the wrong side of the road, had endangered his arriving at the office a quarter of a minute after his time. The public-houses, with gas lights burning inside, were already open. By de grees, other shops began to be unclosed, and a few scattered people were met with. Then came strag gling groups of laborers going to their work: then, men and women with fish-baskets on their heads; donkey-carts laden with vegetables ; chaise-carts till ed with live-stock or whole carcasses of meat; inilk-woiiien with pails; an unbroken concourse of people, trudging out with various supplies to the eastern suburbs of the town. As they approached the City, the noise and traffic gradually increased; when they threaded the streets between Shoreditch and Smith-field, it had swelled into a roar of sound and bustle. It was as light as it was likely to be till night came on again, and the busy morning of half the London population had begun.

Turning down Sun Street and Crown Street, and crossing Finsbury Square, Mr. Sikes struck, by way of Chiswell Street, into Barbican; thence into Long Lane, and so into Smithfield; from which latter place arose a tumult of discordant sounds that filled Oliver Twist with amazement.

It was market-morning. The ground was cover ed, nearly ankle-deep, with filth and mire; a thick steam, perpetually rising from the reeking bodies of the cattle, and mingling with the fog, which seemed to rest upon the chimney-tops, hung heavily above. All the pens in the centre of the large area, and as many temporary pens as could be crowded into the vacant space, were filled with sheep; tied up to posts by the gutter side were long lines of beasts and oxen, three or four deep. Countrymen, butchers, drovers, hawkers, boys, thieves, idlers, and vagabonds of every low grade, were mingled together in a mass; the whistling of drovers, the barking of dogs, the bel lowing and plunging of oxen, the bleating of sheep, the grunting and squeaking of pigs, the cries of hawkers, the shouts, oaths, and quarreling on all sides; the ringing of bells and roar of voices, that issued from every public-house; the crowding, push ing, driving, beating, whooping, and yelling; the hid eous and discordant din that resounded from every corner of the market; and the unwashed, unshaven, squalid, and dirty figures constantly running to and fro, and bursting in and out of the throng, rendered it a stunning and bewildering scene, which quite confounded the senses.

Mr. Sikes, dragging Oliver after him, elbowed his way through the thickest of the crowd, and bestow ed very little attention on the numerous sights and sounds which so astonished the boy. He nodded, twice or thrice, to a passing friend ; and, resisting as many invitations to take a morning dram, pressed steadily onward, they were clear of the, turmoil, i and had made their way through Hosier Lane into Holburn.

ON THE ROAD OUT OF TOJTX.

" Now, young un!" said Sikes, looking up at the clock of St. Andrew's Church,."hard upon seven! you must step out. Come, don't lag behind already, Lazy-legs!"

Mr. Sikes accompanied this speech with a jerk at his little companion's wrist. Oliver, quickening his pace into a kind of trot, between a fast walk and a run, kept up with the rapid strides of the house breaker as well as he could.

They held their course at this rate, until they had passed Hyde Park corner, and were on their way to Kensington ; when Sikes relaxed his pace, until an empty cart, which was at some little distance behind, came up. Seeing " Hounslow " written on it, he ask ed the driver with as much civility as he could as sume, if he would give them a lift as far as Isleworth.

" Jump up," said the man. " Is that your boy V'

" Yes; he's my boy," replied Sikes, loohing hard at Oliver, and putting his hand abstractedly into the pocket where the pistol was.

" Your father walks rather too quick for you, don't he, my man F inquired the driver; seeing that Oliver was out of breath.

" Not a bit of it," replied Sikes, interposing. " He's used to it. Here, take hold of my hand, Ned. In with you!"

Thus -addressing Oliver, he helped him into the cart; and the driver, pointing to a heap of sacks, told him to lie down there and rest himself.

As they passed the different mile-stones, Oliver won dered, more and more, where his companion meant to take him. Kensington, Hammersmith, Chiswick, Kew Bridge, Brentford, were all passed; and yet they went on as steadily as if they had only just begun their journey. At length they came to a public-house called the Coach and Horses ; a little way be yond which, another road appeared to turn off. And here the cart stopped.

Sikes dismounted with great precipitation, holding Oliver by the hand all the while; and, lifting him down directly, bestowed a furious look upon him, and rapped the side-pocket with his list in a signifi cant manner.

" Good-bye, boy," said the man.

" He's sulky," replied Sikes, giving him a shake ; " he's sulky. A young dog! Don't mind him."

" Not I!" rejoined the other, getting into his cart. " It's a fine day, after all." And he drove away.

Sikes waited until he had fairly gone; and then telling Oliver he might look about him if he wanted, once again led him onward on his journey.

They turned rouud to the left, a short way past the public - house; and then, taking a right-hand road, walked on for a long time ; passing many large gardens and gentlemen's houses on both sides of the way, and stopping for nothing but a little beer until they reached a town. Here, against the wall of a house, Oliver saw written up in pretty large letters, " Hampton." They lingered about in the fields for some hours. At length they came back into the town ; and, turning into an old public-house with a defaced sign-board, ordered some dinner by the kitch en fire.

The. kitchen was an old, low-roofed room; with ;> great beam across the middle of the ceiling, and benches, with high backs to them, by the fire; on

which were seated several rough men in smock-frocks, drinking and smoking. They took no notice of Oli ver, and very little of Sikes; and, as Sikes took -very little notice of them, he and his young comrade sat in a corner by themselves, without being much trou bled by their company.

They had some cold meat for dinner, and sat so long after it, while Mr. Sikes indulged himself Avith three or four pipes, that Oliver began to feel quite certain they were not going any farther. Being much tired with the walk, and getting up so early, he dozed a little at first; then, quite overpowered by fatigue and the fumes of the tobacco, fell asleep.

It was quite dark when he was awakened by a push from Sikes. Rousing himself sufficiently to sit up and look about him, he found that worthy in close fellowship and communication with a laboring-man, over a pint of ale.

" So you're going on to Lower Halliford, are you ?" inquired Sikes.

" Yes, I am," replied the man, who seemed a little the worse—or better, as the case might be—for drink ing ; "and not slow about it, neither. My horse hasn't got a load behind him going back, as he had coming up in the mornin'; and he won't be long a-doiug of it. Here's luck to him I Ecod! he's a good un!"

" Could you give my boy and me a lift as far as there ?" demanded Sikes, pushing the ale toward his new friend.

" If you're going directly, I can," replied the man, looking out of the pot. "Are you going to Halli ford?"

" Going on to Shepperton," replied Sikes.

" I'm your man, as far as I go," replied the other. " Is all paid, Becky f'

" Yes, the other gentleman's paid," replied the girl.

" I say!" said the man, with tipsy gravity; " that won't do, you know."

" Why not ?" rejoined Sikes. " You're a-going to accommodate us, and. wot's to prevent my standing treat for a pint or so, in return ?"

The stranger reflected upon this argument with a very profound face; having done so, he seized Sikes by the hand, and declared ho was a real good fellow. To which Mr. Sikes replied, ho was joking; as, if he had been sober, there would have been strong reason to suppose he was.

After the exchange of a few more compliments, they bade the company good-night, and went out; the girl gathering up the pots and glasses as they did so, and lounging out to the door, with her hands full, to see the party start.

The horse, whose health had been drunk in his ab sence, was standing outside, ready harnessed to the cart. Oliver and Sikes got in without any further ceremony; and the man to whom he belonged, hav ing lingered for a minute or tw r o "to bear him up," and to defy the hostler and the •world, to produce his equal, mounted also. Then the hostler was told to give the horse his head; and, his head being given him, he made a very unpleasant use of it—tossing it into the air with great disdain, and running into the parlor windows over the way: after performing those feats, and supporting himself for a short time on his hind-legs, he started off at great speed, and rattled out of the town right gallantly.

OLIVER TWIST.

The night Avas very dark. A damp mist rose from the river and the marshy ground about, and spread itself over the dreary fields. It was piercing cold, too; all was gloomy and black. Not a word was spoken; for the driver had grown sleepy, and Sikes was in no mood to lead him into conversation. Oli ver sat huddled together in a corner of the cart, be wildered with alarm and apprehension ; and figuring strange objects in the gaunt trees, whose branches waved grimly to and fro, as if in some fantastic joy at the desolation of the scene.

As they passed Suubury Church, the clock struck seven. There was a light in the ferry-house win dow opposite, which streamed across the road, and threw into more sombre shadow a dark yew-tree with graves beneath it. There was a dull sound of

the bridge, then turned suddenly down a bank upon the left.

" The water!" thought Oliver, turning sick with fear. "He has brought me to this lonely place to murder me!"

He was about to throw himself on the ground, and make one struggle for his young life, when he saw that they stood before a solitary house, all ruinous and decayed. There was a window on each side of the dilapidated entrance, and one story above, but no light was visible. The house was dark, disman tled ; and, to all appearance, uninhabited.

Sikes, with Oliver's hand still in his, softly ap proached the low porch and raised the latch. The door yielded to the pressure, and they passed in to gether.

, WITH OLIVER'S HAND STILL IN HIS, SOFTLY Al'l'JROAOUEl) T11E LOW POKOU."

falling water not far off; and the leaves of the old tree stirred gently in the night wind. It seemed like quiet music for the repose of the dead.

Sunbury was passed through, and they came again into the lonely road. Two or three miles more, and the cart stopped. Sikes alighted, took Oliver by the hand, and they once again walked on.

They turned into no house at Shepperton, as the weary boy had expected; but still kept walking on, in mud and darkness, through gloomy lanes and over cold open wastes, until they came within sight of the lights of a town at no great distance. On looking intently forward, Oliver saw that the water was just below them, and that they were coming to the foot of a bridge.

Sikes kept straight on until they were close upon

CHAPTER XXII.

THE BURGLARY.

" TTALLOO !" cried a loud, hoarse voice, as soon as Xl_ they set foot in the passage.

" Don't make such a row," said Sikes, bolting the door. " Show a glim, Toby."

"Aha! rny pal!" cried the same voice. "A glim, Barney, a glim! Show the gentleman in, Barney; wake up, first, if convenient."

The speaker appeared to throw a boot-jack, or some such article, at the person he addressed, to rouse him from his slumbers; for the noise of a wooden body, falling violently, was heard; and then an in distinct muttering, as of a man between asleep and awake.

ME. TOBY CRACKIT.

" Do you hear ?" cried the same voice. " There's Bill Sikes iu the passage, with nobody to do the civil to him; and you sleeping there, as if you took lau danum -with your meals, and nothing stronger. Are you any fresher now, or do you want the iron candle stick to wake you thoroughly ?"

A pair of slipshod feet shuffled, hastily, across the bare floor of the room, as this interrogatory was put, and there issued, from a door on the right hand, first, a feeble candle ; and next, the form of the same in dividual who has been heretofore described as labor ing under the infirmity of speaking through his nose, and officiating as waiter at the public-house on Saf fron Hill.

" Bister Sikes!" exclaimed Barney, with real or counterfeit joy; " cub id, sir; cub id."

" Here! you get on first," said Sikes, putting Oli ver in front of him. "Quicker! or I shall tread upon your heels."

Muttering a curse upon his tardiness, Sikes push ed Oliver before him; and they entered a low dark room, with a smoky fire, two or three broken chairs, a table, and a very old couch, on which, with his legs much higher than his head, a man was reposing at full length, smoking a long clay pipe. He was dressed in a smartly-cut snuff- colored coat, with large brass buttons; an orange neckerchief; a coarse, staring, shawl-pattern waistcoat; and drab breeches. Mr. Crackit (for he it was) had no very great quan tity of hair, either upon his head or face; but what he had was of a reddish dye, and tortured into long corkscrew curls, through which he occasionally thrust some very dirty fingers, ornamented with large com mon rings. He was a trifle above the middle size, and apparently rather weak in the legs; but this circumstance by no means detracted from his own admiration of his top-boots, which he contemplated, in their elevated situation, with lively satisfaction.

" Bill, my boy!" said this figure, turning his head toward the door, " I'm glad to see you. I was al most afraid you'd given it up; in which case I should have made a personal wentur. Halloo!"

Uttering this exclamation in a tone of great sur prise, as his eye rested on Oliver, Mr. Toby Crackit brought himself into a sitting posture, and demand ed who that was.

" The boy. Only the boy!" replied Sikes, draw ing a chair toward the fire.

" Wud of Bister Fagid's lads," exclaimed Barney, with a grin.

" Fagin's, eh!" exclaimed Toby, looking at Oliver. " Wot an inwalable boy that'll make for the old ladies' pockets in chapels! His mug is a fortun' to him."

" There—there's enough of that," interposed Sikes, impatiently; and stooping over his recumbent friend, he whispered a few words in his ear, at which Mr. Crackit laughed immensely, and honored Oliver with a long stare of astonishment.

"Now.'" said Sikes, as he resumed his seat, "if you'll give us something to eat and drink while we're waiting, you'll put some heart in us; or in me, at all events. Sit down by the fire, younker, and rest yourself; for you'll have to go out with us again to-night, though not very far off"."

Oliver looked at Sikes, in mute and timid wonder;

and drawing a stool to the fire, sat with his aching head upon his hands, scarcely knowing where he was, or what was passing around him.

" Here," said Toby, as the young Jew placed some fragments of food and a bottle upon the table, " Suc cess to the crack!" He rose to honor the toast, and, carefully depositing his empty pipe in a corner, ad vanced to the table, filled a glass with spirits, and drank off" its contents. Mr. Sikes did the same.

"A drain for the boy," said Toby, half filling a wine-gtiss. " Down with it, Innocence."

" Indeed," said Oliver, looking piteously up into the man's face, " indeed, I—

" Down with it!" echoed Toby. " Do you think I don't know what's good for you I Tell him to drink it, Bill."

" He had better!" said Sikes, clapping his hand upon his pocket. " Burn my body, if he isn't more trouble than a whole family of. Dodgers! Drink it, you perwerse imp! drink it!"

Frightened by the menacing gestures of the two men, Oliver hastily swallowed the contents of the glass, and immediately fell into a violent fit of cough-ing,'which delighted Toby Crackit and Barney, and even drew a smile from the surly Mr. Sikes.

This done, and Sikes having satisfied his appetite (Oliver could eat nothing but a small crust of bread which they made him swallow), the two men laid themselves down on chairs for a short nap. Oliver retained his stool by the fire; Barney, wrapped in a blanket, stretched himself on the floor, close outside the fender.

They slept, or appeared to sleep, for some time; nobody stirring but Barney, who rose once or twice to throw coals upon the fire. Oliver fell into a heavy doze, imagining himself straying along the gloomy lanes, or wandering about the dark church-yard, or retracing some one or other of the scenes of the past day, when he was roused by Toby Crackit jumping up and declaring it was half-past one.

In an instant the other two were on their legs, and all were actively engaged in busy preparation. Sikes and his companion enveloped their necks and chins in large dark shawls, and drew on their great coats ; Barney, opening a cupboard, brought forth several articles, which he hastily crammed into the pockets.

" Barkers foi>me, Barney," said Toby Crackit.

" Here they are," replied Barney, producing a pair of pistols. " You loaded tiiem yourself."

"All right!" replied Toby, stowing them away. " The persuaders ?"

" I've got 'em," replied Sikes.

" Crape, keys, centre-bits, darkies—nothing forgot ten ?" inquired Toby, fastening a small crowbar to a loop inside the skirt of his coat.

"All right," rejoinedhis companion. " Bring them bits of timber, Barney. That's the time of day!"

With these words, he took a thick stick from Bar ney's hands, who, having delivered another to Toby, busied himself in fastening on Oliver's cape.

" Now then!" said Sikes, holding out his hand.

Oliver, who was completely stupefied by the un wonted exercise, and the air, and the drink which had been forced upon him, put his hand mechanically into that which Sikes extended for that purpose.

OLIVER TWIST.

" Take his other hand, Toby," said Sikes. " Look out, Barney."

The man -went to the door, and returned to an nounce that all was quiet. The two robbers issued forth, with Oliver between them. Barney, having made all fast, rolled himself up as before, and was soon asleep again.

It was now intensely dark. The fog was much heavier than it had been in the early part of the night; and the atmosphere was so damp, that, al though no rain fell, Oliver's hair and ejjpbrows, within a few minutes after leaving the house, had become stiff with the half-frozen moisture that was floating about. They crossed the bridge, and kept on toward the lights which he had seen before. They were at no great distance off; and, as they walked pretty briskly, they soon arrived at Chert-sey.

"Slap through the town," whispered Sikes; " there'll be nobody in the way to-night to see us."

Toby acquiesced; and they hurried through the main street of the little town, which at that late hour was wholly deserted. A dim light shone at in tervals from some bedroom window; and the hoarse barking of dogs occasionally broke the silence of the night. But there was nobody abroad. They had cleared the town, as the church-bell struck two.

Quickening their pace, they turned up a road upon the left hand. After walking about a quarter of a mile, they stopped before a detached house sur rounded by a wall, to the top of which, Toby Crack-it, scarcely pausing to take breath, climbed in a twinkling.

" The boy next," said Toby. " Hoist him up; I'll catch hold of him."

Before Oliver had time to look round, Sikes had caught him under the arms; and in three or four seconds he and Toby were lying on the grass on the other side. Sikes followed directly. And they stole cautiously toward the house.

And now, for the first time, Oliver, well-nigh mad with grief and terror, saw that house-breaking and robbery, if not murder, were the objects of the expe dition. He clasped his hands together, and invol untarily uttered a subdued exclamation of horror. A mist came before his eyes; the cold sweat stood upon his ashy face; his limbs failed him, and he sank upon his knees. «

" Get up!" murmured Sikes, trembling with rage, and drawing the pistol from his pocket; " get up, or I'll strew your brains upon the grass!"

" Oh! for God's sake let me go!" cried Oliver; " let me run away and die in the fields. I will nev er come near London; never, never! Oh! pray have mercy on me, and do not make me steal! For the love of all the bright angels that rest in heav en, have mercy upon me!"

The man to whom this appeal was made swore a dreadful oath, and had cocked the pistol, when Toby, striking it from his grasp, placed his hand upon the boy's mouth and dragged him to the house.

" Hush!" cried the man ; " it won't answer here. Say another word, and I'll do your business myself with a crack on the head. That makes no noise, a:ul is quite as certain, and more genteel. Here, Bill, wrench the shutter open. He's game enough

now, I'll engage. I've seen older hands of his age took the same way for a minute or two on a cold night."

Sikes, invoking terrific imprecations upon Fagiu's head for sending Oliver on such an errand, plied the crowbar vigorously, but with little noise. After some delay, and some assistance from Toby, the shutter to which he had referred swung open on its hinges.

It was a little lattice window, about five feet and a half above the ground, at the back of the house, which belonged to a scullery, or small brewing-place, at the end of the passage. The aperture was so small, that the inmates had probably not thought it worth while to defend it more securely; but it was large enough to admit a boy of Oliver's size, nevertheless. A very brief exercise of Mr. Sikes's art sufficed to overcome the fastening of the lattice, and it soon stood wide open also.

" Now listen, you young limb!" whispered Sikes, drawing a dark-lantern from his pocket, and throw ing the glare full on Oliver's face; "I'm a-going to put you through'there. Take this light; go softly up the steps straight afore you, and along the little hall, to the street-door; unfasten it, and let us in."

" There's a bolt at the top you won't be able to reach," interposed Toby. " Stand upon one of the hall chairs. There are three there, Bill, with a jolly large blue unicorn and gold pitchfork on 'em, which is the old lady's arms."

"Keep quiet, can't you?" replied Sikes, with a threatening look. " The room-door is open, is it ?"

" Wide," replied Toby, after peeping in to satisfy himself. "The game of'that is, that they always leave it open with a catch, so that the dog, who's got a bed in here, may walk up and down the pas sage when he feels wakeful. Ha! ha! Barney 'ticed him away to-night. So neat!"

Although Mr. Crackit spoke in a scarcely audible whisper, and laughed without noise, Sikes imperious ly commanded him to be silent, and to get to work. Toby complied, by first producing his lantern, and placing it on the ground; then by planting himself firmly with his head against the wall beneath the window, and his hands upon his knees, so as to make a step of his back. This was no sooner done, than Sikes, mounting upon him, put Oliver gently through the window with his feet first; and, without leaving hold of his collar, planted him safely on the floor in side.

" Take this lantern," said Sikes, looking into the room. " You see the stairs afore you ?"

Oliver, more dead than alive, gasped out, " Yes." Sikes, pointing to the street-door with the pistol-barrel, briefly advised him to take notice that he was within shot all the way; and that if he faltered, he would fall dead that instant.

" It's done iu a minute," said Sikes, in the same low whisper. " Directly I leave go of you, do your work. Hark!"

" What's that ?" whispered the other man.

They listened intently.

"Nothing," said Sikes, releasing his hold of Oli ver. "Now!"

In the short time he had had to collect his senses. the boy had firmly resolved that, whether he died iu

MSS. CORNET.

the attempt or not, he would make one effort to dart up staii-s from the hall and alarm the family. Filled with this idea, he advanced at once, but stealthily.

." Come back!" suddenly cried Sikes, aloud—" back! back!"

Scared by the sudden breaking of the dead still ness of the place, and by a loud cry which followed it, Oliver let his lantern fall, and knew not whether to advance or fly.

The cry was repeated—a light appeared—a vision of two terrified, half-dressed men at the top of the stairs swam before his eyes—a flash—a loud noise— a smoke-—a crash somewhere, but where he knew not—and he staggered back.

CHAPTER XXIII.

WHICH CONTAINS THE SUBSTANCE OF A PLEASANT CON VERSATION BETWEEN MR. BUMBLE AND A LADY; AND SHOWS THAT EVEN A BEADLE MAT BE SUSCEPTIBLE ON SOME POINTS.

THE night was bitter cold. The snow lay on the ground, frozen into a hard thick crust, so that only the heaps that had drifted into by-ways and corners were affected by the sharp wind that howled abroad; which, as if expending increased fury on such prey as it found, caught it savagely up in clouds, and, whirling it into a thousand misty eddies, scat tered it in air. Bleak, dark, and piercing cold, it was

" DIKECTLY I JEA.VE GO OF YOU, DO YOUE WORK. HABK !"

Sikes had disappeared for an instant; but he was up again, and had him by the collar before the smoke had cleared away. He fired his own pistol after the men, who were already retreating, and dragged the boy up.

" Clasp your arm tighter," said Sikes, as he drew him through the window. " Give me a shawl here. They've hit him. Quick! How the boy bleeds!"

Then came the loud ringing of a bell, mingled with the noise of fire-arms, and the shouts of men, and the sensation of being carried over uneven ground at a rapid pace. And then the noises grew confused in the distance ; and a cold deadly feeling crept over the boy's heart; and he saw or heard no more.

a night for the well-housed and fed to draw round the bright fire and thank God they were at home: and for the homeless, starving wretch to lay him down and die. Many hunger-worn outcasts close their eyes in our bare streets at such times, who, let their crimes have been what they may, can hardly open them in a more bitter world.

Such were the aspect of out-of-door affairs, when Mrs. Corney, the matron of the. work-house to which our readers have been already introduced as the birthplace of Oliver Twist, sat herself down before a cheerful fire in her own little room, and glanced, with no small degree of complacency, at a small round table, on which stood a tray of corresponding

OLIVER TWIST.

size, furnished with all necessary materials for the most grateful meal that matrons enjoy. In fact, Mrs. Corney was about to solace herself with a cup of tea. As she glanced from the table to the fire place, where the smallest of all possible kettles was singing a small song in a small voice, her inward sat isfaction evidently increased—so much so, indeed, that Mrs. Corney smiled.

" Well!" said the matron, leaning her elbow on the table, and looking reflectively at the fire; " I'm sure we have all on us a great deal to be grateful for! A great deal, if we did but know it. Ah !"

Mrs. Corney shook her head mournfully, as if de ploring the mental blindness of those paupers who did not know it; and thrusting a silver spoon (pri vate property) into the inmost recesses of a two-ounce tin tea-caddy, proceeded to make the tea.

How slight a thing will disturb the equanimity of our frail minds! The black tea-pot, being very small and easily filled, ran over while Mrs. Corney was moralizing, and the water slightly scalded Mrs. Corney's hand.

" Drat the pot!" said the worthy matron, setting it down very hastily on the hob: " a little stupid thing, that only holds a couple of cups! What use is it of to any body! Except," said Mrs. Corney, pausing, " except to a poor desolate creature like rne. Oh dear!"

With these words, the matron dropped into her chair, and, once more resting her elbow on the table, thought of her solitary fate. The small tea-pot, and the single cup, had awakened in her mind sad recol lections of Mr. Corney (who had not been dead more than five-aud-twenty years); and she was overpow ered.

" I ehall never get another!" said Mrs. Corney, pet tishly ; " I shall never get another—like him!"

Whether this remark bore reference to the hus band, or the tea-pot, is uncertain. It might have been the latter; for Mrs. Corney looked at it as she spoke; and took it up afterward. She had just tasted her first cup, when she was disturbed by a soft tap at the room-door.

" Oh, come in with you!" said Mrs. Corney, sharply. " Some of the old women dying, I suppose. They al ways die when I'm at meals. Don't stand there let ting the cold air in, don't. What's amiss now, eh f" ' " Nothing, ma'am, nothing," replied a man's voice.

"Dear me!" exclaimed the matron, in a much sweeter tone, " is that Mr. Bumble ?"

" At your service, ma'am," said Mr. Bumble, who had been stopping outside to rub his shoes clean, and to shake the snow off his coat; and who now made his appearance, bearing the cocked hat in one hand and a bundle in the other. " Shall I shut the door, ma'am ?"

The lady modestly hesitated to reply, lest there should be any impropriety in holding an interview with Mr. Bumble with closed doors. Mr. Bumble taking advantage of the hesitation, and being very cold himself, shut it without permission.

" Hard weather, Mr. Bumble," said the matron.

" Hard, indeed, ma'am," replied the beadle. " Anti-porochial weather this, ma'am. We have given away, Mrs. Corney, we have given away a matter of twenty quartern loaves and a cheese and a half, this very

blessed afternoon; and yet them paupers are not contented."

" Of course not. When would they be, Mr. Bum ble ?" said the matron, sipping her tea.

" When, indeed, ma'am!" rejoined Mr. Bumble. " Why here's one man that, in consideration of his wife and large family, has a quartern loaf and a good pound of cheese, full weight. Is he grateful, ma'am? Is he grateful? Not a copper farthing's worth of it! What does he do, ma'am, but ask for a few coals; if it's only a pocket-handkerchief full, he says! Coals! What would he do with coals? Toast his cheese with 'em, and then come back for more. That's the way with these people, ma'am; give 'em an apron-ful of coals to-day, and they'll come back for another the day after to-morrow, as brazen as alabaster!"

The matron expressed her entire concurrence in this intelligible simile; and the beadle went on.

" I never," said Mr. Bumble, " see any thing like the pitch it's got to. The day afore yesterday, a man—you have been a married woman, ma'am, and I may mention it to you—a man, with hardly a rag upon his back (here Mrs. Corney looked at the floor), goes to our overseer's door when he has got company coming to dinner; and says, he must be relieved, Mrs. Coruey. As he wouldn't go away, and shocked the company very much, our overseer sent him out a pound of potatoes and half a pint of oatmeal. ' My heart!' says the ungrateful villain,' what's the use of this

to me ? You might as well give me a pair of iron spectacles!' ' Very good,' says our overseer, tak
ing 'em away again,' you won't get any thing else here.' 'Then I'll die in the streets!' says the va
grant. ' Oh no, you won't/ says our overseer."

"Ha! ha! That was very good! So like Mr. Granuett, wasn't it ?" interposed the matron. "
Well, Mr. Bumble ?"

"Well, ma'am," rejoined the beadle, "he went away; and he did die in the streets. There's a
ob stinate pauper for you!"

" It beats any thing I could have believed," ob served the matron, emphatically. " But
don't you think out-of-door relief a very bad thing, any way, Mr. Bumble ? You're a gentleman of
experience, and ought to know. Come."

" Mrs. Corney," said the beadle, smiling as men smile who are conscious of superior
information, "out-of-door relief, properly managed—properly managed, ma'arn—is the porochial
safeguard. The great principle of out-of-door relief is, to give the paupers exactly what they don't
want; and then they get tired of coming."

" Dear me!" exclaimed Mrs. Corney. " Well, that is a good one, too!"

" Yes. Betwixt you and me, ma'am," returned Mr. Bumble, " that's the great principle; and
that's the reason why, if you look at any cases that get into them owdacious newspapers, you'll
always observe that sick families have been relieved with slices of cheese. That's the rule now,
Mrs. Corney, all over the country. But, however," said the beadle, stop ping to unpack his bundle,
" these are official secrets, ma'am; not to be spoken of; except, as I may say, among the porochial
officers, such as ourselves. This is the port-wine, ma'am, that the board ordered for

MRS. CORNET AND MR. BUMBLE.

the infirmary; real, fresh, genuine port-wine; only out of the cask this forenoon; clear as a
bell, and no sediment!"

Having held the first bottle up to the light, and shaken it well to test its excellence, Mr.
Bumble placed them both on the top of a chest of drawers; folded the handkerchief in which they
had been wrapped; put it carefully in his pocket; and took up his hat, as if to go.

" You'll have a very cold walk, Mr. Bumble," said the matron.

" It blows, ma'am," replied Mr. Bumble, turning up his coat-collar, " enough to cut one's
ears off."

The matron looked from the little kettle to the beadle, who was moving toward the door;
and as the beadle coughed, preparatory to bidding her good-night, bashfully inquired whether—w
r hether he wouldn't take a cup of tea ?

Mr. Bumble instantaneously turned back his collar again ; laid his hat and stick upon a
chair; and drew another chair up to the table. As he slowly seated himself, he looked at the lady.
She fixed her eyes upon the little tea-pot. Mr. Bumble coughed again, and slightly smiled.

Mrs. Corney rose to get another cup and saucer from the closet. As she sat down, her eyes
once again encountered those of the gallant beadle: she colored, and applied herself to the task of
making his tea. Again Mr. Bumble coughed—louder this time than he had coughed yet.

" Sweet, Mr. Bumble ?" inquired the matron, tak ing up the sugar-basin.

" Very sweet indeed, ma'am," replied Mr. Bumble. He fixed his eyes on Mrs. Corney as
he said this; and if ever a beadle looked tender, Mr. Bumble was that beadle at that moment.

The tea was made and handed in silence. Mr. Bumble, having spread a handkerchief over
his knees to prevent the crumbs from sullying the splendor of his shorts, began to eat and drink;
varying these amusements, occasionally, by fetching a deep sigh; which, however, had no
injurious effect upon his ap petite, but, on the contrary, rather seemed to facili tate his operations
in the tea-and-toast department.

" You have a cat, ma'am, I see," said Mr. Bumble, glancing at one who, in the centre of her family, was basking before the fire; " and kittens too, I declare!"

" I am so fond of them, Mr. Bumble, you can't think," replied the matron. " They're so happy, so frolicsome, and so cheerful, that they are quite com panions for me."

" Very nice animals, ma'am," replied Mr. Bumble, approvingly; " so very domestic."

" Oh, yes!" rejoined the matron with enthusiasm; " so fond of their home too, that it's quite a pleasure, I'm sure."

" Mrs. Corney, ma'am," said Mr. Bumble, slowly, and marking the time with his tea-spoon, " I mean to say this, ma'am; that any cat, or kitten, that could live with you, ma'am, and not be fond of its home, must be a ass, ma'am."

" Oh, Mr. Bumble!" remonstrated Mrs. Corney.

"It's of no use disguising facts, ma'am,"said Mr. Bumble, slowly flourishing the tea-spoon with a kind of amorous dignity which made him doubly impress ive ; " I would drown it myself with pleasure."

" Then you're a cruel man," said the matron viva ciously, as she held out her hand for the beadle's cup; " and a very hard-hearted man besides."

" Hard-hearted, ma'am ?" said Mr. Bumble. " Hard ?" Mr. Bumble resigned his cup without another word; squeezed Mrs. Corney's little finger as she took it; and inflicting two open-handed slaps upon his laced waistcoat, gave a mighty sigh, and hitched his chair a very little morsel farther from the tire.

It was a round table; and as Mrs. Corney and Mr. Bumble had been sitting opposite each other, with no great space between them, and fronting the fire, it will be seen that Mr. Bumble, in receding from the fire, and still keeping at the table, increased the distance between himself and Mrs. Corney; which proceeding some prudent readers will doubtless be disposed to admire, and to consider an act of great heroism- on Mr. Bumble's part: he being in some sort tempted by time, place, and opportunity, to give ut terance to certain soft nothings, which, however well they may become the lips of the light and thought less, do seem immeasurably beneath the dignity of the judges of the land, members of Parliament, min isters of state, lord mayors, and other great public functionaries, but more particularly beneath the stateliness and gravity of a beadle, who (as is well known) should be the sternest and most inflexible among them all.

Whatever were Mr. Bumble's intentions, however (and no doitbt they were of the best), it iinfortu-nately happened, as has been twice before remarked, that the table was a round one; consequently Mr. Bumble, moving his chair by little and little, soon began to diminish the distance between himself and the matron; and, continuing to travel round the out er edge of the circle, brought his chair, in time, close to that in which the matron was seated. Indeed, the two chairs touched; and when they did so, Mr. Bum ble stopped.

Now, if the matron had moved her chair to the right, she would have been scorched by the fire; and if to the left, she must have fallen into Mr. Bumble's arms; so (being a discreet matron, and no doubt foreseeing these consequences at a glance) she remained where she was, and handed Mr. Bumble an other cup of tea.

"Hard-hearted, Mrs. Corney?" said Mr. Bumble, stirring his tea, and looking up into the matron's face; " are you hard-hearted, Mrs. Corney ?"

" Dear me!" exclaimed the matron, " what a very curious question from a single man! What can you want to know for, Mr. Bumble ?"

The beadle drank his tea to the last drop; finished a piece of toast; whisked the crumbs off his knees; wiped his lips; and deliberately kissed the matron.

" Mr. Bumble!" cried that discreet lady in a whis per ; for the fright was so great, that she had quite lost her voice; " Mr. Bumble, I shall scream!" Mr. Bumble made no reply; but in a slow and dignified manner put his arms round the matron's waist.

As the lady had stated her intention of screaming, of course she would have screamed at this additional boldness, but that the exertion was rendered unnec essary by a hasty knocking at the door: which was no sooner heard, than Mr. Bumble darted, with much agility, to the wine bottles, aoid began dusting theoi

OLIVER TWIST.

•with great violence, while the matron sharply de manded who was there. It is worthy of remark, as a curious physical instance of the efficacy of a sud den surprise in counteracting the effects of extreme fear, that her voice had quite recovered all its official asperity.

" If you please, mistress," said a withered old fe male pauper, hideously ugly, putting her head in at the door, " Old Sally is a-going fast."

" Well, what's that to me ?" angrily demanded the matron. " I can't keep her alive, can I ?"

" No, no, mistress," replied the old woman, " no body can; she's far beyond the reach of help. I've seen a many people die — little babes and great strong men — and I know when death's a - coming well enough. But she's troubled in her mind; and when the tits are not on her—and that's not often, for she is dying very hard — she says she has got something to tell which you must hear. She'll never die quiet till you come, mistress."

At this intelligence, the worthy Mrs. Corney mut tered a variety of invectives against old women who couldn't even die without purposely annoying their betters; and muffling herself in a thick shawl which she hastily caught up, briefly requested Mr, Bumble to stay till she came back, lest any thing particular should occur. Bidding the messenger walk fast, and not be all night hobbling up the stairs, she followed her from the room with a very ill grace, scolding all the way.

Mr. Bumble's conduct on being left to himself was rather inexplicable. He opened the closet, counted the tea-spoons, weighed the sugar-tongs, closely in spected a silver milk-pot to ascertain that it was of the genuine metal, and, having satisfied his curiosity on these points, put on his cocked hat corner-wise, and danced with much gravity four distinct times round the table. Having gone through this very extraordinary performance, he took off the cocked hat again, and, spreading himself before the fire with his back toward it, seemed to be mentally engaged in taking an exact inventory of the furniture.

CHAPTER XXIV

TREATS OF A VERT POOR SUBJECT. BUT IS A SHORT ONE, AND MAT BE FOUND OF IMPORTANCE IN THIS HISTORT.

IT was no unfit messenger of death who had dis turbed the quiet of the matron's room. Her body was bent by age; her limbs trembled with palsy ; her face, distorted into a mumbling leer, resembled more the grotesque shaping of some wild pencil than the work of Nature's hand.

Alas! how few of Nature's faces are left alone, to gladden us with their beauty! The cares, and sor rows, and hungerings, of the world, change them as they change hearts; and it is only when those pas sions sleep, and have lost their hold forever, that the troubled clouds pass off, and leave Heaven's surface clear. It is a common thing for the countenances of the dead, even in that fixed and rigid state, to subside into the long-forgotten expression of sleep ing infancy, and settle into the very look of early

life. So calm, so peaceful, do they grow again, that those Avho knew them in their happy childhood, kneel by the coffin's side in awe, and see the Angel even upon earth.

The old crone tottered along the passages, and up the stairs, nmttering some indistinct answers to the eludings of her companion. Being at length com pelled to pause for breath, she gave the light into her hand, and remained behind to follow as she might; while the more nimble superior made her way to the room where the sick woman lay.

It was a bare garret-room, with a dim light burn ing at the farther end. There was another old wom an watching by the bed; the parish apothecary's ap prentice was standing by the fire, making a tooth pick out of a quill.

" Cold night, Mrs. Corney," said this young gentle man, as the matron entered.

"Very cold, indeed, sir," replied the mistress, in her most civil tones, and dropping a courtesy as she spoke.

" You should get better coals out of your contract ors," said the apothecary's deputy, breaking a lump on the top of the fire with the rusty poker; "these are not at all the sort of thing for a cold night."

" They're the board's choosing, sir," returned the matron. " The least they could do would be to keep us pretty warm; for our places are hard enough."

The conversation was here interrupted by a moan from the sick woman.

" Oh!" said the young man, turning his face to ward the bed, as if he had previously quite forgotten the patient, " it's all U P there, Mrs. Corney."

" It is, is it, sir ?" asked the matron.

"If she lasts a couple of hours, I shall be sur prised," said the apothecary's apprentice, intent upon the tooth-pick's point. " It's a break-up of the system altogether. Is she dozing, old lady ?"

The attendant stooped over the bed, to ascertain, and nodded in the affirmative.

" Then perhaps she'll go off in that way, if you don't make a row," said the young man. " Put the light on the floor. She won't see it there."

The attendant did as she was told, shaking her head meanwhile, to intimate that the woman would not die so easily; having done so, she resumed her seat by the side of the other nurse, who had by this time returned. The mistress, with an expression of impatience, wrapped herself in her shawl, and sat at the foot of the bed.

The apothecary's apprentice, having completed the manufacture of the tooth-pick, planted himself in front of the fire, and made good use of it for ten minutes or so: when apparently growing rather dull, he wished Mrs. Corney joy of her job, and took him self off on tiptoe.

When they had sat in silence for some time, the two old women rose from the bed, and, crouching over the fire, held out their withered hands to catch the heat. The flame threw a ghastly light on their shriveled faces, and made their ugliness appear ter rible, as, in this position, they began to converse in a low voice.

" Did she say any more, Anny dear, while I was gone f' inquired the messenger.

" Not a word," replied the other. " She plucked

A DEATH-BED CONFESSION.

77

and tore at her arms for a little time; but I held her hands, and she soon dropped off. She hasn't much strength in her, so I easily kept her quiet. I ain't so weak for an old woman, although I am on parish allowance ; no, no!"

" Did she drink the hot wine the doctor said she was to have ?" demanded the first.

" I tried to get it down," rejoined the other. " But her teeth were tight set, and she clenched the mug so hard that it was as much as I could do to get it-back again. So / drank it; and it did me good."

Looking cautiously round, to ascertain that they were not overheard, the two hags cowered nearer to the fire, and chuckled heartily.

" I mind the time," said the first speaker, " when she would have done the same, and made rare fun of it afterward."

"Ay, that she would," rejoined the other; "she had a merry heart. A many, many beautiful corpses she laid out, as nice and neat as wax-work. My old eyes have seen them—ay, and those old hands touch ed them too; for I have helped her scores of times."

Stretching forth her trembling fingers as she spoke, the old creature shook them exultingly before her face, and fumbling in her pocket, brought out an old time-discolored tin snuff-box, from which she shook a few grains into the outstretched palm of her com panion, and a few more into her own. While they were thus employed, the matron, who had been im patiently watching until the dying woman should awaken from her stupor, joined them by the fire, and sharply asked how long she was to wait ?"

" Not long, mistress," replied the second woman, looking up into her face. "We have none of us long to wait for Death. Patience, patience! He'll be here soon enough for us all."

" Hold your tongue, you doting idiot!' said the matron, sternly. " You, Martha, tell me; has she been in this way before ?"

" Often," answered the first woman.

". But will never be again," added the second one; " that is, she'll never wake again but once—and mind, mistress, that won't be for long!"

" Long or short," said the matron, snappishly, " she won't find me here when she does wake; take care, both of you, how you worry me again for nothing. It's no part of my duty to see all the old women in the house die, and I won't—that's more. Mind that, you impudent old harridans! If yovi make a fool of me again, I'll soon cure you, I warrant you!"

She was bouncing away, when a cry from the two women, who had turned toward the bed, caused her to look round. The patient had raised herself up right, and was stretching her arms toward them.

" Who's that ?" she cried, in a hollow voice.

" Hush, hush!" said one of the women, stooping over her. " Lie down, lie down!"

" I'll never lie down again alive!" said the woman, struggling. "I will tell her! Come here! Nearer! Let me whisper in your ear."

She clutched the matron by the arm, and forcing her into a chair by the bedside, was aboxit to speak, when, looking round, she caught sight of the two old women bending forward in the attitude of eager listeners.

" Turn them away," said the woman, drowsily; " make haste! make haste!"

The two old crones, chiming in together, began pouring out many piteous lamentations that the poor dear was too far gone to know her best friends; and were uttering sundry protestations that they would never leave her, when the superior pushed them from the room, closed the door, and returned to the bed side. On being excluded, the old ladies changed their tone, and cried through the key-hole that old Sally was drunk; whicli, indeed, was not unlikely; since, in addition to a moderate dose of opium pre scribed by the apothecary, she was laboring under the effects of a final taste of giu-and-water which had been privily administered, in the openness of their hearts, by the worthy old ladies themselves.

" Now listen to me," said the dying woman aloud, as if making a great effort to revive one latent spark of energy. " In this very room—in this very bed— I once nursed a pretty young creetur that was brought into the house with her feet cut and bruised with walking, and all soiled with dust and blood. She gave birth to a boy, and died. Let me think— what was the year again ?"

" Never mind the year," said the impatient audi tor ; " what about her ?"

"Ay," murmured the sick woman, relapsing into her former drowsy state, " what about her ?-—what about—I know!" she cried, jumping fiercely up; her face flushed, and her eyes starting from her head— " I robbed her, so I did! She wasn't cold — I tell you she wasn't cold, when I stole it!"

" Stole what, for God's sake ?" cried the matron, with a gesture as if she would call for help.

"It!" replied the woman, laying her hand over the other's mouth. " The only thing she had. She wanted clothes to keep her warm, and food to eat; but she had kept it safe, and had it in her bosom. It was gold, I tell you! Rich gold, that might have saved her life!"

"Gold!" echoed the matron, bending eagerly over the woman as she fell back. " Go on, go on—yes— what of it ? Who was the mother ? When was it ?"

" She charged me to keep it safe," replied the wom an with a groan, " and trusted me as the only woman about her. I stole it in my heart when she first showed it me hanging round her neck; and the child's death, perhaps, is on me besides! They would have treated him better if they had known it all!"

" Known what ?" asked the other. " Speak!"

" The boy grew so like his mother," said the wom an, rambling on, and not heeding the question, " that I could never forget it when I saw his face. Poor girl! poor girl! She was so young, too! Such a gentle lamb! Wait; there's more to tell. I have not told you all, have I ?"

" No, no," replied the matron, inclining her head to catch the words, as they came more faintly from the dying woman. " Be quick, or it may be too late!"

" The mother," said the woman, making a more violent effort than before; "the mother, when the pains of death first came upon her, whispered in my ear that if her baby was bom alive, and thrived, the day might come when it would not feel so much dis graced to hear its poor young mother named. 'And oh, kind Heaven!' she said, folding her thin hands together, ' whether it be boy or girl, raise up some friends for it in this troubled world, and take pity

OLIVER TWIST.

upon a lonely, desolate child, abandoned to its mer cy!'"

" The boy's name I" demanded the matron.

" They called him Oliver," replied the woman, fee bly. " The gold I stole was—"

" Yes, yes—what ?" cried the other.

She was bending eagerly over the woman to hear her reply; but drew back, instinctively, as she once again rose, slowly and stiffly, ^uto a sitting posture ; then, clutching the coverlid with both hands, mut tered some indistinct sounds in her throat, and fell

lifeless on the bed.

******

" Stone dead!" said one of the old women, hurry ing in as soon as the door was opened.

"And nothing to tell, after all," rejoined the mat ron, walking carelessly away.

The two crones, to all appearance too busily oc cupied in the preparations for their dreadful duties to make any reply, were left alone, hovering about the body.

CHAPTER X£V.

WHEREIN THIS HISTORY REVERTS TO ME. PAGIN AND COMPANY:

WHILE these things were passing in the country work-house, Mr. Fagiu sat in the old den—the same from which Oliver had been removed by the girl— brooding over a dull, smoky fire. He held a pair of bellows upon his knee, with which he had ap parently been endeavoring to rouse it into more cheer ful action; but he had fallen into deep thought; and with his arms folded on them, and his chin resting on his 'thumbs, fixed his eyes abstractedly on the rusty bars.

At a table behind him sat the Artful Dodger, Mas ter Charles Bates, and Mr. Chitliug, all intent upon a game of whist ; the Artful taking dummy against Master Bates and Mr. Chitling.

The countenance of the first-named gentleman, peculiarly intelligent at all times, acquired great additional interest from his close observance of the game, and his attentive pe rusal of Mr. Chitling's hand ; upon which, from time to time, as occasion served, he bestowed a variety of earnest glances: wisely regulating his own play by the result of his observations upon his neighbor's cards. It being a cold night, the Dodger wore his hat, as, indeed, was often his custom within doors. He also sustained a clay pipe between his teeth, which he only removed for a brief space when he deemed it necessary to apply for refreshment to a quart pot upon the table, which stood ready filled with gin-and -water for the accommodation of the company.

Master Bates was also attentive to the play; but being of a more excitable nature than his accom plished friend, it was observable that he more fre quently applied himself to the gin-and-water, and moreover indulged in many jests and irrelevant re marks, all highly unbecoming a scientific rubber. Indeed, the Artful, presuming upon their close at tachment, more than once took occasion to reason gravely with his companion upon these improprie ties : all of which remonstrances Master Bates re

ceived in extremely good part; merely requesting his friend to be " Mowed," or to insert his head in a sack, or replying with some other neatly-turned wit ticism of a similar kind, the happy application of which excited considerable admiration in the mind of Mr. Chitling. It was remarkable that the latter gentleman and his partner invariably lost; and that the circumstance, so far from angering Master Bates, appeared to afford him the highest amusement, inas much as he laughed most uproariously at the end of every deal, and protested that he had never seen such a jolly game in all his born days.

" That's two doubles and the rub," said Mr. Chit-ling, with a very long face, as he drew half a crown from his waistcoat-pocket. " I never see such a fel ler as you, Jack ; you win every thing. Even when we've good cards, Charley and I can't make nothing of 'em."

Either the matter or the manner of this remark, which was made very ruefully, delighted Charley Bates so much, that his consequent shout of laugh ter roused the Jew from his reverie, and induced him to inquire what was the matter.

" Matter, Fagiu!" cried Charley. " I wish you had watched the play. Tommy Chitling hasn't won a point; and I went partners with him against the Artful and dum "

"Ay, ay!" said the Jew, with a grin, which suffi ciently demonstrated that he was at no loss to un derstand the reason. " Try 'em again, Tom; try 'em again."

"No more of it for me, thankee, Fagin," replied Mr. Chitling; " I've had enough. That 'ere Dodger has such a run of luck that there's no standing again' him."

" Ha! ha! my dear," replied the Jew, " you must get up very early in the morning to win against the Dodger."

" Morning!" said Charley Bates; " you must put your boots on over-night, and have a telescope at each eye, and a opera-glass between your shoulders, if you want to come over Mm."

Mr. Dawkins received these handsome compliments with much philosophy, and offered to cut any gentle man in company, for the first picture-card, at a shil ling a time. Nobody accepting the challenge, and his pipe being by this time smoked out, he proceeded to amuse himself by sketching a ground-plan of New gate on the table with the piece of chalk which had served him in lieu of counters ; whistling meantime, with peculiar shrillness.

" How precious dull you are, Tommy !" said the Dodger, stopping short when there had been a long silence, and addressing Mr. Chitling. " What do you think he's thinking of, Fagin ?"

"How should I know, my dear?" replied the Jew, looking round as he plied the bellows. "About his losses, maybe; or the little retirement in the coun try that he's just left, eh ? Ha! ha! Is that it, my dear?"

"Not a bit of it," replied the Dodger, stopping the subject of discourse as Mr. Chitling was about to re ply. " What do you say, Charley ?"

"/should say," replied Master Bates, with a grin, "that he was uncommon sweet upon Betsy. See how he's a-blushiug! Oh, my eye ! here's a merry-

THE DODGER AND FAGIN.

go-rounder! Tommy Chitliug's hi love! Oh, Fagin, Fagin ! what a spree!"

Thoroughly overpowered with the notion of Mr. Chilling being the victim of the tender passion, Mas ter Bates threw himself back in his chair with such violence that he lost his balance and pitched over npon the floor; where (the accident abating nothing of his merriment) he lay at full length until his laugh was over, when he resumed his former posi tion, and began another laugh.

" Never mind him, my dear," said the Jew, wink ing at Mr. Dawkins, and giving Master Bates a re proving tap with the nozzle of the bellows. " Bet sy's a fine girl. Stick up to her, Tom. Stick up to lier."

" What I mean to say, Fagin," replied Mr. Chitling, very red in the face, " is, that that isn't any thing to any body here."

" No more it is," replied the Jew; " Charley will talk. Don't mind him, my dear; don't mind him. Betsy's a fine girl. Do as she bids you, Tom, and you'll make your fortune."

" So I do do as she bids me," replied Mr. Chitling; " I shouldn't have been milled, if it hadn't been for her advice. But it turned out a good job for you; didn't it, Fagiu? And what's six weeks of it? It must come, some time or another, and why not in the winter-time, when you don't want to go out a-walking so much ; eh, Fagin ?"

"Ah, to be sure, my dear," replied the Jew.

" You wouldn't mind it again, Tom, would you," asked the Dodger, winking upon Charley and the Jew, " if Bet was all right ?"

"I mean to say that I shouldn't," replied Tom, angrily. "There now. Ah! Who'll say as much as that, I should like to know; eh, Fagin ?"

" Nobody, my dear," replied the Jew; " not a soul, Tom. I don't know one of 'em that would do it be sides you; not one of 'em, my dear."

" I might have got clear off, if I'd split upon her; mightn't I, Fagin ?" angrily pursued the poor half witted dupe. "A word from me would have done it; wouldn't it, Fagiu ?"

" To be sure it would, my dear," replied the Jew.

" But I didn't blab it; did I, Fagin ?" demanded Tom, pouring question upon question with great volubility.

" No, no, to be sure," replied the Jew, " you were too stout-hearted for that. A deal too stout, my dear!"

" Perhaps I was," rejoined Tom, looking round; "and if I was, what's to laugh at in that; eh, Fa giu ?"

The Jew, perceiving that Mr. Chitling was con siderably roused, hastened to assure him that no body was laughing; and to prove the gravity of the company, appealed to Master Bates, the principal of fender. But, unfortunately, Charley, in opening his j mouth to reply that he was never more serious in ! his life, was unable to prevent the escape of such a ' violent roar, that the abused Mr. Chitling, without \ any preliminary ceremonies, rushed across the room ' and aimed a blow at the offender; who, being skill ful in evading pursuit, ducked to avoid it, and chose liis time so well that it lighted on the chest of the merry old gentleman, and caused him to stagger to

the wall, where he stood panting for breath, while Mr. Chitling looked on in intense dismay.

" Hark!" cried the Dodger at this moment, I heard the tinkler." Catching up the light, he crept softly up stairs.

The bell was rung again, with some impatience, while the party were in darkness.' After a short pause, the Dodger reappeared, and whispered Fagin mysteriously.

" What!" cried the Jew, « alone ?'"

The Dodger nodded in the affirmative, and shad ing the flame of the candle with his hand, gave Charley Bates a private intimation, in dumb show, that he had better not be funny just then. Having performed this friendly office, he fixed his eyes on the Jew's face, and awaited his directions.

The old man bit his yellow fingers, and meditated for some seconds; his face working with agitation the while, as if he dreaded something, and feared to know the worst. At length he raised his head.

" Where is he f he asked.

The Dodger pointed to the floor above, and made a gesture, as if to leave the room.

" Yes," said the Jew, answering the mute inquiry; "bring him down. Hush! Quiet, Charley! Gen tly, Tom! Scarce, scarce!"

This brief direction to Charley Bates, and his re cent antagonist, was softly and immediately obeyed. There was no sound of their whereabout when the Dodger descended the stairs, bearing the light in his hand, and followed by a man in a coarse smock-frock ; who, after casting a hurried glance round the room, pulled off a large wrapper which had con cealed the lower portion of his face, and disclosed, all haggard, unwashed, and unshorn, the features of flash Toby Crackit.

" How are you, Faguey ?" said this worthy, nod ding to the Jew. " Pop that shawl away in my castor, Dodger, so that I may know where to find it when I cut; that's the time of day! You'll be a fine young cracksman afore the old file now."

With these words he pulled up the smock-frock, and, winding it round his middle,,drew a chair to the fire, and placed his feet upon the hob.

" See there, Faguey," he said, pointing disconso lately to his top-boots; " not a drop of Day and Mar tin since, you know when; not a bubble of blacking, by Jove! But don't look at me in that way, man. All in good time. I can't talk about business till I've eat and drank ; so produce the sustanance, and let's have a quiet fill-out for the first time these three days!"

The Jew motioned to the Dodger to place what eat ables there were upon the table; and, seating him self opposite the house-breaker, waited his leisure.

To judge from appearances, Toby was by no means in a hurry to open the conversation. At first, the Jew contented himself with patiently watching his countenance, as if to gain from its .expression some clue to the intelligence he brought; but in vain. He looked tired and worn, but there was the same complacent repose upon his features that they al ways wore; and through dirt, and beard, and whis ker, there still shone, unimpaired^ the self-satisfied smirk of flash Toby Crackit. Then the Jew, in an agony of impatience, watched every morsel he put

OLIVER TWIST.

into his mouth; pacing np and down the room, meanwhile, in irrepressible excitement. It was all of no nse. Toby continued to eat, with the utmost outward indifference, until he could .eat no more; then, ordering the Dodger out, he closed the door, mixed a glass of spirits-and-water, and composed himself for talking.

" First and foremost, Faguey—" said Toby.

"Yes, yes!" interposed the Jew, drawing up his chair.

Mr. Crackit stopped to take a draught of spirits-and-water, and to declare that the gin was excellent; then, placing his feet against the low mantel-piece, so as to bring his boots to about the level of his eye, he quietly resumed.

"First and foremost, Faguey," said the house breaker, " how's Bill ?"

" What!" screamed the Jew, starting from his seat.

"Why, you don't mean to say—" began Toby, turning pale.

" Mean!" cried the Jew, stamping furiously on the ground. "Where are they — Sikes and the boy? * Where are they ? Where have they been ? Where are they hiding ? Why have they iiot been here ?"

" The crack failed," said Toby, faintly.

" I know it," replied the Jew, tearing a newspaper from his pocket, and pointing to it. " What more f'

"They fired and hit the boy. We cut over the fields at the back with him between us— straight as the crow flies — through hedge and ditch. They gave chase. Damme! the whole country was awake, and the dogs upon us."

"The boy?"

" Bill had him on his back, and scudded like the wind. We stopped to take him between us; his head Imng down, and he was cold. They were close upon our heels; every man for himself, and each from the gallows! We parted company, and left the youngster lying in a ditch. Alive or dead, that's all I know about him."

The Jew stopped to hear no more; but uttering a loud yell, and twining his hands in his hair, rushed from the room and from the house.

CHAPTER XXVI.

IN WHICH A MYSTERIOUS CHARACTER APPEARS UPON THE SCENE; AND MANY THINGS INSEPARABLE FROM THIS HISTORY ARE DONE AND PERFORMED.

THE old man had gained the street corner before he began to recover the effect of Toby Crackit's intelligence. He had relaxed nothing of his unusual speed; but was still pressing onward, in the same wild and disordered manner, when the sudden dash ing past of a carriage, and a boisterous cry from the foot-passengers, who saw his danger, drove him back upon the pavement. Avoiding as much as possible all the main streets, and skulking only through the by-ways and alleys, he at length emerged on Snow Hill. Here he walked even faster than before; nor did he linger until he had again turned into a court; when, as if conscious that he was now in his proper element, he fell into his usual shuffling pace, and seemed to breathe more freely.

Near to the spot on which Snow Hill and Holborn Hill meet, there opens, upon the right hand as you come out of the City, a narrow and dismal alley lead ing to Saffron Hill. In its filthy shops are exposed for sale huge bunches of second-hand silk handker chiefs, of all sizes and patterns ; for here reside the traders who purchase them from pickpockets. Hun dreds of these handkerchiefs hang dangling from pegs outside the windows or flaunting from the door posts; and the shelves within are piled with them. Confined as the limits of Field Lane are, it has its barber, its coffee-shop, its beer-shop, and its fried-fish warehouse. It is a commercial colony of itself: the emporium of petty larceny: visited at early morn ing, and setting-ill of dusk, by silent merchants, who traffic in dark back-parlors, and who go as strangely as they come. Here the clothesman, the shoe-varnp-er, and the rag-merchant, display their goods as sign boards to the petty thief; here stores of old iron and bones, and heaps of mildewy fragments of woolen-stuff and linen, rust and rot in the grimy cellars.

It was into this place that the Jew turned. He was well known to the sallow denizens of the lane ; for such of them as were on the look-out to buy or sell, nodded familiarly as he passed along. He re plied to their salutations in the same way ; but be stowed no closer recognition imtil he reached the farther end of the alley, Avhen he stopped to address a salesman of small stature, who had squeezed ;:s much of his person into a child's chair as the chair would hold, and was smoking a pipe at his ware house door.

" Why, the sight of you, Mr. Fagin, would cure the hoptalmy !" said this respectable trader, in acknowl edgment of the Jew's inquiry after his health.

" The neighborhood was a little too hot, Lively," said Fagin, elevating his eyebrows, and crossing his hands upon his shoulders.

"Well, I've heerd that complaint of it once or twice before," replied the trader; " but it soon cools down again ; don't you find it so ?"

Fagin nodded in the affirmative. Pointing in the direction of Saffron Hill, he inquired whether any one was up yonder to-night.

" At the Cripples ?" inquired the man.

The Jew nodded.

"Let me see," pursued the merchant, reflecting. " Yes, there's some half dozen of 'em gone in, that I knows. I don't think your friend's there."

" Sikes is not, I suppose?" inquired the Jew, witli a disappointed countenance.

" Xon istwentus, as the lawyers say," replied the lit tle man, shaking his head, and looking amazingly sly. " Have you got any thing in my line to-night I"

" Nothing to-night," said the Jew, turning away.

"Are you going up to The Cripples, Fagiu?" cried the little man, calling after him. " Stop! I don't mind if I have a drop there with you."

But as the Jew, looking back, waved his hand to intimate that he preferred being alone, and, more over, as the little man could not very easily disen gage himself from the chair, the sign of The Cripples was for a time bereft of the advantage of Mr. Live-ly's presence. By the time he had got upon his legs the Jew had disappeared ; so Mr. Lively, after inef fectually standing on tiptoe, in the hope of catch-

FAGIN AMONG HIS DEVOTED SERVANTS.

81

ing sight of him, again forced himself into the little chair, and, exchanging a shake of the head with a lady in the opposite shop, in which doubt and mis-t rust were plainly mingled, resumed his pipe with a grave demeanor.

The Three Cripples, or rather The Cripples, which was the sign by which the establishment was famil iarly known to its patrons, was the public-house in which Mr. Sikes and his dog have already figured. Merely making a sign to a man at the bar, Fagin walked straight up stairs, and opening the door of a room, and softly insinuating himself into the cham ber, looked anxiously about—shading his eyes with his hand, as if in search of some particular person.

The room was illuminated by two gas-lights; the glare of which was prevented, by the barred shut ters and closely-drawn curtains of faded red, from being visible outside. The ceiling was blackened, to prevent its color from being injured by the flar ing of the lamps ; and the place was so full of dense tobacco smoke, that at first it was scarcely possible to discern any thing more. By degrees, however, as some of it cleared away through the open door, an assemblage of heads, as confused as the noises that greeted the ear, might be made out ; and as the eye grew more accustomed to the scene, the spectator gradually became aware of the presence of a numer ous company, male and female, crowded round a long table, at the upper end of which sat a chair man, with a hammer of office in his hand; while a professional gentleman, with a bluish nose, and his face tied up for the benefit of a toothache, presided at a jingling piano in a remote corner.

As Fagin stepped softly in, the professional gen tleman, running over the keys by way of prelude, occasioned a general cry of order for a song; which having subsided, a young lady proceeded to enter tain the company with a ballad in four verses, be tween each of which the accompanyist played the melody all through, as loud as he could. When this was over, the chairman gave a sentiment, after which the professional gentlemen on the chairman's right and left volunteered a duet, and sang it with great applause.

It was curious to observe some faces which stood out prominently from among the group. There was the chairman himself (the landlord of the house), a coarse, rough, heavy -built fellow, who, while the songs were proceeding, rolled his eyes hither and thither, and, seeming to give himself up to joviality, had an eye for every thing that was done, and an ear for every thing that was said— and sharp ones, too. Near him were the singers, receiving with pro fessional indifference the* compliments of the com pany, and applying themselves, in turn, to a dozen proffered glasses of spirits-and-water, tendered by their more boisterous admirers, whose countenances, expressive of almost every vice, in almost every grade, irresistibly attracted the attention by their very repulsiveness. Cunning, ferocity, and drunk enness in all its stages, were there in their strongest aspects; and women, some with the last lingering tinge of their early freshness almost fading as you looked; others with every mark and stamp of their sex utterly beaten out. and presenting but one loath some blank of profligacy and crime ; some mere girls, F

others but young women, and none past the prime of life; formed the darkest and saddest portion of this dreary picture.

Fagin, troubled by no grave emotions, looked ea gerly from face to face while these proceedings were in progress, but apparently without meeting that of which he was in search. Succeeding at length in catching the eye of the man who occupied the chair, he beckoned to him slightly, and left the room as quietly as he had entered it.

" What can I do for you, Mr. Fagin ?" inquired the man, as he followed him out to the landing. "Won't you join us ? They'll be delighted, every one of'em."

The Jew shook his head impatiently, and said, in a whisper, " Is lie here ?"

" No," replied the man.

"And no news of Barney ?" inquired Fagin.

tf None," replied the landlord of The Cripples; for it was he. " He won't stir till it's all safe. Depend on it, they're on the scent down there; and that if he moved, he'd blow upon the thing at once. He's all right enough, Barney is, else I should have heard of him. I'll pound it, that Barney's managing prop erly. Let him alone for that!"

" Will he be here to-night ?" asked the Jew, laying the same emphasis on the pronoun as before.

"Monks, do you mean?" inquired the landlord, hesitating.

" Hush!" said the Jew. " Yes."

" Certain," replied the man, drawing a gold watch from his fob; " I expected him here before now. If you'll wait ten minutes, he'll be—"

" No, no," said the Jew, hastily; as though, how ever desirous he might be to see the person in ques tion, he was nevertheless relieved by his absence. " Tell him I came here to see him; and that he must come to me to-night. No, say to-morrow. As he is not here, to-morrow will be time enough."

" Good!" said the man. " Nothing more ?"

" Not a word now," said the Jew, descending the stairs.

" I say," said the other, looking over the rails, and speaking in a hoarse whisper; " what a time this would be for a sell! I've got Phil Barker here, so drunk that a boy might take him."

"Aha!, But it's not Phil Barker's time," said the Jew, looking up. " Phil has something more to do before we can afford to part with him; so go back to the company, my dear, and tell them to lead mer ry lives— while they last. Ha! ha! ha!"

The landlord reciprocated the old man's laugh, and returned to his guests. The Jew was no sooner alone, than his countenance resumed its former ex pression of anxiety and thought. After a brief re flection, he called a hack cabriolet, and bade the man drive toward Betlmal Green. He dismissed him within some quarter of a mile of Mr. Sikes's residence, and performed the short remainder of the distance on foot.

" Now," muttered the Jew, as he knocked at the door, " if there is any deep play here, I shall have it out of you, niy girl, cunning as you are."

She was in her room, the \vomau said. Fagin crept softly up stairs, and entered it without any previous ceremony. The girl was alone; lying with her head upon the table, and her hair straggling over it.

OLIVER TWIST.

" She has beeii drinking," thought the Jew, coolly, " or perhaps she is only miserable."

The old man turned to close the door as he made this reflection; the noise thus occasioned roused the girl. She eyed his crafty face narrowly as she in quired whether there was any news, and as she list ened to his recital of Toby Crackit's story. When it was concluded, she sank into her former attitude, but spoke not a word. She pushed the candle im patiently away; and once or twice, as she feverish ly changed her position, shuffled her feet upon the ground; but this was all.

During the silence, the Jew looked restlessly about the room, as if to assure himself that there were no appearances of Sikes having covertly returned. Ap parently satisfied with his inspection, he coughed twice or thrice, and made as many efforts to open a conversation; but the girl heeded him no more than if he had been made of stone. At length he made another attempt; and rubbing his hands together, said, in his most conciliatory tone,

"And where should you think Bill was now, my dear?"

The girl moaned out some half intelligible reply that she could not tell; and seemed, from the smoth ered noise that escaped her, to be crying.

"And the boy, too," said the Jew, straining his eyes to catch a glimpse of her face. ". Poor leetle child! Left in a ditch, Nance; only think!"

"The child!" said the girl, suddenly looking up, " is better where he is than among us; and if no harm comes to Bill from it, I hope he lies dead in the ditch, and that his young bones may rot there."

" What!" cried the Jew, in amazement.

"Ay, I do," returned the girl, meeting his gaze. " I shall be glad to have him away from my eyes, and to know that the worst is over. I can't bear to have him about me. The sight of him turns me against myself, and all of you."

" Pooh!" said the Jew, scornfully. " You're drunk."

"Ami?" cried the girl, bitterly. "It's no fault of yours, if I am not! You'd never have me any thing else, if you had your will, except now;—the humor doesn't suit you, doesn't it ?"

" No!" rejoined the Jew, furiously. " It does not."

"Change it, then!" responded the girl, with a laugh.

" Change it!" exclaimed the Jew, exasperated be yond all bounds by his companion's unexpected ob stinacy, and the vexation of the night. " I WILL change it! Listen to me, you drab! Listen to me, who with six words can strangle Sikes as surely as if I had his bull's throat between my fingers now. If he comes back, and leaves the boy behind him—if he gets off' free, and, dead or alive, fails to restore him to me—murder him yourself if you would have him escape Jack Ketch. And do it the moment he sets foot in this room, or, mind me, it will be too late!"

" What is all this ?" cried the girl, involuntarily.

"What is it?" pursued Fagiu, mad with rage. " When the boy's worth hundreds of pounds to me, am I to lose what chance threw me in the way of getting safely, through the whims of a drunken gang that I could whistle away the lives of? And me bound, too, to a born devil that only wants the will, and has the power to, to—"

Panting for breath, the old man stammered for a word ; and in that instant checked the torrent of his wrath, and changed his whole demeanor. A moment before, his clenched hands had grasped the air, his eyes had dilated, and his face grown livid with pas sion ; but now he shrunk into a chair, and, cowering together, trembled with the apprehension of having himself disclosed some hidden villainy. After a short silence, he ventured to look round at his com panion. He appeared somewhat reassured, on be holding her in the same listless attitude from which he had first roused her.

" Nancy, dear!" croaked the Jew in his usual voice. " Did you mind me, dear ?"

"Don't worry me now, Fagiu!" replied the girl, raising her head languidly. " If Bill has not done it this time, he will another. He has done many a good job for you, and Avill do many more when he can; and when he can't he won't; so no more about that."

" Regarding this boy, my dear ?" said the Jew, rub bing the palms of his hands nervously together.

"The boy must take his chance with the rest," in terrupted Nancy, hastily; " and I say again, I hope he is dead, and out of harm's way, and out of yours —that is, if Bill comes to no harm. And if Toby got clear oif, Bill's pretty sure to be safe; for Bill's worth two of Toby any time."

"And about what I was saying, my dear?" ob served the Jew, keeping his glistening eye steadily upon her.

" You must say it all over again, if it's any thing you want me to do," rejoined Nancy; "and if it is, you had better wait till to-morrow. You put mo up for a minute; but now I'm stupid again."

Fagin put several other questions, all with the same drift of ascertaining whether the girl had prof ited by his unguarded hints; but she answered them so readily, and was withal so utterly unmoved by liis searching looks, that his original impression of her being more than a trifle in liquor was confirmed. Nancy, indeed, was not exempt from a failing which was very common among the Jew's female pupils; and in which, in their tenderer years, they were rath er encouraged than checked. Her disordered ap pearance, and a wholesale perfume of Geneva which pervaded the apartment, afforded strong confirmato ry evidence of the justice of the Jew's supposition ; and when, after indulging in the temporary display of violence above described, she subsided, first into dullness, and afterward into a compound of feelings, under the influence of which she shed tears one min ute, and in the next gave utterance to various ex clamations of " Never sajfc die !" and divers calcula tions as to what might be the amount of the odds so long as a lady or gentleman was happy, Mr. Fagin, who had had considerable experience of such matters in his time, saw, with great satisfaction, that she was very far gone indeed.

Having eased his mind by this discovery; and having accomplished his twofold object of imparting to the girl what he had that night heard, and of as certaining with his own eyes that Sikes had not re turned, Mr. Fagin again turned his face homeward, leaving his young Mend asleep, with her head upon the table.

FAGIN AND HIS VISITOR.

8;5

It was withiii an hour of midnight. The weather being dark and piercing cold, lie had no great temp tation to loiter. The sharp wind that scoured the streets seemed to have cleared them of passengers, as of dust and mud, for few people were abroad, and they were to all appearance hastening fast home. It blew from the right quarter for the Jew, however, and straight before it he went, trembling, and shiv ering, as every fresh gnst drove him rudely on his way.

He had reached the corner of his own street, and was already fumbling in his pocket for the door-key, when a dark figure emerged from a projecting en trance which lay in deep shadow, and, crossing the road, glided up to him unperceived.

" Fagiu!" whispered a voice close to his ear.

remarking that he had better say what he had got to say under cover; for his blood was chilled with standing about so long, and the wind blew through him.

Fagin looked as if he could have willingly excused himself from taking home a visitor at that unseason able hour; and, indeed, muttered something about having no fire; but his companion repeating his re quest in a peremptory manner, he unlocked the door, and requested bim to close it softly, while he got a light.

" It's as dark as the grave," said the man, groping forward a few steps. " Make haste!"

" Shut the door," whispered Fagiu, from the end of the passage. As he spoke, it closed with a loud noise.

FAGIN !' WHISPERED A VOICE CLOSE TO HIS EAE."

"Ah!" said the Jew, turning quickly round, "is that

"Yes!" interrupted the stranger. "I have been lingering here these two hours. Where the devil have you been?"

" On your business, my dear," replied the Jew, glancing uneasily at his companion, and slackening his pace as he spoke. " On your business, all night."

" Oh, of course," said the stranger, with a sneer. " Well; and what's come of it ?"

" Nothing good," said the Jew.

" Nothing bad, I hope ?" said the stranger, stopping short and turning a startled look on his companion.

The Jew shook his head, and was about to reply, when the stranger, interrupting him, motioned to the house, before which they had by this time arrived;

" That wasn't my doing," said the other man, feel ing his way. " The wind blew it to, or it shut of its own accord, one or the other. Look sharp with the light, or I shall knock my brains out against some thing in this confounded hole."

Fagin stealthily descended the kitchen stairs. Af ter a short absence, he returned with a lighted cau dle, and the intelligence that Toby Crackit was asleep in the back room below, and that the boys were in the front one. Beckoning the man to follow him, he led the way up stairs.

" We can say the few words we've got to say in here, my dear," said the Jew, throwing open a door on the first floor; " and as there are holes in the shut ters, and we never show lights to our neighbors, we'll set the candle on the stairs. There!"

OLIVER TWIST.

With those words, the Jew, stooping down, placed the candle on an upper flight of stairs exactly oppo site to the room-door. This done, he led the way into the apartment; which was destitute of all mov ables save a broken arm-chair, and an old couch or sofa, without covering, which stood behind the door. Upon this piece of furniture the stranger sat himself with the air of a weary man; and the Jew, drawing up the arm-chair opposite, they sat face to face. It was not quite dark; the door was partially open, and the candle outside threw a feeble reflection on the opposite wall.

They conversed for some time in whispers. Though nothing of the conversation was distinguishable be yond a few disjointed words here and there, a listen er might easily have perceived that Fagiii appeared to be defending himself against some remarks of the stranger, and that the latter was in a state of con siderable irritation. They might have been talking thus for a quarter of an hour or more, when Monks— by which name the Jew had designated the strange man several times in the course of their colloquy— said, raising his voice a little,

" I tell you again, it w r as badly planned. Why not have kept him here among the rest, and made a sneak ing, sniveling pickpocket of him at once ?"

" Only hear him!" exclaimed the Jew, shrugging his shoulders.

"Why, do you mean to say you couldn't have done it if you had chosen ?" demanded Monks, stern ly. " Haven't you done it with other boys scores of times ? If you had had patience for a twelvemonth at most, couldn't you have got him convicted, and sent safely out of the kingdom—perhaps for life ?"

" Whose turn would that have served, my dear ?" inquired the Jew, humbly.

" Mine," replied Monks.

" But not mine," said the Jew, submissively. " He might have become of use to me. W T hen there are two parties to a bargain, it is only reasonable that the interests of both should be consulted; is it, my good friend f"

" What then ?" demanded Monks.

" I saw it was not easy to train him to the busi ness," replied the Jew; " he was not like other boys in the same circumstances."

" Curse him, no!" muttered the man, " or he would have been a thief long ago."

"I had no hold upon him to make him worse," pursued the Jew, anxiously watching the counte nance of his companion. " His hand was not in. I had nothing to frighten him with; which we always must have in the beginning, or we labor in vain. What could I do ? Send him out with the Dodger and Charley ? We had enough of that at first, my dear; I trembled for us all."

" That was not my doing," observed Monks.

" No, no, my dear!" renewed the Jew. "And I don't quarrel with it now; because, if it had never hap pened, you might never have clapped eyes upon the hoy to notice him, and so led to the discovery that it was him you were looking for. W T ell! I got him hack for you by means of the girl; and then she be gins to favor him."

" Throttle the girl!" said Monks, impatiently.

Why, we can't afford to do that just now, my dear," replied the Jew, smiling; "and, besides, that sort of thing is not in our way; or, one of these d:i vs. I might be glad to have it done. I know what these girls are, Monks, well. As soon as the boy begins to harden, she'll care no more for him than for a block of wood. You want him made a thief. If he is alive, I can make him one from this time; and if—if—" said the Jew, drawing nearer to the other" it's not likely, mind—but if the worst comes to the worst, and he is dead—"

"It's no fault of mine if he is!" interposed the oth er man, with a look of terror, and clasping the Jew's arm with trembling hands. "Mindthat, Fagiii! I had no hand in it. Any thing but his death, I told you from the first. I won't shed blood; it's always found out, and haunts a man besides. If they shot him dead, I was not the cause; do you hear me ? Fire this infernal don! What's that ?"

"What!" cried the Jew, grasping the coward round the body with both arms, as he sprung to his feet. " Where ?"

"Yonder!" replied the man, glaring at the oppo site wall. " The shadow! I saw the shadow of a woman, in a cloak and bonnet, pass along the wain scot like a breath!"

The Jew released his hold, and they rushed tu-multuously from the room. The candle, wasted by the draught, was standing where it had been placed. It showed them only the empty staircase and their own white faces. They listened intently: a pro found silence reigned throughout the house.

"It's your fancy," said the Jew, taking up the light and turning to his companion.

" I'll swear I saw it!" replied Monks, trembling. " It was bending forward when I saw it first; and when I spoke it darted away."

The Jew glanced contemptuously at the pale face of his associate, and telling him he could follow if he pleased, ascended the stairs. They looked into all the rooms; they were cold, bare, and empty. They descended into the passage, and thence into the cel lars below. The green damp hung upon the low walls; the tracks of the snail and slug glistened in the light of the candle; but all was still as death.

" What do you think, now ?" said the Jew, when they had regained the passage. " Besides ourselves, there's not a creature in the house except Toby arid the boys; and they're safe enough. See here!"

As a proof of the fact, the Jew drew forth two keys from his pocket; and explained, that when he first went down stairs he had locked them in, to pre vent any intrusion on the conference.

This accumulated testimony effectually staggered Mr. Monks. His protestations had gradually become less and less vehement as they proceeded in their search without making any discovery; and now he gave vent to several very grim laughs, and con fessed it could only have been his excited imagina tion. He declined any renewal of the conversation, however, for that night, suddenly remembering that it as past one o'clock. And so the amiable couple parted.

BUMBLE FURTHER ALLAYS HIS CURIOSITY.

CHAPTER XXVII.

ATONES FOR THE UNPOLITENESS OF A FORMER CHAPTER, WHICH DESERTED A LADY MOST UNCEREMONIOUSLY.

AS it would be by no means seemly in a humble author to keep so mighty a personage as a bea dle waiting, with his back to the fire, and the skirts of his coat gathered up under his arms, until such time as it«might suit his pleasure to relieve him; and as it would still less become his station or his gal lantry to involve in the same neglect a lady on whom that beadle had looked with an eye of tenderness and affection, and in whose ear he had whispered sweet words, which, coming from such a quarter, might well thrill the bosom of maid or matron of whatso ever degree; the historian whose pen traces these words—trusting that he knows his place, and that he entertains a becoming reverence for those upon earth to whom high and important authority is del egated — hastens to pay them that respect which their position demands, and to treat them with all that duteous ceremony which their exalted rank, and (by consequence) great virtues, imperatively claim at his hands. Toward this end, indeed, he had purposed to introduce, in this place, a dissertation touching the divine right of beadles, and elucidative of the position that a beadle can do no wrong; which could not fail to have been both pleasurable and profitable to the right-minded reader, but which he is unfortunately compelled, by want of time and space, to postpone to some more convenient and fit ting opportunity; on the arrival of which, he will be prepared to show, that a beadle properly consti tuted—that is to say, a parochial beadle, attached to a parochial work-house, and attending in his official capacity the parochial church—is, in right and virtue of his office, possessed of all the excellences and best qualities of humanity; and that to none of those excellences can mere companies' beadles, or court-of-law beadles, or even chapel-of-ease beadles (save the last, and they in a very lowly and inferior degree), lay the remotest sustainable claim.

Mr. Bumble had re-counted the tea-spoons, re-weighed the sugar-tongs, made a closer inspection of the milk-pot, and ascertained to a nicety the ex act condition of the furniture, down to the very horse-hair seats of the chairs; and had repeated each process full half a dozen times, before he began to think that it was time for Mrs. Comey to return. Thinking begets thinking: as there were no sounds of Mrs. Corney's approach, it occurred to Mr. Bumble that it would be an innocent and virtuous way of spending the time, if he were further to allay his curiosity by a cursory glance at the interior of Mrs. Corney's chest of drawers.

Having listened at the key-hole, to assure himself that nobody was approaching the chamber, Mr. Bum ble, beginning at the bottom, proceeded to make him self acquainted with the contents of the three long drawers; which, being filled with various garments of good fashion and texture, carefully preserved be-tweeu two layers of old newspapers, speckled with dried lavender, seemed to yield him exceeding sat isfaction. Arriving, in course of time, at the right-hand corner drawer (in which was the key), and be holding therein a small padlocked box, which, being

shaken, gave forth a pleasant sound, as of the chink ing of coin, Mr. Bumble returned with a stately walk to the fire-place; and, resuming his old attitude, said, with a grave and determined air, " I'll do it!" He followed up this remarkable declaration, by shaking his head in a waggish manner for ten minutes, as though he were remonstrating with himself for be ing such a pleasant dog; and then he took a view of his legs in profile, with much seeming pleasure and interest.

He was still placidly engaged in this latter survey, when Mrs. Corney, hurrying into the room, threw her self, in a breathless state, on a chair by the fireside, and covering her eyes with one hand, placed the oth er over her heart, and gasped for breath.

" Mrs. Comey," said Mr. Bumble, stooping over the matron, " what is this, ma'am ? Has any thing hap pened, ma'am? Pray answer me. I'm on—on— Mr. Bumble, in his alarm, could not immediately think of the word " tenter-hooks," so he said " broken bottles."

" Oh, Mr. Bumble!" cried the lady, " I have been so dreadfully put out!"

" Put out, ma'am!" exclaimed Mr. Bumble; " who has dared to ? I know!" said Mr. Bumble, check ing himself, with native majesty, " this is them wi-cious paupers!"

"It's dreadful to think of!" said the lady, shud dering.

"Then don't think of it, ma'am," rejoined Mr. Bumble.

" I can't help it," whimpered the lady.

" Then take something, ma'am," said Mr. Bumble, soothingly. " A little of the wine ?"

"Not for the world!" replied Mrs. Corney. "I couldn't—oh! The top shelf in the right-hand cor ner— oh!" Uttering these words, the good lady pointed, distractedly, to the cupboard, and under went a convulsion from internal spasms. Mr. Bum ble rushed to the closet; and, snatching a pint green-glass bottle from the shelf thus incoherently indi cated, filled a tea-cup with its contents, and held it to the lady's lips.

" I'm better now," said Mrs. Corney, falling back, after drinking half of it.

Mr. Bumble raised his eyes piously to the ceiling in thankfulness; and, bringing them down again to the brim of the cup, lifted it to his nose.

" Peppermint," exclaimed Mrs. Corney, in a faint voice, smiling gently on the beadle as she spoke. "Try it! There's a little—a little something else in it."

Mr. Bumble tasted the medicine with a doubtful look; smacked his lips; took another taste; and put the cup down empty.

" It's very comforting," said Mrs. Corney.

"Very much so, indeed, ma'am," said the beadle. As he spoke, he drew a chair beside the matron, and tenderly inquired what had happened to distress her.

" Notliing," replied Mrs. Corney. " I am a foolish, excitable, weak creetur."

" Not weak, ma'am," retorted Mr. Bumble, drawing his chair a little closer. "Are you a weak creetur, Mrs. Corney ?"

"We are all weak creeturs," said Mrs. Corney, lay ing down a general principle.

OLIVER TWIST.

" So we are," said the beadle.

Nothing was said, on either side, for a minute or two afterward. By the expiration of that time, Mr. Bumble had illustrated the position by removing his left arm from the back of Mrs. Corney's chair, where it had previously rested, to Mrs. Corney's apron-string, round which it gradually became entwined.

"We are all weak creeturs," said Mr. Bumble.

Mrs. Corney sighed.

" Don't sigh, Mrs. Corney," said Mr. Bumble.

" I can't help it," said Mrs. Coriiey. And she sigh ed again.

" This is a very comfortable room, ma'am," said

"And candles," replied Mrs. Corney, slightly re turning the pressure.

"Coals, candles, and house-rent free," said Mr. Bumble. " Oh, Mrs. Corney, what a angel you are !"

The lady was not proof against this burst of feel ing. She sank into Mr. Bumble's arms; and that gentleman, in his agitation, imprinted a passionate kiss upon her chaste nose.

" Such porochial perfection!" exclaimed Mr. Bum ble, rapturously. " You know that Mr. Slout is worse to-night, my fascinator ?"

" Yes," replied Mrs. Coruey, bashfully.

" He can't live a week, the doctor says," pursued

" 'DON'T SIGH, MBS. CORNEY,' SAID MR. BUMBLE."

Mr. Bumble, looking round. "Another room, and this, ma'am, would be a complete thing."

" It would be too much for one," murmured the lady.

" But not for two, ma'am," rejoined Mr. Bumble, in soft accents. " Eh, Mrs. Corney ?"

Mrs. Corney drooped her head when the beadle said this; the beadle drooped his, to get a view of Mrs. Corney's face. Mrs. Coruey, with great propri ety, turned her head away, and released her hand to get at her pocket-handkerchief; but insensibly re placed it in that of Mr. Bumble.

" The board allow you coals, don't they, Mrs. Cor ney ?" inquired the beadle, affectionately pressing her hand.

Mr. Bumble. "He is the master of this establish ment ; his death will cause a wacancy: that wacan-cy must be filled up. Oh, Mrs. Corney, what a pros pect this opens! What a opportunity for a jiniug of hearts and housekeepings!"

Mrs. Corney sobbed.

" The little word f' said Mr. Bumble, bending over the bashful beauty. " The one little, little, little word, my blessed Corney ?"

" Ye ye yes!" sighed out the matron.

" One more," pursued the beadle; " compose your darling feelings for only one more. When is it to come off?"

Mrs. Corney twice essayed to speak, and twice fail-

MR. CLAY POLE AXD THE OYSTERS.

ed. At length summoning up courage, she threw her arms roimcl Mr. Bumble's neck, and said it might be as soon as ever he pleased, and that he was a irresistible duck."

Matters being thus amicably and satisfactorily ar ranged, the contract was solemnly ratified in anoth er tea-cupful of the peppermint mixture; which was rendered the more necessary by the flutter and agi tation of the lady's spirits. While it was being dis posed of, she acquainted Mr. Bumble with the old woman's decease.

" Very good," said that gentleman, sipping his pep permint ; " I'll call at Sowerberry's as I go home, and tell him to send to-morrow morning. Was it that as frightened yon, love ?"

" It wasn't any thing particular, dear," said the lady, evasively.

" It must have been something, love," urged Mr. Bumble. " Won't you tell your own B. ?"

" Not now," rejoined the lady; " one of these days. After we're married, dear."

"After we're married!" exclaimed Mr. Bumble. " It wasn't any impudence from any of them male paupers as :

" No, no, love!" interposed the lady, hastily.

" If I thought it was," continued Mr. Bumble; " if I thought as any one of 'em had dared to lift his wul-gar eyes to that lovely countenance— :

" They wouldn't have dared to do it, love," re sponded the lady.

" They had better not!" said Mr. Bumble, clenching his list. " Let me see any man, porochial or extra-porochial, as would presume to do it; and I can tell lihn that he wouldn't do it a second time!"

Unembellished by any violence of gesticulation, this might have seemed no very high compliment to the lady's charms; but, as Mr. Bumble accompanied the threat with many warlike gestures, she was much touched with this proof of his devotion, and pro tested, with great admiration, that he was indeed a dove.

The dove then turned up his coat-collar, and put on his cocked hat; and, having exchanged a long and affectionate embrace with his future partner, once again braved the cold wind of the night, mere ly pausing, for a few minutes, in the male paupers' ward, to abuse them a little, with the view of satis-lying himself that he could fill the office of work house master with needful acerbity. Assured of his qualifications, Mr. Bumble left the building with a light heart, and bright visions of his future promo tion, which served to occupy his mind until he reach ed the shop of the undertaker.

Now Mr. and Mrs. Sowerberry having gone out to tea and supper, and Noah Claypole not being at any time disposed to take upon himself a greater amount of physical exertion than is necessary to a conven ient performance of the two functions of eating and drinking, the shop was not closed, although it was past the usual hour of shutting up. Mr. Bumble tapped with his cane on the counter several times; but, attracting no attention, and beholding a light shining through the glass-window of the little par lor at the back of the shop, he made bold to peep in and see what was going forward; and when he saw what u-as going forward, he was not a little surprised.

The cloth was laid for supper; the table was cov ered with bread-and-butter, plates and glasses, a por ter-pot, and a wine-bottle. At the upper end of the table Mr. Noah Claypole lolled negligently in an easy-chair, with his legs thrown over one of the arms, an open clasp-knife in one hand, and a mass of buttered bread in the other. Close beside him stood Charlotte, opening oysters from a barrel, which Mr. Claypole condescended to swallow with remarkable avidity. A more than ordinary redness in the re gion of the young gentleman's nose, and a kind of fixed wink in his right eye, denoted that he was in a slight degree intoxicated; these symptoms were con firmed by the intense relish with which he took his oysters, for which nothing but a strong appreciation of their cooling properties, in cases of internal fever, could have sufficiently accounted.

" Here's a delicious fat one, Noah, dear!" said Char lotte ; " try him, do; only this one."

"What a delicious thing is a oyster!" remarked Mr. Claypole, after he had swallowed it. "What a pity it is, a number of 'em should ever make you feel uncomfortable; isn't it, Charlotte f'

" It's quite a cruelty," said Charlotte.

"So it is," acquiesced Mr. Claypole. "A'n't yer fond of oysters ?"

" Not overmuch," replied Charlotte. " I like to see you eat 'em, Noah dear, better than eating 'em myself."

" Lor*!" said Noah, reflectively; " how queer!"

" Have another," said Charlotte. " Here's one with such a beautiful, delicate beard!"

" I can't manage any more," said Noah. " I'm very sorry. Come here, Charlotte, and I'll kiss yer."

"What!" said Mr. Bumble, bursting into the room. " Say that again, sir."

Charlotte uttered a scream, and hid her face in her apron. Mr. Claypole, without making any further change in his position than suffering his legs to reach the ground, gazed at the beadle in drunken terror.

" Say it again, you wile, owdacious fellow!" said Mr. Bumble. " How dare you mention such a thing, sir ? And how dare you encourage him, you insolent minx ? Kiss her!" exclaimed Mr. Bumble, in strong indignation. " Faugh!"

" I didn't mean to do it!" said Noah, blubbering. " She's always a-kissiug of me, whether I like it or not,"

" Oh, Noah!" cried Charlotte, reproachfully.

" Yer are; yer know yer are!" retorted Noah. " She's always a-doing of it, Mr. Bumble, sir; she chucks me under the chin, please, sir; and makes all manner of love!"

" Silence!" cried Mr. Bumble sternly. " Take your self down stairs, ma'am. Noah, you shut up the shop; say another word till your master comes home at your peril; and, when he does come home, tell him that Mr. Bumble said he was to send a old wom an's shell after breakfast to-morrow morning. Do you hear, sir ? Kissing!" cried Mr. Bumble, holding up his hands. " The sin and wickedness of the low er orders in this porochial district is frightful! If Parliament don't take their abominable courses un der consideration, this country's ruined, and the char acter of the peasantry gone forever!" With these

words, the beadle strode, vith a lofty and gloomy air, from the undertaker's premises.

And now that we have accompanied him so far on his road home, and have made all necessary prepara tions for the old woman's funeral, let us set on foot a few inquiries after young Oliver Twist, and ascer tain whether he be still lying in the ditch where Toby Crackit left him.

CHAPTER XXVIII.

LOOKS AFTER OLIVER, AND PROCEEDS WITH HIS ADVEN TURES.

" YT7OLVES tear your throats!" muttered Sikes,

T V grinding his teeth. "I wish I was among some of you; you'd howl the hoarser for it."

As Sikes growled forth this imprecation, with the most desperate ferocity that his desperate nature was capable of, he rested the body of the wounded boy across his bended knee, and turned his head, for an instant, to look back at his pursuers.

There was little to be made out, in the mist and darkness; but the loud shouting of men vibrated through the air, and the barking of the neighboring dogs, roused by the sound of the alarm-bell, resound ed in every direction.

" Stop, you white-livered hound!" cried the robber, shouting after Toby Crackit, who, making the best use of his long legs, was already ahead. " Stop!"

The repetition of the word brought Toby to a dead stand-still. For he was not quite satisfied that he was beyond the range of pistol-shot; and Sikes was in no mood to be played with.

" Bear a hand with the boy," cried Sikes, beckon ing furiously to his confederate. " Come back!"

Toby made a show of returning; but ventured, in a low voice, broken for want of breath, to intimate considerable reluctance as he came slowly along.

" Quicker!" cried Sikes, laying the boy in a dry ditch at his feet, and drawing the pistol from his pocket. " Don't play booty with me!"

At this moment the noise grew louder. Sikes, again looking round, could discern that the men who had given chase were already climbing the gate of the field in which he stood; and that a couple of dogs were some paces in advance of them.

" It's all up, Bill!" cried Toby; " drop the kid, and show 'em your heels." With this parting advice, Mr. Crackit, preferring the chance of being shot by his friend to the certainty of being taken by his ene mies, fairly turned tail, and darted off at full speed. Sikes clenched his teeth; took one look around; threw over the prostrate form of Oliver the cape in which he had been hurriedly muffled; ran along the front of the hedge, as if to distract the attention of those behind from the spot where the boy lay: paused for a second before another hedge which met it at right angles; and, whirling his pistol high into the air, cleared it at a bound, and was gone.

" Ho, ho, there!" cried a tremulous voice in the rear. " Pincher! Neptune! Come here, come here!"

The dogs, who, in common with their masters, seemed to have no particular relish for the sport in which they were engaged, readily answered to the

command. Three men, who had by this time ad vanced some distance into the field, stopped to take counsel together.

" My advice, or, leastways, I should say, my orders, is," said the fattest man of the party, " that we 'me diately go home again."

" I am agreeable to any thing which is agreeable to Mr. Giles," said a shorter man; who was by no means of a> slirn figure, and who was very pale in the face, and very polite; as frightened men frequently are.

" I shouldn't wish to appear ill-mannered, gentle men," said the third, who had called the dogs back; " Mr. Giles ought to know."

" Certainly," replied the shorter man; " and what ever Mr. Giles says, it isn't our place to contradict him. No, no, I know my sitiwation! Thank my stars, I know my sitiwation." To tell the truth, the little man did seem to know his situation, and to know perfectly well that it was by no means a de sirable one; for his teeth chattered in his head as he spoke.

' You are afraid, Brittles," said Mr. Giles.

I a'n't," said Brittles.

' You are," said Giles.

' You're a falsehood, Mr. Giles," said Brittles.

' You're a lie, Brittles," said Mr. Giles.

Now these four retorts arose from Mr. Giles's taunt; and Mr. Giles's taunt had arisen from his indignation at having the responsibility of going home again imposed upon himself under cover of a compliment. The third man brought the dispute to a close, most philosophic ally.

"I'll tell you what it is, gentlemen," said he, " we're all afraid."

" Speak for yourself, sir," said Mr. Giles, who Avns the palest of the party.

" So I do," replied the man. " It's natural and proper to be afraid, under such circumstances. I am."

" So am I," said Brittles; " only there's no call to tell a man he is, so bounceably."

These frank admissions softened Mr. Giles, who at once owned that lie was afraid; upon which they all three faced about, and ran back again with the completest unanimity, until Mr. Giles (who had the shortest wind of the party, and was encumbered with a pitchfork) most handsomely insisted on stop ping, to make an apology for his hastiness of speech.

" But it's wonderful," said Mr. Giles, when he had explained," what a man will do when his blood is up. I should have committed murder—I know I should—if we'd caught one of them rascals."

As the other two were impressed with a similar presentiment; and as their blood, like his, had all gone down again; some specTilation ensued upon the cause of this sudden change in their temperament.

" I know what it was," said Mr. Giles; " it was the gate."

" I shouldn't wonder if it was," exclaimed Brittles, catching at the idea.

" You may depend upon it," said Giles, " that that gate stopped the flow of the excitement. I felt all mine suddenly going away as I was climbing over it."

Bv a remarkable coincidence, the other two had

OLITEE'S HELPLESS CONDITION.

been visited with the same unpleasant sensation at that precise moment. It was quite obvious, there fore, that it was the gate; especially as there was no doubt regarding the time at which the change had taken place, because all three remembered that they had come in sight of the robbers at the instant of its occurrence.

This dialogue was held between the two men who had surprised the burglars, and a traveling tinker who had been sleeping in an out-house, and who had been roused, together with his two mongrel curs, to join in the pursuit. Mr. Giles acted in the double capacity of butler and steward to the old lady of the mansion; Brittles was a lad-of-all-work, who, hav ing entered her service a mere child, was treated as a promising young boy still, though he was some thing past thirty.

Encouraging each other with such converse as this; but, keeping very close together, notwithstand ing, and looking apprehensively round, whenever a fresh gust rattled through the boughs, the three men hurried back to a tree, behind which they had left their lantern, lest its light should inform the thieves in what direction to fire. Catching up the light, they made the best of their way home at a good round trot; and long after their dusky forms had ceased to be discernible, the light might have been seen twinkling and dancing in the distance, like some exhalation of the damp and gloomy atmos phere through which it was swiftly borne.

The air grew colder as day came slowly on; and the mist rolled along the ground like a dense cloud of smoke. The grass was wet; the pathways and low places were all mire and water; the damp breath of an unwholesome wind went languidly by, with a hollow moaning. Still, Oliver lay motionless and insensible on the spot where Sikes had left him.

Morning drew on apace. The air became more sharp and piercing, as its first dull hue— the death of night, rather than the birth of day—glimmered faintly in the sky. The objects which had looked dim and terrible in the darkness grew more and more defined, and gradually resolved into their fa miliar shapes. The rain came down, thick and fast, and pattered noisily among the leafless bushes. But Oliver felt it not, as it beat against him; for he still lay stretched, helpless and unconscious, on his bed of clay.

At length, a low cry of pain broke the stillness that prevailed.; and uttering it, the boy awoke. His left arm. rudely bandaged in a shawl, hung heavy and useless at his side: the bandage was saturated with blood. He was so weak, that he could scarcely raise himself into a sitting posture; when he had done so, he looked feebly round for help, and groaned with pain. Trembling in every joint, from cold and ex haustion, he made an effort to stand upright; but, shuddering from head to foot, fell prostrate on the ground.

After a short return of the stupor in which he had so long plunged, Oliver, urged by a creeping sickness at his heart, which seemed to warn him tliat. if he lay there, he must surely die, got upon his feet, and essayed to walk. His head was dizzy, and lie staggered to and fro like a drunken man. But he kept up, nevertheless, and, with his head drooping languidly on his breast, went stumbling onward, he knew not whither.

And now, hosts of bewildering and confused ideas canie crowding on his mind. He seemed to be still walking between Sikes and Crackit, who were an grily disputing—for the very words they said sound ed in his ears; and when he caught his own atten tion, as it were, by making some violent effort to save himself from falling, he found that he was talk ing to them. Then he was alone with Sikes, plod ding on as on the previous day; and as shadowy people passed them, he felt the robber's grasp upon his wrist. Suddenly, he started back at the report of fire-arms; there rose into the air loud cries aud shouts; lights gleamed before his eyes; all was noise and tumult, and some unseen hand bore him hurried ly away. Through all these rapid visions, there ran an undefined, uneasy consciousness of pain, which wearied and tormented him incessantly.

Thus he staggered on, creeping almost mechanic ally, between the bars of gates, or through hedge-gaps, as they came in his way, until he reached a road. Here the rain began to fall so heavily, that it roused him.

He looked about, and saw that at no great distance there was a house, which perhaps he could reach. Pitying his condition, they might have compassion on him; and if they did not, it would be better, he thought, to die near human beings than in the lone ly open fields. He summoned up all his strength for one last trial, and bent his faltering steps toward it.

As he drew nearer to this house, a feeling came over him that he had seen it before. He remember ed nothing of its details; but the shape aud aspect of the building seemed familiar to him.

That garden wall! On the grass inside, he had fallen on his knees last night, and prayed the two men's mercy. It was the very house they had at tempted to rob.

Oliver felt such fear come over him when he rec ognized the place, that, for the instant, he forgot the agony of his wound, and thought only of flight. Flight! He could scarcely stand; and if he were in full possession of all the best powers of his slight and youthful frame, whither could he fly ? He pushed against the garden - gate; it was unlocked, and swung open on its hinges. He tottered across the lawn; climbed the steps; knocked faintly at the door; and, his whole strength failing him, sunk down against one of the pillars of the little portico.

It happened that about this time, Mr. Giles, Brit-ties, and the tinker, were recruiting themselves, after the fatigues and terrors of the night, with tea and sundries, in the kitchen. Not that it was Mr. Giles's habit to admit to too great familiarity the humbler servants: toward whom it was rather his wont to deport himself with a lofty affability, which, while it gratified, could not fail to remind them of his su perior position in society. But death, fires, and bur glary, make all men equals; so Mr. Giles sat with his legs stretched out before the kitchen fender, leaning his left arm on the table, while, with his right, he illustrated a circumstantial and minute account of the robbery, to which his hearers (but especially the cook and house-maid, who were of the party) listened with breathless interest.

OLIVER TWIST.

" It was about half-past two," said Mr. Giles, " or I wouldn't swear that it mightn't have been a little nearer three, when I woke up, and, turning round in my bed, as it might be so (here Mr. Giles turned | round in his chair, and pulled the corner of the ta- j ble-cloth over him to imitate bed-clothes), I fancied I heerd a noise."

At this point of the narrative the cook turned pale, and asked the house-maid to shut the door: who ask ed Brittles, who asked the tinker, who pretended not to hear.

" —Heerd a noise," continued Mr. Giles. " I says, at first, ' This is illusion;' and was composing my self off to sleep, when I heerd the noise again, dis tinct."

" What sort of a noise ?" asked the cook.

"A kind of a busting noise," replied Mr. Giles, looking round him.

" More like the noise of powdering a iron bar on a nutmeg-grater," suggested Brittles.

" It was, when you heerd it, sir," rejoined Mr. Giles; " but at this time it had a busting sound. I turned down the clothes," continued Giles, rolling back the table-cloth, " sat up in bed, and listened."

The cook and house-maid simultaneously ejacu lated " Lor!" and drew their chairs closer together.

"I heerd it now, quite apparent," resumed Mr. Giles. " ' Somebody,' I says,' is forcing of. a door, or window; what's to be done ? I'll call up that poor lad, Brittles, and save him from being murdered in his bed; or his throat,' I says, ' may be cut from his right ear to his left, without his ever knowing it.' "

Here all eyes were turned upon Brittles, who fixed his upon the speaker, and stared at him with his mouth wide open, and his face expressive of the most unmitigated horror.

"I tossed off the clothes," said Giles, throwing away the table-cloth, and looking very hard at the cook and house-maid, " got softly out of bed, drew on a pair of—"

" Ladies present, Mr. Giles," murmured the tinker.

" —Of shoes, sir," said Giles, turning upon him, and laying great emphasis on the word; " seized the loaded pistol that always goes up stairs with the plate-basket; and walked on tiptoes to his room. ' Brittles,' I says, when I had woke him, ' don't be frightened!'"

" So you did," observed Brittles, in a low voice.

" ' We're dead men, I think, Brittles,' I says," con tinued Giles; " ' but don't be frightened.' "

" Was he frightened ?" asked the cook.

" Not a bit of it," replied Mr. Giles. " He was as firm—ah! pretty near as firm as I was."

" I should have died at once, I'm sure, if it had been me," observed the house-maid.

" You're a woman," retorted Brittles, plucking up a little.

" Brittles is right," said Mr. Giles, nodding his head, approvingly ; " from a woman nothing else was to be expected. We, being men, took a dark lantern that was standing on Brittles's hob, and groped our way down stairs in the pitch dark—as might be so."

Mr. Giles had risen from his seat, and taken two steps with his eyes shut, to accompany his descrip tion with appropriate action, when he started vio

lently, in common with the rest of the company, and hurried back to his chair. The cook and house-maid screamed.

" It was a knock," said Mr. Giles, assuming perfect serenity. " Open the door, somebody." Nobody moved.

" It seems a strange sort of a thing, a knock com ing at such a time in the morning," said Mr. Giles, surveying the pale faces which surrounded him, and looking very blank himself; "but the door must be opened. Do you hear, somebody ?"

Mr. Giles, as he spoke, looked at Brittles; but that young man, being naturally modest, probably con sidered himself nobody, and so held that the inquiry could not have any application to him; at all events, he tendered no reply. Mr. Giles directed an appeal ing glance at the tinker; but he had suddenly fallen asleep. The women were out of the question.

" If Brittles would rather open the door in the presence of witnesses," said Mr. Giles, after a short silence, " I am ready to make one."

" So am I," said the tinker, waking up as suddenly as he had fallen asleep.

Brittles capitulated on these terms; and the par ty being somewhat reassured by the discovery (made on throwing open the shutters) that it was now broad day, took their way up stairs, with the dogs in front. The two women, who were afraid to stay below, brought up the rear. By the advice of Mr. Giles, they all talked very loud, to warn any evil-disposed person outside that they were strong in numbers; and by a master-stroke of policy, origi nating in the brain of the same ingenious gentle man, the dogs' tails were well pinched, in the hall, to make them bark savagely.

These precautions having been taken, Mr. Giles held on fast by the tinker's arm (to prevent his run ning away, as he pleasantly said), and gave the word of command to open the door. Brittles obeyed; the group, peeping timorously over each other's shoul ders, beheld no more formidable object than poor little Oliver Twist, speechless and exhausted, who raised his heavy eyes and mutely solicited their com passion.

"A boy!" exclaimed Mr. Giles, valiantly pushing the tinker into the background. " What's the mat ter with the— Eh ? Why—Brittles—look here— don't you know ?"

Brittles, who had got behind the door to open it, no sooner saw Oliver, than he uttered a loud cry. Mr. Giles, seizing the boy by one leg and one arm (fortunately not the broken limb) lugged him straight into the hall, and deposited him at full length on the floor thereof.

" Here he is!" bawled Giles, calling, in a state of great excitement, up the staircase; " here's one of the thieves, ma'am! Here's a thief, miss! Wound ed, miss! I shot him, miss; and Brittles held the light."

" —In a lantern, miss," cried Brittles, applying one hand to the side of his mouth, so that his voice might travel the better.

The two women-servants ran up stairs to carry the intelligence that Mr. Giles had captured a rob ber; and the tinker busied himself in endeavoring to restore Oliver, lest he should die before he could

THE DOCTOR AEEIVE8.

be banged. In the midst of all tins noise and com motion there was beard a sweet female voice, which quelled it in an instant.

" Giles!" whispered the voice from the stairhead.

"I'm here, miss," replied Mr. Giles. "Don't be frightened, miss; I ain't much injured. He didn't make a very desperate resistance, miss! I was soon too many for him."

"Hush!" replied the young lady; "you frighten my aunt as much as the thieves did. Is the poor creature much hurt f"

" Wounded desperate, miss," replied Giles, with in describable complacency.

" He looks as if he was a-going, miss," bawled Brittles, in the same manner as before. " Wouldn't you like to come and look at him, miss, in case he should ?"

"Hush, pray; there's a good man!" rejoined the lady. " Wait quietly only one instant, while I speak to aunt."

With a footstep as soft and gentle as the voice, the speaker tripped away. She soon returned, with the direction that the wounded person was to be carried carefully up stairs to Mr. Giles's room; and that Brittles was to saddle the pony and betake him self instantly to Chertsey; from which place he was to dispatch, with all speed, a constable and doctor.

" But won't you take one look at him first, miss ?" asked Mr. Giles, with as much pride as if Oliver were some bird of rare plumage that he had skillfully brought down. " Not one little peep, miss ?"

" Not now, for the world," replied the young lady. " Poor fellow ! Oh! treat him kindly, Giles, for my sake!"

The old servant looked up at the speaker, as she turned away, with a glance as proud and admiring as if she had been his own child. Then, bending over Oliver, he helped to carry him up stairs, with the care and solicitude of a woman.

CHAPTER XXIX.

HAS AX INTRODUCTORY ACCOUNT OF THE INMATES OF THE HOUSE TO WHICH OLIVER RESORTED.

IN a handsome room, though its furniture had rather the air of old-fashioned comfort than of modern elegance, there sat two ladies at a well-spread breakfast-table. Mr. Giles, dressed with scru pulous care in a full suit of black, was in attendance upon them. He had taken his station some half-way between the sideboard and the breakfast-table; and, with his body drawn up to its full height, his head thrown back, and inclined the merest trifle on one side, his left leg advanced, and his right hand thrust into his waistcoat, while his left hung down by his side, grasping a waiter, looked like one who labored under a very agreeable sense of his own merits and importance.

Of the two ladies, one was well advanced in years ; but the high-backed oaken chair in which she sat was not more upright than she. Dressed with the utmost nicety and precision, in a quaint mixture of by-gone costume, with some slight concessions to the prevailing taste, which rather served to point

the old style pleasantly than to impair its effect, she sat, in a stately manner, with her hands folded on the table before her. Her eyes (and age had dimmed but little of their brightness) were attentively fixed upon her young companion.

The younger lady was in the lovely bloom and spring-time of womanhood; at that age when, if ever angels be for God's good purposes enthroned in mortal forms, they may be, without impiety, sup posed to abide in such as hers.

She was not past seventeen. Cast in so slight and exquisite a mould; so mild and gentle; so pure and beautiful; that earth seemed not her element, nor its rough creatures her fit companions. The very intelligence that shone in her deep blue eye, and was stamped upon her noble head, seemed scarce ly of her age, or of the world; and yet the changing expression of sweetness and good-humor, the thou sand lights that played about the face, and left no shadow there; above all, the smile, the cheerful, happy smile, were made for Home, and fireside peace and happiness.

She was busily engaged in the little offices of the table. Chancing to raise her eyes as the elder lady was regarding her, she playfully put back her hair, which was simply braided on her forehead, and threw into her beaming look such an expression of affection and artless loveliness, that blessed spirits might have smiled to look upon her.

" And Brittles has been gone upward of an hour, has he f" asked the old lady, after a pause.

" An hour and twelve minutes, ma'am," replied Mr. Giles, referring to a silver watch, which he drew forth by a black ribbon.

" He is always slow," remarked the old lady.

" Brittles always was a slow boy, ma'am," replied the attendant. And seeing, by-the-bye, that Brittles had been a slow boy for upward of thirty years, there appeared no great probability of his ever being a fast one.

" He gets worse instead of better, I think," said the elder lady.

" It is very inexcusable in him if he stops to play with any other boys," said the young lady, smiling.

Mr. Giles was apparently considering the proprie ty of indulging in a respectful smile himself, when a gig drove up to the garden-gate, out of which there jumped a fat gentleman, who ran straight up to the door; and who, getting quickly into the house by some mysterious process, burst into the room, and nearly overturned Mr. Giles and the breakfast-table together.

" I never heard of such a thing!" exclaimed the fat gentleman. " My dear Mrs. May lie — bless my soul—in the silence of night, too—I never heard of such a thing!"

With these expressions of condolence, the fat gen tleman shook hands with both ladies, and, drawing up a chair, inquired how they found themselves.

" You ought to be dead, positively dead with the fright," said the fat gentleman. " Why didn't you send ? Bless me, my man should have come in a minute; and so would I; and my assistant would have been delighted; or any body, I'm sure, under such circumstances. Dear, dear! So unexpected! In the silence of night, too!"

OLIVER TWIST.

The doctor seemed especially troubled by the fact of the robbery having been unexpected, and at tempted in the night-time; as if it were the estab lished custom of gentlemen in the house-breaking way to transact business at noon, and to make an appointment, by post, a day or two previous.

" And you, Miss Rose," said the doctor, turning to the young lady, " I—"

" Oh! very much so, indeed," said Rose, interrupt ing him; "but there is a poor creature up stairs whom aunt wishes you to see."

" Ah! to be sure," replied the doctor, " so there is. That was your handiwork, Giles, I understand."

Mr. Giles, who had been feverishly putting the tea-cups to rights, blushed very red, and said that he had had that honor.

"Honor, eh?" said the doctor; "well, I don't know; perhaps it's as honorable to hit a thief in a back kitchen as to hit your man at twelve paces. Fancy that he fired in the air, and you've fought a duel, Giles."

Mr. Giles, who thought this light treatment of the matter an unjust attempt at diminishing his glory, answered respectfully, that it was not for the like of him to judge about that; but he rather thought it was no joke to the opposite party.

"Gad, that's true!" said the doctor. "Where is he? Show me the way. I'll look in again, as I come down, Mrs. Maylie. That's the little window that he got in at, eh ? Well, I couldn't have be lieved it!"

Talking all the way, he followed Mr. Giles up stairs; and while he is going up stairs, the reader may be informed that Mr. Losberne, a surgeon in the neighborhood, known through a circuit of ten miles round as " the doctor," had grown fat, more from good humor than from good living; and was as kind and hearty, and withal as eccentric an old bachelor, as will be found in five times that space by any explorer alive.

The doctor was absent much longer than either he or the ladies had anticipated. A large flat box was fetched out of the gig; and a bedroom bell was rung very often; and the servants ran up and down stairs perpetually; from which tokens it was justly concluded that something important was going on above. At length he returned ; and in reply to an anxious inquiry after his patient, looked very mys terious, and closed the door carefully.

" This is a very extraordinary thing, Mrs. Maylie," said the doctor, standing with- his back to the door, as if to keep it shut.

" He is not in danger, I hope ?" said the old lady.

"Why, that would not be an extraordinary thing, under the circumstances," replied the doctor; "though I don't think he is. Have you seen this thief?"

" No," rejoined the old lady.

" Nor heard any thing about him ?"

"No."

" I beg your pardon, ma'am," interposed Mr. Giles; " but I was going to tell you about him when Doctor Losberne came in."

The fact was, that Mr. Giles had not, at first, been able to bring his mind to the avowal that he had only shot a boy. Such commendations had been be

stowed upon his bravery, that he could not, for the life of him, help postponing the explanation for a few delicious minutes; during which he had flour ished in the very zenith of a brief reputation for un daunted courage.

" Rose wished to see the man," said Mrs. Maylie, " but J wouldn't hear of it."

"Humph!" rejoined the doctor. "There is noth ing very alarming in his appearance. Have you any objection to see him in my presence ?"

" If it be necessary," replied the old lady, " cer tainly not."

" Then I think it is necessary," said the doctor; " at all events, I am quite sure that you would deep ly regret not having done so if you postponed it. He is perfectly quiet and comfortable now. Allow me—Miss Rose, will you permit me ? Not the slight est fear, I pledge you my honor!"

CHAPTER XXX.

RELATES WHAT OLIVER'S NEW VISITORS THOUGHT OF HIM.

WITH many loquacious assurances that they would be agreeably surprised in the aspect of the criminal, the doctor drew the young lady's arm through one of his; and offering his disengaged hand to Mrs. Maylie, led them, with much ceremony and stateliness, up stairs.

" Now," said the doctor, in a whisper, as he softly turned the handle of the bedroom-door, " let us hear what you think of him. He has not been shaved very recently, but he don't look at all ferocious, not withstanding. Stop, though! Let me first see that he is in visiting-order."

Stepping before them, he looked into the room. Motioning them to advance, he closed the door when they had entered, and gently drew back the cur tains of the bed. Upon it, in lieu of the dogged, black-visaged ruffian they had expected to behold, there lay a mere child: worn with pain and exhaus tion, and sunk into a deep sleep. His wounded arm, bound and splintered up, was crossed iipou his breast; his head reclined upon the oth,er arm, which was half hidden by his long hair, as it streamed over the pillow.

The honest gentleman held the curtain in his hand, and looked on for a minute or so in silence. While he was watching the patient thus, the younger lady glided softly past, and seating herself in a chair by the bedside, gathered Oliver's hair from his face. As she stooped over him, her tears fell upon his fore head.

The boy stirred, and smiled in his sleep, as though these marks of pity and compassion had awakened some pleasant dream of a love and affection he had never known. Thus, a strain of gentle music, or the rippling of water in a silent place, or the odor of a flower, or the mention of a familiar word, will some times call up sudden dim remembrances of scenes that never were, in this life ; which vanish like a breath; which some brief memory of a happier ex istence, long gone by, would seem to have awakened; which no voluntary exertion of the mind can ever recall.

THE DOCTOR PRESCRIBES.

" What can this mean f' exclaimed the elder lady. " This poor child can never have been the pupil of robbers!"

" Vice," sighed the surgeon, replacing the curtain, " takes up her abode in many temples; and who can say that a fair outside shall not enshrine her ?"

" But at so early an age!" urged Rose.

"My dear young lady," rejoined the surgeon, mournfully shaking his head; " crime, like death, is not confined to the old and withered alone. The youngest and fairest are too often its chosen vic tims."

" But can you—oh! can you really believe that this delicate boy has been the voluntary associate of the worst outcasts of society?" said Rose.

The surgeon shook his head, in a manner which intimated that he feared it was very possible ; and observing that they might disturb the patient, led the way into an adjoining apartment.

" But even if he has been wicked," pursued Rose, "think how young he is; think that he may never have known a mother's love, or the comfort of a home ; that ill-usage and blows, or the want of bread, may have driven him to herd with men who have forced him to guilt. Aunt, dear aunt, for mercy's sake, think of this, before you let them drag this sick child to a prison, which in any case must be the grave of all his chances of amendment. Oh! as you love me, and know that I have never felt the want of parents in your goodness and affection, but that I might have done so, and might have been equally helpless and unprotected with this poor child, have pity upon him before it is too late!"

" My dear love," said the elder lady, as she folded the weeping girl to her bosom, "do you think I would harm a hair of his head f

" Oh, no!" replied Rose, eagerly.

"No, surely," said the old lady; "my days are drawing to their close; and may mercy be shown to me as I show it to others! What can I do to save him, sir ?"

" Let me think, ma'am," said the doctor; " let me think."

Mr. Losberne thrust his hands into his pockets, and took several turns up and down the room; often stopping, and balancing himself on his toes, and frowning frightfully. After various exclamations of "I've got it now," and "no, I haven't," and as many renewals of the walking and frowning, he at length made a dead halt, and spoke as follows:

" I think if you give me a full and unlimited com mission to bully Giles, and that little boy Brittles, I can manage it. Giles is a faithful fellow and an old servant, I know; but you can make it up to him in a thousand ways, and reward him for being such a good shot besides. You don't object to that ?"

" Unless there is some other way of preserving the child," replied Mrs. Maylie.

" There is no other," said the doctor. " No other, take my word for it."

" Then my aunt invests you with full power," said Rose, smiling through her tears; " but pray don't be harder upon the poor fellows than is indispensably necessary. 7 '

" You seem to think," retorted the doctor, " that every body is disposed to be hard-hearted to-day, ex

cept yourself, Miss Rose. I only hope, for the sake of the rising male sex generally, that you may be found in as vulnerable and soft-hearted a mood by the first eligible young fellow who appeals to your compassion; and I wish I were a young fellow, that I might avail myself on the spot of such a favora ble opportunity for doing so as the present."

" You are as great a boy as poor Brittles himself," returned Rose, blushing.

" Well," said the doctor, laughing heartily, " that is no very difficult matter. But to return to this boy. The great point of our agreement is yet to come. He will wake in an hour or so, I dare say; and although I have told that thick-headed consta ble fellow down stairs that he mustn't be moved or spoken to, on peril of his life, I think we may con verse with him without danger. Now I make this stipulation—that I shall examine him in your pres ence, and that if, from what he says, we judge, and I can show to the satisfaction of your cool reason, that he is a real and thorough bad one (which is more than possible), he shall be left to his fate, without any further interference on my part, at all events."

" Oh no, aunt!" entreated Rose.

" Oh yes, aunt!" said the doctor. " Is it a bar gain!"

" He can not be hardened in vice," said Rose. " It is impossible."

" Very good," retorted the doctor; " then so much the more reason for acceding to my proposition."

Finally the treaty was entered into ; and the par ties thereunto sat down to wait, with some impa tience, until Oliver should awake.

The patience of the two ladies was destined to un dergo a longer trial than Mr. Losberne had led them to expect; for hour after hour passed on, and still Oliver slumbered heavily. It was evening, indeed, before the kind-hearted doctor brought them the in telligence that he was at length sufficiently restored to be spoken to. The boy was very ill, he said, and weak from the loss of blood; but his mind was so troubled with anxiety to disclose something, that he deemed it better to give him the opportunity, than to insist upon his remaining quiet until next morn ing, which he should otherwise have done.

The conference was a long one. Oliver told them all his simple history, and was often compelled to stop, by pain and want of strength. It was a sol emn thing to hear, in the darkened room, the feeble voice of the sick child recounting a weary catalogue of evils and calamities which hard men had brought upon him. Oh! if when we oppress and grind our fellow-creatures, we bestowed but one thought on the dark evidences of human error, which, like dense and heavy clouds, are rising, slowly, it is true, but not less surely, to Heaven, to pour their after-ven geance on our heads ; if we heard but one instant, in imagination, the deep testimony of dead men's voices, which no power can stifle, and no pride shut out; where would be the injury and injustice, the suffering, misery, cruelty, and wrong, that each day's life brings with it!

Oliver's pillow was smoothed by gentle hands that night; and loveliness and virtue watched him ;is In-slept. He felt calm and happy, and could have died without a murmur.

OLIVER TWIST.

The momentous interview was no sooner concluded, and Oliver composed to rest again, than the doctor, after wiping his eyes, and condemning them for be ing weak all at once, betook himself down stairs to open upon Mr. Giles. And finding nobody about the parlors, it occurred to him that he could perhaps originate the proceedings with better effect in the kitchen; so into the kitchen he went.

There were assembled, in that lower house of the domestic Parliament, the women-servants, Mr. Brit-ties, Mr. Giles, the tinker (who had received a special invitation to regale himself for the remainder of the day, in consideration of his services), and the consta ble. The latter gentleman had a large staff, a large head, large features, and large half-boots; and he looked as if he had been taking a proportionate al lowance of ale—as indeed he had.

The adventures of the previous night were still under discussion ; for Mr. Giles was expatiating upon his presence of iniud, when the doctor entered; Mr. Brittles, with a mug of ale in his hand, was corrob orating every thing, before his superior said it.

" Sit still!" said the doctor, waving his hand.

" Thank you, sir," said Mr. Giles. " Misses wished some ale to be given out, sir; and as I felt no ways inclined for my own little room, sir, and was disposed for company, I am taking mine among 'em here."

Brittles headed a low murmur, by which the la dies and gentlemen generally were understood to ex press the gratification they derived from Mr. Giles's condescension. Mr. Giles looked round with a pat ronizing air, as much as to say that, so long as they behaved properly, he would never desert them.

" How is the patient to-night, sir ?" asked Giles.

" So-so ;" returned the doctor. " I am afraid you have got yourself into a scrape there, Mr. Giles."

" I hope you don't mean to say, sir," said Mr. Giles, trembling, "that he's going to die. If I thought it, I should never be happy again. I wouldn't cut a boy off—no, not even Brittles here—not for all the plate in the county, sir."

" That's not the point," said the doctor, mysterious ly. " Mr. Giles, are you a Protestant f'

" Yes, sir, I hope so," faltered Mr. Giles, who had turned very pale.

"And what are you, boy?" said the doctor, turning sharply upon Brittles.

" Lord bless me, sir!" replied Brittles, starting vio lently ; " I'm—the same as Mr. Giles, sir."

"Then tell me this," said the doctor, "both of you, both of yon! Are you going to take upon your selves to swear that that boy up stairs is the boy that was put through the little window last night ? Out with it! Come! We are prepared for you!"

The doctor, who was universally considered one of the best-tempered creatures on earth, made this demand in such a dreadful tone of anger, that Giles and Brittles, who were considerably muddled by ale and excitement, stared at each other in a state of stupefaction.

" Pay attention to the reply, constable, will you ?" said the doctor, shaking his forefinger with great solemnity of manner, and tapping the bridge of his nose with it, to bespeak the exercise of that worthy's utmost acuteness. " Something may come of this before long."

The constable looked as wise as he could, and took up his staff of office, which had been reclining indo lently in the chimney-corner.

" It's a simple question of identity, you will ob serve," said the doctor.

"That's what it is, sir," replied the constable, coughing with great violence; for he had finished his ale in a hurry, and some of it had gone the wrong way.

" Here's a house broken into," said the doctor, ".and a couple of men catch one moment's glimpse of a boy, in the midst of gunpowder-smoke, and in all the distraction of alarm and darkness. Here's a boy comes to that very same house next morning, and because he happens to have his arm tied up, these men lay violent hands upon him—by doing which, they place his life in great danger — and s\.'ear he is the thief. Now the question is, whether these men are justified by the fact; if not, in what situation do they place themselves ?"

The constable nodded profoundly. He said, if that wasn't law, he would be glad to know what was.

" I ask you again," thundered the doctor, " are you, on your solemn oaths, able to identify that boy ?"

Brittles looked doubtfully at Mr. Giles; Mr. Giles looked doubtfully at Brittles; the constable put his hand behind his ear to catch the reply; the two women and the tinker leaned forward to listen; the doctor glanced keenly round; when a ring was heard at the gate, and at the same moment the sound of wheels.

" It's the runners!" cried Brittles, to all appearance much relieved.

" The what ?" exclaimed the doctor, aghast, in his turn.

"The Bow Street officers, sir," replied Brittles, taking up a candle; " me and Mr. Giles sent for 'em this morning."

" What ?" cried the doctor.

"Yes," replied Brittles; "I sent a message up by the coachman, and I only wonder they weren't here before, sir."

" You did, did you ? Then confound your—slow coaches down here; that's all," said the doctor, walk ing away.

CHAPTER XXXI.

INVOLVES A CRITICAL POSITION.

" TTHO'S that ?" inquired Brittles, opening the

V door a little way w r ith the chain up, and peep ing out, shading the candle with his hand.

" Open the door," replied a man outside; " it's the officers from Bow Street as was sent to to-day."

Much comforted by this assurance, Brittles opeued the door to its full width and confronted a portly man in a great-coat, who walked in without saying any thing more, and wiped his shoes on the mat as coolly as if he lived there.

" Just send somebody out to relieve my mate, will you, young man ?" said the officer; " he's in the gig, a-miiiding the prad. Have you got a coach-'us here that you could put it up in for five or ten minutes f'

Brittles replying in the affirmative, and pointing out the building, the portly man stepped back to the garden-gate and helped his companion to put up the gig, while Brittles lighted them, in a state of great admiration. This done, they returned to the house, and, being shown into a parlor, took off their great coats and hats, and showed like what they were.

The man who had knocked at the door was a stout personage of middle height, aged about fifty, with shiny black hair cropped pretty close, half-whiskers, a round face, and sharp eyes. The other was a red headed, bony man in top-boots, with a rather ill-fa vored countenance, and a turned-up, sinister-look ing nose.

" Tell your governor that Blathers and Duff Is here,

several muscular affections of the limbs, and forced the head of his stick into his mouth, with some em barrassment.

" Now, with regard to this here robbery, master," said Blathers. " What are the circumstances ?"

Mr. Losberne, who appeared desirous of gaining time, recounted them at great length, and with much circumlocution. Messrs. Blathers and Duff looked very knowing meanwhile, and occasionally ex changed a nod.

"I can't say for certain till I see the work, of course," said Blathers; " but my opinion at once is —I don't mind committing myself to that extent— that this wasn't done by a yokel—eh, Duff?"

" Certainly not," replied Duff.

"JUST SEMD SOMEBODY OUT TO BELIEVE MY MATE, WILL YOU, YOUNG MAS "

will you?" said the stouter man, smoothing down hi.s hair, and laying a pair of handcuffs on the table. " Oh! good-evening, master. Can I have a word or two with you in private, if you please ?"

This was addressed to Mr. Losberne, who now made his appearance; that gentleman, motioning Brittles to retire, brought in the two ladies and shut the, door.

" This is the lady of the house," said Mr. Losberne, motioning toward Mrs. Maylie.

Mr. Blathers made a bow. Being desired to sit down, he put his hat on the floor, and, taking a chair, motioned Duff to do the same. The latter gentle man, who did not appear quite so much accustomed to good society, or quite so much at his ease in it— one of the two — seated himself, after undergoing

"And translating the word yokel for the benefit of the ladies, I apprehend your meaning to be, that this attempt was not made by a countryman ?" said Mr. Losberne, with a smile.

" That's it, master," replied Blathers. " This is all about the robbery, is it ?"

"All," replied the doctor.

" Now, what is this about this here boy that the servants are a-talking on ?" said Blathers.

" Nothing at all," replied the doctor. " One of the frightened servants chose to take it into his head that he had something to do with this attempt to break into the house; but it's nonsense, sheer ab surdity."

"Wery easy disposed of, if it is," remarked Duff.

"What he says is quite correct," observed Blath-

ers, nodding his head in a confirmatory way, and playing carelessly with the handcuffs as if they were a pair of castanets. " Who is the boy ? What ac count does he give of himself ? Where did he come from? He didn't drop out of the clouds, did he, master ?"

" Of course not," replied the doctor, with a nerv ous glance at the two ladies. " I know his whole history; hut we can talk about that presently. You would like first to see the place where the thieves made their attempt, I suppose ?"

"Certainly," rejoined Mr. Blathers. "We had better inspect the premises first, and examine the servants arterward. That's the usual way of doing business."

Lights were then procured; and Messrs. Blathers and Duff, attended by the native constable, Brittles, Giles, and every body else, in short, went into the lit-cle room at the end of the passage and looked out at the Avindow, and afterward went round by way of the lawn and looked in at the window; and after that, had a caudle handed out to inspect the shutter with; and after that, a lantern to trace the footsteps with; and after that, a pitchfork to poke the bushes with. This done, amidst the breathless interest of all beholders, they came in again; and Mr. Giles and Brittles were put through a melodramatic repre sentation of their share in the previous night's ad ventures, which they performed some six times over, contradicting each other in not more than one im portant respect the first time, and in not more than a dozen the last. This consummation being arrived at, Blathers and Duff cleared the room and held a long council together, compared with which, for se crecy and solemnity, a consultation of great doctors on the knottiest point in medicine would be mere child's play.

Meanwhile, the doctor walked up and down the next room in a very uneasy state, and Mrs. Maylie and Rose looked on with anxious faces.

" Upon my word," he said, making a halt after a great number of very rapid turns, " I hardly know what to do."

" Surely," said Eose, " the poor child's story, faith fully repeated to these men, will be sufficient to ex onerate him."

" I doubt it, my dear young lady," said the doctor, shaking his head. " I don't think it would exoner ate him, either with them or with legal functionaries of a higher grade. What is he, after all, they would say ? A runaway. Judged by mere worldly con siderations and probabilities, his story is a very doubtful one."

" You believe it, surely ?" interrupted Rose.

" believe it, strange as it is; and perhaps I may be an old fool for doing so," rejoined the doctor; " but I don't think it is exactly the tale for a prac ticed police officer, nevertheless."

" Why not ?" demanded Rose.

" Because, my pretty cross-examiner," replied the doctor, " because, viewed with their eyes, there are many ugly points about it; he can only prove the parts that look ill, and none of those that look well. Confound the fellows, they will have the why and the wherefore, and will take nothing for granted. On his own showing, you see, he has been the com

panion of thieves for some time past; he has been carried to a police-office on a charge of picking a gentleman's pocket; he has been taken away forci bly from that gentleman's house to a place which he can not describe or point out, and of the situation of which he has not the remotest idea. He is brought down to Chertsey by men who seem to have taken a violent fancy to him, whether he will or no, and is put through a window to rob a house; and then, just at the very moment when he is going to alarm the inmates, and so do the very thing that would set him all to rights, there rushes into the way a blun dering dog of a half-bred butler and shoots him! As if on purpose to prevent his doing any good for him self! Don't you see all this ?"

" I see it, of course," replied Rose, smiling at the doctor's impetuosity; "but still I do not see any thing in it to criminate the poor child."

" No," replied the doctor; " of course not! Bless the bright eyes of your sex! They never see, wheth er for good or bad, more than one side of any ques tion ; and that is always the one which first presents itself to them."

Having given vent to this result of experience, the doctor put his hands into his pockets, and Avalkod up and down the room with even greater rapidity than before.

" The more I think of it," said the doctor, " the more I see that it will occasion endless trouble and difficulty if we put these men in possession of the boy's real story. I am certain it will not be be lieved ; and even if they can do nothing to him in the end, still the dragging it forward, and giving publicity to all the doubts that will be cast upon it, must interfere materially with your benevolent plan of rescuing him from misery."

"Oh! what is to be done?" cried Rose. "Dear, dear! why did they send for these people ?"

" Why, indeed!" exclaimed Mrs. Maylie. " I would not have had them here for the world."

"All I know is," said Mr. Losbeme, at last sitting down with a kind of desperate calmness, " that we must try and carry it oif with a bold face. The ob ject is a good one, and that must be our excuse. The boy has strong symptoms of fever upon him, and is in no condition to be talked to any more; that's one comfort. We must make the best of it; and if bad be the best, it is no fault of ours. Come in!"

" Well, master," said Blathers, entering the room, followed by his colleague, and making the door fast before he said any more. "This warn't a put-up thing."

"And what the devil's a put-up thing?" demanded the doctor, impatiently.

" We call it a put-up robbery, ladies," said Blath ers, turning to them, as if he pitied their ignorance, but had a contempt for the doctor's, " when the serv ants is in it."

" Nobody suspected them in this case," said Mrs. Maylie.

" Wery likely not, ma'am," replied Blathers; " but they might have been in it, for all that."

" More likely on that wery account," said Duff.

" We find it was a town hand," said Blathers, con tinuing his report; "for the style of work is first-rate."

SPYERS AND CHICKWEED.

" Wery pretty iudeed it is," remarked Daft', in an uuder-tone.

There was two of 'em in it," continued Blathers; " and they had a boy with 'em; that's plain from the size of the window. That's all to be said at present. We'll see this lad that you've got up stairs at once, if you please."

" Perhaps they will take something to drink, first, Mrs. Maylie f' said the doctor, his face brightening as if some new thought had occurred to him.

" Oh! to be sure!" exclaimed Rose, eagerly. " You shall have it immediately, if you will."

" Why, thank you, miss!" said Blathers, drawing his coat-sleeve across his mouth; "it's dry work, this sort of duty. Any thing that's handy, miss; don't put yourself out of the way on our accounts."

" What shall it be ?" asked the doctor, following the young lady to the sideboard.

"A little drop of spirits, master, if it's all the same," replied Blathers. " It's a cold ride from Lon don, ma'am; and I always find that spirits comes home warmer to the feelings."

This interesting communication was addressed to Mrs. Maylie, who received it very graciously. While it was being conveyed to her, the doctor slipped out of the room.

Ah!" said Mr. Blathers; not holding his wine glass by the stem, but grasping the bottom between the thumb and forefinger of his left hand, and plac ing it in front of his chest; " I have seen a good many pieces of business like this in my time, ladies."

" That crack down in the back lane at Edmonton, Blathers," said Mr. Duff, assisting his colleague's memory.

" That was something in this way, warn't it ?" re joined Mr. Blathers; "that was done by Conkey duckweed, that was."

" You always gave that to him," replied Duff. " It was the Family Pet, I tell you. Conkey hadn't any more to do with it than I had."

" Get out!" retorted Mr. Blathers; " I know better. Do you mind that time when Conkey was robbed of his money, though ? What a start that was! Bet ter than any novel-book / ever see!"

" What was that ?" inquired Rose: anxious to en courage any symptoms of good-humor in the unwel come visitors.

" It was a robbery, miss, that hardly any body would have been down upon," said Blathers. " This here Conkey Chickweed"

" Coukey means Nosey, ma'am," interposed Duff.

" Of course the lady knows that, don't she ?" de manded Mr. Blathers. "Always interrupting, you are, partner! This here Conkey Chickweed, miss, kept a public-house over Battlebridge way, and he had a cellar, where a good many young lords went to see cock-fighting, and badger-drawing, and that; and a wery intellectual manner the sports was con ducted in, for I've seen 'em off'eu. He warn't one of the family at that time; and one night he was rob-bed of three hundred and twenty-seven guineas in a canvas bag, that was stole out of his bedroom in the dead of night, by a tall man with a black patch over his eye, who had concealed himself under the bed, and after committing the robbery, jumped slap out of window, which was only a storv high. He was G

wery quick about it. But Conkey was quick, too; for he was woke by the noise, and darting out of bed, he fired a blunderbuss arter him, and roused the neighborhood. They set up a hue-aud-cry directly, and when they came to look about 'em, found that Conkey had hit the robber; for there was traces of blood all the way to some palings a good distance off; and there they lost 'em. However, he had made off with the blunt; and, consequently, the name of Mr. Chickweed, licensed witler, appeared in the Ga zette among the other bankrupts; and all manner of benefits and subscriptions, and I don't know what all, was got up for the poor man, who was in a wery low state of mind about his loss, and went up and down the streets, for three or four days, a pulling his hair off in such a desperate manner that many people was afraid he might be going to make away with himself. One day he come up to the office, all in a hurry, and had a private interview with the magistrate, who, after a deal of talk, rings the bell, and orders Jem Spyers in

(Jem was a active officer), and tells him to go and assist Mr. Chickweed in ap prehending the man as robbed his house. 'I see him, Spyers,' said Chickweed, 'pass my house yes terday morning.' 'Why didn't you up, and collar him ?' says Spyers. ' I was so struck all of a heap, that you might have fractured my skull with a tooth pick,' says the poor man; 'but we're sure to have him; for between ten and eleven o'clock at night he passed again.' Spyers no sooner heard this than he put some clean linen and a comb in his pocket, in case he should have to stop a day or two; and away he goes, and sets himself down at one of the public-house windows behind the little red curtain, with his hat on, all ready to bolt out at a moment's no tice. He was smoking his pipe here, late at night, when all of a sudden Chickweed roars out ' Here he is! Stop thief! Murder!' Jem Spyers dashes out; and there he sees Chickweed, a-tearing down the street full cry. Away goes Spyers; on goes Chick-weed ; round turns the people; every body roars out, ' Thieves!' and Chickweed himself keeps on shouting, all the time, like mad. Spyers loses sight of him a minute as he turns a corner; shoots round; sees a lit tle crowd; dives in ; ' Which is the man ?' ' D— me!' says Chickweed,' I've lost him again!' It was a re markable occurrence, but he warn't to be seen no where, so they went back to the public-house. Next morning, Spyers took his old place, and looked out from behind the curtain for a tall man with a black patch over his eye, till his own two eyes ached again. At last he couldn't help shutting 'em, to ease 'em a minute; and the very moment he did so, he hears Chickweed a-roaring out,' Here he is!' Off he starts once more, with Chickweed half way down the street ahead of him; and after twice as long a run as the yesterday's one, the man's lost again! This was done, once or twice more, till one-half the neighbors gave out that Mr. Chickweed had been robbed by the devil, who was playing tricks with him arter-ward ; and the other half, that poor Mr. Chickweed had gone mad with grief."

" What did Jem Spyers say ?" inquired the doctor; who had returned to the room shortly after the com mencement of the story.

"Jem Spyers," resumed the officer, "for a long

OLIVER TWIST.

time said nothing at all, and listened to every thing without seeming to, which showed he understood his business. But, one morning, he walked into the bar, and taking out his snuff-box, says,' Chickweed, I've found out who done this here robbery.' ' Have you ?' said Chickweed. ' Oh, my dear Spyers, only let me have wengeauce, and I shall die contented! Oh, my dear Spyers, where is the villain!' ' Come!' said Spy ers, offering him a pinch of snuff,' none of that gam mon ! You did it yourself.' So he had; and a good bit of money he had made by it, too; and nobody would never have found it out, if he hadn't been so precious anxious to keep up appearances," said Mr. Blathers, putting down his wine-glass, and clinking the handcuffs together.

" Very curious, indeed," observed the doctor. " Now, if you please, you can walk up stairs."

" If you please, sir," returned Mr. Blathers. Close ly following Mr. Losberue, the two officers ascended to Oliver's bedroom ; Mr. Giles preceding the party with a lighted caudle.

Oliver had been dozing; but looked worse, and was more feverish than he had appeared yet. Being assisted by the doctor, he managed to sit up in bed for a minute or so; and looked at the strangers with out at all understanding what was going forward— in fact, without seeming to recollect where he was, or what had been passing.

" This," said Mr. Losberne, speaking softly, but with great vehemence notwithstanding, " this is the lad, who, being accidentally wounded by a spring-gun in some boyish trespass on Mr. What-d'ye-call-him's grounds at the back here, comes to the house for assistance this morning, and is immediately laid hold of and maltreated by that ingenious gentleman with the candle in his hand, who has placed his life in considerable danger, as I can professionally cer tify."

Messrs. Blathers and Duff looked at Mr. Giles, as he was thus recommended to their notice. The bewil dered butler gazed from them toward Oliver, and from Oliver toward Mr. Losberne, with a most ludi crous mixture of fear and perplexity.

" You don't mean to deny that, I suppose ?" said the doctor, laying Oliver gently down again.

" It was all done for the—for the best, sir," an swered Giles. " I am sure I thought it was the boy, or I wouldn't have meddled with him. I am not of an inhuman disposition, sir."

" Thought it was what boy ?" inquired the senior officer.

"The house-breaker's boy, sir!" replied Giles. " They—they certainly had a boy."

" Well ? Do you think so now ?" inquired Blath-. ers.

" Think what, now ?" replied Giles, looking vacant ly at his questioner.

" Think it's the same boy, Stupid-head ?" rejoined Blathers, impatiently.

" 1 don't know; I really don't know," said Giles, with a rueful countenance. " I couldn't swear to him."

" What do you think'?" asked Mr. Blathers.

" I don't know what to think," replied poor Giles. " I don't think it is the boy; indeed, I'm almost cer tain that it isn't. You know it can't be."

" Has this man been a-drinkiug, sir ?" inquired Blathers, turning to the doctor.

" What a precious muddle-headed chap you are!" said Duff, addressing Mr. Giles, with supreme con tempt.

Mr. Losberne had been feeling the patient's pulse during this short dialogue; but he now rose from the chair by the bedside, and remarked, that if the offi cers had any doubts upon the subject, they would perhaps like to step into the next room, and have Brittles before them.

Acting upon this suggestion, they adjourned to a neighboring apartment, where Mr. Brittles, being called in, involved himself and his respected superior in such a wonderful maze of fresh contradictions and impossibilities as tended to throw no particular light on any thing but the fact of his own strong mysti fication; except, indeed, his declarations that he shouldn't know the real boy if he were put before him that instant; that he had only taken Oliver to be he, because Mr. Giles had said he was; and that Mr. Giles had, five minutes previously, admitted in the kitchen that he began to be very much afraid he had been a little too hasty.

Among other ingenious surmises, the question was then raised, whether Mr. Giles had really hit any body; and upon examination of the fellow pistol to that which he had fired, it turned out to have no more destructive loading than gunpowder and brown paper: a discovery which made a considerable im pression on every body but the doctor, who had drawn the ball about ten minutes before. Upon no one, how ever, did it make a greater impression than on Mr. Giles himself; who, after laboring, for some hours, under the fear of having mortally wounded a fellow-creature, eagerly caught at this new idea, and favored it to the utmost. Finally, the officers, without trou bling themselves very much about Oliver, left the Chertsey constable in the house, and took up their rest for that night in the town, promising to return next morning.

With the next morning, there came a rumor that two men and a boy were in the cage at Kingston, who had been apprehended overnight under suspi cious circumstances; and to Kingston Messrs. Blathers and Duff journeyed accordingly. The suspicious cir cumstances, however, resolving themselves, on inves tigation, into the one fact, that they had been dis covered sleeping under a hay-stack; which, although a great crime, is only punishable by imprisonment, and is, in the merciful eye of the English law, and its comprehensive love of all the king's subjects, held to be no satisfactory proof, in the absence of all other evidence, that the sleeper, or sleepers, have committed burglary accompanied with violence, and have there fore rendered themselves liable to the punishment of death; Messrs. Blathers and Duff came back again, as wise as they went.

In short, after some more examination, and a great deal more conversation, a neighboring magistrate was readily induced to take the joint bail of Mrs. Maylie and Mr. Losberne for Oliver's appearance if he should ever be called upon; and Blathers and Duff, being rewarded with a couple of guineas, re turned to town with divided opinions on the subject of their expedition: the latter gentleman, oil a ma-

A FALSE ALARM.

ture consideration of all the circumstances, inclining to the belief that the burglarious attempt had origi nated with the Family Pet; and the former being equally disposed to concede the full merit of it to the great Mr. Conkey Chickweed.

Meanwhile, Oliver gradually throve and prospered under the united care of Mrs. Maylie, Rose, and the kind-hearted Mr. Losberue. If fervent prayers, gush ing from hearts overcharged with gratitude, be heard in heaven—and if they be not, what prayers are!— the blessings which the orphan child called down upon them sunk into their souls, diffusing peace and happiness.

CHAPTER XXXII.

OF THE HAPPY LIFE OLIVER BEGAN TO LEAD WITH HIS KIND FRIENDS.

OLIVER'S ailings were neither slight nor few. In addition to the pain and delay attendant on a broken limb, his exposure to the wet and cold had brought on fever and ague; which hung about him for many weeks, and reduced him sadly. But at length he began, by slow degrees, to get better, and to be able to say, sometimes, in a few tearful words, how deeply he felt the goodness of the two sweet la dies, and how ardently he hoped that when he grew strong and well again, he could do something to show his gratitude: only something which would let them see the love and duty with which his breast was full; something, however slight, which would prove to them that their gentle kindness had not been cast away; but that the poor boy whom their charity had rescued from misery or death was eager to serve them with his whole heart and soul.

" Poor fellow!" said Rose, when Oliver had been one day feebly endeavoring to utter the words of thankfulness that rose to his pale lips; " you shall have many opportunities of serving us, if you will. We are going into the country, and my aunt intends that you shall accompany us. The quiet place, the pure air, and all the pleastires and beauties of spring, will restore you in a few days. We will employ you in a hundred ways, when you can bear the trouble."

" The trouble!" cried Oliver. " Oh! dear lady, if I could but work for you; if I could only give you pleasure by watering your flowers, or watching your birds, or running up and down the whole day long, to make you happy; what would I give to do it!"

" You shall give nothing at all," said Miss Maylie, smiling; " for, as I told yon before, we shall employ you in a hundred ways; and if you only take half the trouble to please us that you promise now, you will make me very happy indeed."

" Happy, ma'am!" cried Oliver; " how kind of you to s;iy so!"

" You will make me happier than I can tell you," replied the young lady. "To think that my dear good aunt should have been the means of rescuing any one from such sad misery as you have described to us, would be an unspeakable pleasure to me; but to know that the object of her goodness and com passion was sincerely grateful and attached in con sequence, would delight me more than you can well

imagine. Do you understand me ?" she inquired, watching Oliver's thoughtful face.

"Oh yes, ma'am, yes!" replied Oliver, eagerly; "but I was thinking that I am ungrateful now."

" To whom f' inquired the young lady.

" To the kind gentleman and the dear old nurse who took so much care of me before," rejoined Oli ver. " If they knew how happy I am, they would be pleased, I am sure."

" I am sure they would," rejoined Oliver's bene factress; "and Mr. Losberne has already been kind enough to promise that when you are well enough to bear the journey, he will carry you to see them."

" Has he, ma'am ?" cried Oliver, his face brighten ing with pleasure. " I don't know what I shall do for joy when I see their kind faces once again."

In a short time Oliver was sufficiently recovered to undergo the fatigue of this expedition. One morn ing he and Mr. Losberne set out, accordingly, in a lit tle carriage which belonged to Mrs. Maylie. When they came to Chertsey Bridge, Oliver turned very pale, and uttered a loud exclamation.

" What's the matter with the boy ?" cried the doc tor ; as usual, all in a bustle. " Do you see any thing —hear any thing—feel any thing—eh ?"

" That, sir," cried Oliver, pointing out of the car riage window. " That house!"

" Yes; well, what of it ? Stop, coachman. Pull up here," cried the doctor. " W T hat of the house, my man; eh ?"

" The thieves—the house they took me to!" whis pered Oliver.

"The devil it is!" cried the doctor. "Halloo, there! let me out!"

But, before the coachman could dismount from his box, he had tumbled out of the coach by some means or other; and, running down to the deserted tene ment, began kicking at the door like a madman.

"Halloo!" said a little ugly humpbacked man, opening the door so suddenly that the doctor, from the very impetus of his last kick, nearly fell forward into the passage. " What's the matter here ?"

" Matter!" exclaimed the other, collaring him, with out a moment's reflection. "A good deal. Robbery is the matter."

" There'll be murder the matter, too," replied the humpbacked man, coolly, "if you don't take your hands off. Do you hear me ?"

" I hear you," said the doctor, giving his captive a hearty shake. "Where's — confound the fellow, what's his rascally name ?—Sikes; that's it. Where's Sikes, you thief?"

The humpbacked man stared, as if in excess of amazement and indignation; then twisting himself dexterously from the doctor's grasp, growled forth a volley of horrid oaths, and retired into the house. Before he could shut the door, however, the doctor had passed into the parlor without a word of parley. He looked anxiously round; not an article of furni ture ; not a vestige of any thing, animate or inani mate—not even the position of the cupboards, an swered Oliver's description.

" Now!" said the humpbacked man, who had watch ed him keenly, "what do you mean by coming into my house in this violent way ? Do you want to rob me, or to murder me ? Which is it ?"

OLIVER TWIST.

" Did you ever know a man come out to do either in a chariot and pair, you ridiculous old vampire I" said the irritable doctor.

" What do you want, then ?" demanded the hunch back. " Will you take yourself off before I do you a mischief ? Curse you!"

"As soon as I think proper," said Mr. Losberne, looking into the other parlor; which, like the first, bore no resemblance whatever to Oliver's account of it. " I shall find you out some day, my friend."

" Will you ?" sneered the ill-favored cripple. " If you ever want me, I'm here. I haven't lived here mad and all alone for five-and-twenty years, to be scared by you. You shall pay for this; you shall pay for this." And so saying, the misshapen little demon set up a yell, and danced upon the ground as if wild with rage.

" Stupid enough, this!" muttered the doctor to him self; "the boy must have made a mistake. Here! Put that in your pocket, and shut yourself up again." With these words he flung the hunchback a piece of money, and returned to the carriage.

The man followed to the chariot door, uttering the wildest imprecations and curses all the way; but as Mr. Losberne turned to speak to the driver, he looked into the carriage, and eyed Oliver for an instant with a glance so sharp and fierce, and at the same time so furious and vindictive, that, waking or sleeping, he could not forget it for months afterward. He con tinued to utter the most fearful imprecations, until the driver had resumed his seat; and when they were once more on their way, they could see him some dis tance behind, beating his feet upon the ground and tearing his hair, in transports of real or pretended rage.

" I am an ass!" said the doctor, after a long silence. " Did you know that before, Oliver ?"

"No, sir."

" Then don't forget it another tune."

"An ass," said the doctor again, after a further si lence of some minutes. " Even if it had been the right place, and the right fellows had been there, what could I have done single-handed? And if I had had assistance, I see no good that I should have done, except leading to my own exposure, and an unavoidable statement of the manner in which I have hushed up this business. That would have served me right, though. I am always involving myself in some scrape or other by acting on impulse. It might have done me good."

Now the fact was, that the excellent doctor had never acted upon any thing but impulse all through his life, and it was no bad compliment to the nature of the impulses which governed him, that, so far from being involved in any peculiar troubles or misfor tunes, he had the warmest respect and esteem of all who knew him. If the truth must be told, he was a little out of temper for a minute or two, at being disappointed in procuring corroborative evidence of Oliver's story, on the very first occasion on which he had a chance of obtaining any. He soon came round again, however; and finding that Oliver's replies to his questions were still as straightforward and con sistent, and still delivered with as much apparent sincerity and truth as they had ever been, he made up his mind to attach full credence to them, from that tune forth.

As Oliver knew the name of the street in which Mr. Browulow resided, they were enabled to drive straight thither. When the coach turned into it, his heart beat so violently that he could scarcely draw his breath.

" Now, my boy, which house is it ?" inquired Mr. Losberne.

"That! That!" replied Oliver, pointing eagerly out of the window. " The white house. Oh! make haste! Pray, make haste! I feel as if I should die; it makes me tremble so."

" Come, come!" said the good doctor, patting him on the shoulder. " You will see them directly, and they will be overjoyed to find you safe and well."

" Oh, I hope so!" cried Oliver. " They were so good to me; so very, very good to me!"

The coach rolled on. It stopped. No; that was the wrong house; the next door. It went on a few paces, and stopped again. Oliver looked up at the windows, with tears of happy expectation coursing dowu his face.

Alas! the white house was empty, and there was a bill in the window—" To Let."

" Knock at the next door," cried Mr. Losberne, tak ing Oliver's arm in his. "What has become of Mr. Brownlow, who used to live in the adjoining house, do you know ?"

The servant did not know, but would go and in quire. She presently returned, and said that

Mr. Browulow had sold off his goods and gone to the West Indies six weeks before. Oliver clasped his hands, and sank feebly backward.

" Has his housekeeper gone, too ?" inquired Mr. Losberne, after a moment's pause.

" Yes, sir," replied the servant. " The old gentle man, the housekeeper, and a gentleman who was a friend of Mr. Browulow's, all went together."

" Then turn toward home again," said Mr. Los berne to the driver; "and don't stop to bait the horses till you get out of this confounded London!"

" The book-stall keeper, sir ?" said Oliver. " I know the way there. See him, pray, sir! Do see him!"

" My poor boy, this is disappointment enough for one day," said the doctor. " Quite enough for both of us. If we go to the book-stall keeper's, we shall certainly find that he is dead, or has set his house on fire, or run away. No ; home again straight!" And in obedience to the doctor's impulse home they went.

This bitter disappointment caused Oliver much sorrow and grief, even in the midst of his happiness; for he had pleased himself, many times -during his illness, with thinking of all that Mr. Brownlow and Mrs. Bedwin would say to him, and what delight it would be to tell them how many long days and nights he had passed in reflecting on what they had done for him, and in bewailing his cmel separation from them. The hope of eventually clearing him self with them, too, and explaining how he had been forced away, had buoyed him up, and sustained him, under many of his recent trials; and now, the idea that they should have gone so far, and carried with them the belief that he was an impostor and a rob ber—a belief which might remain uncontradicted to his dying day—was almost more than he could bear.

The circumstance occasioned no alteration, how-

ever, in the behavior of his benefactors. After an other fortnight, -when the fine warm weather had fairly begun, and every tree and flower was putting forth its young leaves and rich blossoms, they made preparations for quitting the house at Chertsey for some months. Sending the plate, which had so ex cited Fagiu's cupidity, to the banker's; and leaving Giles and another servant in care of the house, they departed to a cottage at some distance in the coun try, and took Oliver with them.

Who can describe the pleasure and delight, the peace of mind and soft tranquillity, the sickly boy felt in the balmy air, and among the green hills and rich woods of an inland village! Who can tell how scenes of peace and quietude sink into the minds of pain-worn dwellers in close and noisy places, and carry their own freshness deep into their jaded hearts! Men who have lived in crowded, pent-up streets, through lives of toil, and who have never wished for change; men, to whom custom has indeed been second nature, and who have come almost to love each brick and stone that formed tho narrow boundaries of their daily walks; even they, with the hand of death upon them, have been known to yearn at last for one short glimpse of Nature's face; and, carried far from the scenes of their old pains and pleasures, have seemed to pass at once into a new state of being. Crawling forth from day to day, to some green sunny spot, they have had such memories wakened up within them by the sight of sky, and hill and plain, and glistening water, that a foretaste of heaven itself has soothed their quick decline, and they have sunk into their tombs as peacefully as the sun, whose setting they watched from their lonely chamber window but a few hours before, faded from their dim and feeble sight! The memories which peaceful country scenes call up are not of this world, nor of its thoughts and hopes. Their gentle in fluence may teach us how to weave fresh garlands for the graves of those we loved—may purify our thoughts, and bear down before it old enmity and hatred; but beneath all this there lingers, in the least reflective mind, a vague and half-formed con sciousness of having held such feelings long before, in some remote and distant time, which calls up sol emn thoughts of distant times to come, and bends down pride and worldliness beneath it.

It was a lovely spot to which they repaired. Oli ver, whose days had been spent among squalid crowds, and in the midst of noise and brawling, seemed to enter on a new existence there. The rose and hon eysuckle clung to the cottage walls; the ivy crept round the trunks of the trees; and the garden-flow ers perfumed the air with delicious odors. Hard by was a little church-yard; not crowded with tall un sightly grave-stones, but full of humble mounds, cov ered with fresh turf and moss: beneath which the old people of the village lay at rest. Oliver often wandered here ; and, thinking of the wretched grave in which his mother lay, would sometimes sit him down and sob unseen; but when he raised his eyes to the deep sky overhead, he would cease to think of her as lying in the ground, and would weep for her, sadly, but without pain.

It was a happy time. The days were peaceful and serene; the nights brought with them neither fear

nor care; no languishing in a wretched prison, or associating with wretched men; nothing but pleas ant and happy thoughts. Every morning he went to a white-headed old gentleman, who lived near the" little church, who taught Mm to read better, and to write; and who spoke so kindly, and took such pains, that Oliver could never try enough to please him. Then he would walk with Mrs. Maylie and Rose, and hear them talk of books; or perhaps sit near them in some shady place, and listen while the young lady read, which he could have done until it grew too dark to see the letters. Then he had his own lesson for the next day to prepare; and at this he would work hard, in a little room which looked into the garden, till evening came slowly on, when the ladies would walk out again, and he with them; list ening with such pleasure to all they said; and so happy, if they wanted a flower, that he could climb to reach, or had forgotten any thing he could run to fetch; that he could never be quick enough about it. When it became quite dark, and they returned home, the young lady would sit down to the piano, and play some pleasant air, or sing, in a low and gen tle voice, some old song which it pleased her aunt to hear. There would be no candles lighted at such times as these; and Oliver would sit by one of the windows, listening to the sweet music in a perfect rapture.

And when Sunday came, how differently the day was spent, from any way in which he had ever spent it yet! and how happily too; like all the other days in that most happy time! There was the little church in the morning, with the green leaves fluttering at the windows; the birds singing without; and the sweet-smelling air stealing in at the low porch, and filling the homely building with its fragrance. The poor people were so neat and clean, and knelt so rev erently in prayer, that it seemed a pleasure, not a tedious duty, their assembling there together; and though the singing might be rude, it was real, and sounded more musical (to Oliver's ears at least) than any he had ever heard in church before. Then there were the walks as usual, and many calls at the clean houses of the laboring men; and at night Oliver read a chapter or two from the Bible, which he had been studying all the week, and in the performance of which duty he felt more proud and pleased than if he had been the clergyman himself.

In the morning Oliver would be afoot by six o'clock, roaming the fields, and plundering the hedges far and wide for nosegays of wild flowers, with which he would return laden home; and which it took great care and consideration to arrange, to the best advantage, for the embellishment of the breakfast-table. There was fresh groundsel, too, for Miss Maylie's birds, with which Oliver, who had been studying the subject under the able tuition of the village clerk, would decorate the cages in the most approved taste. When the birds were made all spruce and smart for the day, there was usually some little commission of charity to execute in the village; or, failing that, there was rare cricket-playing, some times, on the green; or, failing that, there was al ways something to do in the garden, or about the plants, to which Oliver (who had studied this science also, under the same master, who was a gardener by

OLIVER TWIST.

trade), applied himself with hearty good-will, until Miss Rose made her appearance: when there were a thousand commendations to be bestowed on all he had done.

So three mouths glided away; three months which, in the life of the most blessed and favored of mor tals, might have been uumingled happiness, and which, in Oliver's, were true felicity. With the pur est and most amiable generosity on one side; and the truest, warmest, soul-felt gratitude on the other; it is no wonder that, by the end of that short time, Oliver Twist had become completely domesticated

and health; and stretching forth their green arms over the thirsty ground, converted open and naked spots into choice nooks, where was a deep and pleas ant shade from which to look upon the wide pros pect, steeped in sunshine, which lay stretched be yond. The earth had donned her mantle of bright est green, and shed her richest perfumes abroad. It was the prime and vigor of the year; all things were glad aud nourishing.

Still, the same quiet life went on at the little cot tage, and the same cheerful serenity prevailed among its inmates. Oliver had long since grown stout and

' WHEN IT BECAME QUITE DAi'.K, AND THEY BKTUBNED HOME, THE YOUNG LADY WOULD SIT DOWN TO THE PIANO AND PLAY SOME
PLEASANT AIK."

with the old lady and her niece, and that the fer vent attachment of his young and sensitive heart was repaid by their pride in, and attachment to,himself.

CHAPTER XXXIII.

VHEREIN THE HAPPINESS OF OLIVER AND HIS FRIENDS EXPERIENCES A SUDDEN CHECK.

SPRING flew swiftly by, and summer came. If the village had been beautiful at first, it was now in the full glow and luxuriance of its richness. The great trees, which had looked shrunken and bare iu the earlier mouths, had now burst into strong life

healthy; but health or sickness made no difference iu his warm feelings to those about him, "though they do in the feelings of a great many people. He AMIS still the same gentle, attached, affectionate creature that he had been when pain and suffering had wasted his strength, and when he was dependent for every slight attention and comfort on those who tended him.

One beautiful night they had taken a longer walk than was customary with them; for the day had been unusually warm, and there was a brilliant moon, and a light wind had sprung up, which was unusually refreshing. Rose had been in high spir its, too, and they had walked on, in merry conver sation, uutil they had far exceeded their ordinary

A SEAL ALARM.

bounds. Mrs. Maylie beiiig fatigued, they returned more slowly home. The young lady, merely throw ing off her simple bonnet, sat down to the piano as usual. After running abstractedly over the keys for a few minutes, she fell into a low and very sol emn air; and as she played it, they heard a sound as if she were weeping.

" Rose, my dear!" said the elder lady.

Rose made no reply, but played a little quicker, as though the words had roused her from some painful thoughts.

" Rose, my love!" cried Mrs. Maylie, rising hastily, and bending over her. " What is this ? In tears! My dear child, what distresses you ?"

"Nothing, aunt; nothing," replied the young lady. "I don't know what it is; I can't describe it; but I feel—

" Not ill, my love ?" interposed Mrs. Maylie.

" No, no! Oh, not ill!" replied Rose, shuddering as though some deadly dullness were passing over her while she spoke; "I shall be better presently. Close the window, pray!"

Oliver hastened to comply with her request. The young lady, making an effort to recover her cheer fulness, strove to play some livelier tune; but her fingers dropped powerless on the keys. Covering her face with her hands, she sank upon a sofa, and gave vent to the tears which she was now unable to repress.

"My child!" said the elderly lady, folding her anus about her. " I never saw you so before."

" I would not alarm you if I could avoid it," re joined Rose; "but indeed I have tried very hard, and can not help this. I fear I am ill, aunt."

She was, indeed; for, when caudles were brought, they saw that in the very short time which had elapsed since their return home, the hue of her coun tenance had changed to a marble whiteness. Its ex pression had lost nothing of its beauty, but it was changed; and there was an anxious, haggard look about the gentle face, which it had never worn be fore. Another minute, and it was suffused with a crimson flush, and a heavy wildness came over the soft blue eye. Again this disappeared, like the shad ow thrown by a passing cloud; and she was once more deadly pale.

Oliver, who watched the old lady anxiously, ob served that she was alarmed by these appearances; and so, in truth, was he; but seeing that she affected to make light of them, he endeavored to do the same, and they so far succeeded that, when Rose was per suaded by her aunt to retire for the night, she was iu better spirits, and appeared even in better health; assuring them that she felt certain she should rise in the morning quite well.

" I hope," said Oliver, when Mrs. Maylie returned, " that nothing is the matter ? She don't look well to-night, but—"

The old lady motioned to him not to speak; and sitting herself down in a dark corner of the room, remained silent for some time. At length she said, in a trembling voice:

"I hope not, Oliver. I have been very happy with her for some years—too happy, perhaps. It may be time that I should meet with some misfor tune ; but I hope it is not this."

" What ?" inquired Oliver.

" The heavy blow," said the old lady, " of losing the dear girl who has so long been my comfort and happiness."

" Oh! God forbid!" exclaimed Oliver, hastily.

"Amen to that, my child!" said the old lady, wringing her hands.

" Surely there is no danger of any thing so dread ful f' said Oliver. " Two hours ago she was quite well."

" She is very ill now," rejoined Mrs. Maylie; " and will be worse, I am sure. My dear, dear Rose! Oh, what should I do without her ?"

She gave way to such great grief, that Oliver, suppressing his own emotion, ventured to remon strate with her, and to beg earnestly that, for the sake of the dear young lady herself, she would be more cahn.

"And consider, ma'am," said Oliver, as the tears forced themselves into his eyes, despite of his efforts to the contrary—"oh! consider how young and good she is, and what pleasure and comfort she gives to all about her. I am sure—certain—quite certain—that, for your sake, who are so good your self; and for her own; and for the sake of all she makes so happy; she will not die.. Heaven will never let her die so young."

" Hush!" said Mrs. Maylie, laying. her hand on Oliver's head. " You think like a child, poor boy. But you teach me my duty, notwithstanding. I had forgotten it for a moment, Oliver, but I hope I may be pardoned, for I am old, and have seen enough of illness and death to know the agony of separation from the objects of our love. I have seen enough, too, to know that it is not always the youngest and best who are spared to those that love them; but this should give us comfort in our sorrow; for Heav en is just; and such things teach us, impressively, that there is a brighter world than this; and that the passage to it is speedy. God's will be done! I love her; and He knows how well!"

Oliver was surprised to see that as Mrs. Maylie said these words, she checked her lamentations as though by one effort; and drawing herself up as slit-spoke, became composed and firm. He was still more astonished to find that this firmness lasted; and that, under all the care and watching which en sued, Mrs. Maylie was ever ready and collected: per forming all the duties which devolved upon her, steadily, and, to all external appearances, even cheer fully. But he was young, and did not know what strong minds are capable of, under trying circum stances. How should he, when their possessors so seldom know themselves ?

An anxious night ensued. When morning came, Mrs. Maylie's predictions were but too well verified. Rose was in the first stage of a high and dangerous fever.

" We must be active, Oliver, and not give way to useless grief," said Mrs. Maylie, laying her finger on her lip, as she looked steadily into his face; " this letter must be sent, with all possible expedition, to Mr. Losberue. It must be carried to the market-town, which is not more than four miles off by the foot-path across the fields, and thence dispatched, by an express on horseback, straight to Chertsey. The

OLIVER TWIST.

people at the inu will undertake to do this; and I can trust to you to see it done, I know."

Oliver could make no reply, but looked his anx iety to be gone at once.

" Here is another letter," said Mrs. Maylie, pausing to reflect; " but whether to send it now, or wait un til I see how Kose goes on, I scarcely know. I would not forward it unless I feared the worst."

" Is it for Chertsey, too, ma'am ?" inquired Oliver, impatient to execute his commission, and holding out his trembling hand for the letter.

" No," replied the old lady, giving it to him me chanically. Oliver glanced at it, and saw that it was directed to Harry Maylie, Esquire, at some great lord's house in the country; where, he could not make out.

" Shall it go, ma'am ?" asked Oliver, looking up, impatiently.

" I think not," replied Mrs. Maylie, taking it back. " I will Avait until to-morrow."

With these words she gave Oliver her purse, and he started off, without more delay, at the greatest speed he could muster.

Swiftly he ran across the fields, and down the lit tle lanes which sometimes divided them; now al most hidden by the high corn on either side, and now emerging on an open field, where the mowers and hay-makers were busy at their work; nor did he stop once, save now and then, for a few seconds, to recover breath, until he came, in a great heat, and covered with dust, on the little market-place of the market-town.

Here he paused and looked about for the inn. There were a white bank, and a red brewery, and a yellow town-hall; and in one corner there was a large house, with all the wood about it painted green, before which was the sign of " The George." To this he hastened, as soon as it caught his eye.

He spoke to a postboy who was dozing under the gate-way; and who, after hearing what he wanted, referred him to the hostler; who, after hearing all he had to say again, referred him to the landlord, who was a tall gentleman in a blue neckcloth, a white hat, drab breeches, and boots with tops to match, leaning against a pump by the stable-door, picking his teeth with a silver tooth-pick.

This gentleman walked with much deliberation into the bar to make out the bill, which took a long time making out; and after it was ready and paid, a horse had to be saddled, and a man to be dressed, which took up ten good minutes more. Meanwhile Oliver was in such a desperate state of impatience and anxiety, that he felt as if he could have jumped upon the horse himself, and galloped away, full tear, to the next stage. At length all was ready, and the little parcel having been handed up, with many in junctions and entreaties for its speedy delivery, the man set spurs to his horse, and rattling over the uneven paving of the market-place, was out of the town, and galloping along the turnpike-road, in a couple of minutes.

As it was something to feel certain that assist ance was sent for, and that 110 time had been lost, Oliver hurried up the inn-yard with a somewhat lighter heart. He was turning out of the gate-way when he accidentally stumbled against a tall man

wrapped in a cloak, who was at that moment com ing out of the inn door.

" Hah!" cried the man, fixing his eyes on Oliver, and suddenly recoiling. " What the devil's this ?"

" I beg your pardon, sir," said Oliver; " I was in a great hurry to get home, and didn't see you were coming."

" Death!" muttered the man to himself, glaring at the boy with his large dark eyes. "Who would have thought it! Grind him to ashes! He'd start up from a stone coffin, to come in my way!"

" I am sorry," stammered Oliver, confused by the strange man's wild look. " I hope I have not hurt you!"

" Eot you!" murmured the man, in a horrible pas sion, between his clenched teeth ; " if I had only had the courage to say the word, I might have been free of you in a night. Curses on your head, and black death on your heart, you imp! What are you doing here f'

The man shook his fist as he uttered these words incoherently. He advanced toward Oliver, as if with the intention of aiming a blow at him, but fell violently on the ground, writhing and foaming, in a fit.

Oliver gazed, for a moment, at the struggles of the madman (for such he supposed him to be), and then darted into the house for help. Having seen him safely carried into the hotel, he turned his face homeward, running as fast as he could, to make up for lost time, and recalling with a great deal of as tonishment and some fear the extraordinary behav ior of the person from whom he had just parted.

The circumstance did not dwell in his recollection long, however; for when he reached the cottage, there was enough to occupy his mind, and to drive all considerations of self completely from his memory.

Rose Maylie had rapidly grown worse ; before mid night she was delirious. A medical practitioner, who resided on the spot, was in constant attendance upon her; and after first seeing the patient, he had taken Mrs. Maylie aside, and pronounced her disor der to be one of a most alarming nature. " In fact," he said, " it would be little short of a miracle if she recovered."

How often did Oliver start from his bed that night, and stealing out, with noiseless footstep, to the stair case, listen for the slightest sound from the sick-chamber ! How often did a tremble shake his frame, and cold drops of terror start upon his brow, when a sudden trampling of feet caused him to fear that something too dreadful to think of had even then occurred! And what had been the fervency of all the prayers he had ever uttered, compared with those he poured forth now, in the agony and pas sion of his supplication for the life and health of the gentle creature who was tottering on the deep grave's verge!

Oh! the suspense, the fearful, acute suspense, of standing idly by while the life of one we dearly love is trembling in the balance! Oh! the racking thoughts that crowd upon the mind, and make the heart beat violently, and the breath come thick, by the force of the images they conjure up before it; the desperate anxiety io be doing something to relieve the pain, or lessen the danger, which we have no

FLO WEBS FOB THE SICK-CHAMJ3EB.

power to alleviate; the sinkiiig of soul and spirit, which the sad remembrance of our helplessness pro duces ; what tortures can equal these; what reflec tions or endeavors can, in the full tide and fever of the time, allay them!

Morning came; and the little cottage was lonely and still. People spoke in whispers; anxious faces appeared at the gate, from time to time; women and children went away in tears. All the livelong day, and for hours after it had grown dark, Oliver paced softly up and down the garden, raising his eyes every instant to the sick-chamber, and shuddering to see the darkened window, looking as if death lay stretched inside. Late at night Mr. Losberne ar rived. " It is hard," said the good doctor, turning away as he spoke; " so young; so much beloved; but there is very little hope."

Another morning. The sun shone brightly—as brightly as if it looked upon no misery or care; and, with every leaf and flower in full bloom about her; with life and health, and sounds and sights of joy, surrounding her on every side, the fair young crea ture lay, wasting fast. Oliver crept away to the old church-yard, and sitting down on one of the green mounds, wept and prayed for her in silence.

There was such peace and beauty in the scene; so much of brightness and mirth in the sunny land scape ; such blithesome music in the songs of the summer birds; such freedom in the rapid flight of the rook, careering overhead; so much of life and joyousness in all; that, when the boy raised his acMng eyes and looked about, the thought instinct ively occurred to him, that this was not a tune for death; that Rose could surely never die when hum bler things were all so glad and gay; that graves were for cold and cheerless winter; not for sunlight and fragrance. He almost thought that shrouds were for the old and shrunken; and that they never wrapped the young and graceful form in their ghast ly folds.

A knell from the church-bell broke harshly on these youthful thoughts. Another! Again! It was tolling for the funeral service. A group of humble mourners entered the gate, wearing white favors, for the corpse was young. They stood uncovered by a grave; and there was a mother—a mother once — among the weeping train. But the sun shone brightly, and the birds sang on.

Oliver turned homeward, thinking on the many kindnesses he had received from the young lady, and wishing that the time could come over again, that he might never cease showing her how grateful and attached he was. He had no cause for self-reproach on the score of neglect or want of thought, for he had been devoted to her service; and yet a hundred little occasions rose up before him on which he fancied he might have been more zealous and more earnest, and wished he had been. We need be careful how we deal with those about us, when every death carries to some small circle of survivors thoughts of so much omitted, and so lit tle done—of so many things forgotten, and so many more which might have been repaired! There is no remorse so deep as that which is unavailing; if we would be spared its tortures, let us remember this in time.

When he reached home Mrs. Maylie was sitting in the little parlor. Oliver's heart sank at sight of her; for she had never left the bedside of her niece, and he trembled to think what change could have driven her away. He learned that she had fallen into a deep sleep, from which she would waken, either to recovery and life, or to bid them farewell and die.

They sat, listening, and afraid to speak for hours. The uutasted meal was removed, with looks which showed that their thoughts were elsewhere, they watched the sun as he sank lower and lower, and at length cast over sky and earth those brilliant hues which herald his departure. Their quick ears caught the sound of an approaching footstep. They both involuntarily darted to the door, as Mr. Los berne entered.

" What of Eose ?" cried the old lady. " Tell me at onee! I can bear it; any thing but suspense! Oh, tell me! in the name of Heaven!"

" You must compose yourself," said the doctor, sup porting her. " Be calm, my dear ina'ain, pray."

" Let me go, in God's name! My dear child! She is dead! She is dying!"

"No!" cried the doctor, passionately. "As He is good and merciful, she will live to bless us all for years to come."

The lady fell upon her knees, and tried to fold her hands together; but the energy which had support ed her so long, fled up to Heaven with her first thanksgiving; and she sank into the MeQdly anus which were extended to receive her.

CHAPTER XXXIV.

CONTAINS SOME INTRODUCTORY PARTICULARS RELATIVE TO A YOUNG GENTLEMAN WHO NOW ARRIVES UPON THE SCENE, AND A NEW ADVENTURE WHICH HAPPENED TO OLIVER.

IT was almost too much happiness to bear. Oliver felt stunned and stupefied by the unexpected in telligence ; he could not weep, or speak, or rest. He had scarcely the power of understanding any thing that had passed, until, after a long ramble in the quiet evening air, a burst of tears came to his relief, and he seemed to awaken, all at once, to a full sense of the joyful change that had occurred, and the al most insupportable load of anguish which had been taken from his breast.

The night was fast closing in when he returned homeward, laden with flowers which he had culled, with peculiar care, for the adornment of the sick-chamber. As he walked briskly along the road, he heard behind him the noise of some vehicle, ap proaching at a furious pace. Looking round, he saw that it was a post-chaise, driven at great speed; and as the horses were galloping, and the road was nar row, he stood leaning against a gate until it should have passed him.

As it dashed on, Oliver caught a glimpse of a man in a white night-cap, whose face seemed familiar to him, although Ms view was so brief that he could not identify the person. In another second or two, the night-cap was thrust out of the chaise-window,

and a stentorian voice bellowed to the driver to stop; which he did, as soon as he could pull up his horses. Then the night-cap once again appeared, aud the same voice called Oliver by his name.

" Here!" cried the voice. " Oliver, what's the news ? Miss Rose! Master O-li-ver!"

"Is it you,Giles?" cried Oliver,running up to the chaise-door.

Giles popped out his night-cap again, preparatory to making some reply, when he was suddenly pulled back by a young gentleman who occupied the other corner of the chaise, and who eagerly demanded what was the news.

"In a word!" cried the gentleman, "better or worse ?"

"Better—much better!" replied Oliver,hastily.

The tears stood in Olivers eyes as he recalled the scene which was the beginning of so much happi ness ; and the gentleman turned his face away, and remained silent for some minutes. Oliver thought he heard him sob more than once; but he feared to interrupt him by any fresh remark—for he could well guess what his feelings were—and so stood apart, feigning to be occupied with his nosegay.

All this time Mr. Giles, with the white night-cap on, had been sitting on the steps of the chaise, sup porting an elbow on each knee, and wiping his eyes with a blue cotton pocket-handkerchief dotted with white spots. That the honest fellow had not been feigning emotion, was abundantly demonstrated by the very red eyes with which he regarded the young gentleman when he turned round and addressed him.

" LOOKING BOTTNJ, HE SAW THAT IT WAS A PORT-OHAISE, DRIVEN AT GREAT SPEED.

" Thank Heaven!" exclaimed the gentleman. " You are sure ?"

" Quite, sir," replied Oliver. "The change took place only a few hours ago; and Mr. Losberne says that all danger is at an end."

The gentleman said not another word, but, open ing the chaise-door, leaped out, and taking Oliver hurriedly by the arm, led him aside.

" You are quite certain ? There is no possibility of any mistake on your part, my boy, is there I" demanded the gentleman, in a tremulous voice. " Do not deceive me, by awakening hopes that are not to be fulfilled."

" I would not for the world, sir," replied Oliver. " Indeed you may believe me. Mr. Losberue's words were, that she would live to bless us all for many years to come. I heard him say so."

" I think you had better go on to my mother's in the chaise, Giles," said he. " I would rather walk slowly on, so as to gain a little time before I see her. You can say I am coming."

" I beg your pardon, Mr. Harry," said Giles, giving a final polish to his ruffled countenance with the handkerchief; "but if you would leave the postboy to say that, I should be very much obliged to you. It wouldn't be proper for the maids to see me in this state, sir ; I should never have any more authority with them if they did."

" Well," rejoined Harry Maylie, smiling, " you can do as you like. Let him go on with the luggage, if you wish it, and do you follow with us. Only first exchange that night-cap for some more appropriate covering, or we shall be taken for madmeu."

AX AVOWAL OF LOVE.

Mr. Giles, reminded of his unbecoming costume, snatched off and pocketed his night-cap, and substi tuted a hat, of grave and sober shape, which he took out of the chaise. This done, the postboy drove off; Giles, Mr. Maylie, and Oliver, followed at their leisure.

As they walked along, Oliver glanced from time to time with much interest and curiosity at the new comer. He seemed about tive-and-tweuty years of age, and was of the middle height; his countenance was frank and handsome, and his demeanor easy and prepossessing. Notwithstanding the difference between youth and age, he bore so strong a likeness to the old lady, that Oliver would have had no great difficulty in imagining their relationship, if he had not already spoken of her as his mother.

Mrs. Maylie was anxiously waiting to receive her sou when he reached the cottage. The meeting did not take place without great emotion oil both sides.

" Mother!" whispered the young man; " why did you not write before ?"

" I did," replied Mrs. Maylie ; " but, on reflection, I determined to keep back the letter until I had heard Mr. Losberue's opinion."

" But why," said the young man, " why run the chance of that occurring which so nearly happened ? If Rose had—I can not utter that word now—if this illness had terminated differently, how could you ever have forgiven yourself! How could I ever Lave known happiness again!"

" If that had been the case, Harry," said Mrs. May-lie, " I fear your happiness would have been effectual ly blighted, and that your arrival here, a day sooner or a day later, would have been of very, very little import."

"And who can wonder if it be so, mother?" rejoined the young man ; " or why should I say iff —it is—it is—you know it, mother—you must know it!"

" I know that she deserves the best and purest love the heart of man can offer,"said Mrs. Maylie; " I know that the devotion and affection of her na ture require no ordinary return, but one that shall be deep and lasting. If I did not feel this, and know, besides, that a changed behavior in one she loved would break her heart, I should not feel my task so difficult of performance, or have to encounter so many struggles in my own bosom, when I take what seems to me to be the strict line of duty."

" This is unkind, mother," said Harry. " Do you still suppose that I am a boy ignorant of my own mind, and mistaking the impulses of my own soul ?"

" I think, my dear sou," returned Mrs. Maylie, lay ing her hand upon his shoulder," that youth has many generous impulses which do not last; and that among them are some which, being gratified, become only the more fleeting. Above all, I think,"said the lady, fixing her eyes ou her son's face," that if an enthusiastic, ardent, and ambitious man marry a wife on whose name there is a stain, which, though it originate in no fault of hers, may be visited by ••old and sordid people upon her, and upon his chil dren also ; and, in exact proportion to his success in the world, be cast in his teeth, and made the subject of sneers against him; he may, no matter how gen erous and good his nature, one day repent of the coii-nei-tion he formed in early life. And she may have the pain of knowing that he does so."

"Mother," said the young man, impatiently, "he would be a selfish brute, unworthy alike of the name of man and of the woman you describe, who acted thus."

" You think so now, Harry," replied his mother. "And ever will!" said the young man. "The mental agony I have suffered, during the last two days, wrings from me the avowal to you of a passion which, as you well know, is not one of yesterday, nor one I have lightly formed. On Rose, sweet, gentle girl! my heart is set as firmly as ever heart of man was set on woman. I have no thought, no view, no hope in life, beyond her; and if you oppose me in this great stake, you take my peace and happiness in your hands, and cast them to the wind. Mother, think better of this and of me, and do not disre gard the happiness of which you seem to think so little."

" Harry," said Mrs. Maylie, " it is because I think so much of warm and sensitive hearts, that I would spare them from being wounded. But we have said enough, and more than enough, on this matter, just now."

" Let it rest with Rose, then," interposed Harry. " You will not press these overstrained opinions of yours so far as to throw any obstacle in my way .'"

" I will not," rejoined Mrs. Maylie; " but I would have you consider—"

" I have considered!" was the impatient reply; " mother, I have considered years and years. I have considered ever since I have been capable of serious reflection. My feelings remain unchanged, as they ever will; and why should I suffer the pain of a de lay in giving them vent, which can be productive of no earthly good? No! Before I leave this place, Rose shall hear me."

" She shall," said Mrs. Maylie. " There is something in your manner which would almost imply that she will hear me coldly, mother," said the young man.

" Not coldly," rejoined the old lady; " far from it." "How then?" urged the young man. "She has formed no other attachment ?"

" No, indeed," replied his mother; " you have, or I mistake, too strong a hold on her affections already. What I would say," resumed the old lady, stopping her son as he was about to speak, " is this. Before you stake your all on this chance—before you suffer yourself to be carried to the highest point of hope— reflect for a few moments, my dear child, on Rose's history, and consider what effect the knowledge of her doubtful birth may have on her decision; de voted as she is to us, with all the intensity of her noble mind, and with that perfect sacrifice of self which, in all matters, great or trifling, has always been her characteristic." " What do you mean ?"

"That I leave you to discover," replied Mrs. May-lie. " I must go back to her. God bless you!"

" I shall see you again to-night ?" said the young man, eagerly.

"By-aud-by," replied the lady; "when I leave Rose."

" You will tell her I am here ?" said Harry.

" Of course," replied Mrs. Maylie.

"And say how anxious I have been, and how much

OLIVER TWIST.

I have suffered, and how I long to see her. You will not refuse to do this, mother f

" No," said the old lady; " I will tell her all." Aud pressing her sou's hand affectionately, she has tened from the room.

Mr. Losberne and Oliver had remained at another end of the apartment while this hurried conversa tion was proceeding. The former now held out his hand to Harry Maylie, and hearty salutations were exchanged between them. The doctor then com municated, in reply to multifarious questions from his young friend, a precise account of his patient's situation, which was quite as consolatory and full of promise as Oliver's statement had encouraged him to hope; and to the whole of which Mr. Giles, who af fected to be busy about the luggage, listened with greedy ears.

" Have you shot any thing particular lately, Giles ?" inquired the doctor, when he had concluded.

" Nothing particular, sir," replied Mr. Giles, color ing up to the eyes.

"Nor catching any thieves, nor identifying any housebreakers ?" said the doctor.

"None at all, sir," replied Mr. Giles, with much gravity.

" Well," said the doctor, " I am sorry to hear it, because you do that sort of thing admirably. Pray how is Brittles ?"

" The boy is very well, sir," said Mr. Giles, recov ering his usual tone of patronage, " and sends his re spectful duty, sir."

" That's well," said the doctor. " Seeing you here reminds me, Mr. Giles, that on the day before that on which I was called away so hurriedly, I executed, at the request of yotir good mistress, a small com mission in your favor. Just step into this corner a moment, will you t"

Mr. Giles walked into the corner with much im portance and some wonder, and was honored with a short whispering conference with the doctor, on the termination of which he made a great many bows, and retired with steps of unusual stateliuess. The subject-matter of this conference was not disclosed in the parlor, but the kitchen was speedily enlight ened concerning it, for Mr. Giles walked straight thither, and, having called for a mug of ale, an nounced, with an air of majesty, which was highly effective, that it had pleased his mistress, in consid eration of his gallant behavior on the occasion of that attempted robbery, to deposit, in the local sav ings bank, the sum of five-aud-twenty pounds for his sole use and benefit. At this the two women-servants lifted up their hands and eyes, and supposed that Mr. Giles would begin to be quite proud now; whereuuto Mr. Giles, pulling out his shirt-frill, re plied, " No, no;" and that if they observed that he was at all haughty to his inferiors, he would thank them to tell him so. And then he made a great many other remarks, no less illustrative of his hu mility, which were received with equal favor and applause, and were, withal, as original and as much to the purpose as the remarks of great men common ly are.

Above stairs the remainder of the evening passed cheerfully away; for the doctor was in high spirits, and however fatigued or thoughtful Harry Maylie

might have been at first, he was not proof against the worthy gentleman's good-humor, which display ed itself in a great variety of sallies and professional recollections, and an abundance of small jokes, which struck Oliver as being the drollest things he had ever heard, and caused him to laugh proportionate ly, to the evident satisfaction of the doctor, who laughed immoderately at himself, and made Harry laugh almost as heartily by the very force of sympa thy. So they were as pleasant a party as, under the circumstances, they could well have been, and it was late before they retired, with light and thankful hearts, to take that rest of which, after the doubt and suspense they had recently undergone, they stood much in need.

Oliver rose next morning in better heart, and went about his usual early occupations with more hope and pleasure than he had known for many days. The birds were once more hung out to sing in their old places, and the sweetest wild flowers that could be found were once more gathered to gladden Rose with their beauty. The melancholy which had seemed to the sad eyes of the anxious boy to hang, for days past, over every object, beautiful as all were, was dispelled by magic. The dew seemed to sparkle more brightly on the green leaves, the air to rustle among them with a sweeter music, and the sky itself to look more blue and bright. Such is the influence which the condition of bur own thoughts exercises, even over the appearance of external objects. Men who look on nature and their fellow-men, and cry that all is dark and gloomy, are in the right; but the sombre colors are reflections from their own jaundiced eyes and hearts. The real hues are deli cate, and need a clearer vision.

It is worthy of remark, and Oliver did not fail to note it at the time, that his morning expeditions were no longer made alone. Harry Maylie, after the very first morning when he met Oliver coming laden home, was seized with such a passion for flowers, and displayed such a taste in their arrangement, as left his young companion far behind. If Oliver were behindhand in these respects, however, he knew where the best were to be found; and morning af ter morning they scoured the country together, and brought home the fairest that blossomed. The win dow of the young lady's chamber was opened now. for she loved to feel the rich summer air stream in and revive her with its freshness, but there always stood in water, just inside the lattice, one particular little bunch, which was made np with great care ev ery morning. Oliver could not help noticing that the withered flowers were never thrown away, al though the little vase was regularly replenished; nor could he help observing that, whenever the doc tor came into the garden, he invariably cast his eyes up to that particular corner, and nodded his head most expressively as he set forth on his morning's walk. Pending these observations, the days were flying by, and Rose was rapidly recovering.

Nor did Oliver's time hang heavily on his hands, although the young lady had not yet left her cham ber, and there were no evening walks, save now and then for a short distance with Mrs. Maylie. He ap plied himself with redoubled assiduity to the instruc tions of the white-headed old gentleman, and labored

OLIVER SLEEP-WAKIXG.

so hard that his quick progress surprised even him self. It was while he was engaged in this pursuit that he was greatly startled aud distressed by a most unexpected occurrence.

The little room in which he was accustomed to sit when busy at his books was on the ground-floor at the back of the house. It was quite a cottage-room, with a lattice-window, around which were clusters of jessamine and honeysuckle that crept over the casement and filled the place with their delicious perfume. It looked into a garden, whence a wicket-gate opened into a small paddock; all beyond was fine meadow-laud aud wood. There was no other dwelling near in that direction, and the prospect it commanded was very extensive.

One beautiful evening, when the first shades of twilight were beginning to settle upon the earth, Oliver sat at this window intent upon his books. He had been poring over them for some time, and as the day had been uncommonly sultry, and he had exerted himself a great deal, it is no disparagement to the authors, whoever they may have been, to say that gradually and by slow degrees he fell asleep.

There is a kind of sleep that steals upon us some times, which, while it holds the body prisoner, does not free the mind from a sense of things about it and enable it to ramble at its pleasure. So far as an overpowering heaviness, a prostration of strength, and an utter inability to control our thoughts or power of motion can be called sleep, this is it; and yet we have a consciousness of all that is going on about us, and, if we dream at such a time, words which are really spoken, or sounds which really ex ist at the moment, accommodate themselves with surprising readiness to our visions, until reality and imagination become so strangely blended that it is afterward almost matter of impossibility to separate the two. Nor is this the most striking phenome non incidental to such a state. It is an undoubted fact, that although our senses of touch and sight be for the time dead, yet our sleeping thoughts and the visionary scenes that pass before us, will be influ enced, and materially influenced, by the mere silent presence of some external object which may not have been near us when we closed our eyes, and of whose vicinity we have had no waking consciousness.

Oliver knew perfectly well that he was in his own little room; that his books were lying on the table before him; that the sweet air was stirring among the creeping plants outside. And yet he was asleep. Suddenly the scene changed; the air became close and confined; and he thought, with a glow of terror, that he was in the Jew's house again. There sat the hideous old man, in his accustomed corner, pointing at him, and whispering to another man, with his face averted, who sat beside him.

" Hush, my dear!" he thought he heard the Jew say ; " it is he, sure enough. Come away."

" He !" the other man seemed to answer; " could I mistake him, think you ? If a crowd of ghosts were to put themselves into his exact shape, and he stood among them, there is something that would tell me how to point him out. If you buried him fifty feet deep, aud took me across his grave, I fancy I should know, if there wasn't a mark above it, that he lay buried there!"

The man seemed to say this with such dreadful hatred, that Oliver awoke with the fear, and started up.

Good Heaven! what was that which sent the blood tingling to his heart, and deprived him of his voice, and of power to move! There—there—at the win dow—close before him—so close that he could have almost touched him before he started back, with his eyes peering into the room, and meeting his, there stood the Jew! And beside him, white with rage or fear, or both, were the scowling features of the very man who had accosted him in the inn-yard.

It was but an instant, a glance, a flash, before his eyes; and they were gone. But they had recognized him, and he them ; and their look was as firmly im pressed upon his memory as if it had been deeply carved in stone, and set before him from his birth. He stood transfixed for a moment; then, leaping from the window into the garden, called loudly for help.

CHAPTER XXXV.

CONTAINING THE UNSATISFACTORY RESULT OF OLIVER'S ADVENTURE, AND A CONVERSATION OF SOME IMPOR TANCE BETWEEN HARRY MAYLIE AND ROSE.

WHEN the inmates of the house, attracted by Oliver's cries, hurried to the spot from which they proceeded, they found him, pale and agitated, pointing in the direction of the meadows behind the house, and scarcely able to articulate the words, " The Jew! the Jew!"

Mr. Giles was at a loss to comprehend what this outcry meant; but Harry Maylie, whose perceptions were something quicker, and who had heard Oliver's history from his mother, understood it at once.

" What direction did he take ?" he asked, catching up a heavy stick which was standing in a corner.

" That," replied Oliver, pointing out the course the man had taken ; " I missed them in an instant."

" Then they are in the ditch!" said Harry. " Fol low ! And keep as near me as you can." So saying, he sprang over the hedge, and darted off with a speed which rendered it matter of exceeding difficulty for the others to keep near him.

Giles followed as well as he could, and Oliver fol lowed too; and in the course of a minute or two, Mr. Losberne, who had been out walking, and just then returned, tumbled over the hedge after them, and picking himself up with more agility than he could have been supposed to possess, struck into the same course at no contemptible speed, shouting all the while most prodigiously to know what was the mat ter.

On they all went; nor stopped they once to breathe until the leader, striking off into an angle of the field indicated by Oliver, began to search narrowly the ditch and hedge adjoining, which afforded time for the remainder of the party to come up, and for Oli ver to communicate to Mr. Losberne the circum stances that had led to so vigorous a pursuit.

The search was all in vain. There were not even the traces of recent footsteps to be seen. They stood now on the summit of a little hill commanding the open fields in every direction for three or four

OLIVER TWIST.

miles. There was the Tillage in the hollow on the left; but, in order to gain that, after pursuing the truck Oliver had pointed out, the men must have made a circuit of open ground, which it was impos sible they could have accomplished in so short a time. A thick wood skirted the* meadow-land in an other direction, but they could not have gained that covert for the same reason.

" It must have been a dream, Oliver," said Harry Maylie.

"Oh no, indeed, sir!" replied Oliver, shuddering at the very recollection of the old wretch's counte nance ; " I saw him too plainly for that. I saw them both as plainly as I see you uow."

" Who was the other f" inquired Harry and Mr. Losberne together.

" The very same man I told yon of, who came so suddenly upon me at the inn," said Oliver. "We had our eyes fixed full upon each other; and I could swear to him."

" They took this way ?" demanded Harry : " are you sure ?"

" As I am that the men were at the window," re plied Oliver, pointing down as he spoke to the hedge which divided the cottage garden from the meadow. " The tall man leaped over just there; and the Jew, running a few paces to the right, crept through that gap."

The two gentlemen watched Oliver's earnest face as he spoke, and, looking from him to each other, seemed to feel satisfied of the accuracy of what he said. Still in no direction were there any appear ances of the trampling of men in hurried flight. The grass was long, but it was trodden down nowhere, save where their own feet had crushed it. The sides aud brinks of the ditches were of damp clay; but in no one place could they discern the print of men's shoes, or the slightest mark which Avould indicate that any feet had pressed the ground for hours before.

" This is strange!" said Harry.

" Strange !" echoed the doctor. " Blathers and Duff themselves could make nothing of it!"

Notwithstanding the evidently useless nature of their search, they did not desist until the coming on of night rendered its further prosecution hopeless; and even then they gave it up with reluctance. Giles was dispatched to the different ale-houses in the village, furnished with the best description Oli ver could give of the appearance and dress of the strangers. Of these the Jew was, at all events, suf ficiently remarkable to be remembered, supposing he had been seen drinking or loitering about; but Giles returned without any intelligence calculated to dis pel or lessen the mystery.

On the next day fresh search was made, and the inquiries renewed, but with no better success. On the day following, Oliver and Mr. Maylie repaired to the market-town, in the hope of seeing or hearing something of the men there; but this effort was equally fruitless. After a few days the affair began to be forgotten, as most affairs are, when wonder, having no fresh food to support it, dies away of it self.

Meanwhile Kose was rapidly recovering. She had left her room; was able to go out; and, mixing once more with the family, carried joy into the hearts of all.

But although this happy change had a visible ef fect on the little circle, and although cheerful voices and merry laughter were once more heard in the cot tage, there was at times an unwonted restraint upon some there, even upon Rose herself, which Oliver could not fail to remark. Mrs. Maylie and her son were often closeted together for fi long time ; and more than once Rose appeared with traces of tears upon her face. After Mr. Losberne had fixed a day for his departure to Chertsey these symptoms in creased; and it became evident that something was in progress which affected the peace of the young lady, and of somebody else besides.

At length, one morning, when Rose was alone in the breakfast - parlor, Harry Maylie entered; and, with some hesitation, begged permission to speak with her for a few moments.

" A few—a very few—will suffice, Rose," said the young man, drawing his chair toward her. " What I shall have to say has already presented itself-to your mind; the most cherished hopes of my heart are not unknown to you, though from my lips you have not yet heard them stated."

Rose had been very pale from the moment of his entrance, but that might have been the effect of her recent illness. She merely bowed, and, bending over some plants that stood near, waited in silence for him to proceed.

"I — I — ought to have left here before," said Harry.

" You should, indeed," replied Rose. "Forgive me for saying so, but I wish you had."

"I was brought here by the most dreadful and agonizing of all apprehensions," said the young man : " the fear of losing the one dear being on whom my every wish and hope are fixed. You had been dy ing— trembling between earth and heaven. AVe know that when the young, the beautiful, and good are visited with sickness, their pure spirits insensibly turn toward their bright home of lasting rest; we know, Heaven help us! that the best and fairest of our kind too often fade in blooming."

There were tears in the eyes of the gentle girl as these words were spoken ; and when one fell upon the flower over which she bent, and glistened bright ly in its cup, making it more beautiful, it seemed as though the outpouring of her fresh young heart claimed kindred naturally with the loveliest things in nature.

" A creature," continued the young man, passion ately—" a creature as fair and innocent of guile as one of God's own angels, fluttered between life and death. Oh! who could hope, when the distant world to which she was akin half opened to her view, that she would return to the sorrow and ca lamity of this! Rose, Rose, to know that you were passing away like some soft shadow which a light from above casts upon the earth; to have no hope that you would be spared to those who linger here ; hardly to know a reason why you should be ; to feel that you belonged to that bright sphere whither so many of the fairest and the best have winged their early flight; and yet to pray, amidst all these con solations, that you might be restored to those who loved you—these were distractions almost too great to bear. They were mine, by day and night: and

A LOVE SCENE.

Ill

with them came such a rushing torrent of fears, and apprehensions, and selfish regrets, lest you should die, and never know how devotedly I loved you, as almost bore down sense and reason in its course. You recovered. Day by day, and almost hour by hour, some drop of health came back, and, mingling with the spent and feeble stream of life which cir culated languidly within you, swelled it again to a high and rushing tide. I have watched you change almost from death to life with eyes that turned blind with their eagerness and deep atfection. Do not tell me that you wish I had lost this; for it has softened in v heart to all mankind."

your hand, as in redemption of some old mute con tract that had been sealed between us! That time has not arrived; but here, with no fame won, and no young vision realized, I offer you the heart so long your ow r n, and stake my all upon the words with which you greet the offer."

"Your behavior has ever been kind and noble," said Rose, mastering the emotions by which she was agitated. "As you believe that I am not insensible or ungrateful, so hear my answer."

" It is, that I may endeavor to deserve you; it is, dear Rose ?"

"It is,"replied Rose, "that you must endeavor to

'A FEtf—A VEKY FEW—WILL SUFFICE, BO8E," SAID TI1E YOUNG MAN, DBAWING UI8 O11AIB TOWABJ) IIEK.

" I did not mean that," said Rose, weeping ; " I only wish you had left here, that you might have turned to high and noble pursuits again ; to pursuits well worthy of you."

" There is no pursuit more worthy of me, more worthy of the highest nature that exists, than the struggle to win such a heart as yours," said the young man, taking her hand. " Rose, my own dear Rose! For years—for years—I have loved you; hoping to win my way to fame, and then come proudly home and tell you it had been pursued only for you to share ; thinking, in my day-dreams, how I would re mind you, in that happy moment, of the many silent tokens I had given of a boy's attachment, and claim

forget me; not as your old and dearly-attached com panion, for that would wound me deeply, but as the object of your love. Look into the world; think how many hearts you would be proud to gain are there. Confide some other passion to me, if you will; I will be the truest, warmest, and most faith ful friend you have."

There was a pause, during which Rose, who had covered her face with one hand, gave free vent to her tears. Harry still retained the other.

"And your reasons, Rose," he said at length, in a low voice; " your reasons for this decision ?"

" You have a right to know them," rejoined Rose. " You can say nothing to alter my resolution. It is

OLIVER TWIST.

a duty that I must perform. I owe it alike to oth ers and to myself."

"To yourself?"

" Yes, Harry. I owe it to myself, that I, a friend less, portionless girl, with a blight upon my name, should not give your friends reason to suspect that I had sordidly yielded to your first passion, and fast ened myself, a clog, on all your hopes and projects. I owe it to you and yours, to prevent you from op posing, in the warmth of your generous nature, this great obstacle to your progress in the world."

"If your inclinations chime with your sense of duty—" Harry began.

" They do not," replied Rose, coloring deeply.

" Then you return my love ?" said Harry. " Say but that, dear Eose; say but that, and soften the bitterness of this hard disappointment!"

" If I could have done so, without doing heavy wrong to him I loved," rejoined Rose, " I could have—"

" Have received this declaration very differently," said Harry. " Do not conceal that from me, at least, Rose."

" I could," said Rose. " Stay!" she added, disen gaging her hand, "why should we prolong this pain ful interview ? Most painful to me, and yet produc tive of lasting happiness, notwithstanding; for it icill be happiness to know that I once held the high place in your regard which I now occupy, and every triumph you achieve in life will animate me with new fortitude and firmness. Farewell, Harry! As we have met to-day, we meet no more; but in oth er relations than those in which this conversation would have placed us, we may be long and happily entwined; and may every blessing that the prayers of a true and earnest heart can call down from the source of all truth and sincerity cheer and prosper you!"

"Another word, Rose," said Harry. " Your reason in your own words. From your own lips let me hear it!"

" The prospect before you," answered Rose, firmly, " is a brilliant one. All the honors to which great talents and powerful connections can help men in public life are in store for you. But those connec tions are proud; and I will neither mingle with such as may hold in scorn the mother who gave me life, nor bring disgrace or failure on the son of her who has so well supplied that mother's place. In a word," said the young lady, turning away, as her temporary firmness forsook her, "there is a stain upon my name which the world visits on innocent heads. I will carry it into no blood but my own; and the reproach shall rest alone on me."

" One word more, Rose. Dearest Rose, one more!" cried Harry, throwing himself before her. " If I had been less—less fortunate, the world would call it— if some obscure and peaceful life had been my des tiny—if I had been poor, sick, helpless—would you have turned from me then? Or has my probable advancement to riches and honor given this scruple birth?"

" Do not press me to reply," answered Rose. " The question does not arise, and never will. It is unfair, almost unkind, to urge it."

" If your answer be whai I almost dare to hope it

is," retorted Harry, " it will shed a gleam of happi ness upon my lonely way, and light the path before me. It is not an idle thing to do so much, by the ut terance of a few brief words, for one who loves you beyond all else. Oh, Rose! in the name of my ar dent and enduring attachment; in the name of all I have suffered for you, and all you doom me to under go, answer me this one qucstion!"

" Then, if your lot had been differently cast," re joined Rose; " if you had been even a little, but not so far, above me; if I could have been a help and comfort to you in any humble scene of peace and re tirement, and not a blot and drawback in ambitious and distinguished crowds, I should have been spared this trial. I have every reason to be happy, very happy, now; but then, Harry, I own I should have been happier."

Busy recollections of old hopes, cherished as a girl long ago, crowded into the mind of Rose while mak ing this avowal; but they brought tears with them, as old hopes will when they come back .withered; and they relieved her.

" I can not help this weakness, and it makes my purpose stronger," said Rose, extending her hand. " I must leave you now, indeed."

" I ask one promise," said Harry. " Once, and only once more—say within a year, but it may be much sooner—I may speak to you again on this subject for the last time."

"Not to press me to alter my right determination," replied Rose, with a melancholy smile; " it will be useless."

" No," said Harry; " to hear you repeat it, if you will—finally repeat it! I will lay at your feet what ever of station or fortune I may possess; and if you still adhere to your present resolution, will not seek, by word or act, to change it."

"Then let it be so," rejoined Rose ; "it is but one pang the more, and by that time I may be enabled to bear it better."

She extended her hand again. But the young man caught her to his bosom, and imprinting one kiss on her beautiful forehead, hurried from the room.

CHAPTER XXXVI.

IS A VERY SHORT ONE, AND MAY APPEAR OF NO GREAT IMPORTANCE IN ITS PLACE; BUT IT SHOULD BE READ NOTWITHSTANDING, AS A SEQUEL TO THE LAST, AND A KEY TO ONE THAT WILL FOLLOW WHEN ITS TIME AR RIVES.

ND so you are resolved to be my traveling coni-. panion this morning, eh ?" said the doctor, as Harry Maylie joined him and Oliver at the breakfast-table. " Why, you are not in the same mind or in tention two half hours together!"

"You will tell me a different tale one of these days," said Harry, coloring, without any perceptible reason.

" I hope I may have good cause to do so," replied Mr. Losberne; " though I confess I don't think I shall. But yesterday morning you had made up your mind, in a great hurry, to stay here, and to ac company your mother, like a dutiful sou, to the sea-

side. Before noon yon announce that you are going to do me the honor of accompanying me as far as I go, on your road to London. And at night you urge inc. with great mystery, to start before the ladies are stirring; the consequence of which is, that young Oliver here is pinned down to his breakfast, when he ought to be ranging the meadows after botanical phenomena of all kinds. Too bad, isn't it, Oliver ?"

" I should have been very sorry not to have been at home when you and Mr. Maylie went away, sir," rejoined Oliver.

" That's a fine fellow!" said the doctor; " you shall come and see me when you return. But, to speak seriously, Harry, has any communication from the great nobs produced this sudden anxiety on your part to be gone ?"

" The great nobs," replied Harry, " under which designation, I presume, you include my most stately uncle, have not communicated with me at all since I have been here; nor, at this time of the year, is it likely that any thing would occur to render necessa ry my immediate attendance among them."

" Well," said the doctor, " you are a queer fellow. But of course they will get you into Parliament at the election before Christmas, and these sudden sniffings and changes are no bad preparation for po litical life. There's something in that. Good train ing is always desirable, whether the race be for place, cup, or sweepstakes."

Harry Maylie looked as if he could have followed up this short dialogue by one or two remarks that would have staggered the doctor not a little; but he contented himself with saying, " We shall see," and pursued the subject no further. The post-chaise droA~e up to the door shortly afterward; and Giles coming in for the luggage, the good doctor bustled out, to see it packed.

" Oliver," said Harry Maylie, in a low voice," let me speak a word with you."

Oliver walked into the window-recess to which Mr. Maylie beckoned him; much surprised at the mixture of sadness and boisterous spirits which his whole behavior displayed.

" You can write well now ?" said Harry, laying his hand upon his arm.

" I hope so, sir," replied Oliver.

" I shall not be at home again, perhaps, for some time ; I wish you would write to me—say once a fortnight, every alternate Monday, to the General Post-office in London. \Vill you ?"

" Oh! certainly, sir; I shall be proud to do it," ex claimed Oliver, greatly delighted with the commis sion.

" I should like to know how—how my mother and Miss Maylie are," said the young man; "and you can fill up a sheet by telling me what walks you take, and what you talk about, and whether she— they, I mean—seem happy and quite well. You un derstand me?"

"OhT quite, sir, quite," replied Oliver.

" I would rather you did not mention it to them," said Harry, hurrying over his words; " because it might make my mother anxious to write to me ofteu-er, and it is a trouble and worry to her. Let it be a sccn-t between you and me; and mind you tell me every thing! I depend unon you." H

Oliver, quite elated and honored by a sense of his importance, faithfully promised to be secret and ex plicit in his communications. Mr. Maylie took leave of him, with many assurances of his regard and pro tection.

The doctor was in the chaise; Giles (who it had been arranged, should be left behind) held the door open in his hand, and the women-servants were in the garden, looking on. Harry cast one slight glance at the latticed window, and jumped into the car riage.

"Drive on!" he cried, "hard, fast, full gallop! Nothing short of flying will keep pace with me to day."

" Halloo!" cried the doctor, letting down the front glass in a great hurry, and shouting to the postilion; " something very short of flying will keep pace with me. Do you hear ?"

Jingling and clattering, till distance rendered its noise inaudible, and its rapid progress only percepti ble to the eye, the vehicle wound its way along the road, almost hidden in a cloud of dust: now wholly disappearing, and now becoming visible again, as in tervening objects, or the intricacies of the way, per mitted. It was not until even the dusty cloud was no longer to be seen that the gazers dispersed.

And there was one looker-on, who remained with eyes fixed upon the spot where the carriage had dis appeared long after it was many miles away; for, behind the white curtain which had shrouded her from view when Harry raised his eyes toward the window, sat Eose herself.

" He seems in high spirits and happy," she said, at length. " I feared for a time he might be otherwise. I was mistaken. I am very, very glad."

Tears are signs of gladness as well as grief; but those which coursed down Rose's face as she sat pen sively at the window, still gazing in the same direc tion, seemed to tell more of sorrow than of joy.

CHAPTER XXXVII.

IN WHICH THE READER MAY PERCEIVE A CONTRAST NOT UNCOMMON IN MATRIMONIAL CASES.

MR. BUMBLE sat in the work-house parlor, with his eyes moodily fixed on the cheerless grate, whence, as it was summer-time, no brighter gleam proceeded than the reflection of certain sickly rays of the sun, which were sent back from its cold and shining surface. A paper fly-cage dangled from the ceiling, to which he occasionally raised his eyes in gloomy thought; and, as the heedless insects hov ered round the gaudy net-work, Mr. Bumble would heave a deep sigh, while a more gloomy shadow overspread his countenance. Mr. Bumble was med itating; it might be that the insects brought to mind some painful passage in his own past life.

Nor was Mr. Bumble's gloom the only thing calcu lated to awaken a pleasing melancholy in the bosom of a spectator. There were not wanting other ap pearances, and those closely connected with his own person, which announced that a great change had taken place in the position of his affairs. The laced ccat and the cocked hat, where were they ? He still

wore knee-breeches, aiid dark cotton stockings on his nether limbs ; but they were not the breeches. The coat was wide-skirted; and in that respect like the coat, but, oh, how different! The mighty cocked hat was replaced by a modest round one. Mr. Bumble was no longer a beadle.

There are some promotions in life, which, inde pendent of the more substantial rewards they offer, acquire peculiar value and dignity from the coats and waistcoats connected with them. A field-mar shal has his uniform; a bishop his silk apron; a counselor his silk gown; a beadle his cocked hat. Strip the bishop of his apron, or the beadle of his hat and lace, what are they? Men. Mere men. Dignity, and even holiness too, sometimes, are more questions of coat and waistcoat than some people imagine.

Mr. Bumble had married Mrs. Corney, and was master of the work-house. Another beadle had come into power. On him the cocked hat, gold-laced coat, and staff had all three descended.

"And to-morrow two months it was done!" said Mr. Bumble, with a sigh. " It seems a age."

Mr. Bumble might have meant that he had con centrated a whole existence of happiness into the short space of eight weeks; but the sigh—there was a vast deal of meaning in the sigh.

" I sold myself," said Mr. Bumble, pursuing the same train of reflection, " for six tea-spoons, a pair of sugar-tongs, and a milk-pot, with a small quan tity of second-hand furniture, and twenty pound in money. I went very reasonable. Cheap, dirt cheap!"

" Cheap!" cried a shrill voice in Mr. Bumble's ear: " you would have been dear at any price; and dear enough I paid for you, Lord above knows that!"

Mr. Bumble turned, and encountered the face of his interesting consort, who, imperfectly compre hending the few words she had overheard of his complaint, had hazarded the foregoing remark at a venture.

"Mrs. Bumble, ma'am!" said Mr. Bumble, with sentimental sternness.

" Well!" cried the lady.

" Have the goodness to look at me," said Mr. Bum ble, fixing his eyes upon her. (" If she stands such a eye as that," said Mr. Bumble to himself, " she can stand any thing. It is a eye I never knew to fail with paupers. If it fails with her, my power is gone.")

Whether an exceedingly small expansion of eye be sufficient to quell paupers, who, being lightly fed, are in no very high condition, or whether the late Mrs. Corney was particularly proof against eagle glances, are matters of opinion. The matter of fact is, that the matron was in no way overpowered by Mr. Bumble's scowl, but, on the contrary, treated it with great disdain, and even raised a laugh thereat which sounded as though it were genuine.

On hearing this most unexpected sound, Mr. Bum ble looked, first incredulous, and afterward amazed. He then relapsed into his former state, nor did he rouse himself until his attention was again awakened by the voice of his partner.

"Are you going to sit snoring there all day ?" in quired Mrs. Bumble.

" I am going to sit here as long as I think proper,

ma'am," rejoined Mr. Bumble; " and although I was not snoring, I shall snore, gape, sneeze, laugh, or cry, as the humor strikes me; such being my preroga tive."

" Tour prerogative !" sneered Mrs. Bumble, with ineffable contempt.

" I said the word, ma'am," said Mr. Bumble. " The prerogative of a man is to command."

"And what's the prerogative of a woman, in the name of Goodness f' cried the relict of Mr. Corney deceased.

" To obey, ma'am," thundered Mr. Bumble. " Your late unfortunate husband should have taught it you; and then, perhaps, he might have been alive now. I wish he was, poor man!"

Mrs. Bumble seeing at a glance that the decisive moment had now arrived, and that a blow struck for the mastership on one side or other must necessarily be final and conclusive, no sooner heard this allusion to the dead and gone than she dropped into a chair, and with a loud scream that Mr. Bumble was a hard hearted brute, fell into a paroxysm of tears.

But tears were not the things to find their way to Mr. Bumble's soul; his heart was water-proof. Like washable beaver hats that improve with rain, his nerves were rendered stouter and more vigorous by showers of tears, which, being tokens of weakness, and so far tacit admissions of his own power, pleased and exalted him. He eyed his good lady with looks of great satisfaction, and begged, in an encouraging manner, that she should cry her hardest: the exer cise being looked upon by the faculty as strongly conducive to health.

" It opens the lungs, washes the countenance, ex ercises the eyes, and softens down the temper," said Mr. Bumble. " So cry away."

As he discharged himself of this pleasantry, Mr. Bumble took his hat from a peg, and putting it on, rather rakishly, on one side, as a man might who felt he had asserted his superiority in a becoming man ner, thrust his hands into his pockets, and sauntered toward the door, with much ease and waggishuess depicted in his whole appearance.

Now, Mrs. Corney that was had tried the tears, because they were less troublesome than a manual assault; but she was quite prepared to make trial of the latter mode of proceeding, as Mr. Bumble was not long in discovering.

The first proof he experienced of the fact was con veyed in a hollow sound, immediately succeeded by the sudden flying off of his hat to the opposite end of the room. This preliminary proceeding laying bare his head, the expert lady, clasping him tightly round the throat with one hand, inflicted a shower of blows (dealt with singular vigor and dexterity) upon it with the other. This done, she created a little variety by scratching his face and tearing his hair; and having, by this time, inflicted as much punishment as she deemed necessary for the offense, she pushed him over a chair, which was luckily well situated for the purpose, and defied him to talk about his prerogative again, if he dared.

" Get up!" said Mrs. Bumble, in a voice of com mand. "And take yourself away from here, unless you want me to do something desperate."

Mr. Bumble rose with a very rueful countenance,

THE MIGHTY FALLEN.

wondering much what something desperate might be. Picking up his hat, he looked toward the door.

"Are you going ?" demanded Mrs. Bumble.

" Certainly, my dear, certainly," rejoined Mr. Bum ble, making a quicker motion toward the door. " I didn't intend to—I'm going, my dear! You are so very violent, that really I—

At this instant Mi's. Bumble stepped hastily for ward to replace the carpet, which had been kicked up in the scuffle. Mr. Bumble immediately darted out of the room, without bestowing another thought on his unfinished sentence, leaving the late Mrs. Cor-iiey in full possession of the field.

Mr. Bumble was fairly taken by surprise, and fair ly beaten. He had a decided propensity for bully ing; derived no inconsiderable pleasure from the exercise of petty cruelty ; and, consequently, was (it is needless to say) a coward. This is by no means a disparagement to his character ; for many official personages, who are held in high respect and admi ration, are the victims of similar infirmities. The remark is made, indeed, rather in his favor than oth erwise, and with a view of impressing the reader with a just sense of his qualifications for office.

But the measure of his degradation was not yet full.* After making a tour of the house, and think ing, for the first time, that the poor-laws really were too hard on people; and that men who ran away from their wives, leaving them chargeable to the parish, ought, in justice, to be visited with no pun ishment at all, but rather rewarded as meritorious individuals who had suffered much; Mr. Bumble came to a room where some of the female paupers were usually employed in washing the parish linen ; whence the sound of voices in conversation now pro ceeded.

" Hem!" said Mr. Bumble, summoning up all his native dignity. " These women at least shall con tinue to respect the prerogative. Halloo! halloo there! What do you mean by this noise, you hus-sics ?"

With these words, Mr. Bumble opened the door, and walked in with a very fierce and angry manner; which was at once exchanged for a most humiliated and cowering air, as his eyes unexpectedly rested on the form of his lady wife.

" My dear," said Mr. Bumble, " I didn't know you \vere here."

" Didn't know I was here!" repeated Mrs. Bumble. " What do you do here f'

" I thought they were talking rather too much to be doing their work properly, my dear," replied Mr. Bumble, glancing distractedly at a couple of old women at the wash-tub, who were comparing notes of admiration at the work-house master's humility.

" Ton thought they were talking too much ?" said Mrs. Bumble. " What business is it of yours ?"

"Why, my dear—" urged Mr. Bumble, submis sively.

"What business is it of yours?" demanded Mrs. Bumble again.

" It's very true, you're matron here, my dear," sub mitted Mr. Bumble; " but I thought you mightn't be iu the way just then."

" I'll tell you what, Mr. Bumble," returned his lady, " we don't want any of your interference. You're a great deal too fond of poking your nose into things that don't concern you, making every body in the house laugh the moment your back is turned, and making yourself look like a fool every hour in the day. Be off; come!"

Mr. Bumble, seeing with excruciating feelings the delight of the two old paupers, who were tittering together most rapturously, hesitated for an instant. Mrs. Bumble, whose patience brooked no delay, caught up a bowl of soap-suds, and motioning him toward the door, ordered him instantly to depart, on pain of receiving the contents upon his portly person.

What could Mr. Bumble do ? He looked deject edly round, and slunk away; and, as he reached the door, the titterings of the paupers broke into a shrill chuckle of irrepressible delight. It wanted but this. He was degraded in their eyes; he had lost caste and station before the very paupers; he had fallen from all the height and pomp of beadleship to the lowest depth of the most snubbed hen-peckery.

"All in two months!" said Mr. Bumble, filled with dismal thoughts. "Two months! No more than two months ago, I was not only my own master, but every body else's, so far as the porochial work-house was concerned, and now!—"

It was too much. Mr. Bumble boxed the ears of the boy who opened the gate for him (for he had reached the portal in his reverie), and walked dis tractedly into the street.

He walked up one street, and down another, until exercise had abated the first passion of his grief; and then the revulsion of feeling made him thirsty. He passed a great many public-houses, but at length paused before one in a by-way, whose parlor, as he gathered from a hasty peep over the blinds, was de serted, save by one solitary customer. It began to rain heavily at the moment. This determined him. Mr. Bumble stepped in, and, ordering something to drink as he pas§ed the bar, entered the apartment into which he had looked from the street.

The man who was seated there was tall and dark, and wore a large cloak. He had the air of a stranger, and seemed, by a certain haggardness in his look, as well as by the dusty soils on his dress, to have trav eled some distance. He eyed Bumble askance as he entered, but scarcely deigned to nod his head in ac knowledgment of his salutation.

Mr. Bumble had quite dignity enough for two: supposing even that the stranger had been more fa miliar ; so he drank his gin-and-water in silence, and read the paper with great show of pomp and circum stance.

It so happened, however, as it will happen very often when men fall into company under such cir cumstances, that Mr. Bumble felt every now and then a powerful inducement, which he could not resist, to steal a look at the stranger; and that whenever he did so, he withdrew his eyes, in some confusion, to find that the stranger was at that moment stealing a look at him. Mr. Bumble's awkwardness was en hanced by the very remarkable expression of the stranger's eye, which was keen and bright, but shad owed by a scowl of distrust and suspicion, unlike any thing he had ever observed before, and repulsive to behold.

When they had encountered each other's glance
OLIVER TWIST.
several times in this way, the stranger, in a harsh, deep voice, broke silence.

" Were you looking for me,' ; he said, " when you peered in at the window ?"

" Not that I am aware of, unless you're Mr. — Here Mr. Bumble stopped short; for he was curious to know the stranger's name, and thought, in his im patience, he might supply the blank.

"I see you were not," said the stranger, an ex pression of quiet sarcasm playing about his mouth ; "or you would have known my name. You don't know it. I would recommend you not to ask for it."

" I meant no harm, young man," observed Mr. Bumble, majestically.

"And have done none," said the stranger.

looking keenly into Mr. Bumble's eyes as he raised them in astonishment at the question. " Don't scru ple to answer freely, man. I know you pretty well, you see."

" I suppose, a married man," replied Mr. Bumble, shading his eyes with his hand, and surveying the stranger from head to foot in evident perplexity, " is not more averse to turning an honest penny when he can, than a single one. Porochial officers are not so well paid that they can afford to refuse any little extra fee, when it comes to them in a civil and prop er manner."

The stranger smiled, and nodded his head again; as much as to say, he had not mistaken his man ; then rang the bell.

YOC LOOKING FORME," , "WHEN YOU PEERED IN AT TUR WIN

Another silence succeeded this short dialogue, which was again broken by the stranger.

" I have seen you before, I think ?" said he. " You were differently dressed at that time, and I only passed you in the street, but I should know you again. You were beadle here once, were you not ?"

" I was," said Mr. Bumble, in some surprise—" po-rochial beadle."

" Just so," rejoined the other, nodding his head. " It was in that character I saw you. What are you now ?"

" Master of the work-house," rejoined Mr. Bumble, slowly and impressively, to check any undue famil iarity the stranger might otherwise assume. " Mas ter of the work-house, young man!"

" You have the same eye to your own interest that you always had, I doubt not T" resumed the stranger.

" Fill this glass again," he said, handing Mr. Bmn-ble's empty tumbler to the landlord. "Let it be strong and hot. You like it so, I suppose ?"

" Not too strong," replied Mr. Bumble, with a deli cate cough.

" You understand what that means, landlord!" said the stranger, dryly.

The host smiled, disappeared, and shortly after ward returned with a steaming jorum, of which the first gulp brought the water into Mr. Bumble's eyes.

" Now listen to me," said the stranger, after clos ing the door and window. "I came down to this place to-day to find you out; and, by one of those chances which the devil throws in the way of his friends sometimes, you walked into the very room I was sitting in while you were uppermost in my mind.

AXD HlS. BUMBLE.

I want some information from you. I don't ask you • to give it for nothing, slight as it is. Put up that, to begin with."

As he spoke, he pushed a couple of sovereigns across the table to his companion carefully, as though unwilling that the chinking of money should be heard without. When Mr. Bumble had scrupulously ex amined the coins, to see that they were genuine, and had put them up, with much satisfaction, in his waistcoat-pocket, he went on :

" Carry your memory back—let me see—twelve years, last winter."

" It's a long time," said Mr. Bumble. " Very good. I've done it."

" The scene, the work-house."

"Good!"

" And the time, night."

" Yes."

"And the place, the crazy hole, wherever it was, in which miserable drabs brought forth the life and health so often denied to themselves—gave birth to puling children for the parish to rear; and hid their shame, rot 'em, in the grave."

" The lying-in room, I suppose ?" said Mr. Bumble, not quite following the stranger's excited descrip tion.

" Yes," said the stranger. "A boy was born there."

"A many boys," observed Mr. Bumble, shaking his head despondingly.

"A murrain on the young devils!" cried the stranger; "I speak of one; a meek-looking, pale-faced boy, who was apprenticed down here to a cof-tiu-maker—I wish he had made his coffin, and screwed his body in it—and who afterward ran away to Lon don, as it was supposed."

" Why, you mean Oliver! Young Twist!" said Mr. Bumble ; " I remember him, of course. There wasn't a obstinater young rascal—"

" It's not of him I want to hear ; I've heard enough of him," said the stranger, stopping Mr. Bumble in the outset of a tirade on the subject of poor Oliver's vices. " It's of a woman; the hag that nursed bis mother. Where is she ?"

" Where is she ?" said Mr. Bumble, whom the gin-und-water had rendered facetious. " It would be hard to tell. There's no midwifery there, which ever place she's gone to; so I suppose she's out of employment, any way."

" What do you mean ?" demanded the stranger, sternly.

" That she died last winter," rejoined Mr. Bumble.

The man looked fixedly at him when he had given this information ; and although he did not withdraw his eyes for some time afterward, his gaze gradually became vacant and abstracted, and he seemed lost in thought. For some time he appeared doubtful whether he ought to be relieved or disappointed by the intelligence; but at length he breathed more freely, and, withdrawing his eyes, observed that it was no great matter. With that he rose, as if to depart.

But Mr. Bumble was cunning enough ; and he at once saw that an opportunity was opened for the lucrative disposal of some secret in the possession of his better half. He well remembered the night of

old Sally's death, which the occurrences of that day had given him good reason to recollect, as the occa sion on which he had proposed to Mrs. Corney ; and although that lady had never confided to him the disclosure of which she had been the solitary witness, he had heard enough to know that it related to some thing that had occurred in the old woman's attend ance, as work-house nurse, upon the young mother of Oliver Twist. Hastily calling this' circumstance to mind, he informed the stranger, with an air of mystery, that one woman had been closeted with the old harridan shortly before she died; and that she could, as he had reason to believe, throw some light on the subject of his inquiry.

" How can I find her f" said the stranger, thrown off his guard ; and plainly showing that all his fears (whatever they were) were aroused afresh by the in telligence.

" Only through me," rejoined Mr. Bumble.

" When ?" cried the stranger, hastily.

" To-morrow," rejoined Bumble.

"At nine in the evening/' said the stranger, pro ducing a scrap of paper, and writing down upon it an obscure address by the water-side, in characters that betrayed his agitation; " at nine in the evening bring her to me there. I needn't tell you to be se cret. It's your interest."

With these words, he led the way to the door, after stopping to pay for the liquor that had been drunk. Shortly remarking that their roads were different, he departed, without more ceremony than an ejn-phatic repetition of the hour of appointment for the following night.

On glancing at the address, the parochial function ary observed that it contained no name. The stran ger had not gone far, so he made after him to ask it.

"What do you want?" cried the man, turning quickly round, as Bumble touched him on the arm. " Following me !"

" Only to ask a question," said the other, pointing to the scrap of paper. " What name am I to ask for ?"

"Monks!" rejoined the man; and strode hastily away.

CHAPTER XXXVin.

CONTAINING AN ACCOUNT OF WHAT PASSED BETWEEN MR. AND MRS. BUMBLE AND MR. MONKS AT THEIR NOCTUR NAL INTERVIEW.

IT was a dull, close, overcast summer evening. The clouds, which had been threatening all day. spread out in a dense and sluggish mass of vapor, already yielded large drops of rain, and seemed to presage a violent thunder-storm, when Mr. and Mrs. Bumble, turning out of the main street of the town, directed their course toward a scattered little colony of ruinous houses, distant from it some mile and a half, or thereabout, and erected on a low unwhole some swamp bordering upon the river.

They were both wrapped in old and shabby outer garments, which might', perhaps, serve the double purpose of protecting their persons from the rain and sheltering them from observation. The husband carried a lantern, from which, however, no light yet shone, and trudged on a few paces in front, as though

OLIVER TWIST.

—the way being dirty—to give his wife the benefit of treading in his heavy foot-prints. They went on in profound silence ; every now and then Mr. Bum ble relaxed his pace, and turned his head as if to make sure that Ms helpmate was following; then discovering that she was close at his heels, he mend ed his rate of walking, and proceeded, at a considera ble increase of speed, toward their place of destination.

This was far from being a place of doubtful char acter ; for it had long been known as the residence of none but low ruffians, who, under various pre tenses of living by their labor, subsisted chiefly on plunder and crime. It was a collection of mere hov els, some hastily built with loose bricks, others of old worm-eaten ship-timber, jumbled together with out any attempt at order or arrangement, and plant ed, for the most part, within a few feet of the river's bank. A few leaky boats drawn up on the mud, and made fast to the dwarf wall which skirted it; and here and there an oar or coil of rope, appeared, at first, to indicate that the inhabitants of these miser able cottages pursued some avocation on the river; but a glance at the shattered and useless condition of the articles thus displayed would have led a pass er-by, without much difficulty, to the conjecture that they were disposed there rather for the preservation of appearances than with any view to their being actually employed.

In the heart of this cluster of huts, and skirting the river, which its upper stories overhung, stood a large building, formerly used as a manufactory of some kind. It had, in its day, probably furnished employment to the inhabitants of the surrounding tenements. But it had long since gone to ruin. The rat, the worm, and the action of the damp, had weak ened and rotted the piles on which it stood; and a considerable portion of the building had already sunk down into the water; while the remainder, tottering and bending over the dark stream, seemed to wait a favorable opportunity of following its old compan ion, and involving itself in the same fate.

It was before this ruinous building that the wor thy couple paused, as the first peal of distant thun der reverberated in the air, and the rain commenced pouring violently down.

" The place should be somewhere here," said Bum ble, consulting a scrap of paper he held in his hand.

" Halloo there!" cried a voice from above.

Following the sound, Mr. Bumble raised his head, and descried a man looking out of a door, breast-high, on the second story.

" Stand still a minute," cried the voice; " I'll be with you directly." With which the head disap peared,'and the door closed.

" Is that the man ?" asked Mr. Bumble's good lady.

Mr. Bumble nodded in the affirmative.

" Then mind what I told yon," said the matron; " and be careful to say as little as you can, or you'll betray us at once."

Mr. Bumble, who had eyed the building with very rueful looks, was apparently about to express some doubts relative to the advisability of proceeding any farther with the enterprise just then, when he was prevented by the appearance of Monks, who opened a small door, near which they stood, and beckoned them inward.

" Come in!" he cried, impatiently, stamping his foot upon the ground. " Don't keep me here!"

The woman, who had hesitated at first, walked boldly in, without any other invitation. Mr. Bum ble, who was ashamed or afraid to lag behind, fol lowed ; obviously very ill at ease, and with scarcely any of that remarkable dignity which was usually his chief characteristic.

" What the devil made you stand lingering there in the wet ?" said Monks, turning round and address ing Bumble, after he had bolted the door behind them.

" We—we were only cooling ourselves," stammer ed Bumble, looking apprehensively about him.

" Cooling yourselves!" retorted Monks. " Not all the rain that ever fell, or ever will fall, will put as much of hell's fire out as a man can carry about with him. You won't cool yourselves so easily; don't think it!"

With this agreeable speech, Monks turned short upon the matron, and bent his gaze upon her, till even she, who was not easily cowed, was fain to withdraw her eyes, and turn them toward the ground.

" This is the woman, is it ?" demanded Monks.

" Hem! That is the woman," replied Mr. Bumble, mindful of his wife's caution.

" You think women never can keep secrets, I sup pose ?" said the matron, interposing, and returning, as she spoke, the searching look of Monks.

" I know they will always keep one till it's found out," said Monks.

" And what may that be ?" asked the matron.

" The loss of their own good name," replied Monks. " So, by the same rule, if a woman's a party to a se cret that might hang or transport her, I'm not afraid of her telling it to any body; not I! Do you under stand, mistress ?"

" No," rejoined the matron, slightly coloring as she spoke.

" Of course you don't!" said Monks. " How should you?"

Bestowing something half-way between a smile and a frown upon his two companions, and again beckoning them to follow him, the man hastened across the apartment, which was of considerable ex tent, but low in the roof. He was preparing to as cend a steep staircase, or rather ladder, leading to another floor of warehouses above, when a bright flash of lightning streamed down the aperture, and a peal of thunder followed, which shook the crazy building to its centre.

" Hear it!" he cried, shrinking back. " Hear it! Rolling and crashing on as if it echoed through a thousand caverns where the devils were hiding from it. I hate the sound!"

He remained silent for a few moments; and then, removing his hands suddenly from his face, showed, to the unspeakable discomposure of Mr. Bumble, that it was much distorted and discolored.

" These fits come over me, now and then," said Monks, observing his alarm; " and thunder some times brings them on. Don't mind me now; it's all over for this once."

Thus speaking, he led the way up the ladder; and hastily closing the window-shutter of the room into which it led, lowered a lantern which hung at the

MRS. BUMBLE MANAGES THE CONFERENCE.

end of a rope and pulley passed through one of the heavy beams in the ceiling; and which cast a dim light upon an old table and three chairs that were placed beneath it.

" Now," said Monks, when they had all three seat ed themselves, " the sooner we come to our business, the better for all. The woman knows what it is, does she ?"

The question was addressed to Bumble; but his wife anticipated the reply, by intimating that she was perfectly acquainted with it.

" He is right in saying that you were with this hag the night she died; and that she told you something— :

"About the mother of the boy you named," replied the matron, interrupting him. " Yes."

"The first question is, of what nature was her communication ?" said Monks.

" That's the second," observed the woman, with much deliberation. "The first is, what may the communication be worth ?"

"Who the devil can tell that, without knowing of •what kind it is ?" asked Monks.

" Nobody better than you, I am persuaded," an swered Mrs. Bumble; who did not want for spirit, as her yoke-fellow could abundantly testify.

" Humph!" said Monks significantly, and with a look of eager inquiry; " there may be money's worth to get, eh f

" Perhaps there may," was the composed reply.

" Something that was taken from her," said Monks. " Something that she wore. Something that—

" You had better bid," interrupted Mrs. Bumble. " I have heard enough, already, to assure me that you are the man I ought to talk to."

Mr. Bumble, who had not yet been admitted by his better half into any greater share of the secret than he had originally possessed, listened to this dia logue with outstretched neck and distended eyes; which he directed toward his wife and Monks, by turns, in undisguised astonishment; increased, if possible, when the latter sternly demanded what sum was required for the disclosure.

"What's it worth to you?" asked the woman, as collectedly as before.

" It may be nothing; it may be twenty pounds," replied Monks. " Speak out, and let me know which."

"Add five pounds to the sum you have named; give me five-and-twenty pounds in gold," said the woman, " and I'll tell you all I know. Not before."

" Five-and-twenty pounds!" exclaimed Monks, drawing back.

" I spoke as plainly as I could," replied Mrs. Bum ble. " It's not a large sum, either."

" Not a large sum for a paltry secret that may be nothing when it's told!" cried Monks, impatiently; "and which has been lying dead for twelve years past or more!"

" Such matters keep well, and, like good wine, oft en double their value in course of time," answered the matron, still preserving the resolute indifference she had assumed. " As to lying dead, there are those who will lie dead for twelve thousand years to come, or twelve million, for any thing you or I know, who will tell strange tales at last!"

" What if I pay it for nothing ?" asked Monks, hes itating.

" You can easily take it away again," replied the matron. " I ain but a woman, alone here, and un protected."

"Not alone, my dear, nor unprotected neither," submitted Mr. Bumble, in a voice tremulous with fear: "J am here, my dear. And besides," said Mr. Bumble, his teeth chattering as he spoke, "Mr. Monks is too much of a gentleman to attempt any violence on porochial persons. Mr. Monks is aware that I am not a young man, my dear, and also that I am a little run to seed, as I may say; but he has heerd—I say I have no doubt Mr. Monks has heerd, my dear— that I am a very determined officer, with very un common strength, if I'm once roused. I only want a little rousing; that's all."

As Mr. Bumble spoke, he made a melancholy feint of grasping his lantern with fierce determination, and plainly showed, by the alarmed expression of ev ery feature, that he did want a little rousing, and not a little, prior to making any very warlike demonstra tion—unless, indeed, against paupers, or other per son or persons trained down for the purpose.

"You are a fool," said Mrs. Bumble, in reply; "and had better hold your tongue."

" He had better have cut it out, before he came, if he can't speak in a lower tone," said Monks, grimly. " So! He's your husband, eh ?"

" He my husband!" tittered the matron, parrying the question.

" I thought as much, when you came in," rejoined Monks, marking the angry glance which the lady darted at her spouse as she spoke. ""So much the better; I have less hesitation in dealing with two people, when I find that there's only one will be tween them. I'm in earnest. See here!"

He thrust his hand into a side-pocket; and pro ducing a canvas bag, told out twenty-five sovereigns on the table, and pushed them over to the woman.

" Now," he said, " gather them up; and when this cursed peal of thunder, which I feel is coming up to break over the house-top, is gone, let's hear your story."

The thunder, which seemed in fact much nearer, and to shiver and break almost over their heads, having subsided, Monks, raising his face from the table, bent forward to listen to what the woman should say. The faces of the three nearly touched, as the two men leaned over the small table in their eagerness to hear, and the woman also leaned for ward to render her whisper audible. The sickly rays of the suspended lantern falling directly upon them, aggravated the paleness and anxiety of their countenances, which, encircled by the deepest gloom and darkness, looked ghastly in the extreme.

"When this woman,that we called old Sally,died," the matron began, " she and I were alone."

" Was there no one by ?" asked Monks, in the same hollow whisper; "no sick wretch or idiot in some other bed ? No one who could hear, and might, by possibility, understand f"

" Not a soul," replied the woman; " we were alone. / stood alone beside the body when death came over it."

"Good!" said Monks, regarding her attentively. " Go on."

"She spoke of a young creature," resumed the

OLIVER TWIST.

matron, " who had brought a child into the world some years before ; not merely in the same room, but in the same bed, in which she then lay dying."

"Ay?" said Monks, with quivering lip, and glan cing over his shoulder. " Blood! How things come about!"

"The child was the one you named to him last night," said the matron, nodding carelessly toward her husband ; " the mother this nurse had robbed."

" In life ?" asked Monks.

" In death," replied the woman, with something like a shudder. " She stole from the corpse, when it had hardly turned to one, that which the dead moth er had prayed her, with her last breath, to keep for the infant's sake."

" She sold it ?" cried Monks, with desperate eager ness ; " did she sell it ? Where ? When ? To whom ? How long before ?"

"As* she told me, with great difficulty, that she had done this," said the matron, " she fell back and died."

" Without saying more ?" cried Monks, in a voice which, from its very suppression, seemed only the more furious. " It's a lie! I'll not be played with. She said more. I'll tear the life out of you both, but I'll know what it was."

" She didn't utter another word," said the woman, to all appearance unmoved (as Mr. Bumble was very far from being) by the strange man's violence ; " but she clutched my gown violently with one hand, which was partly closed; and when I saw that she was dead, and sd removed the hand by force, I found it clasped a scrap of dirty paper."

" Which contained— " interposed Monks, stretch ing forward.

" Nothing," replied the woman; " it was a pawn broker's duplicate."

" For what ?" demanded Monks.

" In good time I'll tell you," said the woman. " I judge that she had kept the trinket for some time, iu the hope of turning it to better account, and then had pawned it; and had saved or scraped together money to pay the pawnbroker's interest year by year, and prevent its running out; so that if any thing came of it, it could still be redeemed. Nothing had come of it; and, as I.tell you, she died with the scrap of paper, all worn and tattered, in her hand. The time was out in two days; I thought something might one day come of it too, and so redeemed the pledge."

"Where is it now ?" asked Monks, quickly.

" There" replied the woman. And, as if glad to be relieved of it, she hastily threw upon the table a .small kid bag scarcely large enough for a French watch, which Monks pouncing upon, tore open with trembling hands. It contained a little gold locket, in which were two locks of hair and a plain gold wedding-ring.

" It has the word ' Agnes' engraved on the in-wide," said the woman. " There is a blank left for the surname; and then follows the date, which is within a year before the child was born. I found out that,"

" And this is all ?" said Monks, after a close and eager scrutiny of the contents of the little packet.

"All," replied the woman.

Mr. Bumble drew a long breath, as if he were glad to find that the story was over, and no mention made of taking the tive-and-twenty pounds back again; and now he toek courage to wipe off the per spiration which had been trickling over his nose un checked during the whole of the previous dialogue.

" I know nothing of the story beyond what I can guess at," said his wife, addressing Monks, after a short silence, " and I want to know nothing ; for it's safer not. But I may ask you two questions, may I F

" You may ask," said Monks, with some show of surprise; " but whether I answer or not is another question."

" — Which makes three," observed Mr. Bumble, essaying a stroke of facetiousness.

" Is that what you expected to get from me ?" de manded the matron.

" It is," replied Monks. " The other question ?"

" What you propose to do with it ? Can it be used against me ?"

" Never," rejoined Monks, " nor against me either. See here! But don't move a step forward, or your life is not worth a bulrush."

With these words, he suddenly wheeled the table aside, and pulling an iron ring in the boarding, threw back a large trap-door which opened close at Mr. Bumble's feet, and caused that gentleman to re tire several paces backward with great precipitation.

" Look down," said Monks, lowering the lantern into the gulf. " Don't fear me. I could have let you down, quietly enough, when you were seated | over it, if that had been my game."

Thus encouraged, the matron drew near to the brink; and even Mr. Bumble himself, impelled by curiosity, ventured to do the same. The turbid water, swollen by the heavy rain, was rushing rapid ly on below; and all other sounds were lost iu the noise of its plashing and eddying against the green and slimy piles. There had once been a water-mill beneath; the tide, foaming and chafing round the few rotten stakes and fragments of machinery that yet remained, seemed to dart onward, with a new impulse, when freed from the obstacles which had unavailingly attempted to stem its headlong course.

" If you flung a man's body down there, where would it be to-morrow morning ?" said Monks, swinging the lantern to and fro in the dark well.

" Twelve miles down the river, and cut to pieces besides," replied Bumble, recoiling at the thought.

Monks drew the little packet from his breast, where he had hurriedly thrust it, and tying it to a leaden weight), which had formed a part of some pulley and was lying on the floor, dropped it into the stream. It fell straight, and true as a die, clove * the water with a scarcely audible splash, and was gone.

The three, looking into each other's faces, seemed to breathe more freely.

" There!" said Monks, closing the trap-door, which fell heavily back into its former position. " If the sea ever gives up its dead, as books say it will, it will keep its gold and silver to itself, and that trash among it. We have nothing more to say, and may break up our pleasant party."

" By all means," observed Mr. Bumble, with great alacrity.

MR. SIRES AND HIS NURSE.

" You'll keep a quiet tongue in your head, will you ?" said Monks, with a threatening look. I'm not afraid of your wife."

" You may depend upon me, young man," answered Mr. Bumble, bowing himself gradually toward the ladder with excessive politeness. " On every body's account, young man; 011 my own, you know, Mr. Monks." '

" I am glad, for your sake, to hear it," remarked Monks. " Light your lantern, and get away from here as fast as you can."

It was fortunate that the conversation terminated at this point, or Mr. Bumble, who had bowed himself to within six inches of the ladder, would infallibly have pitched headlong into the room below. He lighted his lantern from that which Monks had de tached from the rope and now carried in his hand; and, making no effort to prolong the discourse, de scended in silence, followed by his wife. Monks brought up the rear, after pausing on the steps to satisfy himself that there were no other sounds to be heard than the beating of the rain without, and the rushing of the water.

They traversed the lower room slowly, and with caution, for Monks started at every shadow; and Mr. Bumble, holding his lantern a foot above the ground, walked not only with remarkable care, but with a marvelously light step for a gentleman of his h'gure, looking nervously about him fbr hidden trap doors. The gate at which they had entered was softly unfastened and opened by Monks; merely ex changing a nod with their mysterious acquaintance, the married couple emerged into the wet and dark ness outside.

They were no sooner gone than Monks, who ap peared to entertain an invincible repugnance to be ing left alone, called to a boy who had been hidden somewhere below. Bidding him go first and bear the light, he rerarued to the chamber he had just quitted.

CHAPTER XXXIX.

INTRODUCES SOME RESPECTABLE CHARACTERS WITH WHOM THE READER IS ALREADY ACQUAINTED, AND SHOWS HOW MONKS AND THE JEW LAID THEIR WORTHY HEADS TOGETHER.

ON the evening following that upon which the three worthies mentioned in the last chapter disposed of their little matter of business as therein narrated, Mr. William Sikes, awakening from a nap, drowsily growled forth an inquiry what time of night it was.

The room in which Mr. Sikes propounded this question was not one of those he had tenanted pre vious to the Chertsey expedition, although it was in the same quarter of the town, and was situated at no great distance from his former lodgings. It was not, in appearance, so desirable a habitation as his old quarters, being a mean and badly-furnished apartment, of very limited size, lighted only by one small window in the shelving roof, and abutting on a close and dirty lane. Nor were there wanting oth er indications of the good gentleman's having gone down in the world of late; for a great scarcity of

furniture, and total absence of comfort, together with the disappearance of all such small movables as spare clothes and linen, bespoke a state of ex treme poverty, while the meagre and attenuated condition of Mr. Sikss himself would have fully con firmed these symptoms, if they had stood in any need of corroboration.

The house-breaker was lying on the bed, wrapped in his white great-coat, by way of dressing-gown, and displaying a set of features in no degree improved by the cadaverous hue of illness, and the addition of a soiled night-cap, and a stiff black beard of a week's growth. The dog sat at the bedside, now eying his master with a wistful look, and now prick ing his ears and uttering a low growl as some noise in the street, or in the lower part of the house, at tracted his attention. Seated by the window, busi ly engaged in patching an old waistcoat which form ed a portion of the robber's ordinary dress, was a fe male, so pale and reduced with watching and pri vation, that there would have been considerable dif ficulty in recognizing her as the same Nancy who has already figured in this tale, but for the voice in which she replied to Mr. Sikes's question.

" Not long gone seven," said the girl. " How do you feel to-night, Bill ?"

"As weak as water," replied Mr. Sikes, with an imprecation on his eyes and limbs. "Here, lend us a hand, and let me get off this thundering bed, any how."

Illness had not improved Mr. Sikes's temper; for, as the girl raised him up and led him to a chair, he muttered various curses on her awkwardness, and struck her.

" Whining, are you?" said Sikes. "Come? don't stand sniveling there. If you can't do any thing better than that, cut off altogether. D'ye hear me ?"

"I hear you," replied the girl, turning her face-aside, and forcing a laugh. " What fancy have you got in your head now ?"

" Oh! you've thought better of it, have you ?" growled Sikes, marking the tear which trembled in her eye. "All the better for you, you have."

" WTiy, you don't mean to say you'd be hard upon me to-night, Bill," said the girl, laying her hand upon his shoulder.

" No!" cried Mr. Sikes. " Why not ?"

" Such a number of nights," said the girl, with a touch of woman's tenderness which communicated something like sweetness of tone even to her voice, " such a number of nights as I've been patient with you, nursing and caring for you, as if you'd boon a child; and this the first that I've seen you like yourself—you wouldn't have served me as you did just now, if you'd thought of that, would you? Come, come; say you wouldn't."

" Well, then," rejoined Mr. Sikes, " I wouldn't. Why, damme, now the girl's whining again!"

" It's nothing," said the girl, throwing herself into a chair. " Don't you seem to mind me. It'll soon be over."

" What'll be over ?" demanded Mr. Sikes, in a sav age votee. " What foolery are you up to now again ? Get up and bustle about, and don't come over me with your woman's nonsense."

At any other time this remonstrance, and the tone

OLIVER TWIST.

in which it was delivered, would have had the de sired effect; but the girl being really weak and ex hausted, dropped her head over the back of the chair and fainted, before Mr. Sikes could get out a few of the appropriate oaths with which, oil similar occasions, he was accustomed to garnish his threats. Not knowing very well what to do, in this uncom mon emergency—for Miss Nancy's hysterics were usually of that violent kind which the patient fights and struggles out of without much assistance—Mr. Sikes tried a little blasphemy; and finding that mode of treatment wholly ineffectual, called for as sistance.

" What's the matter here, my dear ?" said Fagin, looking in.

" Lend a hand to the girl, can't you ?" replied Sikes, impatiently. " Don't stand chattering and grinning at me!"

With an exclamation of surprise, Fagin hastened to the girl's assistance, while Mr. John Dawkins (oth erwise the Artful Dodger), who had followed his venerable friend into the room, hastily deposited on the floor a bundle with which he was laden; and, snatching a bottle from the grasp of Master Charles Bates, who came close at his heels, uncorked it in a twinkling with his teeth, and poured a portion of its contents down the patient's throat, previously •taking a taste himself, to prevent mistakes.

" Give her a whiff of fresh air with the bellows, Charley," said Mr. Dawkins, "and you slap her hands, Fagin, while Bill undoes the petticuts."

These united restoratives, administered with great energy — especially that department consigned to Master Bates, who appeared to consider his share in the proceedings a piece of unexampled pleasantry—-were not long in producing the desired effect. The girl gradually recovered her senses; and, staggering to a chair by the bedside, hid her face upon the pil low, leaving Mr. Sikes to confront the new-comers in some astonishment at their unlooked-for appearance.

" Why, what evil wind has blowed you here ?" he asked Fagin.

" No evil wind at all, my dear, for evil winds blow nobody any good; and I've brought something good with me, that you'll be glad to see. Dodger, my dear, open the bundle, and give Bill the little trifles that we spent all our money on this morning."

In compliance with Mr. Fagin's request, the Artful untied his bundle, which was of large size and form ed of an old table-cloth, and handed the articles it contained, one by one, to Charley Bates, who placed them on the table, with various encomiums on their rarity and excellence.

" Sitch a rabbit-pie, Bill!" exclaimed that young gentleman, disclosing to view a huge pasty; " sitch delicate creeturs, with sitch tender limbs, Bill, that the wery bones melt in your mouth and there's no occasion to pick 'em; half a pound of seven-and-six-penuy green, so precious strong that if you mix it with boiling water, it'll go nigh to blow the lid of the tea-pot off; a pound and a half of moist sugar that the niggers didn't work at all at, afore they got it up to sitch a pitch of goodness—oh no! Tfc'o half-quartern brans; pound of best fresh; piece of double Glo'ster; and, to wind up all, some of the richest sort you ever lushed!"

Uttering this last panegyric, Master Bates pro duced from one of his extensive pockets a full-sized wine-bottle, carefully corked, Avhile Mr. Dawkins, at the same instant, poured out a wine-glassful of raw spirits from the bottle he carried, which the invalid tossed down his throat without a moment's hesita tion.

"Ah!" said Fagin, rubbing his hands with great satisfaction. " You'll do, Bill; you'll do now."

" Do!" exclaimed Mr. Sikes; " I might have been done for twenty times over afore you'd have done any thing to help me. What do you mean by leav ing a man in this state three weeks and more, you false-hearted wagabond ?"

" Only hear him, boys!" said Fagin, shrugging his shoulders. "And us come to bring him all these beau-ti-ful things."

"The things is well enough in their way," ob served Mr. Sikes, a little soothed, as he glanced over the table; " but what have you got to say for your self, why you should leave me here down in the mouth, health, blunt, and every thing else, and take no more notice of me all this mortal time than if I was that 'ere dog ?—Drive him down, Charley!"

" I never see such a jolly dog as that!" cried Mas ter Bates, doing as he was desired. " Smelling the grub like a old lady a-going to market! He'd make his fortun on the stage, that dog would, and rewive the drayma besides."

" Hold your din!" cried Sikes, as the dog retreated under the bed, still growling angrily. " What have you got to say for yourself, you withered old fence, eh?"

"I was away from London a week and more, my dear, on a plant," replied the Jew.

"And what about the other fortnight ?" demanded Sikes. " What about the other fortnight that you've left me lying here, like a sick rat in his hole ?"

" I couldn't help it, Bill. I can*t go into a long explanation before company; but I couldn't help it, upon my honor."

" Upon your what?" growled Sikes, with excessive disgust. " Here! Cut me off a piece of that pie, one of you boys, to take the taste of that out of my mouth, or it'll choke me dead."

" Don't be out of temper, my dear," urged Fagin, submissively. " I have never forgot you, Bill, never once."

"No! I'll pound it that you han't," replied Sikes, with a bitter grin. "You've been scheming and plotting away every hour that I have laid shivering and burning here; and Bill was to do this, and Bill was to do that, and Bill was to do it, all, dirt cheap, as soon as he got well, and was quite poor enough for your work. If it hadn't been for the girl, I might have died."

"There now, Bill," remonstrated Fagin, eagerly catching at the word. "If it hadn't been for the girl! Who but poor ould Fagin was the means of your halving such a handy girl about you ?"

" He says true enough there," said Nancy, coming hastily forward. " Let him be; let him be."

Nancy's appearance gave a new turn to the con versation ; for the boys, receiving a sly wink from the wary old Jew, began to ply her with liquor, of which, however, she took very sparingly ; while Fa-

MR. CHITLING'S OPINION OF MR. CRACKIT.

gin, assuming an unusual flow of spirits, gradually brought Mr. Sikes into a better temper, by affecting to regasd his threats as a little pleasant banter, and, moreover, by laughing very heartily at one or two rough jokes, which, after repeated applications to the spirit-bottle, he condescended to make.

" It's all very well," said Mr. Sikes; " but I must have some blunt from you to-night."

" I haven't a piece of coin about me," replied the Jew.

"Then you've got lots at home," retorted Sikes; " and I must have some from there."

" Lots!" cried Fagin, holding up his hands. " I haven't so much as would—"

" I don't know how much you've got, and I dare say you hardly know yourself, as it would take a pretty long time to count it," said Sikes, "but I must have some to-night; and that's flat."

"Well, well," said Fagin, with a sigh, "I'll send the Artful round presently."

" You won't do nothing of the kind," rejoined Mr. Sikes. " The Artful's a deal too artful, and would forget to come, or lose his way, or get dodged by traps, and so be perwented, or any thing for an ex cuse, if you put him up to it. Nancy shall go to the ken and fetch it, to make all sure; and I'll lie down and have a snooze while she's gone."

After a great deal of haggling and squabbling, Fa-gin beat down the amount of the required advance from five pounds to three pounds four-and-sixpence, protesting, with many solemn asseverations, that that would only leave him eighteen-peuce to keep house with; Mr. Sikes sullenly remarking that if he couldn't get any more he must be content with that, Nancy prepared to accompany him home, while the Dodger and Master Bates put the eatables in the cupboard. The Jew then, taking leave of his affectionate friend, returned homeward, attended by Nancy and the boys: Mr. Sikes, meanwhile, flinging himself on the bed, and composing himself to sleep away the time until the young lady's return.

In due course they arrived at Fagin's abode, where they found Toby Crackit and Mr. Chitling intent upon their fifteenth game at cribbage, which it is scarcely necessary to say the latter gentleman lost, and with it, his fifteenth and last sixpence, much to the amusement of his young friends. Mr. Crackit, apparently somewhat ashamed at being found relax ing himself with a gentleman so much his inferior in station and mental endowments, yawned, and inquir ing after Sikes, took up his hat to go.

" Has nobody been, Toby ?" asked Fagin.

" Not a living leg," answered Mr. Crackit, pulling up his collar; " it's been as dull as swipes. You ought to stand something handsome, Fagin, to rec ompense me for keeping house so long. Damme, I'm as flat as a juryman ; and should have gone to sleep as fast as Newgate, if I hadn't had the good natur' to amuse this youngster. Horrid dull, I'm blessed if I ain't!"

With these and other ejaculations of the same kind, Mr. Toby Crackit swept up his winnings, and crammed them into his waistcoat .-pocket with a haughty air, as though such small pieces of silver were wholly beneath the consideration of a man of his figure; this done, he swaggered out of the room

with so much elegance and gentility, that Mr. Chit-ling, bestowing numerous admiring glances on his legs and boots till they were out of sight, assured the company that he considered his acquaintance cheap at fifteen sixpences an interview, and that he didn't value his losses the snap of his little finger.

"Wot a rum chap you are, Tom!" said Master Bates, highly amused by this declaration.

"Not a bit of it," replied Mr. Chitling. "Am I, Fagin?"

"A very clever fellow, my dear," said Fagiu, pat ting him on the shoulder, and winking to his other pupils.

"And Mr. Crackit is a heavy swell; ain't he, Fa-gin ?" asked Tom.

" No doubt at all of that, my dear."

"And it i« a creditable thing to have his acquaint ance ; ain't it, Fagin ?" pursued Tom.

"Very much so, indeed, my dear. They're only jealous, Tom, because he won't give it to them."

"Ah!" cried Tom, triumphantly, "that's where it is! He has cleaned me out. But I can go and earn some more when I like; can't I, Fagin ?"

" To be sure you can, and the sooner you go the better, Tom; so make up your loss at once, and don't lose any more time. Dodger! Charley! It's time you were on the lay. Come! It's near ten, and nothing done yet."

In obedience to this hint, the boys, nodding to Nancy, took up their hats and left the room; the Dodger and his vivacious friend indulging, as they went, in many witticisms at the expense of Mr. Chit-ling ; in whose conduct, it is but justice to say, there was nothing very conspicuous or peculiar, inasmuch as there are a great number of spirited young bloods upon town who pay a much higher price than Mr. Chitling for being seen in good society, and a great number of fine gentlemen (composing the good so ciety aforesaid) who establish their reputation upon very much the same footing as flash Toby Crackit.

" Now," said Fagin, when they had left the room, " I'll go and get you that cash, Nancy. This is only the key of a little cupboard where I keep a few odd things the boys get, my dear. I never lock up my money, for I've got none to lock up, my dear—ha! ha! ha!—none to lock up. It's a poor trade, Nancy, and no thanks; but I'm fond of seeing the young people about me, and I bear it all, I bear it all. Hush!" he said, hastily concealing the key in his breast; "who's that? Listen!"

The girl, who was sitting at the table with her arms folded, appeared in no way interested in the arrival, or to care whether the person, whoever he 'was, came or went, until the murmur of a man's voice reached her ears. The instant she caught the sound, she tore off her bonnet and shawl with the rapidity of lightning, and thrust them under the ta ble. The Jew, turning round immediately after ward, she muttered a complaint of the heat in a tone of languor that contrasted very remarkably with the extreme haste and violence of this action, which, however, had been unobserved by Fagin, who had his back toward her at the time.

"Bah!" he whispered, as though nettled by the interruption; " it's the man I expected before; he's coming down stairs. Not a word about the money

OLIVER TWIST.

while he's here, Nance. He won't stop long. Not ten minutes, my clear."

Laying his skinny forefinger upon his lip, the Jew (iu-iied a candle to the door, as a man's step was heard upon the stairs without. He reached it at the same moment as the visitor, who, coming hastily into the room, was close upon the girl before he ob served her.

It was Monks.

" Only one of my young people," said Fagin, ob-' serving that Monks drew back on beholding a stran ger. " Don't move, Nancy."

The girl drew closer to the table, and glancing at Monks with an air of careless levity, withdrew her eyes; but as he turned his toward Fagin, she stole another look, so keen and searching, and full of pur pose, that if there had been any by-stander to ob serve the change, he could hardly have believed the two looks to have proceeded from the same person.

" Any news ?" inquired Fagiu.

"Great."

"And—and—good?" asked Fagin, hesitating as though he feared to vex the other man by being too sanguine.

" Not bad, any way," replied Monks, with a smile. " I have been prompt enough this time. Let me have a word with you.".

The girl drew closer to the table, and made no of fer to leave the room, although she could see that Monks was pointing to her. The Jew, perhaps fear ing she might say something aloud about the mon ey if he endeavored to get rid of her, pointed up ward, and took Monks out of the room.

" Not that infernal hole we were in before," she could hear the man say as they went up stairs. Fa-gin laughed; and making some reply which did not reach her, seemed, by the creaking of the boards, to lead his companion to the second story.

Before the sound of their footsteps had ceased to echo through the house, the girl had slipped off her shoes; and drawing her gown loosely over her head, and muffling her arms in it, stood at the door, listen ing with breathless interest. The moment the noise ceased, she glided from the room, ascended the stairs with incredible softness and silence, and was lost in the gloom above.

The room remained deserted for a quarter of an hour or more; the girl glided back with the same unearthly tread; and, immediately afterward, the two men were heard descending. Monks went at once into the street, and the Jew crawled up stairs again for the money. When he returned, the girl was adj listing her shawl and bonnet, as if preparing to be gone.

" Why, Nance," exclaimed the Jew, starting back as he put down the candle, " how pale you are!"

" Pale!" echoed the girl, shading her eyes with her hands, as if to look steadily at him.

"Quite horrible! What have you been doing to yourself?"

'• Nothing that I know of, except sitting in this close place for I don't know how long and all," re plied the girl, carelessly. " Come! Let me get back; that's a dear."

With a sigh for every piece of money, Fagin told the amount into her hand. They parted without

more conversation, merely interchanging a "•good night,"

When the girl got into the open street, she sat down upon a door-step, and seemed for a few mo-incuts wholly bewildered, and unable to pursue her way. Suddenly she arose ; and hurrying on in a direction quite opposite to that in which Sikes was awaiting her return, quickened her pace, until it gradually resolved into a violent run. After com pletely exhausting herself, she stopped to take breath ; and, as if suddenly recollecting herself, and deploring her inability to do something she was bent upon, wrung her hands and burst into tears.

It might be that her tears relieved her, or that she felt the full hopelessness of her condition; but she turned back, and hurrying with nearly as great ra pidity in the contrary direction, partly to recover lost time, and partly to keep pace with the violent current of her own thoughts, soon reached the dwell ing where she had left the house-breaker.

If she betrayed any agitation when she presented herself to Mr. Sikes, he did not observe it; for mere ly inquiring if she had brought the money, and re ceiving a reply in the affirmative, he uttered a growl of satisfaction, and replacing his head upon the pil low, resumed the slumbers which her arrival had in terrupted.

It was fortunate for her that the possession of money occasioned him so much employment next day in the way of eating and drinking, and withal had so beneficial an effect in smoothing down the as perities of his temper, that he had neither time nor inclination to be very critical upon her behavior and deportment. That she had all the abstracted and nervous manner of one who is on the eve of some bold and hazardous step which it has required no common struggle to resolve upon, would have been obvious to the lynx-eyed Fagin, who would most probably have taken the alarm at once; but Mr. Sikes lacking the niceties of discrimination, and be ing troubled with no more subtle misgivings than those wliich resolve themselves into a dogged rough ness of behavior toward every body; and being, fur thermore, in an unusually amiable condition, as has been already observed, saw nothing unusual in her demeanor, and, indeed, troubled himself so little about her, that, had her agitation been far more per ceptible than it was, it Avould have been very un likely to have awakened his suspicions.

As that day closed in, the girl's excitement in creased ; and, when night came on, and she sat by, watching until the house-breaker should drink him self asleep, there was an unusual paleness in her cheek, and a fire iu her eye, that even Sikes observed with astonishment.

Mr. Sikes being weak from the fever, was lying in bed, taking hot water with his gin to render it less inflammatory, and had pushed his glass toward Nan cy to be replenished for the third or fourth time, when these symptoms first struck him.

" Why, burn my body!" said the man, raising him self on his hands as he stared the girl in the face. " You look like a corpse come to life again. What'.s the matter ?"

" Matter!" replied the girl. " Nothing. What do vou look at me so hard for ?"

A COMPOSING DRAUGHT.

" What foolery is this ?" demanded Sikes, grasping her by the arm aiid shaking her roughly. " What is it ? What do you mean f What are you thinking of ?"

" Of many things, Bill," replied the girl, shivering, and, as she did so, pressing her hands upon her eyes. " But, Lord! What odds in that ?"

The tone of forced gayety in which the last words were spoken seemed to produce a deeper impression on Sikes than the wild and rigid look which had preceded them.

" I tell you wot it is," said Sikes; " if you haven't caught the fever, and got it comiu' on now, there's something more than usual in the wind, and some-

" Now," said the robber, " come and sit aside of me, and put on your own face, or I'll alter it so that you won't know it again when you do want it."

The girl obeyed. Sikes, locking her hand in his, fell back upon the pillow, turning his eyes upon her face. They closed, opened again, closed once more, again opened. He shifted his position restlessly, and after dozing again and again for two or three min utes, and as often springing up with a look of terror and gazing vacantly about him, was suddenly strick en, as it were, while in the very attitude of rising, into a deep and heavy sleep. The grasp of his hand

"THEN, STOOPING SOFTLY OVEB TUB BED, SHE KISSKD

thing dangerous too. You're not a-going to— No, damme! you wouldn't do that!"

" Do what ?" asked the girl.

" There ain't," said Sikes, fixing his eyes upon her, and muttering the words to himself; "there ain't a stauncher-hearted gal going, or I'd have cut her throat three months ago. She's got the fever com ing on; that's it."

Fortifying himself with this assurance, Sikes drained the glass to the bottom, and then, with many grumbling oaths, called for his physic. The girl jumped up with great alacrity, poured it quick ly out, but with her back toward him, and held the vessel to his lips, while he drank off the contents.

relaxed, the upraised arm fell languidly by his side, and he lay like one in a profound trance.

" The laudanum has taken effect at last," murmur ed the girl, as she rose from the bedside. " I may he too late, even now."

She hastily dressed herself in her bonnet and shawl, looking fearfully round from time to time, as if, despite the sleeping draught, she expected every moment to feel the pressure of Sikes's heavy haud upon her shoulder; then, stooping softly over the bed, she kissed the robber's lips, and then opening and closing the room-door with noiseless touch, hur ried from the house.

A watchman was crying half-past nine, down a

OLIVER TWIST.

dark passage through Avhich she had to pass in gaiii-iiig the main thoroughfare.

" Has it long gone the half hour ?" asked the girl.

" It'll strike the hour in another quarter," said the man, raising his lantern to her face.

"And I can not get there in less than an hour or more," muttered Nancy, brushing swiftly past him, and gliding rapidly down the street.

Many of the shops were already closing in the back lanes and avenues through which she tracked her way in making from Spitalfields toward the West-End of London. The clock struck ten, increasing her impatience. She tore along the narrow pave ment, elbowing the passengers from side to side, and darting almost under the horses' heads; crossed crowded streets, where clusters of persons were ea gerly watching their opportunity to do the like.

` " The woman is mad!" said the people, turning to look after her as she rushed away.

When she reached the more wealthy quarter of the town, the streets were comparatively deserted; and here her headlong progress excited a still great er curiosity in the stragglers whom she hurried past.' Some quickened their pace behind, as though to see w r hither she was hastening at such an unusual rate, and a few made head upon her, and looked back, surprised at her undimiuished speed; but they fell off one by one, and when she neared her place of des tination she was alone.

It was a family hotel in a quiet but handsome street near Hyde Park. As the brilliant light of the lamp which burned before its door guided her to the spot, the clock struck eleven. She had loitered for a few paces as though irresolute, and making up her mind to advance, but the sound determined her, and she stepped into the hall. The porter's seat was va cant. She looked round with an air of incertitude, and advanced toward the stairs.

" Now, young woman !" said a smartly-dressed fe male, looking out from a door behind her, " who do you want here ?"

" A lady who is stopping in this house," answered the girl.

"A lady!" was the reply, accompanied with a scornful look. " What lady f'

" Miss Maylie," said Nancy.

The young woman, who had by this time noted her appearance, replied only by a look of virtuous disdain, and summoned a man to answer her. To him Nancy repeated her request.

" W T hat name am I to say ?" asked the waiter.

" It's of no use saying any," replied Nancy.

" Nor business ?" said the man.

" No, nor that neither," rejoined the girl. " I must see the lady."

" Come!" said the man, pushing her toward the door. " None of this. Take yourself off."

" I shall be carried out, if I go!" said the girl, vio lently ; " and I can make that a job that two of you won't like to do. Isn't there any body here," she said, looking round, " that will see a simple message carried for a poor wretch like me ?"

This appeal produced an effect on a good-tempered-faced man-cook, who with some other of the servants was looking on, and who stepped forward to interfere.

" Take it up for her, Joe, can't you ?" said this person.

" What's the good f' replied the man. " You don't suppose the young lady will see such as her, do you ?"

This allusion to Nancy's doubtful character raised a vast quantity of chaste wrath iu the bosoms of four house-maids, who remarked with great fervor that the creature was a disgrace to her sex, and strong ly advocated her being thrown ruthlessly into the kennel.

" Do what you like with me," said the girl, turn ing to the men again; " but do what I ask you first, and I ask you to give this message for God Almighty's sake."

The soft-hearted cook added his intercession, and the result was that the man who had first appeared undertook its delivery.

" What's it to bef said the man, with one foot on the stairs.

" That a young woman earnestly asks to speak to Miss Maylie alone," said Nancy; "and that if the lady will only hear the first word she has to say, she will know whether to hear her business, or to have her turned out-of-doors as an impostor."

" I say," said the man, " you're coming it strong."

" You give the message," said the girl, firmly, " and let me hear the answer."

The man ran up stairs. Nancy remained, pale and almost breathless, listening with quivering lip to the very audible expressions of scorn, of which the chaste hoiise-maids were very prolific, and of which they became still more so when the man returned and said the young woman was to walk up stairs.

" It's no good being proper in this world," said the first house-maid.

" Brass can do better than the gold what has stood the fire," said the second.

The third contented herself with wondering "what ladies was made of;" and the fourth took the first in a quartette of " Shameful!" with which the Dianas concluded.

Regardless of all this, for she had weightier mat ters at heart, Nancy followed the man, with trem bling limbs, to a small antechamber lighted by a lamp from the ceiling. Here he left her, and retired.

CHAPTER XL.

A STRANGE INTERVIEW, WHICH IS A SEQUEL TO THE LAST CHAPTER.

THE girl's life had been squandered in the streets, and among the most noisome of the stews and dens of London, but there was something of the woman's original nature left in her still; and when she heard a light step approaching the door opposite to that by which she had entered, and thought of the wide contrast which the small room would in anoth er moment contain, she felt burdened with the sense of her own deep shame, and shrunk as though she could scarcely bear the presence of her with whom she had sought this interview.

But struggling with these better feelings was pride —the vice of the lowest and most debased creatures no less than of the high and self-assured. The mis erable companion of thieves and ruffians, the fallen outcast of low haunts, the associate of the scourings

of the jails and hulks, living within the shadow of the gallows itself—even this degraded being felt too proud to betray a feeble gleam of the womanly feel ing Avhich she thought a weakness, but which alone connected her with that humanity of which her wast ing life had obliterated so many, many traces when a very child.

She raised her eyes sufficiently to observe that the figure which presented itself was that of a slight and beautiful girl; then, bending them on the ground, she tossed her head with affected carelessness as she said:

" It's a hard matter to get to see you, lady. If I had taken offense and gone away, as many would have done, you'd have been sorry for it one day, and not without reason either."

" I am very sorry if any one has behaved harshly to you," replied Rose. " Do not think of that. Tell me why you wished to see me. I am the person you inquired for."

The kind tone of this answer, the sweet voice, the gentle manner, the absence of any accent of haugh tiness or displeasure, took the girl completely by sur prise, and she burst into tears.

" Oh, lady! lady !" she said, clasping her hands pas sionately before her face, " if there was more like you, there would be fewer like me; there would—there would!"

" Sit down," said Rose, earnestly. " W you are in poverty or affliction, I shall be truly glad to relieve you, if I can—I shall, indeed. Sit down."

" Let me stand, lady," said the girl, still weeping, " and do not speak to me so kindly till you know me better. It is growing late. Is—is—that door shut f"

" Yes," said Rose, recoiling a few steps, as if to be nearer assistance in case she should require it. " Why ?"

" Because," said the girl, " I am about to put my life, and the lives of others, in your hands. I am the girl that dragged little Oliver back to old Fagiu's on the night he went out from the house in Peafconville."

" You!" said Rose Maylie.

" I, lady!" replied the girl. " I am the infamous creature you have heard of, that lives among the thieves, and that never, from the first moment I can recollect my eyes and senses opening on London streets, have known any better life, or kinder words than they have given me, so help me God! Do not mind shrinking openly from me, lady. I am young er than you would think, to look at me, but I am well used to it. The poorest women fall back as I make my way along the crowded pavement."

" What dreadful things are these!" said Rose, in voluntarily falling from her strange companion.

" Thank Heaven upon your knees, dear lady," cried the girl, "•that you had friends to care for and keep you in your childhood, and that you were never in the midst of cold and hunger, and riot and drunken ness, and—and—something worse than all—as I have been from my cradle. I may use the word, for the alley and the gutter were mine, as they will be my death-bed."

" I pity you!" said Rose, in a broken voice. " It wrings my heart to hear you!"

" Heaven bless you for your goodness!" rejoined the girl. " If you knew what I am sometimes, you

would pity me, indeed. But I have stolen away from those who would surely murder me if they knew I had been here to tell you what I have over heard. Do you know a man named Monks f

" No," said Rose.

" He knows you," replied the girl; " and knew you were here, for it was by hearing him tell the place that I found you out."

" I never heard the name," said Rose.

" Then he goes by some other among us," rejoined the girl, " which I more than thought before. Some time ago, and soon after Oliver was put into your house on the night of the robbery, I—suspecting this man—listened to a conversation held between him and Fagin in the dark. I found out, from what I heard, that Monks—the man I asked you about, you know—"

" Yes," said Rose, " I understand."

" —That Monks," pursued the girl, " had seen him accidentally with two of our boys on the day we first lost him, and had known him directly to be the same child that he was watching for, though I couldn't make out why. A bargain was struck with Fagin, that if Oliver was got back he should have a certain sum; and he was to have more for making him a thief, which this Monks wanted for some purpose of his own."

" For what purpose ?" asked Rose.

" He caught sight of my shadow on the wall as I listened, in the hope of finding out," said the girl; "and there are not many people besides me that could have got out of their way in time to escape discovery. But I did; and I saw him no more till last night."

"And what occurred then?"

" I'll tell you, lady. Last night he came again. Again they went up stairs, and I, wrapping myself up so that my shadow should not betray me, again listened at the door. The first words I heard Monks say were these: ' So the only proofs of the boy's identity lie at the bottom of the river, and the old hag that received them from the mother is rotting in her coffin.' They laughed, and talked of his suc cess in doing this; and Monks, talking on about the boy, and getting very wild, said that though he had got the young devil's money safely now, he'd rather have had it the other way; for what a game it would have been to have brought down the boast of the father's will by driving him through every jail in town, and then hauling him up for some cap ital felony which Fagin could easily manage, after having made a good profit of him beside."

" What is all this ?" said Rose.

" The truth, lady, though it comes from my lips," replied the girl. " Then, he said, with oaths com mon enough in my ears, but strange to yours, that if he could gratify his hatred by taking the boy's life without bringing his own neck in danger, he would; but, as he couldn't, he'd be upon the watch to meet him at every turn in life; and if he took advantage of his birth and history, he might harm him yet. ' In short, Fagin,' he says,' Jew as you are, you never laid such snares as I'll contrive for my young broth er Oliver."

" His brother!" exclaimed Rose.

" Those were his words," said Xancy, glancing un-

OLIVER TWIST.

easily round, as she had scarcely ceased to do since she began to speak, for a vision of Sikes haunted her perpetually. "And more. When he spoke of you and the other lady, and said it seemed contrived by Heaveu, or the devil, against him, that Oliver should come into your hands, he laughed, and said there was some comfort in that too, for how many thou sands and hundreds of thousands of pounds would you not give, if you had them, to know who your two-legged spaniel was."

" You do not mean," said Rose, turning very pale, " to tell me that this was said in earnest ?"

" He spoke in hard and angry earnest,if a man ever did," replied the girl, shaking her head. " He is an earnest man when his hatred is up. I know many who do worse things; but I'd rather listen to them all a dozen times than to that Monks once. It is growing late, and I have to reach home without sus picion of having been on such an errand as this. I must get back quickly."

" But what can I do ?" said Rose. " To what use can I turn this communication without you ? Back! Why do you wish to return to companions you paint in such terrible colors ? If you repeat this informa tion to a gentleman whom I can summon in an in stant from the next room, you can be consigned to some place of safety without half an hour's delay."

" I wish to go back," said the girl. " I must go back, because—how can I tell such things to an in nocent lady like you?—because among the men I have told you of there is one—the most desperate among them all—that I can't leave; no, not even to be saved from the life I am leading now."

" Your having interfered in this dear boy's behalf before," said Rose; " your coming here, at so great a risk, to tell me what you have heard; your manner, which convinces me of the truth of what you say; your evident contrition, and sense of shame; all lead me to believe that you might be yet reclaimed. Oh!" said the earnest girl, folding her hands as the tears coursed down her face," do not turn a deaf ear to the entreaties of one of your own sex; the first—the first, I do believe, who ever appealed to you in the voice of pity and compassion. Do hear my words, and let me save you yet for better things."

"Lady," cried the girl, sinking on her knees," dear, sweet, angel lady, you are the first that ever blessed me with such words as these; and if I had heard them years ago, they might have turned me from a life of sin and sorrow; but it is too late, it is too late!"

"It is never too late," said Rose," for penitence and atonement."

" It is!" cried the girl, writhing in the agony of her mind; " I can not leave him now! I could not be his death."

" Why should you be ?" asked Rose.

" Nothing could save him," cried the girl. " If I told others what I have told you, and led to their being taken, he would be sure to die. He is the boldest, and has been so cruel!" .

" Is it possible," cried Rose, " that for such a man as this you can resign every future hope, and the certainty of immediate rescue ? It is madness."

" I don't know what it is," answered the girl; " I only know that it is so, and not with me alone ; but

with hundreds of others as ba4 and wretched as my self. I must go back. Whether it is God's wrath for the wrong I have done, I do not know ; but I am drawn back to him, through every suffering and ill-usage ; and I should be, I believe, if I knew that I was to die by his hand at last." '

"W T hat am I to do?" said Rose. "I should not let you depart from me thus."

" You should, lady, and I know you will," rejoined the girl, rising. " You will not stop my going, be cause I have trusted in your goodness, and forced no promise from you, as I might have done."

"Of what use, then, is the communication you have made ?" said Rose. " This mystery must be in vestigated, or how will its disclosure to me benefit Oliver, whom you are anxious to serve ?"

" You must have some kind gentleman about you that will hear it as a secret and advise you what to do," rejoined the girl. t

" But where can I find you again when it is nec essary ?" asked Rose. " I do not seek to know where these dreadful people live, but where will you be walking or passing at any settled period from this time?"

" Will you promise me that you will have my se cret strictly kept, and come alone, or with the only other person that knows it, and that I shall not be watched or followed ?" asked the girl.

" I promise you solemnly," answered Rose.

" Every Sunday night from eleven until the clock strikes twelve," said the girl, without hesitation, "I will walk on London Bridge, if I am alive."

" Stay another moment," interposed Rose, as the girl moved hurriedly toward the door. " Think once again on your own condition, and the opportunity you have of escaping from it. You have a claim on me, not only as the voluntary bearer of this intelli gence, but as a woman lost almost beyond redemp tion. Will you return to this gang of robbers, and to this man, when a word can save you ? What fas cination Ik it that can take you back and make you cling to wickedness and misery? Oh! is there no chord in your heart that I can touch ? Is there nothing left to which I can appeal against this ter rible infatuation ?"

" When ladies as young, and good, and beautiful as you are," replied the girl, steadily, " give away your hearts, love will carry you all lengths—even such as you, who have home, friends, other admirers, every thing to fill them. When such as I, Avho have no certain roof but the coffin-lid, and no Mend in sickness or death but the hospital nurse, set our rot ten hearts on any man, and let him fill the place that has been a blank through all our wretched lives, who can hope to cure us ? Pity us, lady—pity us for having only one feeling of the woman left, and for having that turned by a heavy judgment from a comfort and a pride, into a new means of vi olence and suffering."

" You will," said Rose, after a pause, " take somo money from me, which may enable you to live with out dishonesty—at all events, until we meet again .'"

" Not a penny," replied the girl, waving her hand.

" Do not close your heart against all my efforts to help you," said Rose, stepping gently fonvard. " I wish to serve you, indeed."

" You would serve me best, lady," replied the girl, wringing her hands, " if you could take my life at once; for I have felt more grief to think of what I am to-night than I ever did before, and it would be something not to die in the hell in which I have lived. God bless you, sweet lady, and send as much happiness on your head as I have brought shame on mine!"

Thus speaking, and sobbing aloud, the unhappy creature turned away; while Rose Maylie, overpow ered by this extraordinary interview, which had more the resemblance of a rapid dream than an actual oc currence, sank into a chair, and endeavored to collect her wandering thoughts.

CHAPTER XLI.

CONTAINING FRESH DISCOVERIES, AND SHOWING THAT SURPRISES, LIKE MISFORTUNES, SELDOM COME ALONE.

HER situation was, indeed, one of no common tri al and difficulty. While she felt the most ea ger and burning desire to penetrate the mystery in which Oliver's history was enveloped, she could not but hold sacred the confidence which the miserable woman with whom she had just conversed had re posed in her, as a young and guileless girl. Her words and manner had touched Rose Maylie's heart; and, mingled with her love for her young charge, and scarcely less intense, in its truth and fervor, was her fond wish to win the outcast back to repentance and hope.

They purposed remaining in London only three days, prior to departing for some weeks to a distant part of the coast. It was now midnight of the first day. What course of action could she determine upon which could be adopted in eight-and-forty hours? Or how could she postpone the journey without exciting suspicion ?

Mr. Losberne was with them, and would be for the next two days; but Rose was too well acquainted with the excellent gentleman's impetuosity, and fore saw too clearly the wrath with which, in the first explosion of his indignation, he would regard the in strument of Oliver's recapture, to trust him with the secret, when her representations in the girl's behalf could be seconded by no experienced person. These were all reasons for the greatest caution and most circumspect behavior in communicating it to Mrs. Maylie, whose first impulse would infallibly be to hold a conference with the worthy doctor on the subject. As to resorting to any legal adviser, even if she had known how to do so, it was scarcely to be thought of for the same reasons. Once the thought occurred to her of seeking assistance from Harry; but this awakened the recollection of their last part ing, and it seemed unworthy of her to call him back, when — the tears rose to her eyes as she pursued this train of reflection—he might have by this time learned to forget her, and to be happier away.

Disturbed by these different reflections; inclining now to one course and then to another, and again recoiling from all, as each successive consideration presented itself to her mind, Rose passed a sleepless and anxious night. After more communing with

herself next day, she arrived at the desperate con clusion of consulting Harry.

" If it be painful to him," she thought, " to come back here, how painful it will be to me! But per haps he will not come; he may write, or he may come himself, and studiously abstain from meeting me—he did when he went away. I hardly thought he would; but it was better for us both." And here Rose dropped the pen and turned away, as though the very paper which was to be her messenger should not see her weep.

She had taken up the same pen and laid it down again fifty times, and had considered and reconsid ered the first line of her letter without writing the first word, when Oliver, who had been walking in the streets, with Mr. Giles for a body-guard, entered the room in such breathless haste and violent agita tion, as seemed to betoken some new cause of alarm.

" What makes you look so flurried ?" asked Rose, advancing to meet him.

" I hardly know how; I feel as if I should be choked," replied the boy. "Oh dear! To think that I should see him at last, and you should be able to know that I have told you all the truth!"

" I never thought you had told us any thing but the truth," said Rose, soothing him. " But what is this ?—of whom do you speak ?"

"I have seen the gentleman," replied Oliver, scarce ly able to articulate, " the gentleman who was so good to me—Mr. Brownlow, that we have so often talked about."

" Where ?" asked Rose.

" Getting out of a coach," replied Oliver, shedding tears of delight, " and going into 'a house. I didn't speak to bim —I couldn't speak to him, for he didn't see me, and I trembled so that I was not able to go up to him. But Giles asked, for me, whether he lived there, and they said he did. Look here," said Oliver, opening a scrap of paper, " here it is; here's where he lives—I'm going there directly! Oh, dear me, dear me! What shall I do when I come to see him and hear him speak again H'

With her attention not a little distracted by these and a great many other incoherent exclamations of joy, Rose read the address, which was Craven Street, in the Strand. She very soon determined upon turn ing the discovery to account.

"Quick!" she'said. "Tell them to fetch a hack ney-coach, and be ready to go with me. I will take you there directly, without a minute's loss of time. I will only tell my aunt that we are going out for an hour, and be ready as soon as you are."

Oliver needed no prompting to dispatch, and in little more than five minutes they were on their way to Craven Street. When they arrived there, Rose left Oliver in the coach, under pretense of preparing the old gentleman to receive him; and sending up her card by the servant, requested to see Mr. Brown-low on very pressing business. The servant soon re turned to beg that she would walk up stairs; and following him into an upper room, Miss. Maylie was presented to an elderly gentleman of benevolent ap pearance, in a bottle-green coat; at no great dis tance from whom was seated another old gentleman, in nankeen breeches and gaiters, who did not look particularly benevolent, and who was sitting with

OLIVER TWIST.

his bauds clasped on the top of a thick stick, and bis cbin propped thereupon.

" Dear me !" said the gentleman in the bottle-green coat, hastily rising with great politeness, " I beg your pardon, youug lady—I imagined it was some impor tunate person who—I beg you will excuse me. Be seated, pray."

" Mr. Brownlow, I believe, sir ?" said Rose, glan cing from the other gentleman to the one who had spoken.

" That is my name," said the old gentleman. " This is my friend, Mr. Griinwig. Grim wig, will you leave us for a few minutes ?"

" I believe," interposed Miss Maylie, " that at this period of our interview I need not give that gentle man the trouble of going away. If I am correctly informed, he is cognizant of the business on which I wish to speak to you."

Mr Brownlow inclined his head. Mr. Grimwig, who had made one very stiff bow, and risen from his chair, made another very stiff bow, and dropped into it again.

" I shall surprise you very much, I have no doubt," said Rose,, naturally embarrassed; " but you once showed great benevolence and goodness to a very dear young Mend of mine, and I am sure you will take an interest in hearing of him again."

" Indeed!" said Mr. Brownlow.

" Oliver Twist you knew him as," replied Rose.

The words no sooner escaped her lips, than Mr. Grimwig, who had been affecting to dip into a large book that lay on the table, upset it with a great crash, and falling back in his chair, discharged from his features every expression but one of unmitigated wonder, and indulged in a prolonged and vacant stare; then, as if ashamed of having betrayed so much emotion, he jerked himself, as it were, by a convulsion into his former attitude, and looking out straight before him, emitted a long deep whistle, which seemed at last not to be discharged on empty air, but to die away in the iunermost recesses of his stomach.

Mr. Brownlow was no less surprised, although his astonishment was not expressed in the same eccen tric manner. He drew his chair nearer to Miss May-lie's, and said,

" Do me the favor, my dear young lady, to leave entirely out of the question that gooduess and benev olence of which you speak, and of which nobody else knows any thing ; and if you have it in your power to produce any evidence which will alter the unfa vorable opinion I was once induced to entertain of that poor child, in Heaven's name put me in posses sion of it."

" A bad one! I'll eat my head if he is not a bad one!" growled Mr. Grimwig, speaking by some ven-triloquial power, without moving a muscle of his face.

" He is a child of a noble nature and a warm heart," said Rose, coloring; "and that Power which has thought fit to try him beyond his years has planted in his breast affections and feelings which would do honor to many who have numbered his days six times over."

" I'm only sixty-one," said Mr. Grimwig, with the same rigid face. "And, as the devil's in it if this

Oliver is not twelve years old at least, I don't see the application of that remark."

" Do not heed my friend, Miss Maylie," said Mr. Brownlow ; "he does not mean Avhafc he says."

" Yes he does," growled Mr. Grimwig.

" No, he does not," said Mr. Browulow, obviously rising in wrath as he spoke.

" He'll eat his head, if he doesn't," growled Mr. Grimwig.

" He would deserve to have it knocked off, if he does," said Mr. Brownlow.

"And he'd uncommonly like to see any man offer to do it," responded Mr. Grimwig, knocking his stick upon the floor.

Having gone thus far, the two old gentlemen sev erally took snuff, and afterward shook hands, accord ing to their invariable custom.

" Now, Miss Maylie," said Mr. Brownlow, " to return to the subject in which your humanity is so much in terested. Will you let me know what intelligence you have of this poor child; allowing me to premise that I exhausted every means in my power of dis covering him, and that since I have been absent from this country, my first impression that he had imposed upon me, and had been persuaded by his former associates to rob me, has been considerably shaken."

Rose, who had had time to collect her thoughts, at once related, in a few natural words, all that had befallen Oliver since he left Mr. Brownlow's house ; reserving Nancy's information for that gentleman's private ear, and concluding with the assurance that his only sorrow for some months past had been the not being able to meet with his former benefactor and friend.

" Thank God!" said the old gentleman. " This is great happiness to me, great happiness. But you have not told me where he is now, Miss Maylie. You must pardon my finding fault with you—but why not have brought him ?"

"He is waiting in a coach at the door,"replied Rose.

"At this door!" cried the old gentleman. With which he hurried out of the room, down the stairs, up the coach-steps, and into the coach, without an other word.

When the room-door closed behind him, Mr. Grim-wig lifted up his head, and converting one of the hind legs of his chair into a pivot, described three distinct circles with the assistance of his stick and the table, sitting in it all the time. After perform ing this evolution, he rose and limped as fast as he could up and down the room at least a dozen times, and then stopping suddenly before Rose, kissed her without the slightest preface.

" Hush!" he said, as the young lady rose in some alarm at this unusual proceeding. " Don't be afraid. I'm old enough to be your grandfather. You're a sweet girl. I like you. Here they are!"

In fact, as he threw himself at one dexterous dive into his former seat, Mr. Brownlow returned, accom panied by Oliver, whom Mr. Grimwig received very graciously; and if the gratification of that moment had been the only reward for all her anxiety and can-in Oliver's behalf, Rose Maylie would have been well repaid.

"There is somebody else who should uot be for gotten, by-the-bye," said Mr. Brownlow, riiiging the bell. " Seud Mrs. Bed win here, if you please."

The old housekeeper auswered the summons with all dispatch; and dropping a courtesy at the door, waited for orders.

" Why, you get blinder every day, Bedwin," said Mr. Brownlow, rather testily.

" Well, that I do, sir," replied the old lady. " Peo ple's eyes, at my time of life, don't improve with age, sir."

" I could have told you that," rejoined Mr. Brown-low ; " but put on your glasses, and see if you can't find out what you were wanted for, will you f'

The old lady began to rummage in her pocket for her spectacles. But Oliver's patience was not proof against this new trial; and yielding to his first im pulse, he sprang into her arms.

" God be good to me!" cried the old lady, embra cing him; " it is my innocent boy!"

" My dear old nurse!" cried Oliver.

" He would come back—I knew he would," said the old lady, holding him in her arms. " How well he looks, and how like a gentleman's son he is dressed again! Where have you been this long, long while ? Ah! the same sweet face, but not so pale; the same soft eye, but not so sad. I have never forgotten them or his quiet smile, but have seen them every day, side by side with those of my own dear children, (lead and gone since I was a lightsome young creature." Euu-uiiig on thus, and now holding Oliver from her to mark how he had grown, now clasping him to her and passing her fingers fondly through his hair, the good soul laughed and wept upon his neck by turns.

Leaving her and Oliver to compare notes at lei sure, Mr. Brownlow led the way into another room, and there heard from' Eose a full narration of her interview with Nancy, which occasioned him no lit tle surprise and perplexity. Rose also explained her reasons for not confiding in her friend Mr. Los-berne in the first instance. The old gentleman con sidered that she had acted prudently, and readily un dertook to hold solemn conference with the worthy doctor himself. To afford him an early opportunity for the execution of this design, it was arranged that he should call at the hotel at eight o'clock that even ing, and that in the mean time Mrs. Maylie should be cautiously informed of all that had occurred. These preliminaries adjusted, Eose and Oliver returned home.

Eose had by no means overrated the measure of the good doctor's wrath. Nancy's history was no sooner unfolded to him, than he poured forth a shower of mingled threats and execrations, threat ened to make her the first victim of the combined in genuity of Messrs. Blathers and Duff, and actually put on his hat preparatory to sallying forth to ob tain the assistance of those worthies. And doubt less he would, in this first outbreak, have carried the intention into effect without a moment's considera tion of the consequences, if he had not been restrain ed in part by corresponding violence on the" side of Mr. Brownlow, who was himself of an irascible tem perament, and partly by such arguments and repre sentations as seemed best calculated to dissuade him from Ms hot-brained purpose.

" Then what the devil is to be done ?" said the im petuous doctor, when they had rejoined the two la dies. " Are we to pass a vote of thanks to all these vagabonds, male and female, and beg them to accept a hundred pounds or so apiece, as a trifling mark of our esteem, and some slight acknowledgment of their kindness to Oliver ?"

" Not exactly that," rejoined Mr. Brownlow, laugh ing, " but we must proceed gently and with great care."

"Gentleness and care!" exclaimed the doctor. " I'd send them, one and all, to—"

" Never mind where," interposed Mr. Brownlow. " But reflect whether sending them anywhere is like ly to attain the object we have in view."

" What object ?" asked the doctor.

" Simply the discovery of Oliver's parentage, and regaining for him the inheritance of which, if this stcry be true, he has been fraudulently deprived."

" Ah!" said Mr. Losberue, cooling himself with his pocket-handkerchief; "I almost forgot that."

" You see," pursued Mr. Brownlow, " placing this poor girl entirely out of the question, and supposing it were possible to bring these scoundrels to justice without compromising her safety, what good should we bring about ?"

" Hanging a few of them, at least, in all probabil ity," suggested the doctor, "and transporting the rest."

" Very good," replied Mr.Brownlow, smiling ; "but no doubt they will bring that about for themselves in the fullness of time; and if we step in to forestall them, it seems to me that we shall be performing a very Quixotic act, in direct opposition to our own in terest—or at least to Oliver's, which is the same thing."

" How ?" inquired the doctor.

" Thus. It is quite clear that we shall have ex treme difficulty in getting to the bottom of this mys tery, unless we can bring this man, Monks, upon his knees. That can only be done by stratagem, and by catching him when he is not surrounded by these people. *For, suppose he were apprehended, we have no proof against him. He is not even (so far as we know, or as the facts appear to us) concerned with the gang in any of their robberies. If he were not discharged, it is very unlikely that he could receive any further punishment than being committed to prison as a rogue and vagabond; and of course ever afterward his mouth would be so obstinately closed that he might as well, for our purposes, be deaf, dumb, blind, and an idiot."

" Then," said the doctor, impetuously, " I put it to you again, whether you think it reasonable that this promise to the girl should be considered binding; a promise made with the best and kindest intentions, but really—

" Do not discuss the point, my dear young lady, pray," said Mr. Brownlow, interrupting Eose as she was about to speak. " The promise shall be kept. I don't think it will, in the slightest degree, interfere with our proceedings. But before we can resolve upon any precise course of action, it will be necessa ry to see the girl, to ascertain from her whether she will point out this Monks, on the understanding that he is to be dealt with by us, and not by the law; or,

if she will not or can not do that, to procure from her such an account of his haunts and description of his person as will enable us to identify him. She can not he seen until next Sunday night; this is Tuesday. I would suggest that in the mean time we remain perfectly quiet, and keep these matters secret even from Oliver himself."

Although Mr. Losherne received with many wry faces a proposal involving a delay of five whole days, he was fain to admit that no better course occurred to him just then; and as both Rose and Mrs. May lie sided very strongly with Mr. Brownlow, that gentle man's proposition was carried unanimously.

" I should like," he said, " to call in the aid of my friend Grimwig. He is a strange creature, but a shrewd one, and might prove of material assistance to us; I should say that he was bred a lawyer, and quitted the Bar in disgust because he had only one brief and a motion of course, in twenty years, though whether that is a recommendation or not, you must determine for yourselves."

" I have no objection to your calling in your friend if I may call in mine," said the doctor.

" We must put it to the vote," replied Mr. Brown-low, " who may he be ?"

" That lady's son, and this young lady's—very old friend," said the doctor, motioning toward Mrs. May-lie, and concluding with an expressive glance at her niece.

Eose blushed deeply, but she did not make any audible objection to this motion (possibly she felt in a hopeless minority); and Harry Maylie and Mr. Grim-wig were accordingly added to the committee.

" We stay in town, of course," said Mrs. Maylie, "while there remains the slightest prospect of pros ecuting this inquiry with a chance of success. I will spare neither trouble nor expense in behalf of the ob ject in which we are all so deeply interested, and I am content to remain here, if it be for twelve mouths, so long as you assure me that any hope remains."

"Good!" rejoined Mr. Brownlow. "And as I see on the faces about me a disposition to inquire how it happened that I was not in the way to corroborate Oliver's tale, and had so suddenly left the kingdom, let me stipulate that I shall be asked no questions until such time as I may deem it expedient to fore stall them by telling my own story. Believe me, I make this request with good reason, for I might oth erwise excite hopes destined never to be realized, and only increase difficulties and disappointments already quite numerous enough. Come! Supper has been announced, and young Oliver, who is all alone in the next room, will have begun to think by this time that we have wearied of his company, and entered into some dark conspiracy to thrust him forth upon the world."

With these words, the old gentleman gave his hand to Mrs. Maylie, and escorted her into the supper-room. Mr. Losberne followed, leading Rose, and the council was, for the present, effectually broken up.

CHAPTER XLII.

AN OLD ACQUAINTANCE OF OLIVER'S, EXHIBITING DE CIDED MAKKS OF GENIUS, BECOMES A PUBLIC CHARAC TER IN THE METROPOLIS.

TTPON the night when Nancy, having lulled Mr. l_J Sikes to sleep, hurried on her self-imposed mis sion to Rose Maylie, there advanced toward London by the Great North Road two persons, upon whom it is expedient that this history should bestow some at tention.

They were a man and woman; or perhaps they would be better described as a male and female : for the former was one of those long-limbed, knock-kneed, shambling, bony people, to whom it is diffi cult to assign any precise age—looking as they do, when they are yet boys, like undergrown men, and when they are almost men, like overgrown boys. The woman was young, but of a robust and hardy make, as she need have been to bear the weight of the heavy bundle which was strapped to her back. Her companion was not iucumbered with much lug-gage, as there merely dangled from a stick which he carried over his shoulder a small parcel wrapped in a common handkerchief, and apparently light enough. This circumstance, added to the length of his legs, which were of unusual extent, enabled him with much ease to keep some half dozen paces in advance of his companion, to whom he occasionally turned with an impatient jerk of the head, as if reproaching her tardiness, and urging her to greater exertion.

Thus they had toiled along the dusty road, taking little heed of any object within sight, save when they stepped aside to allow a wider passage for the mail-coaches which were whirling out of town, un til they passed through Highgate archway; when the foremost traveler stopped and called impatiently to his companion.

" Come on, can't yer ? What a lazybones yer are, Charlotte!"

" It's a heavy load, I can tell you," said the female, coming up, almost breathless with fatigue.

"Heavy! What are yer talking about? What are yer made for ?" rejoined the male traveler, chang ing his own little bundle as he spoke, to the other shoulder. " Oh, there yer are, resting again! Well, if yer ain't enough to tire any body's patience out, I don't know what is!"

" Is it much farther ?" asked the woman, resting herself against a bank, and looking up with the per spiration streaming from her face.

" Much farther! Yer as good as there," said the long-legged tramper, pointing out before him. " Look there! Those are the lights of London."

" They're a good two mile off, at least," said the woman, despondingly.

"Never mind whether they're two mile off, or twenty," said Noah Claypole, for he it was; "but get up and come on, or I'll kick yer, and so I give yer notice."

As Noah's red nose grew redder with anger, and as he crossed the road while speaking, as if fully prepared to put his threat into execution, the wom an rose without any further remark, and trudged on ward by his side.

" Where do you mean to stop for the night, Noah ?"

she asked, after they had walked a few hundred yards.

" How should I know ?" replied Noah, whose tem per had been considerably impaired by walking.

" Near, I hope," said Charlotte.

" No, not near," replied Mr. Claypole. " There ! Not near; so don't think it."

"Why not?"

" When I tell yer that I don't mean to do a thing, that's enough, without any why or because either," replied Mr. Claypole, with dignity.

" Well, you needn't be so cross," said his com panion.

"A pretty thing it would be, wouldn't it, to go and stop at the very first public-house outside the town, so that Sowerberry, if he come up after us, might

" I took it for you, Noah, dear," rejoined Charlotte.

" Did I keep it ?" asked Mr. Claypole.

"No; you trusted in me, and let me carry it, like a dear, and so you are," said the lady, chucking him under the chin, and drawing her arm through his.

This was indeed the case; but as it was not Mr. Claypole's habit to repose a blind and foolish confi dence in any body, it should be observed, in justice to that gentleman, that he had trusted Charlotte to this extent, in order that, if they were pursued, the money might be found on her; which would leave him an opportunity of asserting his innocence of any theft, and would greatly facilitate his chances of es cape. Of course he entered, at this juncture, into no explanation of his motives, and they walked on very lovingly together.

' LOOK THERE ! THOSE AKE THE LIGHTS OP LONDON."

poke in his old nose, and have us taken back in a cart with handcuffs on," said Mr. Claypole, in a jeer ing tone. " No! I shall go and lose myself among the narrowest streets I can find, and not stop till we come to the very out-of-the-wayest house I can set eyes on. 'Cod, yer may thank yer stars I've got a head; for if we hadn't gone at first the wrong road a purpose, and come back across country, yer'd have been locked up hard and fast a week ago, my lady. And serve yer right for being a fool."

" I know I ain't as cunning as you are," replied Charlotte; " but don't put all the blame on me, and say / should have been locked up. You would have been if I had been, any way."

" Yer took the money from the till, yer know yer did," said Mr. Claypole.

In pursuance of this cautious plan, Mr. Claypole went on, without halting, until he arrived at the Angel at Islington, where he wisely judged, from the crowd of passengers and number of vehicles, that London began in earnest. Just pausing to observe which appeared the most crowded streets, and con sequently the most to be avoided, he crossed into Saint John's Road, and was soon deep in the obscu rity of the intricate and dirty ways, which, lying be tween Gray's Inn Lane and Smithfield, render that part of the town one of the lowest and worst that improvement has left in the midst of London.

Through these streets Noah Claypole walked, drag ging Charlotte after him; now stepping into the ken nel to embrace at a glance the whole external char acter of some small public - house, now jogging on

OLIVER TWIST.

again, as some fancied appearance induced him to believe it too public for his purpose. At length he stopped in front of one more humble in appearance and more dirty than any he had yet seen; and, hav ing crossed over and surveyed it from the opposite pavement, graciously announced his intention of put ting up for the night.

" So give us the bundle," said Noah, unstrapping it from the woman's shoulders, and slinging it over his own, " and don't yer speak except when yer spoke to. What's the name of the house—t-h-r— three what ?"

" Cripples," said Charlotte.

" Three Cripples," repeated Noah, " and a very good sign too. Now, then ! Keep close at my heels, and come along." With these injunctions, he pushed the rattling door with his shoulder, and entered the house, followed by his companion.

There was nobody in the bar but a young Jew, who, with his two elbows on the counter, was read ing a dirty newspaper. He stared very hard at Noah, and Noah stared very hard at him. r

If Noah had been attired in his charity-boy's dress, there might have been some reason for the Jew open ing his eyes so wide; but as he had discarded the coat and badge, and wore a short smock-frock over his leath ers, there seemed no particular reason for his appear ance exciting so much attention in a public-house.

" Is this the Three Cripples ?" asked Noah.

" That is the dabe of this ouse," replied the Jew.

"A gentleman we met on the road, coming up from the country, recommended us here," said Noah, nudging Charlotte, perhaps to call her attention to this most ingenious device for attracting respect, and perhaps to warn her to betray no surprise. " We want to sleep here to-night."

" I'b dot certaid you cad," said Barney, who was the attendant sprite; " but I'll idquire."

" Show us the tap, and give us a bit of cold meat and a drop of beer while yer inquiring, will yer ?" said Noah.

Barney complied by ushering them into a small back-room, and setting the required viands before them ; having done which, he informed the travelers that they could be lodged that night, and left the amiable couple to their refreshment.

Now, this back-room was immediately behind the bar, and some steps lower, so that any person con nected with the house undrawing a small curtain, which concealed a single pane of glass fixed in the wall of the last-named apartment about five feet from its flooring, could not only look down upon any guests in the back-room without any great hazard of being observed (the glass being in a dark angle of the wall, between which and a large upright beam the observer had to thrust himself), but could, by applying his ear to the partition, ascertain with tolerable distinctness their subject of conversation. The landlord of the house hud not withdrawn his '•ye from this place of espial for five minutes, and Barney had only just returned from making the com munication above related, when Fagin, in the course of his evening's business, came into the bar to inquire after some of his young pupils.

" Hush!" said Barney : " stradegers id the next roob."

" Strangers!" repeated the old man, in a whisper.

"Ah! Ad rub uds too," added Barney. "Frob the cut-try, but subthig in your way, or I'b bistaked."

Fagiu appeared to receive this communication with great interest. Mounting a stool, he cautiously ap plied his eye to the pane of glass, from which secret post he could see Mr. Claypole taking cold beef from the dish and porter from the pot, and administering homeopathic doses of both to Charlotte, who sat pa tiently by, eating and drinking at his pleasure.

"Aha!" he whispered, looking round to Barney, " I like that fellow's looks. He'd be of use to us; he knows how to train the girl already. Don't make as much noise as a mouse, my dear, and let me hear 'em talk—let me hear 'em."

He again applied his eye to the glass, and turning his ear to the partition, listened attentively, with a subtle and eager look upon his face that might have appertained to some old goblin.

" So I mean to be a gentleman," said Mr. Claypole, kicking out his legs, and continuing a conversation the commencement of which Fagiu had arrived too late to hear. " No more jolly old coffins, Charlotte, but a gentleman's life for me; and, if yer like, yer shall be a lady."

"I should like that well enough, dear," replied Charlotte ; " but tills ain't to be emptied every day,. and people to get clear off after it."

"Tills be blowed!" said Mr. Claypole; "there's more things besides tills to be emptied."

" What do you mean ?" asked his companion.

" Pockets, women's ridicules, houses, mail-coaches, banks!" said Mr. Claypole, rising with the porter.

" But you can't do all that, dear," said Charlotte.

" I shall look out to get into company with them as can," replied Noah. " They'll be able to make us useful someway or another. Why, you yourself are worth fifty women ; I never see siich a precious sly and deceitful creetur as yer can be when I let yer."

" Lor, how nice it is to hear you say so!" exclaim ed Charlotte, imprinting a kiss upon his ugly face.

" There, that'll do; don't yer be too affectionate, in case I'm cross with yer," said Noah, disengaging himself with great gravity. " I should like to be the captain of some band, and have the whopping of 'em, and follering 'em about, unbeknown to them selves. That would suit me, if there was good prof it; and if we could only get in with some gentle men of this sort, I say it would be cheap at that twenty-pound note you've got—especially as we don't very well know how to get rid of it our selves."

After expressing this opinion, Mr. Claypole look ed into the porter-pot with an aspect of deep wis dom ; and having well shaken its contents, nodded condescendingly to Charlotte, and took a draught, wherewith he appeared greatly refreshed. He was meditating another, when the sudden opening of tIn door and the appearance of a stranger interrupted him.

The stranger was Mr. Fagin. And very amiable he looked, and a very low bow he made as he ad vanced, and. setting himself down at the nearest ta- • ble, ordered something to drink of the grinning Bar ney.

"A pleasant night, sir, but cool for the time of

OPENING PRESENTS ITSELF.

135

year," said Fagin, rubbing his bands. " From the country, I see, sir ?"

" How do yer see that ?" asked Noah Claypole.

" We have not so much dust as that in London," replied Fagin, pointing from Noah's shoes to those of his companion, and from them to the two bundles.

"Yer a sharp feller," said Noah. "Ha! ha! only hear that, Charlotte!"

" Why, one need be sharp in this town, my dear," replied the Jew, sinking his voice to a confidential whisper; "and that's-the truth."

Fagin followed up this remark by striking the side of his nose with his right forefinger—a gesture which Noah attempted to imitate, though not with complete success, in consequence of his own nose not being large enough for the purpose. However, Mr. Fagiu seemed to interpret the endeavor as express ing a perfect coincidence with his opinion, and put about the liquor which Barney re-appeared with in a very friendly manner.

" Good stuff that," observed Mr. Claypole, smack ing his lips.

"Dear!" said Fagin. "A man need be always emptying a till, or a pocket, or a woman's reticule, or a house, or a mail-coach, or a bank, if he drinks it regularly."

Mr. Claypole no sooner heard this extract from his own remarks than he fell back in his chair, and looked from the Jew to Charlotte with a counte nance of ashy paleness and excessive terror.

" Don't mind me, my dear," said Fagin, drawing his chair closer. " Ha! ha! it was lucky it was only me that heard you by chance. It was very lucky it was only me."

"I didn't take it," stammered Noah, no longer stretching out his legs like an independent gentle man, but coiling them up as well as he could under his chair; " it was all her doing; yerVe got it now, Charlotte, yer know yer have."

" No matter who's got it, or who did it, my dear!" replied Fagin, glancing, nevertheless, with a hawk's eye at the girl and the two bundles. " I'm in that way myself, and I like you for it."

" In what way ?" asked Mr. Claypole, a little re covering.

" In that way of business," rejoined Fagin; "and so are the people of the house. You've hit the right nail upon the head, and are as safe here as you could be. There is not a safer place in all this town than is The Cripples—that is, when I like to make it so. And I have taken a fancy to you and the young woman; so I've said the word, and you may make your minds easy."

Noah Claypole's mind might have been at ease af ter this assurance, but his body certainly was not; for he shuffled and writhed about into various un couth positions, eying his new friend meanwhile with mingled fear and suspicion.

" I'll tell you more," said Fagin, after he had reas-' sured the girl by dint of friendly nods and muttered encouragements. " I have got a friend that I think ; can gratify your darling wish, and put you in the right way, where you can take whatever department of the business you think will suit you best at first, and be taught all the others."

" Yer speak as if yer were iu earnest," replied Noah.

"What advantage would it be to me to be any thing else ?"• inquired Fagin, shrugging his shoul ders. " Here! Let me have a word with you out side."

" There's no occasion to trouble ourselves to move," said Noah, getting his legs by gradual degrees abroad again. " She'll take the luggage up stairs the while. Charlotte, see to them bundles!"

This mandate, which had been delivered with great majesty, was obeyed without the slightest de mur ; and Charlotte made the best of her way off with the packages while Noah held the door open and watched her out.

" She's kept tolerably well under, ain't she ?" he asked, as he resumed his seat, in the tone of a keeper who has tamed some wild animal.

" Quite perfect," rejoined Fagin, clapping him on the shoulder. " You're a genius, my dear."

"Why, I suppose if I wasn't I shouldn't be here," replied Noah. . " But, I say, she'll be back if yer lose time."

" Now, what do you think ?" said Fagin. " If you was to like my friend, could you do better than join him ?"

" Is he in a good way of business; that's where it is!" responded Noah, winking one of his little eyes.

" The top of the tree; employs a power of hands; has the very best society iu the profession."

" Eegular town-maders ?" asked Mr. Claypole.

" Not a countryman among 'em; and I don't think he'd take you, even on my recommendation, if he didn't run rather short of assistants just now," re plied Fagin.

" Should I have to hand over ?" said Noah, slapping his breeches-pocket.

"It couldn't possibly be done without," replied Fagin, in a most decided manner.

" Twenty pound, though—it's a lot of money!"

" Not when it's in a note you can't get rid of," re torted Fagiu. " Number and date taken, I suppose ? Payment stopped at the bank? • Ah! It's not worth much to him. It'll have to go abroad, and he couldn't sell it for a great deal in the market."

" When could I see him ?" asked Noah, doubtfully.

" To-morrow morning."

" Where ?"

"Here?"

" Urn!" said Noah. " What's the wages ?"

" Live like a gentleman—board and lodging, pipes and spirits free—half of all you earn, and half of all the young woman earns," replied Mr. Fagiu.

Whether Noah Claypole, whose rapacity was none of the least comprehensive, would have acceded even to these glowing terms, had he been a perfectly free agent, is very doubtful; but as he recollected that, iu the event of his refusal, it was in the power of his new acquaintance to give him up to justice immediately (and more unlikely things had come to pass), he gradually relented, and said he thought that would suit him.

" But, yer see," observed Noah, " as she will be able to do a good deal, I should like to take some thing very light."

"A little fancy work ?" suggested Fagin.

"Ah! something of that sort," replied Noah. " What do you think would suit me, now ? Some-

thing not too trying for the strength, and not very dangerous, you know. That's the sort .of thing!"

" I heard you talk of something in the spy way upon the others, my dear," said Fagiii. " My friend wants somebody who would do that well, very much."

" Why, I did mention that, and I shouldn't mind turning my hand to it sometimes," rejoined Mr. Clay-pole, slowly; "but it wouldn't pay by itself, you know."

" That's true!" observed the Jew, ruminating, or pretending to ruminate. " No, it might not."

" What do you think, then ?" asked Noah, anxious ly regarding him. " Something in the sneaking way, where it was pretty sure work, and not much more risk than being at home."

" What do you think of the old ladies ?" asked Fa-gin. " There's a good deal of money made in snatch ing their bags and parcels and running round the corner."

" Don't they holler out a good deal, and scratch sometimes?" asked Noah, shaking his head. "I don't think that would answer my purpose. Ain't there any other line open ?"

" Stop!" said Fagiu, laying his hand on Noah's knee. " The kinchin lay."

" What's that ?" demanded Mr. Claypole.

" The kinchins, my dear," said Fagin, " is the young children that's sent on errands by their moth ers with sixpences and shillings; and the lay is just to take their money away—they've always got it ready in their hands—then knock 'em into the ken nel, and walk off very slow, as if there were nothing else the matter but a child fallen down and hurt it self. Ha! ha! ha!"

"Ha! ha!" roared Mr. Claypole, kicking up his legs in an ecstasy. " Lord, that's the very thing!"

" To be sure it is," replied Fagin; " and you can have a few good beats chalked out in Camden Town, and Battle Bridge, and neighborhoods like that, where they're always going errands; and you can upset as manv kinchins as you want, any hour in the day. Hafha! ha!"

With this, Fagin poked Mr. Claypole in the side, and they joined in a burst of laughter both long and loud.

" Well, that's all right!" said Noah, when he had recovered himself, and Charlotte had returned. " What time to-morrow shall we say ?"

" Will ten do ?" asked Fagin, adding, as Mr. Clay-pole nodded assent, "What name shall I tell my good friend ?"

" Mr. Bolter," replied Noah, who had prepared him self for such an emergency. " Mr. Morris Bolter. This is Mrs. Bolter."

" Mrs. Bolter's humble servant," said Fagiu, bow ing with grotesque politeness. " I hope I shall know her better very shortly."

" Do you hear the gentleman, Charlotte ?" thun dered Mr. Claypole.

" Yes, Noah dear!" responded Mrs. Bolter, extend ing her hand.

" She calls me Noah, as a sort of fond way of talk ing," said Mr. Morris Bolter, late Claypole, turning to Fagin. " You understand?"

" Oh yes, I understand—perfectly," replied Fagin,

telling the truth for once. "Good-night! Good night !"

With many adieus and good wishes, Mr. Fagin went his way. Noah Claypole, bespeaking his good lady's attention, proceeded to enlighten her relative to the arrangement he had made with all that haugh tiness and air of superiority becoming, not only a member of the sterner sex, but a gentleman who ap preciated the dignity of a special appointment on the kinchin lay in London and its vicinity.

CHAPTER XLIIL

WHEREIN IS SHOWN HOW THE ARTFUL DODGER GOT INTO TROUBLE.

" 4 ND so it was you that was your own friend, J_A_ was it ?" asked Mr. Claypole, otherwise Bolter, when, by virtue of the compact entered into between them, he had removed next day to Fagiu's house, " 'Cod, I thought as much last night!"

" Every man's his own friend, rny dear," replied Fagin, with his most insinuating grin. " He hasn't as good an one as himself anywhere."

" Except sometimes," replied Morris Bolter, assum ing the air of a man of the world. " Some people are nobody's enemies but their own, yer know."

" Don't believe that," said Fagin. " When a man's his own enemy, it's only because he's too much his own friend ; not because he's careful for every body but himself. Pooh! pooh! There ain't such a thing in nature."

" There oughtn't to be, if there is," replied Mr. Bolter.

" That stands to reason. Some conjurers say that number three is the magic number, and some say number seven. It's neither, my friend, neither. It's number one."

" Ha! ha!" cried Mr. Bolter. " Number one for ever !"

" In a little community like ours, my dear," said Fagin, who felt it necessary to qualify this position, " we have a general number one; that is, you can't consider yourself as number one, without consider ing me too as the same, and all the other young peo ple."

" Oh, the devil!" exclaimed Mr. Bolter.

" You see," pursued Fagin, affecting to disregard this interruption," we are so mixed up together, and identified in our interests, that it must be so. For instance, it's your object to take care of number one —meaning yourself."

" Certainly," replied Mr. Bolter. " Yer about right there."

" Well! You can't take care of yourself, number one, without taking care of me, number one."

"Number two, you mean," said Mr. Bolter, who was largely endowed with the quality of selfishness.

," No, I don't!" retorted Fagin. " I'm of the same importance to you, as you are to yourself."

" I say," interrupted Mr. Bolter, " yer a very nice man, and I'm very fond of yer; but we ain't quite so thick together as all that comes to."

" Only think," said Fagin, shrugging his shoulders and stretching out his hands," only consider. You've

THE POST OF HONOR IS A NEWGATE STATION.

doiie what's a very pretty thing, and what I love you for doing; but what at the same time would put the cravat round your throat, that's so very easily tied and so very difficult to unloose—in plain English, the halter!"

Mr. Bolter put his hand to his neckerchief, as if he felt it inconveniently tight, and murmured an assent, qualified in tone but not in substance.

" The gallows," continued Fagin," the gallows, my dear, is an ugly finger-post, which points out a very short and sharp turning that has stopped many a bold fellow's career on the broad highway. To keep in the easy road, and keep it at a distance, is object number one with you."

" Of course it is," replied Mr. Bolter. " What do yer talk about such things for ?"

" Only to show you my meaning clearly," said the Jew, raising his eyebrows. " To be able to do that, you depend upon me. To keep my little business all snug, I depend upon you. The first is your number one, the second my number one. The more you value your number one, the more careful you must be of mine; so we come at last to what I told you at first —that a regard for number one-holds us all together, and must do so, unless we would all go to pieces in company."

" That's true," rejoined Mr. Bolter, thoughtfully. " Oh! yer a cunning old codger."

Mr. Fagin saw, with delight, that this tribute to his powers was no mere compliment, but that he had really impressed his recruit with a sense of his wily genius, which it was most important that he should entertain in the outset of their acquaintance. To strengthen an impression so desirable and useful, he followed up the blow by acquainting him, in some detail, with the magnitude and extent of his opera tions, blending truth and fiction together, as best served his purpose, and bringing both to bear with so much art that Mr. Bolter's respect visibly in creased, and became tempered, at the same time, with a degree of wholesome fear which it was high ly desirable to awaken.

" It's this nmtual trust we have in each other that consoles me under heavy losses," said Fagin. ; ' My best hand was taken from me yesterday morn ing."

"You don't mean to say he died?" cried Mr. Bolter.

" No, no," replied Fagin, " not so bad as that. Not quite so bad."

" What; I suppose he was— :

" Wanted," interposed Fagin. " Yes, he was want ed."

" Yery particular ?" inquired Mr. Bolter.

" No," replied Fagin, " not very. He was charged with attempting to pick a pocket, and they found a silver snuff-box on him—his own, my dear, his own, for he took snuff himself, and was very fond of it. They remanded him till to-day, for they thought they knew the owner. Ah! he was worth lifry boxes, and I'd give the price of as many to have him back. You should have known the Dodger, my dear ; you should have known the Dodger."

" Well, but I shall know him, I hope; don't yer think so f' said Mr. Bolter.

" I'm doubtful about it," replied Fagin, with a sigh.

" If they don't get any fresh evidence, it'll only be a summary conviction, and we shall have him back again after six weeks or so; but if they do, it's a case of lagging. They know what a clever lad he is, he'll be a lifer. They'll make the Artful nothing less than a lifer."

" What do yer mean by lagging and a lifer ?" de manded Mr. Bolter. " What's the good of talking in that way to me; why don't yer speak so as I can understand yer ?"

Fagin was about to translate these mysterious ex pressions into the vulgar tongue; and, being inter preted, Mr. Bolter would have been informed that they represented that combination of words, " trans portation for life," when the dialogue was cut short by the entry of Master Bates, with his hands in his breeches-pockets, and his face twisted into a lock of semi-comical woe.

" It's all up, Fagin," said Charley, when he and his new companion had been made known to each other.

" What do you mean ?"

" They've found the gentleman as owns the box; two or three more's a-coming to 'dentify him; and the Artful's booked for a passage out," replied Master Bates. " I must have a full suit of mourning, Fagin, and a hat-band, to wisit him in afore he sets out upon his travels. To think of Jack Dawkins—lum my Jack—the Dodger—the Artful Dodger—going abroad for a common twopenuy-half-penny sneeze-box ! I never thought he'd a done it under a gold watch, chain, and seals, at the lowest. Oh, why didn't he rob some rich old gentleman of all his wal-ables, and go out as a gentleman, and not like a com mon prig, without no honor nor glory!"

With this expression of feeling for his unfortunate friend, Master Bates sat himself on the nearest chair with an aspect of chagrin and despondency.

" What do you talk about his having neither hon or nor glory for!" exclaimed Fagin, darting an angry look at his pupil. "Wasn't he always top-sawyer among you all ? Is there one of you that could touch him or come near him on any scent! Eh ?"

" Not one," replied Master Bates, in a voice render ed husky by regret; " not one."

" Then what do you talk of?" replied Fagin, angri ly ; " what are you blubbering for ?"

" 'Cause it isn't on the rec-ord, is it ?" said Charley, chafed into perfect defiance of his venerable friend by the current of his regrets; " 'cause it can't come out in the 'dictment; 'cause nobody will never know half of what he was. How will he stand in the New gate Calendar ? P'raps not be there at all. Oh, my eye, my eye, wot a blow it is!"

" Ha! ha!" cried Fagiu, extending his right hand, and turning to Mr. Bolter in a fit of chuckling which shook him as though he had the palsy; " see what a pride they take in their profession, my dear. Ain't it beautiful ?"

Mr. Bolter nodded assent; and Fagin, after con templating the grief of Charley Bates for some sec onds with evident satisfaction, stepped up to that young gentleman and patted him on the shoulder.

"Never mind, Charley," said Fagin, soothingly; " it'll come out, it'll be sure to come out. They'll all know what a clever fellow he was; he'll show it him self, and not disgrace his old pals and teachers. Think

OLIVER TWIST.

how young he is too! What a distinction, Charley, to be lagged at his time of life!"

" Well, it is a honor, that is!" said Charley, a little consoled.

" He shall have all he wants," continued the Jew. "He shall be kept in the Stone Jug, Charley, like a gentleman. Like a gentleman! With his beer ev ery day, and money in his pocket to pitch and toss with, if he can't spend it."

"No, shall he, though ?" cried Charley Bates.

"Ay, that he shall," replied Fagin, " and we'll have a big-wig, Charley—one that's got the greatest gift of the gab—to carry on his defense; and he shall make a speech for himself too, if he likes; and we'll road it all in the papers—'Artful Dodger—shrieks of laughter—here the court was convulsed'—eh, Charley, eh ?"

"Ha! ha!" laughed Master Bates, "what a lark that would be, wouldn't it, Fagin ? I say, how the Artful would bother ? em, wouldn't he ?"

" Would!" cried Fagin. " He shall—he will!"

"Ah, to be sure, so he will," repeated Charley, rub bing his hands.

" I think I see him now!" cried the Jew, bending his eyes upon his pupil.

"So do I!" cried Charley Bates. "Ha! ha! ha! so do I! I see it all afore me, upon my soul I do, Fa-gin. What a game! What a regular game! All the big-wigs trying to look solemn, and Jack Daw-kins addressing of 'em as intimate and comfortable as if he was the judge's own son making a speech ar-ter dinner—ha! ha! ha!"

In fact, Mr. Fagin had so well humored his young friend's eccentric disposition, that Master Bates, who had at first been disposed to consider the imprisoned Dodger rather in the light of a victim, now looked upon him as the chief actor in a scene of most un common and exquisite humor, and felt quite impa tient for the arrival of the time when his old com panion should have so favorable an opportunity of displaying his abilities.

" We must know how he gets on to-day, by some handy means or other," said Fagin. " Let me think."

" Shall I go ?" asked Charley.

"Not for the world," replied Fagin. "Are you mad, my dear, stark mad, that you'd walk into the very place where— No, Charley, no. One is enough to lose at a time."

" You don't mean to go yourself, I suppose ?" said Charley, with a humorous leer.

" That wouldn't quite fit," replied Fagin, shaking his head.

" Then why don't you send this new cove ?" asked Master Bates, laying his hand on Noah's arm. " No body knows him."

" Why, if he didn't mind—" observed Fagin.

" Mind !" interposed Charley. " What should lie have to mind ?"

" Really nothing, my dear," said Fagin, turning to Mr. Bolter, " really nothing."

" Oh, I dare say about that, yer know," observed Noah, backing toward the door, and shaking his head with a kind of sober alarm. "No, no—none of that. It's not in my department, that ain't."

"Wot department has he got, Fagiu?" inquired Master Bates, surveying Noah's lank form with much

disgust. " The cutting away when there's any thing wrong, and the eating all the wittles when there's every thing right; is that his branch f'

" Never mind," retorted Mr. Bolter; " and don't yer take liberties with yer superiors, little boy, or yer'll find yerself in the wrong shop."

Master Bates laughed so vehemently at this mag nificent threat, that it was some time before Fagiu could interpose, and represent to Mr. Bolter that he incurred no possible danger in visiting the police-of fice ; that, inasmuch as no account of the little affair in which he had been engaged, nor any description of his person, had yet been forwarded to the metrop olis, it was very probable that he was not even sus pected of having resorted to it for shelter; and that if he were properly disguised, it would be as safe a spot for him to visit as any in London, inasmuch as it would be, of all places, the very last to which he could be supposed likely to resort of his own free wiU.

Persuaded in part by these representations, biit overborne in a much greater degree by his fear of Fagin, Mr. Bolter at length consented, with a very bad grace, to undertake the expedition. By Fagin's directions, he immediately substituted for his own attire a wagoner's frock, velveteen breeches, and leather leggings, all of which articles the Jew had at hand. He was likewise furnished with a felt hat well garnished with turnpike tickets, and a carter's whip. Thus equipped, he was to saunter into the office, as some country fellow from Covent Garden market might be supposed to do for the gratification of his curiosity; and as he was as awkward, ungain ly, and raw-boned a fellow as need be, Mr. Fagiu had no fear but that he would look the part to perfection.

These arrangements completed, he was informed of the necessary signs and tokens by which to recog nize the Artful Dodger, and was conveyed by Master Bates through dark and winding ways to within a very short distance of Bow Street. Having described the precise situation of the office, and accompanied it with copious directions how he was to walk straight up the passage, and when he got into the yard take the door up the steps on the right-hand side, and pull off his hat as he went into the room, Charley Bates bade him hurry on alone, and promised to bide his return on the spot of their parting.

Noah Claypole, or Morris Bolter, as the reader pleases, punctually followed the directions he had received, which—Master Bates being pretty well ac quainted with the locality—were so exact that he was enabled to gain the magisterial presence with out asking any question, or meeting with any inter ruption by the way. He found himself jostled ajnoug a crowd of people, chiefly women, who were huddled together in a dirty, frowsy room, at the upper end of which was a raised platform railed off from the rest, with a dock for the prisoners on the left hand against the wall, a box for the witnesses in the middle, and a desk for the magistrates on the right; the awful locality last named being screened off by a partition which concealed the bench from the common gaze, and left the vulgar to imagine (if they could) the full majesty of justice.

There were only a couple of women in the dock, who were nodding to their admiring friends, Avhile

MR. BOLTER DISGUISED.

the clerk read some depositions to a couple of police men and a man iu plain clothes who leaned over the table. A jailer stood reclining against the dock-rail, tapping his nose listlessly with a large key, except when he repressed an undue tendency to conversa tion among the idlers by proclaiming silence, or look ed sternly up to bid some woman " Take that baby out," when the gravity of justice was disturbed by feeble cries, half-smothered in the mother's shawl, from some meagre infant. The room smelled close and unwholesome; the walls were dirt-discolored, and the ceiling blackened. There was an old smoky bust over the mantel-shelf, and a dusty clock above the dock—the only thing present that seemed to go on as it ought; for depravity, or poverty, or an ha bitual acquaintance with both, had left a taint on all the animate matter, hardly less unpleasant than the thick, greasy scum on every inanimate object that frowned upon it.

Noah looked eagerly about him for the Dodger; but although there were several women who would have done very well for that distinguished charac ter's mother or sister, and more than one man who might be supposed to bear a strong resemblance to his father, nobody at all answering the description given him of Mr. Dawkius was to be seen. He wait ed in a state of much suspense and uncertainty until the women, being committed for trial, went flaunt ing out, and then was quickly relieved by the ap pearance of another prisoner who he felt at once could be no other than the object of his visit.

It was indeed Mr. Dawkins, who, shuffling into the office with the big coat sleeves tucked up as usual, his left hand in his pocket, and his hat in his right hand, preceded the jailer with a rolling gait alto gether indescribable, and, taking his place in the dock, requested, in an audible voice, to know what he was placed in that 'ere disgraceful sitivation for.

" Hold your tongue, will you ?" said the jailer.

" I'm an Englishman, ain't I ?" rejoined the Dodger. " Where are my priwileges ?"

" You'll get your privileges soon enough," retorted the jailer, " and pepper with 'em."

" We'll see wot the Secretary of State for the Home Affairs has got to say to the beaks, if I don't," replied Mr. Dawkins. " Now then! wot is this here business ? I shall thank the madg'strates to dispose of this here little affair, and not to keep me while they read the paper, for I've got an appointment with a genelman iu the City; and as I'm a man of my word, and wery punctual in business matters, he'll go away if I ain't there to my time, and then pr'aps there won't be an action for damage against them as kep me away. Oh no, certainly not!"

At this point, the Dodger, with a show of being very particular with a view to proceedings to be had thereafter, desired the jailer to communicate "the names of them two files as was on the bench;" which so tickled the spectators that they laughed almost as heartily as Master Bates could have done if he had heard the request.

" Silence there!" cried the jailer.

" What is this ?" inquired one of the magistrates.

" A pick-pocketing case, your worship."

"Has the boy ever been here before ?"

" He ought to have been a many times," replied the jailer. " He has been pretty well everywhere else. know him well, your worship."

"Oh! you know me, do you?" cried the Artful, making a note of the statement. "Wery good. That's a case of deformation of character, any way."

Here there w y as another laugh, and another cry of silence.

" Now, then, where are the witnesses ?" said the clerk.

"Ah! that's right," added the Dodger. "Where are they ? I should like to see 'em,"

This wish was immediately gratified, for a police man stepped forward who had seen the prisoner at tempt the pocket of an unknown gentleman in a crowd, and, indeed, take a handkerchief therefrom, which, being a very old one, he deliberately put back again, after trying it on his own countenance. For this reason he took the Dodger into custody as soon as he could get near him, and the said Dodger, being searched, had upon his person a silver snuff box, with the owner's name engraved upon the lid. This gentleman had been discovered on reference to the Court Guide; and being then and there present, swore that the snuff-box was his, and that he had missed it on the previous day, the moment he had disengaged himself from the crowd before referred to. He had also remarked a young gentleman in the throng particularly active in making his way about, and that young gentleman was the prisoner before him.

" Have yon any thing to ask this witness, boy ?" said the magistrate.

" I wouldn't abase myself by descending to hold no conversation with him," replied the Dodger.

" Have you any thing to say at all ?"

" Do you hear his worship ask if you've any thing to say ?" inquired the jailer, nudging the silent Dodger with his elbow.

" I beg your pardon," said the Dodger, looking up with an air of abstraction. " Did you redress your self to me, my man ?"

"I never see such an out-and-out young waga-bond, your worship," observed the officer, with a griu. " Do you mean to say any thing, you young shaver ?"

" No," replied the Dodger, " not here, for this ain't the shop for justice; besides which, my attorney is a-breakfasting this morning with the Wice-president of the House of Commons; but I shall have some thing to say elsewhere, and so will he, and so will a wery numerous and 'spectable circle of acqiiaint-ance as'll make them beaks wish they'd never been born, or that they'd got their footmen to hang 'em up to their own hat-pegs 'afore they let 'em come out this morning to try it on upon me. I'll—

"There! He's fully committed!" interposed the clerk. " Take him away."

" Come on," said the jailer.

" Oh, ah! I'll come on," replied the Dodger, brush ing his hat with the palm of his hand. "Ah 1 (to the Bench) it's no use your looking frightened ; I won't show you no mercy, not a ha'porth of it. You'll pay for this, my fine fellers. I wouldn't be you for something. I wouldn't go free, now, if you was to fall down on your knees and ask me. Here, carry me off to prison! Take me away!"

OLIVER TWIST.

With these last words, the Dodger suffered him self to be led oft" by the collar, threatening, till he got into the yard, to make a parliamentary business of it, and then grinning in the officer's face with great glee and self-approval.

Having seen him locked up by himself in a little cell, Noah made the best of his way back to where he had left Master Bates. After waiting here some time, he was joined by that young gentleman, who had prudently abstained from showing himself until he had looked carefully abroad from a snug retreat aud ascertained that his new friend had not been fol lowed by any impertinent person.

bered that both the crafty Jew and the brutal Sikes had confided to her schemes which had been hidden from all others, in the full confidence that she was trustworthy, and beyond the reach of their suspicion. Vile as those schemes were, desperate as were their originators, and bitter as were her feelings toward Fa-gin, who had led her, step by step, deeper and deeper down into an abyss of crime and misery whence was no escape, still there were times when, even toward him, she felt some relenting lest her disclosure should bring him within the iron grasp he had so long eluded, and he should fall at last—richly as he mer ited such a fate—by her hand.

"WUAT IS THIS?" INQUIRED ONE OP THE MAGISTRATES. A PICK-POCKETING CASE, YOUR WORSHIP."

The two hastened back together, to bear to Mr. Fa-gin the animating news that the Dodger was doing full justice to his bringing up, and establishing for himself a glorious reputation.

CHAPTER XLIV.

THE TIME ARRIVES FOR NANCY TO REDEEM HER PLEDGE TO ROSE MAYLIE. SHE FAILS.

ADEPT as she was in all the arts of cunning and dissimulation, the girl Nancy could not wholly conceal the effect which the knowledge of the step she had taken wrought upon her mind. She remem-

But these were the mere wanderings of a mind un able wholly to detach itself from old companions and associations, though enabled to fix itself steadily on one object, and resolved not to be turned aside by any consideration. Her fears for Sikes would have been more powerful inducements to recoil while there was yet time, but she had stipulated that her secret should be rigidly kept; she had dropped no clue which could lead to his discovery; she had refused, even for his sake, a refuge from all the guilt and wretchedness that encompassed her—and what more could she do! She was resolved.

Though all her mental struggles terminated in this conclusion, they forced themselves upon her again

THE KEY TURNED ON NANCY.

and again, and left their traces too. She grew pale and thin, even within a few days. At times she took no heed of what was passing before her, or no part in conversations where once she would have been the loudest. At other times she laughed without merri ment, and was noisy without cause or meaning. At others—often within a moment afterward—she sat silent and dejected, brooding with her head upon her hands, while the very effort by which she roused herself told, more forcibly than even these indica tions, that she was ill at ease, and that her thoughts were occupied with matters very different and dis tant from those in course of discussion by her com panions.

It was Sunday night, and the bell of the nearest church struck the hour. Sikes and the Jew were talking, but they paused to listen. The girl looked up from the low seat on which she crouched and list ened too. Eleven.

"An hour this side of midnight," said Sikes, rais ing the blind to look out, and returning to his seat. " Dark and heavy it is too. A good night for busi ness this."

"Ah!" replied Fagin. "What a pity, Bill, my dear, that there's none quite ready to be done."

"You're right for once," replied Sikes, gruffly. " It is a pity, for I'm in the humor too."

Fagin sighed, and shook his head despondingly.

"We must make up for lost time when we've got things into a good train. That's all I know," said Sikes.

" That's the way to talk, my dear," replied Fagin, venturing to pat him on the shoulder. " It does me good to hear you."

" Does you good, does it!" cried Sikes. " Well, so be it."

" Ha! ha! ha!" laughed Fagin, as if he were re lieved by even this concession. "You're like your self to-night, Bill! Quite like yourself."

" I don't feel like myself wnen you lay that with ered old claw on my shoulder, so take it away," said Sikes, casting off the Jew's hand.

" It makes you nervous, Bill—reminds you of be ing nabbed, does it ?" said Fagiu, determined not to be offended.

" Eeminds me of being nabbed by the devil," re turned Sikes. " There never was another man with such a face as yours, unless it was your father, and I suppose he is singeing his grizzled red beard by this time, unless you came straight from the old 'un without any father at all betwixt you; which I shouldn't wonder at a bit."

Fagin offered no reply to this compliment; but, pulling Sikes by the sleeve, pointed his finger toward Nancy, who had taken advantage of the foregoing conversation to put on her bonnet, and was now leaving the room.

" Halloo!" cried Sikes. " Nance! Where's the gal going to at this time of night ?"

" Not far."

"What answer's that?" returned Sikes. "Where axe you going ?"

" I say, not far."

"And I say, where ?" retorted Sikes. " Do you hear me ?"

" I don't know where," replied the girl.

" Then I do," said Sikes, more in the spirit of ob stinacy than because he had any real objection to the girl going Avhere she listed. "Now r here. Sit down."

" I'm not well. I told yon that before," rejoined the girl. " I want a breath of air."

" Put your head out of the winder," replied Sikes.

" There's not enough there," said the girl. " I want it in the street."

" Then you won't have it," replied Sikes. With which assurance he rose, locked the door, took the key out, and pulling her bonnet from her head, flung it up to the top of an old press.

" There !" said the robber. " Now stop quietly where you are, will you ?"

" It's not such a matter as a bonnet would keep me," said the girl, turning very pale. "What do you mean, Bill ? Do you know what you're doing ?"

" Know what I'm— Oh!" cried Sikes, turning to Fagin, "she's out of her senses, you know, or she daren't talk to me in that way."

" You'll drive me on to something desperate," mut tered the girl, placing both hands upon her breast as though to keep down by force some violent outbreak. " Let me go, will you—this minute—this instant!"

"No!" said Sikes.

"Tell him to let me go, Fagin. He had better. It'll be better for him. Do you hear me?" cried Nancy, stamping her foot upon the ground.

" Hear you!" repeated Sikes, turning round in his chair to confront her. "Ay! And if I hear you for half a minute longer, the dog shall have such a grip on your throat as'll tear some of that screaming voice out. Wot has come over you, you jade ? Wot is it ?"

" Let me go," said the girl with great earnestness; then sitting herself down on the floor before the door, she said, "Bill, let me go; you don't know what you are doing. You don't, indeed. For only one hour—do—do!"

" Cut my limbs off one by one," cried Sikes, seiz ing her roughly by the arm, " if I don't think the girl's stark raving mad. Get up!"

" Not till you let me go—not till you let me go— never—never!" screamed the girl. Sikes looked on for a minute, watching his opportunity, and sudden ly pinioning her hands, dragged her, struggling and wrestling with him by the way, into a small room ad joining, where he sat himself on a bench, and, thrust ing her into a chair, held her down by force. She struggled and implored by turns until twelve o'clock had struck, and then, wearied and exhausted, ceased to contest the point any further. With a caution, backed by many oaths, to make no more efforts to go out that night, Sikes left her to recover at leisure and rejoined Fagin.

"Whew!" said the house-breaker, wiping the per-: spiration from his face. "Wot a precious strange gal that is!"

" You may say that, Bill," replied Fagin, thought fully. " You may say that."

" Wot did she take it into her head to go out to night for, do you think ?" asked Sikes. " Come ; you should know her better than me. Wot does it mean ?"

"Obstinacy; woman's obstinacy, I suppose, my dear."

OLIVER TWIST.

" Well, I suppose it is," growled Sikes. " I thought I had tained her, but she's as bad as ever."

"Worse," said Fagin, thoughtfully. " I never knew her like this, for such a little cause."

" Nor I," said Sikes. " I thiuk she's got a touch of that fever in her blood yet, and it won't come out —eh?"

" Like enough."

" I'll let her a little blood, without troubling the doctor, if she's took that way again," said Sikes.

Fagin nodded an expressive approval of this mode of treatment.

" She was hanging about me all day, and night too, when I was stretched on my back; and you, like a black-hearted wolf as you are, kept yourself aloof," said Sikes. "We was very poor too, all the time, and I think, one way or other, it's worried and fretted her; and that being shut up here so long has made her restless—eh ?"

" That's it, rny dear," replied the Jew, in a whisper. "Hush!"

As he uttered these words, the girl herself appear ed and resumed her former seat. Her eyes were swollen and red; she rocked herself to and fro, toss ed her head, and, after a little time, burst out laugh ing.

"Why, now she's on the other tack!" exclaimed Sikes, turning a look of excessive surprise on his companion.

Fagin nodded to him to take no further notice just then, and in a few minutes the girl subsided into her accustomed demeanor. Whispering Sikes that there was no fear of her relapsing, Fagin took up his hat and bade him good-night. He paused when he reached the room-door, and, looking round, asked if somebody would light him down the dark stairs.

" Light him down," said Sikes, who was filling his pipe. " It's a pity he should break his neck him self, and disappoint the sight-seers. Show him a light."

Nancy followed the old man down stairs with a candle. When they reached the passage, he laid his finger on his lip, and drawing close to the girl, said, in a whisper,

" What is it, Nancy, dear ?"

"What do you mean?" replied the girl, in the same tone.

" The reason of all this," replied Fagin. " If he " —he pointed with his skinny forefinger up the stairs —" is so hard with you (he's a brute, Nance, a brute-beast), why don't you—

" Well ?" said the girl, as Fagin paused, with his mouth almost touching her ear, and his eyes looking into hers.

. "No matter just now. We'll talk of this again. You have a friend in me, Nance—a staunch friend. I have the means at hand, quiet and close. If you want revenge on those that treat you like a dog— like a dog! worse than his dog, for he humors him sometimes—come to me. I say, come to me. He is the mere hound of a day, but you know me of old, Nance,"

" I know you well," replied the girl, without man ifesting the least emotion. " Good-night."

She shrank back, as Fagin offered to lay his hand

on hers, but said good-night again in a steady voice, and, answering his parting look with a nod of intelli gence, closed the door between them.

Fagin walked toward his own home, intent upon the thoughts that were working within his brain. He had conceived the idea—not from what had just passed, though that had tended to confirm him, but slowly and by degrees—that Nancy, wearied of the house-breaker's brutality, had conceived an attach ment for some new friend. Her altered manner, her repeated absences from home alone, her comparative indifference to the interests of the gang for which she had once been so zealous, and, added to these, her desperate impatience to leave home that night at a particular hour, all favored the supposition, and ren dered it, to him at least, almost matter of certainty. The object of this new liking was not among his myrmidons. He would be a valuable acquisition with such an assistant as Nancy, and must (thus Fa-gin argued) be secured without delay.

There was another and a darker object to be gain ed. Sikes knew too much, and his ruffian taunts had not galled Fagin the less because the wounds were hidden. The girl must know well that, if she shook him off, she could never be safe from his fury, and that it would be surely wreaked—to the maim ing of limbs, or perhaps the loss of life—on the ob ject of her more recent fancy. "With a little per suasion," thought Fagin, " what more likely than that she would consent to poison him? Women have done such things, and worse, to secure the same object before now. There Avould be the dangerous villain, the man I hate, gone; another secured in his place; and my influence over the girl, with a knowl edge of this crime to back it, unlimited."

These things passed through the mind of Fagin during the short time he sat alone in the house-break er's room; and with them uppermost in his thoughts, he had taken the opportunity afterward afforded him of sounding the girl in the broken hints he threw out at parting. There was no expression of surprise, no assumption of an inability to understand his meaning. The girl clearly comprehended it. Her glance at parting showed that.

But perhaps she would recoil from a plot to take the life of Sikes, and that was one of the chief ends to be attained. " How," thought Fagiu, as he crept homeward, " can I increase my influence with her ? what new power can I acquire ?"

Such brains are fertile in expedients. If, without extracting a confession from herself, he laid a watch, discovered the object of her altered regard, and threat ened to reveal the whole history to Sikes (of whom she stood in no common fear) unless she entered into his designs, could he not secure her compliance ?

"I can," said Fagiu, almost aloud. " She durst not refuse me then. Not for her life, not for her life! I have it all. The means are ready, and shall be set to work. I shall have you yet ?"

He cast back a dark look, and a threatening mo tion of the hand, toward the spot where he had left the bolder villain; and went on his way, busying his bony hands in the folds of his tattered garment, which he wrenched tightly in his grasp, as though there were a hated enemy crushed with every mo tion of his fingers.

BOLTER AGAIN IX EEQUEST.

CHAPTER XLV.

NOAH CLATPOLE 18 EMPLOYED BY FAGIN ON A SECRET MISSION.

THE old man was up betimes next morning, and waited impatiently for the appearance of his new associate, who, after a delay that seemed inter minable, at length presented himself, and commenced a voracious assault on the breakfast.

" Bolter," said Fagin, drawing up a chair and seat ing himself opposite Morris Bolter.

"Well, here I am," returned Noah. "What's the matter ? Don't yer ask me to do any thing till I have done eating. That's a great fault in this place. Yer never get time enough over yer meals."

" You can talk as you eat, can't you ?" said Fagin, cursing his dear young friend's greediness from the very bottom of his heart.

" Oh yes, I can talk. I get on better when I talk," said Noah, cutting a monstrous slice of bread. "Where's Charlotte?"

" Out," said Fagin. " I sent her out this morning with the other young woman, because I wanted us to be alone."

" Oh!" said Noah. " I wish yer'd ordered her to make some buttered toast first. W T ell, talk away. Yer won't interrupt me."

There seemed, indeed, no great fear of any thing interrupting him, as he had evidently sat down with a determination to do a great deal of business.

" You did well yesterday, my dear," said Fagin. " Beautiful! Six shillings and ninepence half-pen ny on the very first day! The kinchin lay will be a fortune to you."

" Don't you forget to add three pint-pots and a milk-can," said Mr. Bolter.

" No, no, my dear. The pint-pots were great strokes of genius; but the milk-can was a perfect masterpiece."

" Pretty well, I think, for a beginner," remarked Mr. Bolter, complacently. " The pots I took off airy railings, and the milk-can was standing by itself outside a public-house. I thought it might get rusty with the rain, or catch cold, yer know—eh ? Ha! ha! ha!"

Fagin affected to laugh very heartily; and Mr. Bolter having had his laugh out, took a series of large bites, which finished his first hunk of bread-and-butter, and assisted Mmself to a second.

" I want you, Bolter," said Fagin, leaning over the table, " to do a piece of work for me, my dear, that needs great care and caution."

" I say," rejoined Bolter, " don't yer go shoving me into danger, or sending me to any more o' yer police-offices. That don't suit me, that don't; and so I tell yer."

" There's not the smallest danger in it—not the very smallest," said the Jew; " it's only to dodge a woman."

"An old woman ?" demanded Mr. Bolter.

" A young one," replied Fagiu.

" I can do that pretty well, I know," said Bolter. " I was a regular cunning sneak when I was at school. What am I to dodge her for ? Not to—"

" Not to do any thing, but to tell me where she goes, who she sees, and, if possible, what she says;

to remember the street, if it is a street, or the house, if it is a house; and to bring me back all the in formation you can."

" What'U yer give me ?" asked Noah, setting down his cup and looking his employer eagerly in the face.

"If you do it well, a pound, my dear. One pound," said Fagin, wishing to interest him in the scent as much as possible. "And that's what I nev er gave yet for any job of work where there wasn't valuable consideration to be gained."

" Who is she ?" inquired Noah.

" One of us."

" Oh Lor!" cried Noah, curling up his nose. " Yer doubtful of her, are yer ?"

" She has found out some new friends, my dear, and I must know who they are," replied Fagin.

" I see," said Noah, " Just to have the pleasure of knowing them, if they're respectable people—eh ? Ha! ha! ha! I'm your man."

" I knew you would be," cried Fagin, elated by the success of his proposal.

" Of course, of course," replied Noah. " Where is she? Where am I to wait for her? WTiere am I to go ?"

"All that, my dear, you shall hear from me. I'll point her out at the proper time," said Fagiu. " You keep ready, and leave the rest to me."

That night, and the next, and the next sgain, the spy sat booted and equipped in his carter's dress, ready to turn out at a word from Fagin. Six nights passed—six long weary nights—and on each Fagin came home with a disappointed face, and briefly in timated that it was not yet time. On the seventh he returned earlier, and with an exultation he could not conceal. It was Sunday.

" She goes abroad to-night," said Fagin, " and on the right errand, I'm sure; for she has been alone all day, and the man she is afraid of will not be back much before day-break. Come with me. Quick!"

Noah started up without saying a word; for the Jew was in a state of such intense excitement that it infected him. They left the house stealthily, and, hurrying through a labyrinth of streets, arrived at length before a public-house, which Noah recognized as the same in which he had slept on the night of his arrival in London.

It was past eleven o'clock, and the door was closed. It opened softly on its hinges as Fagin gave a low whistle. They entered without noise, and the door was closed behind them.

Scarcely venturing to whisper, but substituting dumb show for words, Fagin and the young Jew who had admitted them pointed out the pane of glass to Noah, and signed to him to climb up and observe the person in the adjoining room.

" Is that the woman ?" he asked, scarcely above his breath.

Fagin nodded yes.

" I can't see her face well," whispered Noah. " She is looking down, and the candle is behind her."

" Stay there," whispered Fagin. He signed to Bar ney, who withdrew. In an instant the lad entered the room adjoining, and, under pretense of snuffing the candle, moved it in the required position, and, speaking to the girl, caused her to raise her face.

" I see her now," cried the spy.

"Plainly?"

OLIVER TWIST,

" I should know her among a thousand." He hastily descended as the room-door opened, and the girl came out. Fagin drew him behind a small partition which was curtained off, and they held their breaths as she passed within a few feet of their place of concealment and emerged by the door at which they had entered.

" Hist !" cried the lad who held the door. " Dow !" Noah exchanged a look with Fagin, and darted out. "To the left," whispered the lad: "take the left had, and keep od the other side."

He did so ; and, by the light of the lamps, saw the girl's retreating figure, already at some distance be fore him. He advanced as near as he considered pru dent, and kept on the opposite side of the street, the

was that of a woman, who looked eagerly about her as though in quest of some expected object; the other figure was that of a man, who slunk along in the deepest shadow he could find, and, at some distance, accommodated his pace to hers—stopping when she stopped, and, as she moved again, creeping stealthily on, but never allowing himself, in the ardor of his pursuit, to gain upon her footsteps. Thus they cross ed the bridge, from the Middlesex to the Surrey shore, when the woman, apparently disappointed in her anxious scrutiny of the foot-passengers, turned back. The movement was sudden; but he who watched her was not thrown off his guard by it; for, shrink ing into one of the recesses which surmount the piers of the bridge, and leaning over the parapet, the bet-

" WHEN SHE WAS ABOUT THE SAME DISTANCE IN ADVANCE AS SHE HAD BEEN BEFOEE, HE SLIPPED QUIETLY DOWN, AND FOLLOWED HER AGAIN."

better to observe her motions. She looked nervous ly round twice or thrice, and once stopped to let two men who were following close behind her pass on. She seemed to gather courage as she advanced, and to walk with a steadier and firmer step. The spy preserved the same relative distance between them, and followed, with his eye upon her.

THE APPOINTMENT KEPT.

rMHE church clocks chimed three quarters past elev-_L en, as two figures emerged on London Bridge. One, which advanced with a swift and rapid step,

ter to conceal his figure, he suffered her to pass on the opposite pavement. When she was about the same distance in advance as she had been before, he slipped quietly down, and followed her again. At nearly the centre of the bridge she stopped. The man stopped too.

It was a very dark night. The day had been un favorable, and at that hour and place there were few people stirring. Such as there were hurried quickly past, very possibly without seeing, but certainly with out noticing, either the woman or the man who kept her in view. Their appearance was not calculated to attract the importunate regards of such of Lon don's destitute population as chanced to take their way over the bridge that night in search of some cold arch or doorless hovel wherein to lay their

heads; they stood there iu silence, neither speaking nor spoken to by any one who passed.

A mist hung over the river, deepening the red glare of the tires that burned upon the small craft moored oft' the different wharves, and rendering darker and more indistinct the inurky buildings on the banks. The old smoke-stained store-houses on either side rose heavy and dull from the dense mass of roofs and ga bles, and frowned sternly upon water too black to reflect even their lumbering shapes. The tower of old Saint Saviour's Church, and the spire of Saint Magnus, so long the giant-warders of the ancient bridge, were visible in the gloom; but the forest of shipping below bridge, and the thickly scattered spires of churches above, were nearly all hidden from the sight.

The girl had taken a few restless turns to and fro, closely watched meanwhile by her hidden observer, when the heavy bell of St. Paul's tolled for the death of another day. Midnight had come upon the crowd ed city. The palace, the night-cellar, the jail, the mad-house; the chambers of birth and death, of health and sickness, the rigid face of the corpse and the calm sleep of the child—midnight was upon them all.

The hour had not struck two minutes, when a young lady, accompanied by a gray-haired gentle man, alighted from a hackney-carriage within a short distance of the bridge, and, having dismissed the ve hicle, walked straight toward it. They had scarcely set foot upon its pavement, when the girl started, and immediately made toward them.

They walked onward, looking about them with the air of persons who entertained some very slight ex pectation which had little chance of being realized, when they were suddenly joined by this new associ ate. They halted with an exclamation of surprise, but suppressed it immediately; for a man in the garments of a countryman came close up—brushed against them, indeed—at that precise moment.

" Not here," said Nancy, hurriedly, " I am afraid to speak to you here. Come away—out of the public road—down the steps yonder!"

As she uttered these words, and indicated with her hand the direction in which she wished them to proceed, the countryman looked round, and roughly asking what they took up the whole pavement for, passed on.

The steps to which the girl had pointed were those which, on the Surrey bank, and on the same side of the bridge as Saint Saviour's Church, form a landing-stairs from the river. To this spot the man bearing the appearance of a countryman hastened unobserved, and after a moment's survey of the place, he began to descend.

These stairs are a part of the bridge; they consist of three flights. Just below the end of the second, going down, the stone wall on the left terminates in an ornamental pilaster facing toward the Thames. At this point the lower steps widen, so that a person turning that angle of the wall is necessarily unseen by any others on the stairs who chance to be above him, if only a step. The countryman looked hasti ly round when he reached this point; and as there seemed no better place of concealment, and, the tide leing out, there was plenty of room, he slipped aside, with his back to the pilaster, and there waited, pret-ty certain that they would come no lower, and that even if he could not hear what was said, he could follow them again with safety.

So tardily stole the time in this lonely place, and so eager was the spy to penetrate the motives of an interview so different from what he had been led to expect, that he more than once gave the matter up for lost, and persuaded himself either that they had stopped far above, or had resorted to some entirely different spot to hold their mysterious conversation. He was on the point of emerging from his hiding-place and regaining the road above, when he heard the sound of footsteps, and directly afterward of voices almost close at his ear.

He drew himself straight upright against the wall, and, scarcely breathing, listened attentively.

" This is far enough," said a voice, which was evi dently that of the gentleman. " I will not suffer the young lady to go any farther. Many people would have distrusted you too much to have come even so far, but you see I am willing to humor you."

" To humor me!" cried the voice of the girl whom he had followed. " You're considerate, indeed, sir. To humor me! Well, well, it's no matter."

" Why, for what," said the gentleman, in a kinder tone, " for what purpose can you have brought us to this strange place ? Why not have let me speak to you above there, where it is light, and there is some thing stirring, instead of bringing us to this dark and dismal hole ?"

" I told you before," replied Nancy," that I was afraid to speak to you there. I don't know why it is," said the girl, shuddering, " but I have such a fear and dread upon me to-night that I can hardly stand."

"A fear of what ?" asked the gentleman, who seem ed to pity her.

" I scarcely know of what," replied the girl. " I wish I did. Horrible thoughts of death, and shrouds with blood upon them, and a fear that has made me burn as if I was on tire, have been upon me all day. I was reading a book to-night, to while the time away, and the same things came into the print."

" Imagination," said the gentleman, soothing her.

"No imagination," replied the girl, in a hoarse voice. "I'll swear I saw 'coffin' written in every page of the book in large black letters—ay, and they carried one close to me in the streets to-night."

" There is nothing unusual in that," said the gen tleman. " They have passed me often."

" Real ones," rejoined the girl. " This was not."

There was something so uncommon iu her manner. that the flesh of the concealed listener crept as IK heard the girl utter these words, and the blood chill ed within him. He had never experienced a greater relief than in hearing the sweet voice of the young lady as she begged her to be calm, and not allow her self to become the prey of such fearful fancies.

" Speak to her kindly," said the young lady to her companion. " Poor creature! She seems to need it."

"Your haughty religious people would have held their heads up to see me as I am to-night, and preached, of flames and vengeance," cried the girl. " Oh, dear lady, why ar'n't those who claim to be God's own folks as gentle and as kind to us poor wretches as you, who, having youth, and beauty, and all that they have lost, might be a little proud, in stead of so much humbler ?"

"Ah!" said the gentleman. "A Turk turns his face, after washing it well, to the East, when he says his prayers; these good people, after giving their tact's such a rub against the World as to take the smiles off, turn with no less regularity to the darkest side of Heaven. Between the Mussulman and the Pharisee, commend me to the first!"

These words appeared to be addressed to the young lady, and were perhaps uttered with the view of af fording Nancy time to recover herself. The gentle man shortly afterward addressed himself to her.

" You were not here last Sunday night," he said.

" I couldn't come," replied Nancy; " I was kept by force."

" By whom ?"

" Him that I told the young lady of before."

" You were not suspected of holding any commu nication with any body on the subject which has brought us here to-night, I hope ?" asked the old gentleman.

"No," replied the girl, shaking her head. "It's not very easy for me to leave him unless he knows why ; I couldn't have seen the lady when I did, but that I gave him a drink of laudanum before I came away."

" Did he awake before you returned ?" inquired the gentleman.

" No; and neither he nor any of them suspect me."

" Good," said the gentleman. " Now listen to me."

" I am ready," replied the girl, as he paused for a moment.

" This young lady," the gentleman began," has communicated to me, and to some other friends who can be safely trusted, what you told her nearly a fortnight since. I confess to you that I had doubts at first whether you were to be implicitly relied upon, but now I firmly believe you are."

" I am," said the girl, earnestly.

"I repeat that I firmly believe it. To prove ro you that I am disposed to trust you, I tell you, with out reserve, that we propose to extort the secret, whatever it may be, from the fears of this man Monks. But if—if—" said the gentleman," he can not be secured,'or, if secured, can not be acted upon as we wish, yoii must deliver up the Jew."

" Fagin!" cried the girl, recoiling.

" That man must be delivered up by you," said the gentleman.

" I will not do it! I will never do it!" replied the girl. " Devil that he is, and worse than devil as he has been to me, I will never do that."

" Yon will not ?" said the gentleman, who seemed fully prepared for this answer.

" Never!" returned the girl.

" Tell me why ?"

" For one reason," rejoined the girl, firmly," for one reason,that the lady knows and will stand by me in— I know she will, for I have her promise; and for this other reason besides, that, bad life as he has led, I have led a bad life too: there are many of us who have kept the same courses together, and I'll not turn upon them, who might—any of them—have turned upon me, but didn't, bad as they are."

" Then," said the gentleman, quickly, as if this had

been the point he had been aiming to attain, "put Monks into my hands, and leave him to me to deal with."

" What if he turns against the others ?"

" I promise you that in that case, if the truth is forced from him, there the matter will rest; there must be circumstances in Oliver's little history which it would be painful to drag before the public-eye, and, if the truth is once elicited, they shall go scot free."

"And if it is not ?" suggested the girl.

"Then,"pursued the gentleman, " this Fagin shall not be brought to justice without your consent. In such a case I could show you reasons, I think, which would induce you to yield it."

" Have I the lady's promise for that ?" asked the girl.

" You have," replied Rose. " My true and faithful pledge."

" Monks would never learn how you knew what you do ?" said the girl, after a short pause.

" Never," replied the gentleman. " The intelli gence should be so brought to bear upon him that he could never even guess."

" I have been a liar, and among liars from a little child," said the girl, after another interval of silence, " but I will take your words."

After receiving an assurance from both that she might safely do so, she proceeded, in a voice so low that it was often difficult for the listener to discover even the purport of what she said, to describe, by name and situation, the public -house whence she had been followed that night. From the manner in which she occasionally paused, it appeared as if the gentleman were making some hasty notes of the in formation she communicated. When she had thor oughly explained the localities of the place, the best position from which to watch it without exciting ob servation, and the night and hour on which Monks was most in the habit of frequenting it, she seemed to consider for a few moments, for the purpose of re calling his features and appearance more forcibly t<> her recollection.

" He is tall," said the girl, " and a strongly made man, but not stout; he has a lurking \walk ; and. as he walks, constantly looks over his shoulder, first on one side, and then on the other. Don't forget that, for his eyes are sunk in his head so much deeper than any other man's that you might almost tell him by that alone. His face is dark, like his hair and eyes; and, although he can't be more than six or eight and twenty, withered and haggard. His lips are often discolored and disfigured with the marks of teeth ; for lie has desperate fits, and some times even bites his hands and covers them with wounds—why did you start?" said the girl, stopping suddenly.

The gentleman replied, in a hurried manner, that he was not conscious of having done so, and begged her to proceed.

" Part of this," said the girl, " I've drawn out from other people at the house I tell you of, for I have only seen him twice, and both times he was covered up in a large cloak. I think that's all I can give you to know him by. Stay, though." she added. " Upon his throat, so high that you can see a part of it be-

THE SPY MAKES OFF WITH NEJTS.

low his neckerchief when he turns his face, there is—"

"A broad red mark, like a burn or scald," cried the gentleman.

" How's this ?" said the girl. " Yon know him !"

The young lady uttered a cry of surprise, and for a few moments they were so still that the listener could distinctly hear them breathe.

" I think I do," said the gentleman, breaking si lence. " I should by your description. We shall see. Many people are singularly like each other. It may not be the same."

As he expressed himself to this effect with assumed carelessness, he took a step or two nearer the con cealed spy, as the latter could tell from the distinct ness with which he heard him mutter, " It must be he!"

" Now," he said, returning, so it seemed by the sound, to the spot where he had stood before, " you have given us most valuable assistance, young wom an, and I wish you to be the better for it. What can I do to serve you ?"

" Nothing," replied Nancy.

" You will not persist in saying that," rejoined the gentleman, with a voice and emphasis of kindness that might have touched a much harder and more obdurate heart. " Think now. Tell me."

" Nothing, sir," rejoined the girl, weeping. " You can do nothing to help me. I am past all hope, in deed."

" You put yourself beyond its pale," said the gen tleman. "The past has been a dreary waste with you, of youthful energies misspent, and such price less treasures lavished, as the Creator bestows but once and never grants again, but, for the future, you may hope. I do not say that it is in our power to otter you peace of heart and mind, for that must come as you seek it; but a quiet asylum, either in England, or, if you fear to remain here, in some for eign country, it is not only within the compass of our ability but our most anxious wish to secure you. Before the dawn of morning, before this river wakes to the first glimpse of daylight, you shall be placed as entirely beyond the reach of your former asso ciates, and leave as utter an absence of all trace be hind you, as if you were to disappear from the earth this moment. Come! I would not have you go back to exchange one word with any old companion, or take one look at any old haunt, or breathe the very air which is pestilence and death to you. Quit them all, while there is time and opportunity!"

" She will be persuaded now," cried the young lady. " She hesitates, I am sure."

" I fear not, my dear," said the gentleman.

" No, sir, I do not," replied the girl, after a short struggle. " I am chained to my old life. I loathe and hate it now, but I can not leave it. I must have gone too far to turn back—and yet I don't know; for if you had spoken to me so some time ago, I should have laughed it off. But," she said, looking hastily round, "this fear comes over me again. I must go home."

"Home!" repeated the young lady, with great stress upon the word.

" Home, lady," rejoined the girl. " To such a home as I have raised for mvself with the work of

my whole life. Let us part. I shall be watched or seen. Go! Go! If I have done you any service, all I ask is, that you leave me, and let me go my way alone."

" It is useless," said the gentleman, with a sigh. " We compromise her safety, perhaps, by staving here. We may have detained her longer than she expected already."

" Yes, yes," urged the girl. " You have."

" What," cried the young lady, " can be the end of this poor creature's life!"

"What!" repeated the girl. "Look before you, lady. Look at that dark water. How many times do you read of such as I who spring into the tide, and leave no living thing to care for or bewail them. It may be years hence, or it may be only months, but I shall come to that at last."

"Do not speak thus, pray," returned the young lady, sobbing.

" It will never reach your ears, dear lady, and God forbid such horrors should!" replied the girl. " Good-night, good-night!"

The gentleman turned away.

"This purse," cried the young lady. "Take it for my sake, that you may have some resource in an hour of need and trouble!"

" No!" replied the girl. " I have not done this for money. Let me have that to think of. And yet— give me something that you have worn: I should like to have soniethiug—no, no, not a ring—your gloves or handkerchief—any thing that I can keep, as having belonged to you, sweet lady. There. Bless you! God bless you! Good-night, good night !"

The violent agitation of the girl, and the appre hension of some discovery which would subject her to ill-usage and violence, seemed to determine the gentleman to leave her as she requested. The sounds of retreating footsteps were audible, and the voices ceased.

The two figures of the young lady and her com panion soon afterward appeared upon the bridge. They stopped at the summit of the stairs.

"Hark!" cried the young lady, listeuing. "Did she call ? I thought I heard her voice."

"No, my love," replied Mr. Brownlow, looking sad ly back. " She has not moved, and will not till we are gone."

Rose Maylie lingered, but the old gentleman drew her arm through his, and led her, with gentle force, away. As they disappeared, the girl sunk down nearly at her full length upon one of the stone stairs, and vented the anguish of her heart in bitter tears.

After a time she arose, and with feeble and totter ing steps ascended to the street. The astonished listener remained motionless on his post for some minutes afterward, and having ascertained, with many cautions glances round him, that he was again alone, crept slowly from his hiding-place, and return ed stealthily and in the shade of the wall, in the same manner as he had descended.

Peeping out more than once, when he reached the top, to make sure that he was unobserved, Noah Clay-pole darted away at his utmost speed, and made for the Jew's house as fast as his legs would carry him.

OLIVER TWIST.

CHAPTER XLVII.

.FATAL CONSEQUENCES.

IT was nearly two hours before day-break—that time which in the autumn of the year may be truly called the dead of night, when the streets are silent and deserted, when even sounds appear to slumber, and profligacy and riot have staggered home to dream; it was at this still and silent hour that Fagin sat watching in his old lair, with face so distorted and pale, and eyes so red and bloodshot, that he looked leas like a man than like some hid eous phantom moist from the grave, and worried by an evil spirit.

He sat crouching over a cold hearth, wrapped in an old torn coverlet, with his face turned toward a wasting candle that stood upon a table by his side. His right hand was raised to his lips, and as, absorb ed in thought, he bit his long black nails, he dis closed among his toothless gums a few such fangs as should have been a dog's or rat's.

Stretched upon a mattress on the floor lay Noah Claypole, fast asleep. Toward him the old man sometimes directed his eyes for an instant, and then brought them back again to the candle, which with a long-burnt wick drooping almost double, and hot grease falling down in clots upon the table, plainly showed that his thoughts were busy elsewhere.

Indeed they were. Mortification at the overthrow of his notable scheme; hatred of the girl who had dared to palter with strangers; an utter distrust of the sincerity of her refusal to yield him up; bitter disappointment at the loss of his revenge on Sikes; the fear of detection, and ruin, and death; and a fierce and deadly rage kindled by all; these were the passionate considerations which, following close upon each other with rapid and ceaseless whirl, shot through the brain of Fagiu, as every evil thought and blackest purpose lay working at his heart.

He sat without changing his attitude in the least, or appearing to take the smallest heed of time, until his quick ear seemed to be attracted by a footstep in the street.

"At last," he muttered, wiping his dry and fever ed mouth. "At last!"

The bell rang gently as he spoke. He crept up stairs to the door, and presently returned accompa nied by a man muffled to the chin, who carried a bundle under one arm. Sitting down and throwing back his outer coat, the man displayed the burly frame of Sikes.

" There!" he said, laying the bundle on the table. " Take care of that, and do the most you can with it. It's been trouble enough to get; I thought I should have been here three hours ago."

Fagin laid his hand upon the bundle, and locking it in the cupboard, sat down again without speaking. But he did not take his eyes off the robber for an in-stnnt during this action ; and now that they sat over against each other, fact- to face, he looked fixedly at him, with his lips quivering so violently, and his face so altered by the emotions which had mastered him, that the house-breaker involuntarily drew back his chair, and surveyed him with a look of real affright.

" Wot now ?" cried Sikes. " Wot do you look at a man so for?"

Fagin raised his right hand and shook his trem bling forefinger in the air ; but his passion was so great that the power of speech was for the moment gone.

" Damme!" said Sikes, feeling in his breast with a look of alarm. " He's gone mad. I must look to myself here."

" No, no," rejoined Fagin, finding his voice. " It's not— you're not the person, Bill. I've no — no fault to find with you."

" Oh, you haven't, haven't you ?" said Sikes, look ing sternly at him, and ostentatiously passing a pis tol into a more convenient pocket. " That's lucky— for one of us. Which one that is, don't matter."

" I've got that to tell you, Bill," said Fagiu, draw ing his chair nearer, "will make you worse than me."

"Ay?" returned the robber, with an incredulous air. " Tell away ! Look sharp, or Nance will think I'm lost,"

" Lost!" cried Fagin. " She has pretty well set tled that in her own mind already."

Sikes looked with an aspect of great perplexity into the Jew's face, and reading no satisfactory ex planation of the riddle there, clenched his coat-col lar in his huge hand and shook him soundly.

" Speak, will you !" he said ; " or, if you don't, it shall be for want of breath. Open your mouth and say wot you've got to say in plain words. Out with it, you thundering old cur—out with it!"

" Suppose that lad that's lying there— " Fagiu be gan.

Sikes turned round to where Noah was sleeping, as if he had not previously observed him. " Well!" he said, resuming his former position.

" Suppose that lad," pursued Fagin, " was to peach —to blow upon us all—first seeking out the right folks for the purpose, and then having a meeting with 'em in the street to paint our likenesses, de scribe every mark that they might know us by, and the crib where we might be most easily taken. Sup pose he was to do all this, and besides, to blow upon a plant we've all been in more or less—of his own fancy; not grabbed, trapped, tried, ear wished by the parson and brought to it on bread-and-water — but of his own fancy; to please his own taste; steal ing out at nights to find those most interested against us, and peaching to them. Do you hear me ?" cried the Jew, his eyes flashing with rage. " Suppose he-did all this, what then?"

" What then !" replied Sikes, with a tremendous oath. " If he was left alive till I came, I'd grind his skull under the iron heel of my boot into as many grains as there are hairs upon his head."

" What if I did it !" cried Fagiu, almost in a yell. "7, that know so much, and could hang so many be sides myself!"

" I don't know," replied Sikes, clenching his teeth and turning white at the mere suggestion. " I'd do something in the jail that 'ml get me put in irons; and if I was tried along with you, I'd fall upon you with them in the open court, and beat your brains out afore the people. I should have such strength," muttered the robber, poising his brawny arm, " that I could smash your head as if a loaded wagon had gone over it."

" You would ?"

GOADING THE WILD BEAST.

" Would I!" said the house-breaker. " Try me."

" If it was Charley, or the Dodger, or Bet, or— :

" I don't care who," replied Sikes, impatiently. " Whoever it was, I'd serve them the same."

Fagin looked hard at the robber; and, motioning him to be silent, stooped over the bed upon the floor and shook the sleeper to rouse him. Sikes leaned forward in his chair, looking on with his hands upon his knees, as if wondering much what all this ques tioning and preparation was to end in.

" Bolter, Bolter! Poor lad!" said Fagin, looking up with an expression of devilish anticipation, and speaking slowly and with marked emphasis. " He's tired—tired with watching for her so long—watch ing for her, Bill."

" Wot d'ye mean ?" asked Sikes, drawing back.

Fagin made no answer, but bending over the sleep er again, hauled him into a sitting posture. When his assumed name had been repeated several times, Noah rubbed his eyes, and, giving a heavy yawn, looked sleepily about him.

"Tell me that again—once again, just for him to hear," said the Jew, pointing to Sikes as he spoke.

" Tell yer what ?" asked the sleepy Noah, shaking himself pettishly.

" That about— NANCY," said Fagin, clutching Sikes by the wrist, as if to prevent his leaving the house before he had heard enough. " You followed her t"

" Yes."

" To London Bridge ?"

" Yes."

" Where she met two people ?"

" So she did."

"A gentleman and lady that she had gone to of her own accord before, who asked her to give up all her pals, and Monks first, which she did—and to de scribe him, which she did—and to tell her what house it was that we meet at, and go to, which she did— and where it could be best watched from, which she did—and what time the people went there, which she did. She did all this. She told it all, every word, without a threat, without a murmur—she did—did she not ?" cried Fagin, half mad with fury.

"All right," replied Noah, scratching his head. " That's just what it was!"

" What did they say about last Sunday ?"

" About last Sunday ?" replied Noah, considering. " Why I told yer that before."

"Again. 'Tell it again!" cried Fagin, tightening his grasp on Sikes, and brandishing his other hand aloft, as the foam flew from his lips.

" They asked her," said Noah, who, as he grew more wakeful, seemed to have a dawning perception who Sikes was, " they asked her why she didn't come last Sunday, as she promised. She said she couldn't."

" Why—why ? Tell him that."

" Because she was forcibly kept at home by Bill, the man she had told them of before," replied Noah.

" What more of him ?" cried Fagiu. " What more of the man she had told them of before ? Tell him that, tell him that."

" Why, that she couldn't very easily get out-of-doors unless he knew where she was going to," said Noah; " and so the first time she went to see the lady, she—ha! ha! ha! it made me laugh when she said it, that it did—she gave him a diluk of laudauum!"

" Hell's fire!" cried Sikes, breaking fiercely from the Jew. " Let me go!"

Flinging the old man from him, he rushed from the room, and darted, wildly and furiously, up the stairs.

" Bill, Bill!" cried Fagiu, following him hastily. "A word. Only a word."

The word would not have been exchanged, but that the house-breaker was unable to open the door, on which he was expending fruitless oaths and vio lence, when the Jew came panting up.

" Let me out!" said Sikes. " Don't speak to me; it's not safe. Let me out, I say!"

" Hear me speak a word," rejoined Fagin, laying his hand upon the lock. " You won't be—"

" Well," replied the other.

" You won't be—too—violent, Bill ?"

The day was breaking, and there was light enough for the men to see each other's faces. They ex changed one brief glance; there was a fire in the eyes of both which could not be mistaken.

" I mean," said Fagiu, showing that he felt all dis guise was now useless, " not too violent for safety. Be crafty, Bill, and not too bold."

Sikes made no reply; but, pulling open the door of which Fagin had turned the lock, dashed into the silent streets.

Without one pause, or moment's consideration ; without once turning his head to the right or left, or raising his eyes to the sky, or lowering them to the ground, but looking straight before him with savage resolution, his teeth so tightly compressed that the strained jaw seemed starting through his skin, the robber held on his headlong course, nor muttered a word, nor relaxed a muscle, until he reached his own door. He opened it softly with a key, strode lightly up the stairs, and, entering his own room, double-locked the door, and lifting a heavy table against it, drew back the curtain of the bed.

The girl was lying, half-dressed, upon it. He had roused her from her sleep, for she raised herself with a hurried and startled look.

" Get up!" said the man.

" It is you, Bill!" said the girl, with an expression of pleasure at his return.

" It is," was the reply. " Get up!"

There was a candle burning, but the man hastily drew it from the candlestick and hurled it under the grate. Seeing the faint light of early day without, the girl rose to undraw the curtain.

" Let it be," said Sikes, thrusting his hand before her. " There's light enough for wot I've got to do."

" Bill," said the girl, in the low voice of alarm, " why do you look like that at me ?"

The robber sat regarding her for a few seconds with dilated nostrils and heaving breast; and then, grasping her by the head and throat, dragged her into the middle of the room, and looking once toward the door, placed his heavy hand upon her mouth.

"Bill! Bill!" gasped the girl, wrestling with the strength of mortal fear—" I—I won't scream or cry —not once—hear me—speak to me—tell rue what I have done."

" You know, you she-devil!" returned the robber, suppressing his breath. "You were watched to night ; every word you said was heard."

" Then spare my life for the love of Heaven, as I

spared yours," rejoined the girl, clinging to him. " Bill, dear Bill, you can not have the heart to kill me! Oh! think of all I have given up, only this one night, for you. You shall have time to think, and save yourself this crime; I will not loose my hold, you can not throw me off. Bill, Bill, for dear God's sake, for your own, for mine, stop before you spill my blood! I have been true to you, upon my guilty soul I have!"

The man struggled violently to release his arms; but those of the girl were clasped round his, and, tear her as lie would, he could not tear them away.

" Bill," cried the girl, striving to lay her head upon his breast, " the gentleman and that dear lady told me to-night of a home in some foreign country where I could end my days in solitude and peace. Let me see them again, and beg them on my knees to show the same mercy and goodness to you ; and let us both leave this dreadful place, and, far apart, lead better lives, and forget how we have lived, except in prayers, and never see each other more. It is never too late to repent. They told me so—I feel it now; but we must have time—a little, little time!"

The house-breaker freed one arm, and grasped his pistol. The certainty of immediate detection if he tired, flashed across his mind even in the midst of his fury, and he beat it twice, with all the force he could summon, upon the upturned face that almost touched his own.

She staggered and fell, nearly blinded with the blood that rained down from a deep gash in her forehead; but raising herself with difficulty on her knees, drew from her bosom a white handkerchief— Rose Maylie's own—and holding it up, in her folded hands, as high toward heaven as her feeble strength would allow, breathed one prayer for mercy to her Maker.

It was a ghastly figure to look upon. The mur derer staggering backward to the wall, and shutting out the sight with his hand, seized a heavy club and struck her down.

CHAPTER XLVIII.

THE FLIGHT OF SIKES.

OF all bad deed.s that, under cover of the dark ness, had been committed within wide London's bounds since night hung over it, that was the worst. Of all the horrors that rose with an ill scent upon the morning air, that was the foulest and most cruel.

The sun—the bright sun, that brings back, not light alone, but new life, and hope, and freshness to man—burst upon the crowded city in clear and ra diant glory. Through costly-colored glass and pa per - mended window, through cathedral dome and rotten crevice, it shed its equal ray. It lighted up the room where the murdered woman lay. It did. He tried to shut it out, but it would stream in. If the sight had been a ghastly one in the dull morn-iiig, what was it now, in all that brilliant light!

He had not moved; he had been afraid to stir. There had been a moan and motion of the hand, and, with terror added to rage, he had struck and struck again. O:ice he threw a rug over it; but it was worse to fancy the eyes, and imagine them moving

towai'd him, than to see them glaring upward, as if watching the reflection of the pool of gore that quivered and danced in the sunlight on the ceiling. He had plucked it off again. And there was the body — mere flesh and blood, no more — but such flesh, and so much blood!

He struck a light, kindled the fire, and thrust the club into it. There was hair upon the end, which blazed and shrunk into a light cinder, and, caught by the air, whirled up the chimney. Even that fright ened him, sturdy as he was ; but he held the weapon till it broke, and then piled it on the coals to burn away, and smoulder into ashes. He washed himself, and rubbed his clothes; there were spots that would not be removed, but he cut the pieces out, and burned them. How those stains were dispersed about the room! The very feet of the dog were bloody.

All this time he had never once turned his back upon the corpse; no, not for a moment. Such prepa rations completed, he moved backward toward the door, dragging the dog with him, lest he should soil his feet anew and carry out new evidences of the crime into the streets. He shut the door softly, locked it, took the key, and left the house.

He crossed over, and glanced up at the window, to be sure that nothing was visible from the outside. There was the curtain still drawn, which she would have opened to admit the light she never saw again. It lay nearly under there. He knew that. God. how the sun poured down upon the very spot!

The glance was instantaneous. It was a relief to have got free of the room. He whistled on the dog, and walked rapidly away.

lie went through Islington; strode up the hill at Highgate on which stands the stone in honor of Whittingtoii; turned down to Highgate Hill, un steady of purpose, .and uncertain where to go; struck off to the right again almost as soon as he began to descend it; and taking the foot-path across the fields, skirted Caen Wood, and so came out on Hampstead Heath. Traversing the hollow by the Vale of Health, he mounted the opposite bank, and, crossing the road which joins the villages of Hampstead and Highgate, made along the remaining portion of the Heath to the fields at North End, in one of which he laid himself down under a hedge and slepr.

Soon he was up again and away—not far into the country, but back toward London by the high-road— then back again—then over another part of the same ground as he already traversed—then wandering up and down in fields, and lying on ditches' brinks to rest, and starting up to make for some other spot and do the same, and ramble on again.

Where could he go that was near and not too pub lic, to get some meat and drink ? Hendon. That was a good place, not far oft", and out of most peo ple's way. Thither he directed his steps—running sometimes, and sometimes, with a strange perversi ty, loitering at a snail's pace, or stopping altogether and idly breaking the hedges with his stick. But when he got there, all the people he met—the very children at the doors—seemed to view him with sus picion. Back he turned again, without the courage to purchase bit or drop, though he had tasted no food for many hours; and once more he lingered on the Heath, uncertain where to go.

THE PEDDLER OF ALL WARES.

He wandered over miles .and miles of ground, and still came back to the old place. Morning and noon had passed, and the day was on the wane, and still he rambled to and fro, and up and down, and round and round, and still lingered about the same spot. At last he got away, and shaped his course for Hat-tield.

It was nine o'clock at night, when the man, quite tired out, and the dog, limping and lame from the unaccustomed exercise, turned down the hill by the church of the quiet village, and plodding along the little street, crept into a small public-house, whose scanty light had guided them to the spot. There was a fire in the tap-room, and some country-labor-

There was nothing to attract attention or excite alarm in this. The robber, after paying his reckon ing, sat silent and unnoticed in his corner, and had almost dropped asleep, when he was half wakened by the noisy entrance of a new-comer.

This was an antic fellow, half peddler and half mountebank, who traveled about the country on foot to vend hones, strops, razors, wash-balls, har ness-paste, medicine for dogs and horses, cheap per fumery, cosmetics, and such-like wares, which he carried in a case slung to his back. His entrance was the signal for various homely jokes with the countrymen, which slackened not until he had made his supper, and opened his box of treasures, when lie

" HE MOVED UACKWAKI

ers were drinking before it. They made room for the stranger, but he sat down in the farthest corner, and ate and drank alone, or rather with his dog, to whom he cast a morsel of food from time to time.

The conversation of the men assembled here turn ed upon the neighboring laud and fanners; and when those topics were exhausted, upon the age of some old man who had been buried on the previous Sun day ; the young men present considering him very old, and the old men present declaring him to have been quite young—not older, one white-haired grand father said, than he was—with ten or fifteen year of life in him at least—if he had taken care; if he had taken care.

WITH HIM.

ingeniously contrived to unite business with amuse ment.

" And what be that stoof ? Good to eat, Harry ?" asked a grinning countryman, pointing to some com position-cakes in one corner.

" This," said the fellow, producing one, " this is the infallible and invaluable composition for removing all sorts of stain, rust, dirt, mildew, spick, speck, spot, or spatter, from silk, satin, linen, cambric, cloth, crape, stuff, carpet, merino, muslin, bombazine, or woolen stuff. Wine-stains, fruit-stains, beer-stains, water-stains, paint-stains, pitch-stains, any stains, all come out at one rub with the infallible and invaluable composition. If a lady stains her honor, she,has only

OLIVER TWIST.

need to swallow one cake, and she's cured at once— for it's poison. Jf a gentleman wants to prove this, he has only need to bolt one little square, and he has put ic beyond question—for it's quite as satisfacto ry as a pistol-bullet, and a great deal nastier in the flavor, consequently the more credit in taking it. One penny a square. With all these virtues, one penny a square!"

There were two buyers directly, and more of the listeners plainly hesitated. The vender observing this, increased in loquacity.

"It's all bought up as fast as it can be made," said the fellow. " There are fourteen water-mills, six steam-engines, and a galvanic battery, always a-working upon it, and they can't make it fast enough, though the men work so hard that they die off, and the widows is pensioned directly, with twenty pound a year for each of the children, and a premium of fifty for twins. One penny a square! Two half pence is all the same, and four farthings is received with joy. One penny a square ! Wine-stains, fruit-stains, beer-stains, water-stains, paint-stains, pitch-stains, mud-stains, blood-stains! Here is a stain upon the hat of a gentleman id company that I'll take clean out before he can order me a pint of ale."

" Hah!" cried Sikes, starting up. " Give that back!"

" I'll take it clean out, sir," replied the man, wink ing to the company, " before you can come across the room to get it. Gentlemen all, observe the dark stain upon this gentleman's hat, no wider than a shil ling, but thicker than a half-crown. Whether it is a wine-stain, fruit-stain, beer-stain, water-stain, paint-stain, pitch-stain, mud-stain, or blood-stain—"

The man got no farther, for Sikes, with a hideous imprecation, overthrew the table, and, tearing the hat from him, burst out of the house.

With the same perversity of feeling and irresolu tion that had fastened upon him, despite himself, all day, the murderer, finding that he was not followed, and that they most probably considered him some drunken, sullen fellow, turned back up the town, and getting out of the glare of the lamps of a stage coach that was standing in the street, was walking past, when he recognized the mail from London, and saw that it was standing at the little post-office. He almost knew what was to come; but he crossed over, and listened.

The guard was standing at the door, waiting for the letter-bag. A man, dressed like a gamekeeper, came up at the moment, and he handed him a basket which lay ready on the pavement.

" That's for your people," said the guard. " Now, look alive in there, will you! D— that 'ere bag, it warn't ready night afore last; this won't do, you know!"

"Any thing new up in town, Ben ?" asked the gamekeeper, drawing back to the window-shutters, the better to admire the horses.

" No, nothing that I knows on," replied the man, pulling on his gloves. " Corn's up a little. I heerd talk of a murder, too, down Spitalfields way, but I don't reckon much upon it."

" Oh, that's quite true," said a gentleman inside, who was looking out of the window. "And a dread ful murder it was."

"Was it, sir?" rejoined the guard, touching his hat. " Man or woman, pray, sir ?"

"A woman," replied the gentleman. "It is sup posed—

" Now, Ben!" cried the coachman, impatiently.

" D— that 'ere bag," said the guard; " are you gone to sleep in there ?"

" Coming!" cried the officer-keeper, running out.

" Coming!" growled the guard. "Ah, and so's the young ooman of property that's going to take a fan cy to me, but I don't know when. Here, give hold. Allri—ight!"

The horn sounded a few cheerful notes, and the coach was gone.

Sikes remained standing in the street, apparently unmoved by what he had just heard, and agitated by no stronger feeling than a doubt where to go. At length he went back again, and took the road which leads from Hatfield to St. Albaus.

He went on doggedly; but as he left the town be hind him, and plunged into the solitude and dark ness of the road, he felt a dread and awe creeping upon hiifl which shook him to the core. Every ob ject before him, substance or shadow, still or moving, took the semblance of some fearful thing; but these fears were nothing compared to the sense that haunt ed him of that morning's ghastly figure following at his heels. He could trace its shadow in the gloom, supply the smallest item of the outline, and note how stiff and solemn it seemed to stalk alone. He could hear its garments rustling in the leaves, and every breath of wind came laden with that last low cry. If he stopped, it did the same. If he ran, it followed —not running too ; that would have been a relief: but like a corpse endowed with the mere machinery of life, and borne on one slow, melancholy wind that never rose or fell.

At times he turned, with desperate determination, resolved to beat this phantom off, though it should look him dead; but the hair rose on his head, and his blood stood still, for it had turned with him, and was behind him then. He ha<l kept it before him that morning, but it was behind now—always. He leaned his back against a bank, and felt that it stood above him, visibly out against the cold night-sky. He threw himself upon the road—on his back upon the road. At his head it stood, silent, erect, and still —a living grave-stone, with its epitaph in blood.

Let no man talk of murderers escaping justice, and • hint that Providence must sleep. There were twen ty score of violent deaths in one long minute of that • agony of fear.

There was a shed in a field he passed that offered shelter for the night. Before the door were three tall poplar trees, which made it very dark within ; and the wind moaned through them with a dismal wail. He could not walk on till daylight came again : and here he stretched himself close to the wall—to undergo new torture.

For now a vision came before him, as constant and more terrible than that from which he had es caped. Those widely-staring eyes, so lustreless and so glassy, that he had better borne to see them than think upon them, appeared in the midst of the dark ness, bight in themselves, but giving light to nothing. There were but two, but they were everywhere. If

THE CUESE OF CAIN.

he shut out the sight, there came the room with ev ery well-known object—some, indeed, that he Avould have forgotten if lie had gone over its contents from memory—each in its accustomed place. The body was in its place, and its eyes were as he saw them when he stole away. He got up aud rushed into the field without. The figure was behind him. He re-entered the shed, aud shrunk down once more. The eyes were there, before he had lain himself along.

And here he remained in such terror as none but he can know, trembling in every limb, and the cold sweat starting from every pore, when suddenly there arose upon the night-wind the noise of distant shout ing and the roar of voices mingled in alarm and won der. Any sound of men in that lonely place, even though it conveyed a real cause of alarm, was some thing to him. He regained his strength and energy at the prospect of personal danger; and springing to his feet, rushed into the open air.

The broad sky seemed on fire. Rising into the air with showers of sparks, and rolling one above the other, were sheets of flame, lighting the atmosphere for miles round, and driving clouds of smoke in the direction where he stood. The shouts grew louder as new voices swelled the roar, and he could hear the cry of fire, mingled with the ringing of an alarm-bell, the fall of heavy bodies, and the crackling of flames as they twined round some new obstacle, and shot aloft as though refreshed by food. The noise increased as he looked. There were people there— men and women — light, bustle. It was like new life to him. He darted onward—straight, headlong — dashing through brier aud brake, and leaping gate and fence as madly as his dog, who careered with loud and sounding bark before him.

He came upon the spot. There were half-dressed figures tearing to and fro, some endeavoring to drag the frightened horses from the stables, others driv ing the cattle from the yard and out-houses, and oth ers coming laden from the burning pile, amidst a shower of falling sparks and the tumbling down of red-hot beams. The apertures, where doors and win dows stood an hour ago, disclosed a mass of raging fire; walls rocked and crumbled into the burning well; the molten lead and iron poured down, white-hot, upon the ground. Women and children shrieked, and men encouraged each other with noisy shouts and cheers. The clanking of the engine-pumps, and the spirting and hissing of the water as it fell upon the blazing wood, added to the tremendous roar. He shouted, too, till he was hoarse ; and flying from memory and himself, plunged into the thickest of the throng.

Hither and thither he dived that night — now working at the pumps, and now hurrying through the smoke and flame, but never ceasing to engage himself wherever noise and men were thickest. Up and down the ladders, upon the roofs of buildings, over floors that quaked and trembled with his weight, under the lee of falling bricks and stones, in every part of that great fire, was he ; but he bore a charmed life, and had neither scratch nor bruise, nor weari ness nor thought, till morning dawned again, and only smoke and blackened ruins remained.

This mad excitement over, there returned, with tenfold force, the dreadful consciousness of his crime. He looked suspiciously about him, for the men were conversing in groups, and he feared to be the subject of their talk. The dog obeyed the significant beck of his finger, and they drew off, stealthily, together. He passed near an engine where some men were seated, and they called to him to share in their re freshment. He took some bread and meat; and, as he drank a draught of beer, heard the firemen, who were from London, talking about the murder. " He has gone to Birmingham, they say," said one; " but they'll have him yet, for the scouts are out, and by to-morrow night .there'll be a cry all through the country."

He hurried off, and walked till he almost dropped upon the ground ; then lay down in a lane, and had a long, but broken and uneasy sleep. He wandered on again, irresolute and undecided, and oppressed with the fear of another solitary night.

Suddenly, he took the desperate resolution of go ing back to London.

" There's somebody to speak to there, at all events," he thought. "A good hiding-place, too. They'll never expect to nab me there, after this country scent. Why can't I lie by for a week or so, and, forcing blunt from Fagin, get abroad to France ? Damme, I'll risk it."

He acted upon this impulse without delay, and choosing the least frequented roads, began his jour ney back, resolved to lie concealed within a short distance of the metropolis, and, entering it at dusk by a circuitous route, to proceed straight to that part of it which he had fixed on for his destina tion.

The dog, though. If any descriptions of him were out, it would not be forgotten that the dog was miss ing, and had probably gone with him. This might lead to his apprehension as he passed along the streets. He resolved to drown him, and walked on, looking about for a pond, picking up a heavy stone and tying it to his handkerchief as he went.

The animal looked up into his master's face while these preparations were making: whether his in stinct apprehended something of their purpose, or the robber's sidelong look at him was sterner than ordinary, he skulked a little farther in the rear than usual, and cowered as he came more slowly along. When his master halted at the brink of a pool, and looked round to call him, he stopped outright.

" Do you hear me call ? Come here!" cried Sikes.

The animal came up from the very force of hab it ; but as Sikes stooped to attach the handkerchief to his throat, he uttered a low growl and started back.

" Come back!" said the robber.

The dog wagged his tail, but moved not. Sikes made a running noose and called him again.

The dog advanced, retreated, paused an instant, turned, aud scoured away at his hardest speed.

The man whistled again and again, and sat down and waited in the expectation that he would return. But no dog appeared, and at length he resumed his journey.

OLIVER TWIST.

CHAPTER XLIX.

MONKS AND MR. BROWNLOW AT LENGTH MEET. THEIR CONVERSATION, AND THE INTELLIGENCE THAT INTER RUPTS IT.

THE twilight was beginning to close in, when Mr. Browulow alighted from a hackney-coach at his own door, and knocked softly. The door being open ed, a sturdy man got out of the coach and stationed himself on one side of the steps, while another man, who had been seated on the box, dismounted too, and stood upon the other side. At a sign from Mr. Brownlow they helped out a third man, and taking him between them, hurried him into the house. This man was Monks.

They walked in the same manner up the stairs, without speaking; and Mr. Browulow, preceding them, led the way into a back-room. At the door of this apartment Monks, who had ascended w y ith ev ident reluctance, stopped. The two men looked to the old gentleman as if for instructions.

" He knows the alternative," said Mr. Brownlow. " If he hesitates or moves a finger but as you bid him, drag him into the street, call for the aid of the police, and impeach him as a felon in my name."

" How dare you say this of me ?" asked Monks.

" How dare you urge me to it, young man ?" re plied Mr. Brownlow, confronting him with a steady look. "Are you mad enough to leave this house? Unhand him. There, sir. You are free to go, and we to follow. But I warn you, by all I hold most solemn and most sacred, that the instant you set foot in the street, that instant will I have you appre hended on a charge of fraud and robbery. I am res olute and immovable. If you are determined to be the same, your blood be upon your own head!"

" By what authority am I kidnapped in the street, and brought here by these dogs ?" asked Monks, look ing from one to the other of the men who stood be side him.

" By mine," replied Mr. Brownlow. " Those per sons are indemnified by me. If you complain of be ing deprived of your liberty—you had power and opportunity to retrieve it as you came along, but you deemed it advisable to remain quiet — I say again, throw yourself for protection on the law. I will appeal to the law too; but when you have gone too far to recede, do not sue to me for leniency, when the power will have passed into other hands; and do not say I plunged you down the gulf into which you rushed yourself."

Monks was plainly disconcerted, and alarmed be sides. He hesitated.

" You Avill decide quickly," said Mr. Brownlow, with perfect firmness and composure. " If you wish me to prefer my charges publicly, and consign you to a punishment the extent of which, although I can, with a shudder, foresee, I can not control—once more, I say, you know the way. If not, and you appeal to my forbearance and the mercy of those you have deeply injured, seat yourself, without a word, in that chair. It has waited for you two whole days."

Monks muttered some unintelligible words, but wavered still.

"You will be prompt," said Mr. Brownlow. "A word from me, and the alternative has gone forever."

(Still the man hesitated.

" I have not the inclination to parley," said Mr. Brownlow, " and, as I advocate the dearest interests of others, I have not the right."

"Is there—" demanded Monks, with a faltering tongue—" is there—no middle course?"

" None."

Monks looked at the old gentleman with an anx ious eye; but reading in his countenance nothing but severity and determination, Avalked into the room, and, shrugging his shoulders, sat down.

" Lock the door 011 the outside," said Mr. Brown-low to the attendants, " and come when I ring."

The men obeyed, and the two were left alone to gether.

" This is pretty treatment, sir," said Monks, throw ing down his hat and cloak, " from my father's old est friend."

"It is because I was your father's oldest friend, young man," returned Mr. Browulow; " it is because the hopes aud wishes of young and happy years were bound up with him and that fair creature of his blood and kindred who rejoined her God in youth, and left me here a solitary, lonely man; it is because he kuelt with me beside his only sister's death-bed when he was yet a boy, on the morning that would —but Heaven willed otherwise—have made her my young wife; it is because my seared heart clung to him, from that time forth, through all his trials and errors, till he died; it is because old recollections and associations filled my heart, and even the sight of you brings with it old thoughts of him; it is be cause of all these things that I am moved to treat you gently now—yes, Edward Leeford, even now — and blush for your unworthiness who bear the name."

" What has the name to do with it ?" asked the other, after contemplating, half in silence, and half in dogged wonder, the agitation of his companion. " What is the name to me ?"

" Nothing," replied Mr. Brownlow; " nothing to you. But it was hers, and, even at this distance of time, brings back to me, an old man, the glow and thrill which I once felt, only to hear it repeated by a stranger. I am very glad you have changed it— very—very."

" This is all mighty fine," said Monks (to retain his assumed designation), after a long silence, during which he had jerked himself in sullen defiance to and fro, and Mr. Brownlow had sat shading his face with his hand. " But what do you want with me f

" You have a brother," said Mr. Brownlow, rousing himself—" a brother, the whisper of whose name in your ear when I came behind you in the street was, in itself, almost enough to make you accompany me hither, in wonder and alarm."

" I have no brother," replied Monks. " You know I was an only child. Why do you talk to me of brothers ? You know that, as well as I."

"Attend to what I do know, and you may not," said Mr. Brownlow. I shall interest you by-and-by. I know that of the wretched marriage into which family pride, and the most sordid and narrowest of all ambition, forced your unhappy father when a mere boy, you were the sole and most unnatural issue."

" I don't care for hard names," interrupted Monks,

with a jeering laugh. " You kuow the fact, and that's enough for me."

"But I also kuow," pursued the old gentleman, "the misery, the slow torture, the protracted an guish, of that ill-assorted union. I kuow how list lessly and wearily each of that wretched pair drag ged on their heavy chain through a world that was poisoned to them both. I know how cold formalities were succeeded by open taunts; how indifference gave place to dislike, dislike to hate, and hate to loathing, until at last they wrenched the clanking bond asunder, and retiring a wide space apart, car ried each a galling fragment, of which nothing but death could break the rivets, to hide it in new so ciety beneath the gayest looks they could assume. Your mother succeeded—she forgot it soon. But it rusted and cankered at your father's heart for years." •• Well, they were separated," said Monks; "and what of that?"

•• When they had been separated for some time," returned Mr. Browulow, " and your mother, wholly given up to continental frivolities, had utterly for gotten the young husband, ten good years her junior, who, with prospects blighted, lingered on at home, he fell among new friends. This circumstance, at least, you know already."

" Not I," said Monks, turning away his eyes and beating his foot upon the ground, as a man who is determined to deny every thing. " Not I."

" Your manner, no less than your actions, assures me that you have never forgotten it, or ceased to think of it with bitterness," returned Mr. Brownlow. " I speak of fifteen years ago, when you were not more than eleven years old, and your father but one-and-thirty—for he was, I repeat, a boy when his fa ther ordered him to marry. Must I go back to events which cast a shade upon the memory of your parent, or will you spare it, and disclose to me the truth ?"

" I have nothing to disclose," rejoined Monks. " You must talk on if you will."

"These new friends, then," said Mr. Brownlow, " were a naval officer, retired from active service, whose wife had died some half a year before, and left him with two children—there had been more, but, of all their family, happily but two survived. They were both daughters; one a beautiful creature of nineteen, and the other a mere child of two or three years old."

" What's this to me ?" asked Monks. " They resided," said Mr. Brownlow, without seem ing to hear the interruption, " in a part of the coun try to which your father in his wandering had re paired, and where he had taken up his abode. Ac quaintance, intimacy, friendship, fast followed on each other. Your father was gifted as few men are. He had his sister's soul and person. As the old offi cer knew him more and more, he grew to love him. I would that it had ended there. His daughter did the same."

The old gentleman paused—Mcnks was biting his lips, with his eyes fixed upon the floor. Seeing this, he immediately resumed:

" The end of a year found him contracted, sol emnly contracted, to that daughter—the object of tin- first, true, ardent, only passion of a guileless girl."

" Your tale is o*f the longest," observed Monks, moving restlessly in his chair.

"It.is a true tale of grief and trial and sorrow, young man," returned Mr. Browulow; " and such tales usually are : if it were one of unmixed joy and happiness, it would be very brief. At length one of those rich relations, to strengthen whose interest and importance your father had been sacrificed, as others are often—it is no uncommon case—died, and, to re pair the misery he had been instrumental in occasion ing, left him his panacea for all griefs—Money. It was necessary that he should immediately repair to Rome, whither this man had sped for health, and where he had died, leaving his affairs in great confu sion. He went, was seized with mortal illness there; was followed the moment the intelligence reached Paris by your mother, who carried you with her; he died the day after her arrival, leaving no will— no will —so that the whole property fell to her and you."

At this part of the recital, Monks held his breath and listened with a face of intense eagerness, though his eyes were not directed toward the speaker. As Mr. Brownlow paused, he changed his position with the air of one who has experienced a sudden relief, and wiped his hot face and hands.

" Before he went abroad, and as he passed through London on his way," said Mr. Brownlow, slowly, and fixing his eyes upon the other's face, " he came to me."

" I never heard of that," interrupted Monks, in a tone intended to appear incredulous, but savoring more of disagreeable surprise.

" He came to me, and left with me, among some other things, a picture—a portrait painted by him self—a likeness of this poor girl—which he did not wish to leave behind, and could not carry forward on his hasty journey. He was worn, by anxiety and re morse, almost to a shadow; talked in a wild, dis tracted way of ruin and dishonor worked by himself; confided to me his intention to convert his whole property, at any loss, into money, and, having set tled on his wife and you a portion of his recent ac quisition, to fly the country—I guessed too well he would not fly alone—and never see it more. Even from me, his old and early friend, whose strong at tachment had taken root in the earth that covered one most dear to both—even from me he withheld any more particular confession, promising to write and tell me all, and after that to see me once again for the last time on earth. Alas! That was the last time. I had no letter, and I never saw him more.

" I went," said Mr. Browulow, after a short pause; " I went, when all was over, to the scene of his—I will vise the term the world would freely use, for worldly harshness or favor are now alike to him—of his guilty love, resolved that if my fears were real ized, that erring child should find one heart and home to shelter and compassionate her. The family had left that part a week before; they had called in such trifling debts as were outstanding, discharged them, and left the place by night. Why, or whither, none can tell."

Monks drew his breath yet more freely, and looked round with a smile of triumph.

" When your brother," said Mr. Brownlow, draw ing nearer to the other's chair—" when your broth-

OLIVER TWIST.

er — a feeble, ragged, neglected (fliild — was cast in my way by a stronger hand than chance, and res cued by me from a life of vice and infamy—

" What ?" cried Monks.

" By me," said Mr. Brownlow. " I told you I should interest you before long. I say by me—I see that your cunning associate suppressed my name, although, for aught he knew, it would be quite strange to your ears. When he was rescued by me, then, and lay recover ing from sickness in my house, his strong resemblance to this picture I have spoken of struck me with as tonishment. Even when I first saw him in all his dirt and misery, there was a lingering expression in his face that came upon me like a glimpse of some old friend flashing on one in a vivid dream. I need not tell you he was snared away before I knew his history—

" Why not ?" asked Monks, hastily.

" Because you know it well." a j j»

" Denial to me is vain," replied Mr. Brownlow. " I shall show you that I know more than that."

" You—you—can't prove any thing against me," stammered Monks. " I defy you to do it!"

" We shall see," returned the old gentleman, with a searching glance. " I lost the boy, and no efforts of mine could recover him. Your mother being dead, I knew that you alone could solve the mystery if any body could; and as when I had last heard of you you were on your own estate in the West Indies —whither, as you well know, you retired upon your mother's death to escape the consequences of vicious courses here—I made the voyage. You had left it months before, and were supposed to be in London; but no one could tell where. I returned. Your agents had no clue to your residence. You came and went, they said, as strangely as you had ever done—some times for days together and sometimes not for mouths —keeping, to all appearance, the same low haunts, and mingling with the same infamous herd who had been your associates when a fierce, ungovern able boy. I wearied them with new applications. I paced the streets by night and day, but, until two hours ago, all my efforts were fruitless, and I never saw you for an instant."

"And now you do see me," said Monks, rising bold ly, " what then ? Fraud and robbery are high-sound-iug words—justified, you think, by a fancied resem blance in some young imp to an idle daub of a dead man's. Brother! you don't even know that a child was born of this maudlin pair; you don't even know that,"

" I did not," replied Mr. Brownlow, rising too; " but within the last fortnight I have learned it all. You have a brother: you know it and him. There was a will, which your mother destroyed, leaving the secret and the gain to you at her own death. It contained a reference to some child likely to be the result of this sad connection, which child was born, and acci dentally encountered by you, when your suspicions were first awakened by his resemblance to his father. You repaired to the place of his birth. There exist ed proofs—proofs long suppressed—of his birth and parentage. Those proofs were destroyed by you, and now, in your own words to your accomplice the Jew, l tlw only proofs of the boy's identity lie at the bottom of

the river, and the old hay that received them from tlic mother is rotting in her coffin. 1 Unworthy son, coward, liar—you, who hold your councils with thieves and murderers in dark rooms at night—you, whose plots and wiles have brought a violent death upon the head of one worth millions such as you—you, who from your cradle were gall and bitterness to your own father's heart, and in whom all evil passions, vice, and profligacy festered, till they found a vent in a hideous disease which has made your face an index even to your mind—you, Edward Leeford, do you still brave me!"

"No, no, no!" returned the coward, overwhelmed by these accumulated charges.

" Every word!" cried the old gentleman, " every word that has passed between you and this detested villain is known to me. Shadows on the wall have caught your whispers, and brought them to my ear; the sight of the persecuted child has turned vice it self, and given it the courage and almost the attri butes of virtue. Murder has been done, to which you were morally if not really a party."

" No, no," interposed Monks. " I—I—know noth ing of that; I was going to inquire the truth of the story when you overtook me. I didn't know the cause. I thought it was a common quarrel."

" It was the partial disclosure of your secrets," re plied Mr. Browillow. " Will you disclose the whole f'

"Yes,I will."

" Set your hand to a statement of truth and facts, and repeat it before witnesses ?"

" That I promise too."

"Remain quietly here until such a document is drawn up, and proceed with me to such a place as I may deem most advisible, for the purpose of attest ing it ?"

" If you insist upon that, I'll do that also," replied Monks.

" You must do more than that," said Mr. Brown-low. "Make restitution to an innocent and unof fending child; for such he is, although the offspring of a guilty and most miserable love. You have not forgotten the provisions of the will. Carry them into execution so far as your brother is concerned, and then go where you please. In this world you need meet no more."

While Monks was pacing up and down, meditating with dark and evil looks on this proposal and the possibilities of evading it—torn by his fears on the one hand and his hatred on the other—the door was hurriedly unlocked, and a gentleman (Mr. Losberue) entered the room in violent agitation.

" The man will be taken," he cried. " He will be taken to-night."

" The murderer ?" asked Mr. Brownlow.

" Yes, yes," replied the other. " His dog has been seen lurking about some old haunt, and there seems little doubt that his master either is, or will be, there. under cover of the darkness. Spies are hovering about in every direction. I have spoken to the men who are charged with his capture, and they tell me he can not escape. A reward of a hundred pounds is proclaimed by Government to-night."

" I will give fifty more," said Mr. Brownlow, " and proclaim it with my own lips upon the spot, if I can reach it. Where is Mr. May lie ?"

JACOB'S ISLAND—FOLLY DITCH.

157

" Harry ? As soon as he had seen your friend here, safe in a coach with you, he hnrried off to where he heard this," replied the doctor, " and, mounting his horse, sallied forth to join the first party at some place in the outskirts agreed upon between them."

" Fagiu ?" said Mr. Brownlow; " what of him ?"

" When I last heard, he had not been taken, but he will be, or is, by this time. They're sure of him."

" Have you made up your mind?" asked Mr. Brown-low, in a low voice, of Monks.

"Yes," he replied. "You—you—will be secret with me ?•"

" I will. Remain here till I return. It is your only hope of safety."

They left the room, and the door was again locked.

" What have you done ?" asked the doctor, in a whisper.

"All -that I could hope to do, and even more. Coupling the poor girl's intelligence with my previ ous knowledge, and the result of our good friend's inquiries on the spot, I left him no loop-hole of es cape, and laid bare the whole villainy which by these lights became plain as day. Write and ap point the evening after to-morrow, at seven, for the meeting. We shall be down there a few hours be fore, but shall require rest, especially the young lady, who may have greater need of firmness than either you or I can quite foresee just now. But my blood boils to avenge this poor murdered creature. Which way have they taken ?"

" Drive straight to the office and you will be in time," replied Mr. Losberne. " I will remain here."

The two gentlemen hastily separated, each in a fever of excitement wholly uncontrollable.

CHAPTER L.

THE PURSUIT AND ESCAPE.

"VTEAR to that part of the Thames on which the J_ i church at Rotherhithe abuts, where the build ings on the banks are dirtiest and the vessels on the river blackest with the dust of colliers and the smoke of close-built low-roofed houses, there exists the filthiest, the strangest, the most extraordinary of the many localities that are hidden in London, wholly unknown, even by name, to the great mass of its in habitants.

To reach this place the visitor has to penetrate through a maze of close, narrow, and muddy streets, thronged by the roughest and poorest of water-side people, and devoted to the traffic they may be sup posed to occasion. The cheapest and least delicate provisions are heaped in the shops; the coarsest and commonest articles of wearing apparel dangle at the salesman's door, and stream from the house parapet and windows. Jostling with unemployed laborers of the lowest class, ballast-heavers, coal-whippers, brazen women, ragged children, and the raff and ref use of the river, he makes his way with difficulty along, assailed by offensive sights and smells from the narrow alleys which branch off on the right and left, and deafened by the clash of ponderous wagons that bear great piles of merchant! ise from the stacks of warehouses that rise from every corner. Arriv

ing, at length, in streets remoter and less frequented than those through which he has passed, he walks beneath tottering house-fronts projecting over the pavement, dismantled walls that seem to totter as he passes, chimneys half crushed, half hesitating to fall, windows guarded by rusty iron bars that time and dirt have almost eaten away, and every imagi nable sign of desolation and neglect.

In such a neighborhood, beyond Dockhead, in the borough of Southwark, stands Jacob's Island, sur rounded by a muddy ditch, six or eight feet deep and fifteen or twenty wide when the tide is in, once called Mill Pond, but known in the days of this sto ry as Folly Ditch. It is a creek or inlet from the Thames, and can always be filled at high water by opening the sluices at the Lead Mills, from which it took its old name. At such times a stranger, look ing from one of the wooden bridges thrown across it at Mill Lane, will see the inhabitants of the houses on either side lowering from their backdoors and windows, buckets, pails, domestic utensils of all kinds, in which to haul the water up; and when his eye is turned from these operations to the houses themselves, his utmost astonishment will be excited by the scene before him. Crazy wooden galleries common to the backs of half a dozen houses, with holes from which to look upon the slime beneath; windows, broken and patched, with poles thrust out, on which to dry the linen that is never there; rooms so small, so filthy, so confined, that the air would seem too tainted even for the dirt and squalor which they shelter; wooden chambers thrusting themselves out above the mud, and threatening to fall into it— as some have done; dirt-besmeared walls and decay ing foundations; every repulsive lineament of pov erty, every loathsome indication of filth, rot, and gar bage ; all these ornament the banks of Folly Ditch.

In Jacob's Island the warehouses are roofless and empty; the walls are crumbling down; the windows are windows no more; the doors are falling into the streets; the chimneys are blackened, but they yield no smoke. Thirty or.forty years ago, before losses and chancery suits came upon it, it was a thriving place; but now it is a desolate island indeed. The houses have no owners; they are broken open and entered upon by those who have the courage; and there they live and there they die. They must have powerful motives for a secret residence, or be reduced to a destitute condition indeed, who seek a refuge in Jacob's Island.

In an upper room of one of these houses—a de tached house of fair size, ruinous in other respects, but strongly defended at door and window, of which house the back commanded the ditch in manner al ready described—there were assembled three men, who, regarding each other every now and then with looks expressive of perplexity and expectation, sat for some time in profound and gloomy silence. One of these was Toby Crackit, another Mr. Chitling. and the third a robber of fifty years, whose nose had been almost beaten in, in some old scuffle, and whose face bore a frightful scar which might probably be traced to the same occasion. This man was a returned transport, and his name was Kags.

" I wish," said Toby, turning to Mr. Chitling, " that you had picked out some other crib when the two

OLIVER TWIST.

old ones got too warm, and had not come here, my fine feller."

" Why didn't yon, blunderhead ?" said Kags.

" Well, I thought you'd have been a little more glad to see me than this," replied Mr. Chitling, with a melancholy air.

"Why look'e, young gentleman," said Toby, "when a man keeps himself so very ex- elusive as I have done, and by that means has a snug house over his head, with nobody a-pryiug and smelling about it, it's rather a startling thing to have the honor of a wisit from a young gentleman (however respectable and pleasant a person he may be to play cards with at conweniency) circumstanced as you are."

" Especially when the exclusive young man has got a friend stopping with him that's arrived sooner than was expected from foreign parts, and is too modest to want to be presented to the Judges ou his return," added Mr. Kags.

There was a short silence, after which Toby Crack-it, seeming to abandon as hopeless any further eifort to maintain his usual devil-may-care swagger, turn ed to Chitliug and said,

" When was Fagin took, then ?"

"Just at dinner-time—two o'clock this afternoon. Charley and I made our lucky up the wash'us chim ney, and Bolter got into the empty water-butt, head downward; but his legs were so precious long that they stuck out at the top, and so they took him too."

"And Bet?"

" Poor Bet! She went to see the Body, to speak to who it was," replied Chitling, his countenance falling more and more, " and went off mad, scream ing and raving, and beating her head against the boards ; so they put a strait-weskut on her and took her to the hospital—and there she is."

" Wot's come of young Bates ?" demanded Kags.

" He hung about, not to come over here afore dark; but he'll be here soon," replied Chitliug. " There's nowhere else to go to now, for the people at The Cripples are all in custody, and the bar of the ken— I went up there and see it with my own eyes—is filled with traps."

" This is a smash!" observed Toby, biting his lips. " There's more than one will go with this."

" The Sessions are on," said Kags. " If they get the inquest over, and Bolter turns king's evidence— as of course he will, from what he's said already— they can prove Fagin an accessory before the fact, and get the trial on on Friday, and he'll swing in six days from this, by G—!"

" You should have heard the people groan," said Chitling; " the officers fought like devils, or they'd have torn him away. He was down once, but they made a ring round him, and fought their way along. You should have seen how he looked about him, all muddy and bleeding, and clung to them as if they were his dearest friends. I can see 7 em now, not able to stand upright with the pressing of the mob, and dragging him along among 'em; I can see the people jumping up, one behind another, and snarl ing with their teeth and making at him like wild beasts; I can see the blood upon his hair and beard, and hear the cries with which the women worked themselves into the centre of the crowd at the street corner, and swore they'd tear his heart out!"

The horror-stricken witness of this scene pressed his hands upon his ears, and Avith his eyes closed got up and paced violently to and fro, like one distracted.

While he was thus engaged, and the two men sat by in silence with their eyes fixed upon the floor, a pattering noise was heard upon the stairs, and Sikes's dog bounded into the room. They ran to the win dow, down stairs, and into the street. The dog had jumped in at an open window; he made no attempt to follow them, nor was his master to be seen.

" What's the meaning of this ?" said Toby, when they had returned. " He can't be coming here. I— I—hope not."

" If he was coming here, he'd have come with the dog," said Kags, stooping down to examine the ani mal, who lay panting on the floor. " Here! Give us some water for him ; he has run himself faint."

" He's drunk it all up, every drop," said Chitling, after watching the dog for some time in silence. "Covered with mud—lame — half blind — he must have come a long way."

" Where can he have come from!" exclaimed Toby. " He's been to the other kens of course, and finding them filled with strangers, come on here, where he's been many a time and often. But where can he have come from first, and how comes he here alone without the other!"

" He!"—(none of them called the murderer by his old name)—" he can't have made away with himself. What do you think ?" said Chitling.

Toby shook his head.

" If he had," said Kags, " the dog 'ud want to lead us away to where he did it. No. I think he's got out of the country, and left the dog behind. He must have given him the slip somehow, or he wouldn't be so easy."

This solution, appearing the most probable one, was adopted as the right; and the dog creeping un der a chair, coiled himself up to sleep, without more notice from any body.

It being now dark, the shutter was closed, and a candle lighted and placed upon the table. The ter rible events of the last two days had made a deep impression on all three, increased by the danger and uncertainty of their own position. They drew their chairs closer together, starting at every sound. They spoke little, and that in whispers, and were as silent and awe-stricken as if the remains of the murdered woman lay in the next room.

They had sat tints some time, when suddenly was heard a hurried knocking at the door below.

" Young Bates," said Kags, looking angrily round, to check the fear he felt himself.

The knocking came again. No. it wasn't he. He never knocked like that.

Crackit went to the window, and, shaking all over, drew in his head. There was no need to tell them who it was; his pale face was enough. The dog. too, was on the alert in an instant, and ran whining to the door.

"We must let him in," he said, taking up the candle.

" Isn't there any help for it ?" asked the other man in a hoarse voice.

" None. He must come in."

" Don't leave us in the dark," said Kags, taking

SIKES AXD THE BOY CHARLEY.

159

down a candle from the chimney-piece, and lighting it, with such a trembling hand that the knocking was twice repeated before he had finished.

Crackit went down to the door, and returned fol lowed by a man with the lower part of his face buried in a handkerchief and another tied over his head under his hat. He drew them slowly off. Blanched face, sunken eyes, hollow cheeks, beard of three days' growth, wasted flesh, short thick breath; it was the very ghost of Sikes.

He laid his hand upon a chair which stood in the middle of the room, but, shuddering as he was about to drop into it, and seeming to glance over his shoul der, dragged it back close to the wall—as close as it would go—ground it against it—and sat down.

Not a word had been exchanged. He looked from one to another in silence. If an eye were furtively raised and met his, it was instantly averted. When his hollow voice broke silence, they all three started. They seemed never to have heard its tones before.

" How came that dog here ?" he asked.

"Alone. Three hours ago."

" To-night's paper says that Fagin's taken. Is it true, or a lie ?"

" True."

They were silent again.

"D— you all!" said Sikes, passing his hand across his forehead. " Have yon nothing to say to me f"

There was an uneasy movement among them, but nobody spoke.

" You that keep this house," said Sikes, turning his face to Crackit, " do yon mean to sell me, or to let me lie here till this hunt is over ?"

" You may stop here, if you think it safe," returned the person addressed, after some hesitation.

Sikes carried his eyes slowly up the wall behind him, rather trying to turn his head than actually doing it, and said, " Is—it—the body—is it buried ?"

They shook their heads.

" Why isn't it ?" he retorted, with the same glance behind him. "Wot do they keep such ugly things above the ground for ?—Who's that knocking ?"

Crackit intimated, by a motion of his hand as he left the room, that there was nothing to fear; and directly came back with Charley Bates behind him. Sikes sat opposite the door, so that the moment the boy entered the room he encountered his figure.

" Toby," said the boy, falling back, as Sikes turned his eyes toward him, "why didn't you tell me this down stairs ?"

There had been something so tremendous in the shrinking off of the three, that the wretched man was willing to propitiate even this lad. According ly he nodded, and made as though he would shake hands with him.

" Let me go into some other room," said the boy, retreating still farther.

" Charley!" said Sikes, stepping forward. " Don't you—don't you know me ?"

" Don't come nearer me," answered the boy, still retreating, and looking, with horror in his eyes, upon the murderer's face. " You monster !"

The man stopped half-way, and they looked at each other; but Sikes's eyes sunk gradually to the ground.

" Witness you three," cried the boy, shaking his

clenched fist, and becoming more and more excited as he spoke. "Witness you three—I'm not afraid of him—if they come here after him, I'll give him np; I will. I tell you out at once. He may kill me for it if he likes, or if he dares, but if I'm here I'll give him up. I'd give him up if he was to be boiled alive. Murder! Help ! If there's the pluck of a man among you three, you'll help me. Murder! Help ! Down with him !"

Pouring out these cries, and accompanying them with violent gesticulation, the boy actually threw himself, single-handed, upon the strong man, and in the intensity of his energy and the suddenness of his surprise, brought him heavily to the ground.

The three spectators seemed quite stupefied. They offered no inteference, and the boy and man rolled on the ground together; the former, heedless of the blows that showered upon him, wrenching his hands tighter and tighter in the garments about the mur derer's breast, and never ceasing to call for help with all his might.

The contest, however, was too unequal to last long. Sikes had him down, and his knee was on his throat, when Crackit pulled him back with a look of alarm, and pointed to the window. There were lights gleaming below, voices in loud and earnest conversation, the tramp of hurried footsteps—end less they seemed in number—crossing the nearest wooden bridge. One man on horseback seemed to be among the crowd; for there was the noise of hoofs rattling on the uneven pavement. The gleam of lights increased; the footsteps came more thickly and noisily on. Then came a loud knocking at the door, and then a hoarse murmur from such a multi tude of angry voices as would have made the bold est quail.

" Help!" shrieked the boy, in a voice that rent the air. "He's here! Break down the door!"

" In the king's name," cried the voices without; and the the hoarse cry arose again, but louder.

" Break down the door!" screamed the boy. " I tell you they'll never open it! Run straight to tin-room where the light is. Break down the door!"

Strokes thick and heavy rattled upon the door and lower window-shutters as he ceased to speak. and a loud huzzah burst from the crowd, giving the listener, for the first time, some adequate idea of its immense extent.

" Open the door of some place where I can lock this screeching hell-babe!" cried Sikes, fiercely, running to and fro, and dragging the boy now as easily as it he were an empty sack. " That door. Quick!" He flung him in, bolted it, and turned the key. " Is the down stairs door fast ?"

"Double-locked and chained," replied Crackit, who, with the other two men, still remained quite helpless and bewildered.

' The panels—are they strong ?" Lined with sheet-iron." And the windows too f"

' Yes, and the windows."

' D— you!" cried the desperate ruffian, throwing up the sash and menacing the crowd. " Do your worst! I'll cheat you yet!"

Of all the terrific yells that ever fell on mortal ears, none could exceed the cry of the infuriated

throng. Some shouted to those who were nearest to set the house on lire; others roared to the officers to shoot him dead. Among them all, none showed snch fury as the man on horseback, who, throwing himself out of the saddle, and bursting through the crowd as if he were parting water, cried, beneath the window, in a voice that rose above all others, " Twenty guineas to the man who brings a ladder!" The nearest voices took up the cry, and hundreds echoed it. Some called for ladders, some for sledge hammers ; some ran with torches to and fro as if to seek them, and still came back and roared again; some spent their breath in impotent curses and exe crations ; some pressed forward with the ecstasy of madmen, and thus impeded the progress of those be low; some among the boldest attempted to climb

room where the boy was locked, and that was too small even for the passage of his body. But, from this aperture, he had never ceased to call on those without to guard the back; and thus, when the mur derer emerged at last on the house-top by the door in the roof, a loud shout proclaimed the fact to those in front, who immediately began to pour round, press ing upon each other in one unbroken stream.

He planted a board, which he had carried up with him for the purpose, so firmly against the door that it must be matter of great difficulty to open it from the inside; and creeping over the tiles, looked over the low parapet.

The water was out, and the ditch a bed of mud.

The crowd had been hushed during these few mo ments, watching his motions and doubtful of hispur-

"AND CHEEPING OVER THE TILES, LOOKED OVEU THE LOW PAKAPET."

up by the water-spoilt and crevices in the wall; and all waved to and fro, in the darkness beneath, like a field of corn moved by an angry wind, and joined from time to time in one loud furious roar.

"The tide," cried the murderer, as he staggered back into the room, and shut the faces out, " the tide was in as I came up. Give me a rope, a long rope. They're all in front. I may drop into the Folly Ditch, aud clear off that way. Give me a rope, or I shall do three more murders and kill myself."

The panic-stricken men pointed to where such ar ticles were kept; the murderer, hastily selecting the longest and strongest cord, hurried up to the house top.

All the windows in the rear of the house had been long ago bricked up, except one small trap in the

pose, but the instant they perceived it and knew it was defeated they raised a cry of triumphant exe cration to which all their previous shouting had been whispers. Again and again it rose. Those who were at too great a distance to know its mean ing took up the sound ; it echoed and re-echoed; it seemed as though the whole city had poured its pop ulation out to curse him.

On pressed the people from the front—on, on, on, in a strong struggling current of angry faces, with here and there a glaring torch to light them up, and show them out in all their wrath and passion. The houses on the opposite side of the ditch had been en tered by the mob; sashes were thrown up, or torn bodily out; there were tiers and tiers of faces in ev ery window, and cluster upon cluster of people cling-

OLIVER EE'VISITS HIS BIRTHPLACE.

131

ing to every house-top. Each little bridge (arid there were three in sight) beiit beneath the weight of the crowd upon it. Still the current poured on to find some nook or hole from which to vent their shouts, and only for an instant see the wretch.

" They have him now!" cried a man on the nearest bridge. " Hurrah!"

The crowd grew light with uncovered heads; and again the shout uprose.

" I will give fifty pounds," cried an old gentleman from the same quarter, " to the man who takes him alive. I will remain here till he comes to ask me for it."

There was another roar. At this moment the word was passed among the crowd that* the door was forced at last, and that he who had first called for the ladder had mounted into the room. The stream abruptly turned as this intelligence ran from mouth to mouth; and the people at the windows, seeing those upon the bridges pouring back, quitted their stations, and, running into the street, joined the concourse that now thronged pell-mell to the spot they had left, each man crushing and striving with his neighbor, and all panting with impatience to get near the door, and look npoii the criminal as the of ficers brought him out. The cries and shrieks of those who were pressed almost to suffocation, or trampled down and trodden under foot in the con fusion, were dreadful; the narrow ways were com pletely blocked up; and at this time, between the rush of some to regain the space in front of the house, and the unavailing struggles of others to ex- • tricate themselves from the mass, the immediate at tention was distracted from the murderer, although the universal eagerness for his capture was, if possi ble, increased.

The man had shrank down, thoroughly quelled by the ferocity of the crowd and the impossibility of escape; but seeiug this sudden change with no less rapidity than it had occurred, he sprang upon his feet, determiued to make one last effort for his life by dropping into the ditch, and, at the risk of being stifled, endeavoring to creep away in the darkness and confusion.

Roused into new strength and energy, and stimu lated by the noise within the house, which announced that an entrance had really been effected, he set his foot against the stack of chimneys, fastened one end of the rope tightly and firmly round it, and with the other made a strong running noose, by the aid of his hands and teeth, almost in a second. He could let himself down by the cord to within a less distance of the ground than his own height, and had his knife ready in his hand to cut it then and drop.

At the very instant when he brought the loop over his head previous to slipping it beneath his armpits, and when the old gentleman before mentioned (who had clung so tight to the railing of the bridge as to resist the force of the crowd, and retain his position) earnestly warned those about him that the man was about to lower himself down—at that very instant the murderer, looking behind him on the roof, threw his arms above his head and uttered a yell of terror.

" The eyes again!" he cried, in an unearthly screech.

Staggering as if struck by lightning, he lost his L

balance and tumbled over the parapet. The noose was on his neck. It ran up with his weight tight as a bow-string, and swift as the arrow it speeds. He fell for five-aud-thirty feet. There was a sudden jerk, a terrific convulsion of the limbs; and there he hung, with the open knife clinched in his stiffening hand.

The old chimney quivered with the shock, but stood it bravely. The murderer swung lifeless against the wall; and the boy, thrusting aside the dangling body which obscured his view, called to the people to come and take him out, for God's sake.

A dog which had lain concealed till now ran back ward and forward on the parapet with a dismal howl, and collecting himself for a spring, jumped for the dead man's shoulders. Missing his aim, he fell into the ditch, turning completely over as he went, and striking his head against a stone, dashed out his brains.

CHAPTER LI.

AFFORDING AN EXPLANATION OF MORE MYSTERIES THAN ONE, AND COMPREHENDING A PROPOSAL OF MARRIAGE WITH NO WORD OF SETTLEMENT OR PIN-MONEY.

THE events narrated in the last chapter were yet but two days old when Oliver found himself, at three o'clock in the afternoon, in a traveling-carnage rolling fast toward his native town. Mrs. Maylie, and Rose, and Mrs. Bedwiu, and the good doctor, were with him; and Mr.

Brownlow followed in a post-chaise, accompanied by one other person, whose name had not been mentioned.

They had not talked much upon the way; for Ol iver was in a flutter of agitation and uncertainty which deprived him of the power of collecting his thoughts, and almost of speech, and appeared to have scarcely less effect on his companions, who shared it in at least an equal degree. He and the two ladies had been very carefully made acquainted by Mr. Brownlow with the nature of the admissions which had been forced from Monks; and although they knew that the object of their present journey was to complete the work which had been so well begun, still the whole matter was enveloped in enough of doubt and mystery to leave them in en durance of the most intense suspense.

The same kind friend had, with Mr. Losberne's as sistance, cautiously stopped all channels of commu nication through which they could receive intelli gence of the dreadful occurrences that had so recent ly taken place. " It was quite true," he said, " that they must know them before long, but it might be at a better time than the present, and it could not be at a worse." So they traveled on in silence, each busied with reflections on the object which had brought them together, and no one disposed to give utterance to the thoughts which crowded upon all.

But if Oliver, under these influences, had remained silent while they journeyed toward his birthplace by a road he had never seen, how the whole current of his recollections ran back to old times, and what a crowd of emotions were wakened up in his breast. when they turned into that which he had traversed

OLIVER TWIST.

on foot—a poor houseless, wandering boy, without a friend to help him, or a roof to shelter his head.

" See there, there! cried Oliver, eagerly clasping the hand of Rose, and pointing out at the carriage window; " that's the stile I caine over; there are the hedges I crept behind, for fear any one should over take me arid force me back! Yonder is the path across the iields, leading to the old house where I was a little child! Oh Dick, Dick, my dear old friend, if I could only see you now!"

" You will see him soon," replied Rose, gently tak ing his folded hands between her own. " You shall tell him how happy you are, and how rich you have grown, and that in all your happiness you have none so great as the coming back to make him happy too."

" Yes, yes." said Oliver, " and we'll—we'll take him away from here, and have him clothed and taught, and send him to some quiet country place where he may grow strong and well—shall we ?"

Rose nodded " yes;" for the boy was smiling through such happy tears that she could not speak.

" You will be kind and good to him, for you are to every one," said Oliver. "It will make you cry, I know, to hear what he can tell; but never mind, never mind: it will be all over, and you will smile again—I know that too—to think how changed he is; you did the same with me. He said ' God bless you' to me when I ran away," cried the boy, with a burst of affectionate emotion, " and I will say ' God bless you' now, and show him how I love him for it!"

As they approached the town, and at length drove through its narrow streets, it became matter of no small difficulty to restrain the boy within reasonable bounds. There was Sowerberry's, the undertaker's, just as it used to be, only smaller and less imposing in appearance than he remembered it—there were all the well-known shops and houses, with almost ev ery one of which he had some slight incident con nected—there was Gamfield's cart, the very cart he used to have, standing at the old public-house door— there was the work-house, the dreary prison of his youthful days, with its dismal windows frowning on the street—there was the same lean porter standing at the gate, at sight of whom Oliver involuntarily shrunk back, and then laughed at himself for being so foolish, then cried, then laughed again—there were scores of faces at the doors and windows that he knew quite well—there was nearly every thing as if he had left it but yesterday, and all his recent life had been but a happy dream.

But it was pure, earnest, joyful reality. They drove straight to the door of the chief hotel (which Oliver used to stare up at with awe, and think a mighty palace, but which had somehow fallen off in grandeur and size); and here was Mr. Grim wig all ready to receive them, kissing the young lady, and the old one too, when they got out of the coach, as if he were the grandfather of the whole party, all smiles and kindness, and not offering to eat his head—no, not once; not even when he contradicted a very old postboy about the nearest road to London, and main tained he knew it best, though he had only come that way once, and that time fast asleep. There was din ner prepared, and there were bedrooms ready, and every thing was arranged as if by magic.

Notwithstanding all this, when the hurry of the first half hour was over, the same silence and con straint prevailed that had marked their journey down. Mr. Brownlow did not join them at dinner, but remained in a separate room. The two other gentlemen hurried in and out with anxious faces, and during the short intervals when they were pres ent conversed apart. Once Mrs. Maylie was called away, and, after being absent for nearly an hour, re turned with eyes swollen with weeping. All these things made Rose and Oliver, who were not in any new secrets, nervous and uncomfortable. They sat wondering, in silence; or, if they exchanged a few words, spoke in whispers, as if they were afraid to hear the sound of their own voices.

At length, when nine o'clock had come, and they began to think they were to hear no more that night, Mr. Losberne and Mr. Grimwig entered the room, fol lowed by Mr. Brownlow and a man whom Oliver al most shrieked with surprise to see; for they told him it was his brother, and it was the same man he had met at the market-town, and seen looking in with Fagin at the window of his little room. Monks cast a look of hate, which, even then, he could not dissem ble, at the astonished boy, and sat down near the door. Mr. Brownlow, who had papers in his hand, walked to a table near which Rose and Oliver were seated.

" This is a painful task," said he, " but these dec larations, which have been signed in London before many gentlemen, must be in substance repeated here. I would have spared you the degradation, but we must hear them from your own lips before we part, and you know why."

" Go on," said the person addressed, turning away his face. " Quick. I have almost done enough, I think. Don't keep me here."

" This child," said Mr. Brownlow, drawing Oliver to him, and laying his hand upon his head, " is your half-brother; the illegitimate son of your father, my dear friend Edwin Leeford, by poor young Agnes Fleming, who died in giving him birth."

" Yes," said Monks, scowling at the trembling boy, the beating of whose heart he might have heard. " That is their bastard child."

"The term you use," said Mr.Brownlow, sternly, "is a reproach to those who long since passed be yond the feeble censure of the world. It reflects disgrace on no one living, except you who use it. Let that pass. He was born in this town."

" In the work-house of this town," was the sullen reply. " You have the story there." He pointed im patiently to the papers as he spoke.

"I must have it here,too," said Mr. Brownlow, looking round upon the listeners.

" Listen then! You !" returned Monks. " His fa ther being taken ill at Rome, was joined by his wife, my mother, from whom he had been long separated, who went from Paris and took me with her—to look after his property, for what I know, for she had no great affection for him, nor he for her. He knew nothing of us, for his senses were gone, and he slum bered on till next day, when he died. Among the papers in his desk were two, dated on the night his illness first came on, directed to yourself—" he ad dressed himself to Mr. Brownlow—" and inclosed in a few short lines to you, with an intimation on the

RELUCTANT ADMISSIONS.

cover of the package that it was not to be forwarded till after he was dead. One of these papers was a letter to this girl Agnes ; the other a will."

" What of the letter ?" asked Mr. Brownlow.

" The letter ?A sheet of paper crossed and cross ed again, with a penitent confession, and prayers to God to help her. He had palmed a tale on the girl that some secret mystery—to be explained one day —prevented his marrying her just then; and so she had gone on; trusting patiently to him, until she trusted too far, and lost what none could ever give her back. She was at that time within a few months of her confinement. He told her all he had meant to do to hide her shame if he had lived, and prayed her, if he died, not to curse his memory, or think the consequences of their sin would be visited on her or their young child; for all the guilt was his. He re minded her of the day he had given her the little locket and the ring with her Christian name en graved upon it, and a blank left for that which he hoped one day to have bestowed upon her—prayed her yet to keep it, and wear it next her heart, as she had done before—and then ran on wildly in the same words, over and over again, as if he had gone dis tracted. I believe he had."

" The will," said Mr. Brownlow, as Oliver's tears fell fast.

Monks was silent.

"The will," said Mr. Brownlow, speaking for him, " was in the same spirit as the letter. He talked of miseries which his wife had brought upon him; of the rebellious disposition, vice, malice, and prema ture bad passions of you, his only son, who had been trained to hate him; and left you and your mother each an annuity of eight hundred pounds. The bulk of his property he divided into two equal portions— one for Agues Fleming, and the other for their child, if it should be born alive and ever come of age. If it were a girl, it was to inherit the money uncondition ally ; but if a boy, only on the stipulation that in his minority he should never have stained his name with any public act of dishonor, meanness, cowardice, or wrong. He did this, he said, to mark his confidence in the mother, and his conviction—only strengthen ed by approaching death—that the child would share her gentle heart and noble nature. If he were dis appointed in this expectation, then the money was to come to you; for then, and not till then, when both children were equal, would he recognize your prior claim upon his purse, who had none upon his heart, but had, from an infant, repulsed him with coldness and aversion.

"My mother," said Monks, in a louder tone, "did what a woman should have done. She burned this will. The letter never reached its destination ; but that and other proofs she kept, in case they ever tried to lie away the blot. The girl's father had the truth from her with every aggravation that her vio lent hate—I love her for it now—could add. Goad ed by shame and dishonor, he fled with his children into a remote corner of Wales, changing his very name, that his friends might never know of his re treat ; and here, no great while afterward, he was found dead in his bed. The girl had left her home, in secret, some weeks before; he had searched for her, on foot, in every town and village near; it was

on the night when he returned home, assured that she had destroyed herself to hide her shame and his, that his old heart broke.

There was a short silence here, until Mr. Brown-low took up the thread of the narrative.

" Years after this," he said, " this man's—Edward Leeford's — mother came to me. He had left her when only eighteen; robbed her of jewels and mon ey; gambled, squandered, forged, and fled to Lon don, where for two years he had associated with the lowest outcasts. She was sinking under a painful and incurable disease, and wished to recover him be fore she died. Inquiries were set on foot, and strict searches made. They were unavailing for a long time, but ultimately successful; and he went back with her to France."

" There she died," said Monks, " after a lingering illness; and on her death-bed she bequeathed these secrets to me, together with her unquenchable and deadly hatred of all whom they involved — though she need not have left me that, for I had inherited it long before. She would not believe that the girl had destroyed herself and the child too, but was filled with the impression that a male child had been born, and was alive. I swore to her, if ever it cross ed my path, to hunt it down ; never to let it rest ; to pursue it with the bitterest and most unrelenting animosity; to vent upon it the hatred that I deeply felt, and to spit upon the empty vaunt of that insult ing will by dragging it, if I could, to the very gal lows-foot. She was right. He came in my way at last. I began well ; and, but for babbling drabs, I would have finished as I began !"

As the villain folded his arms tight together, and muttered curses on himself in the impotence of baf fled malice, Mr. Brownlow turned to the terrified group beside him, and explained that the Jew, who had been his old accomplice and confidant, had a large reward for keeping Oliver ensnared, of which some part was to be given up in the event of his be ing rescued, and that a dispute on this head had led to their visit to the country house for the purpose of identifying him.

" The locket and ring ?" said Mr. Brownlow, turn ing to Monks.

" I bought them from the man and woman I told you of, who stole them from the nurse, who stole them from the corpse," answered Monks, without raising his eyes. " You know what became of them."

Mr. Brownlow merely nodded to Mr. Grimwig, who, disappearing with great alacrity, shortly returned, pushing in Mrs. Bumble, and dragging her unwilling consort after him.

" Do my hi's deceive me !" cried Mr. Bumble, with ill-feigned enthusiasm, " or is that little Oliver ? Oh Ol-i-ver, if you know'd how I've been a-grieving for you— "

" Hold your tongue, fool !" murmured Mrs. Bumble.

"Isn't natur natur, Mrs. Bumble?" remonstrated the work-house master. " Can't I be supposed to feel—/ as brought him up porochially—when I see him a setting here among ladies and gentlemen of the very affablest description! I always loved that boy as if he'd been my— my—my own grandfather," said Mr. Bumble, halting for an appropriate compar ison. " Master Oliver, my dear, you remember the

OLIVER TWIST.

blessed gentleman in the white waistcoat ? Ah! he went to heaven last week, in a oak coffin with plated handles, Oliver."

" Come, sir," said Mr. Grimwig, tartly; " suppress your feelings."

" I will do my endeavors, sir," replied Mr. Bumble. " How do you do, sir ? I hope you are very well."

This salutation was addressed to Mr. Brownlow, who had stepped up to within a short distance of the respectable couple. He inquired, as he pointed to Monks:

" Do you know that person ?"

li No," replied Mrs. Bumble, flatly.

" Perhaps you don't ?" said Mr. Brownlow, address ing her spouse.

" I never saw him in all my life," said Mr. Bum ble.

" Nor sold him any thing, perhaps ?"

" No," replied Mrs. Bumble.

"You never had, perhaps, a certain gold locket and ring ?" said Mr. Brownlow.

" Certainly not," replied the matron. " Why are we brought here to answer to such nonsense as this ?"

Again Mr. Brownlow nodded to Mr. Grimwig; and again that gentleman limped away with extraordi nary readiness. But not again did he return with a stout man and his wife; for this time he led in two palsied women, who shook and tottered as they walked.

"You shut the door the night old Sally died," said the foremost one, raising her shriveled hand, " but you couldn't shut out the sound, nor stop the chinks."

" No, no," said the other, looking round her and wagging her toothless jaws. " No, no, no."

" We heard her try to tell you what she'd done, and saw you take a paper from her hand, and watch ed you too, next day, to the pawnbroker's shop," said the first.

"Yes," added the second, "and it was a 'locket and gold ring.' We found out that, and saw it given you. We were by. Oh! we were by."

"And we know more than that," resumed the first, " for she told us often, long ago, that the young moth er had told her that, feeling she should never get over it, she was on her way, at the time she was tak en ill, to die near the grave of the father of the child."

" Would you like to see the pawnbroker himself?" asked Mr. Grimwig, with a motion toward the door.

" No," replied the woman; " if he "—she pointed to Monks—" has been coward enough to confess, as I see he has, and you have sounded all these hags till you have found the right ones, I have nothing more to say. I did sell them, and they're where you'll never get them. What then ?"

" Nothing," replied Mr. Brownlow, " except that it remains for us to take care that neither of you is em ployed in a situation of trust again. You may leave the room."

" I hope," said Mr. Bumble, looking about him with great ruefulness, as Mr. Grimwig disappeared with the two old women—" I hope that this unfortunate little circumstance will not deprive me of my poro-chial office ?"

" Indeed it will," replied Mr. Brownlow. " You may make up your mind to that, and think yourself well off besides."

" It was all Mrs. Bumble. She would do it," urged Mr. Bumble, first looking round to ascertain that his partner had left the room.

" That is no excuse," replied Mr. Brownlow. " You were present on the occasion of the destruction of these trinkets, and indeed are the more guilty of the two, in the eye of the law; for the law supposes that your wife acts under your direction."

"If the law supposes that," said Mr. Bumble, squeezing his hat emphatically in both hands, " the law is a ass— a idiot. If that's the eye of the law, the law is a bachelor; and the worst I wish the law is, that his eye may be opened by experience— by ex perience."

Laying great stress on the repetition of these two words, Mr. Bumble fixed his hat on very tight, and, putting his hands in his pockets, followed his help mate down stairs.

"Young lady," said Mr. Brownlow, turning to Rose, "give me your hand. Do not tremble. You need not fear to hear the few remaining words we have to say."

" If they have—I do not know how they can, but if they have—any reference to me," said Rose, " pray let me hear them at some other time. I have not strength or spirits now."

" Nay," returned the old gentleman, drawing her arm through his; "you have more fortitude than this, I am sure. Do you know this young lady, sir ?"

" Yes," replied Monks.

" I never saw you before," said Rose, faintly.

" I have seen you often," returned Monks.

" The father of the unhappy Agnes had two daugh ters," said Mr. Brownlow. " What was the fate of the other—the child?"

" The child," replied Monks; " when her father died in a strange place, in a strange name, without a letter, book, or scrap of paper that yielded the faint est clue by which his friends or relatives could be traced— the child was taken by some wretched cot tagers, who reared it as their own."

" Go on," said Mr. Brownlow, signing to Mrs. May-lie to approach. " Go on!"

" You couldn't find the spot to which these people had repaired," said Monks; " but where friendship fails, hatred will often force a way. My mother found it, after a year of cunning search—ay, and found the child."

"She took it, did she?"

" No. The people were poor and began to sicken —at least the man did—of their fine humanity; so she left it with them, giving them a small present of money which would not last long, and promising more, which she never meant to send. She didn't quite rely, however, on their discontent and poverty for the child's unhappiness, but told the histoiy of her sister's shame, with such alterations as suited her ; bade them take good heed of the child, for she came of bad blood; and told them she was illegiti mate, and sure to go wrong at one time or other. The circumstances countenanced all this; the people believed it; and there the child dragged on an ex istence, miserable enough even to satisfy us, until a widow lady, residing then at Chester, saw the girl by chance, pitied her, and took her home. There was some cursed spell, I think, against us ; for in spite of

OLIVER FINDS A NEW RELATION.

all our efforts she remained there and was happy. I lost sight of her two or three years ago, and saw her no more until a few months back."

" Do you see her now ?"

" Yes. Leaning on your arm."

" But not the less my niece," cried Mrs. Maylie, folding the fainting girl in her arms; " not the less my dearest child. I would not lose her now for all the treasures of the world. My sweet companion, my own dear girl!"

" The only friend I ever had," cried Rose, clinging to her. " The kindest, best of friends. My heart will burst. I can not bear all this!"

" You have borne more, and have been through

Joy and grief were mingled in the cup ; but there were no bitter tears : for even grief itself arose so softened, and clothed in such sweet and tender rec ollections, that it became a solemn pleasure, and lost all character of pain.

They were a long, long time alone. A soft tap at the door at length announced that some one was without. Oliver opened it, glided away, and gave place to Harry Maylie.

" I know it all," he said, taking a seat beside the lovely girl. " Dear Rose, I know it all."

" I am not here by accident," he added, after a lengthened silence; "nor have I heard all this to night, for I knew it yesterday—only yesterday. Do

"DO YOU KNOW THIS YOITNG LADJT, SIR?"

all the best and gentlest creature that ever shed happiness on every one she knew," said Mrs. Maylie, embracing her tenderly. " Come, come, my love, re member who this is who waits to clasp you in his arms, poor child! See here—look, look, my dear !"

" Not aunt," cried Oliver, throwing his arms about her neck ; " I'll never call her aunt—sister, my own dear sister, that something taught my heart to love so dearly from the first ! Rose! dear, darling Rose!"

Let the tears which fell, and the broken words which were exchanged in the long close embrace be tween the orphans, be sacred. A father, sister, and mother were gained and lost in that one moment.

you guess that I have come to remind you of a promise ?"

" Stay," said Rose. " You do know all."

"All. You gave me leave, at any time within a year, to renew the subject of our last discourse."

" I did."

" Not to press you to alter your determination," pursued the young man, " but to hear you repeat it, if you would. I was to lay whatever of station or fortune I might possess at your feet; and if you still adhered to your former determination, I pledged my self, by no word or act, to seek to change it."

" The same reasons which influenced nie then will influence me now," said Rose, firmly. "If I ever

OLIVER TWIST.

owed a strict and rigid duty to her whose goodness saved me from a life of indigence and suffering, when should I ever feel it as I should to-night ? It is a struggle," said Rose, " but one I am proud to make; it is a pang, but one my heart shall bear."

" The disclosure of to-night—" Harry began.

" The disclosure of to-night/' replied Rose, softly, " leaves me in the same position, with reference to you, as that in which I stood before."

" You harden your heart against me, Rose," urged her lover.

" Oh, Harry, Harry," said the young lady, bursting into tears, " I wish I could, and spare myself this pain."

" Then why inflict *t on yourself?" said Harry, tak ing her hand. " Think, dear Rose, think what you have heard to-night."

" And what have I heard! What have I heard!" cried Rose. " That a sense of his deep disgrace so worked upon my own father that he shunned all— there, we have said enough, Harry, we have said enough."

" Not yet, not yet," said the young man, detaining her as she rose. " My hopes, my wishes, prospects, feelings—every thought in life except my love for you—have undergone a change. I offer you, now, no distinction among a bustling crowd ; no mingling with a world of malice and detraction, where the blood is called into honest cheeks by aught but real disgrace and shame ; but a home—a heart and home yes, dearest Rose; and those, and those alone, are all I have to offer."

" What do you mean ?" she faltered.

" I mean but this—that when I left you last, I left you with a firm determination to level all fancied barriers between yourself and me; resolved that if my world could not be yours, I would make yours mine; that no pride of birth should curl the lip at you, for I would turn from it. This I have 'done. Those who have shrunk from me because of this, have shrunk from you, and proved you so far right. Such power and patronage, such relatives of influence and rank, as smiled upon me then, look coldly now; but there are smiling fields and waving trees in En gland's richest county; and by one village church-mine, Rose, my own!—there stands a rustic dwelling which you can make me prouder of than all the hopes I have renounced, measured a thousand-fold. This is my rank and station now, and here I lay it down!"

" It's a trying thing waiting supper for lovers," said Mr. Grimwig, waking up, and pulling his pock et-handkerchief from over his head.

Truth to tell, the supper had been waiting a most unreasonable time. Neither Mrs. Maylie, nor Harry, nor Rose (who all came in together), could offer a word in extenuation.

"I had serious thoughts of eating my head to night," said Mr. Grimwig, " for I began to think I should get nothing else. I'll take the liberty, if you'll allow me, of saluting the bride that is to be."

Mr. Grimwig lost no time in carrying this notice into effect upon the blushing girl; and the example being contagious, was followed both by the doctor and Mr. Brownlow: some people affirm that Harry

Maylie had been observed to set it, originally, in a dark room adjoining; but the best authorities con sider this downright scandal, he being young and a clergyman.

" Oliver, my child," said Mrs. Maylie, " where have you been, and why do you look so sad ? There are tears stealing down your face at this moment. What is the matter ?"

It is a world of disappointment often to the hopes we most cherish, and hopes that do our nature the greatest honor.

Poor Dick was dead!

CHAPTER LII.

FAGIN'S LAST NIGHT ALIVE.

rTIHE court was paved from floor to roof with hu-i man faces. Inquisitive and eager eyes peered from every inch of space. From the rail before the dock, away into the sharpest angle of the smallest corner in the galleries, all looks were fixed upon one man—Fagin. Before him and behind—above, be low, on the right and on the left — he seemed to stand surrounded by a firmament all .bright with gleaming eyes.

He stood there, in all this glare of living light, with one hand resting on the wooden slab before him, the other held to his ear, and his head thrust forward to enable him to catch with greater dis tinctness every word that fell from the presiding judge, who was delivering his charge to the jury. At times he turned his eyes sharply upon them, to observe the effect of the slightest feather-weight in his favor; and when the points against him were stated with terrible distinctness, looked toward his counsel, in mute appeal that he would, even then, urge something in his behalf. Beyond these mani festations of anxiety, he stirred not hand or foot. He had scarcely moved since the trial began; and now that the judge ceased to speak, he still remain ed in the same strained attitude of close attention, with his gaze bent on him, as though he listened still.

A slight bustle in the court recalled him to him self. Looking round, he saw that the jurymen had turned together, to consider of their verdict. As his eyes wandered to the gallery, he could see the people rising above each other to see his face, some hastily applying their glasses to their eyes, and others whis pering their neighbors with looks expressive of ab horrence. A few there were who seemed unmindful of him, and looked only to the jury, in impatient wonder how they could delay. But in no one face —not even among the women, of whom there were many there — could he read the faintest sympathy with himself, or any feeling but one of all-absorbing interest that he should be condemned.

As he saw all this in one bewildered glance, the death-like stillness came again, and looking back, he saw that the jurymen had turned toward the judge. Hush!

They only sought permission to retire.

He looked wistfully into their faces, one by one, when they passed out, as though to see which way

WAXDEHIXG MIND AXD IMPRISONED BODY.

the greater number leaned; but that was fruitless. The jailer touched him on the shoulder. He follow ed mechanically to the end of the dock, and sat down on a chair. The man pointed it out, or he would not have seen it.

He looked up into the gallery again. Some of the people were eating, and some fanning themselves with handkerchiefs; for the crowded place was very hot. There was one young man sketching his face in a little note-book. He wondered whether it was like, and looked on when the artist broke his pencil-point and made another with his knife, as any idle spectator might have done.

In the same way, when he turned his eyes toward the judge, his mind began to busy itself with the fashion of his dress, and what it cost, and how he put it on. There was an old fat gentleman on the bench, too, who had gone out some half an hour before, and now come back. He wondered within himself whether this man had been to get his dinner, what he had had, and where he had had it; and pur sued this train of careless thought until some new object caught his eye and roused another.

Not. that, all this time, his mind was for an instant free from one oppressive, overwhelming sense of the grave that opened at his feet: it was ever present to him, but in a vague and general way, and he could not fix his thoughfs upon it. Thus, even while he trembled, and turned burning hot at the idea of speedy death, he fell to counting the iron spikes be fore him, and wondering how the head of one had been broken off, and whether they would mend it, or leave it as it was. Then he thought of all the hor rors of the gallows and the scaffold—and stopped to watch a man sprinkling the floor to cool it — and then went on to think again.

At length there was a cry of silence, and a breath less look from all toward the door. The jury re turned, and passed him close. He could glean noth ing from their faces; they might as well have been of stone. Perfect stillness ensued—not a rustle—not a breath—Guilty.

The building rang with a tremendous shout, and another, and another, and then it echoed loud groans, that gathered strength as.they swelled out, like an gry thunder. It was a peal of joy from the populace outside, greeting the news that he would die on Monday.

The noise subsided, and he was asked if he had any thing to say why sentence of death should not be passed upon him. He had resumed his listening attitude, and looked intently at his questioner while the demand was made; but it was twice repeated before he seemed to hear it, and then he only mut tered that he was an old man—an old man—an old man—and so, dropping into a whisper, was silent again.

The judge assumed the black cap, and the prisoner still stood with the same air and gesture. A woman in the gallery uttered some exclamation, called forth by this dread solemnity; he looked hastily up as if angry at the interruption, and bent forward yet more attentively. The address was solemn and impress ive, the sentence fearful to hear. But he stood like a marble figure, without the motion of a nerve. His . haggard face was still thrust forward, lib uuder-jaw

hanging down, and his eyes staring out before him, | when the jailer put his hand upon his arm, and beck oned him away. He gazed stupidly about him for an instant, and obeyed.

They led him through a paved room under the court, where some prisoners were waiting till their turns came, and others were talking to their friends, who crowded round a grate which looked into the open yard. There was nobody there to speak to him; but, as he passed, the prisoners fell back to ren der him more visible to the people who were cling ing to the bars; and they assailed him with oppro brious names, and screeched and hissed. He shook his fist, and would have spat upon them; but his conductors hurried him on, through a gloomy pas sage lighted by a few dim lamps, into the interior of the prison.

Here he was searched, that he might not have | about him the means of anticipating the law; this j ceremony performed, they led him to one of the con demned cells, and left him there— alone.

He sat down on a stone bench opposite the door, which served for seat and bedstead ; and casting his blood-shot eyes upon the ground, tried to collect his thoughts. After a while he began to remember a few disjointed fragments of what the judge had said, though it had seemed to him at the time that he could not hear a word. These gradually fell into their proper places, and by degrees suggested more; so that in a little time he had the whole, almost as it was delivered. To be hanged by the neck till he was dead—that was the end. To be hanged by the neck till he was dead.

As it came on very dark, he began to think of all the men he had known who had died upon the scaf fold—some of them through his means. They rose up in such quick succession that he could hardly count them. He had seen some of them die—and had joked, too, because they died with prayers upon their lips. With what a rattling noise the drop went down ! and how suddenly they changed from strong and vigorous men to dangling heaps of clothes!

Some of them might have inhabited that very cell —sat upon that very spot. It was very dark; why didn't they bring a light ? The cell had been built for many years. Scores of men must have passed their last hours there. It was like sitting in a vault strewn with dead bodies — the cap, the noose, the pinioned arms, the faces that he knew, even beneath that hideous veil.—Light! light!

At length, when his hands were raw with beating against the heavy door and walls, two men appeared, one bearing a candle, which he thrust into an iron candlestick fixed against the wall, the other dragging in a mattress on which to pass the night; for the prisoner was to be left alone no more.Then came night — dark, dismal, silent night. Other watchers are glad to hear the church-clocks strike, for they tell of life and coming day. To him they brought despair. The boom of every iron bell came laden with the one deep, hollow sound—Death. What availed the noise and bustle of cheerful morn ing, which penetrated even there, to him ? It was another form of knell, with mockery added to the warning.

OLIVER TWIST.

The day passed off. Day ? There was no day ; it was gone as soon as come — and night came on again ; night so long, and yet so short ; long in its dreadful silence, and short in its fleeting hours. At one time he raved and blasphemed ; and at another howled and tore his hair. Venerable men of his own persuasion had come to pray beside him, but he had driven them away with curses. They renewed their charitable efforts, and he beat them off.

Saturday night. He had only one night more to live. And as he thought of this, the day broke— Sunday.

It was not until the night of this last awful day, that a withering sense of his helpless, desperate state came in its full intensity upon his blighted soul ; not that he had ever held any denned or positive hope.of

his head was bandaged with a linen cloth. His red hair hung down upon his bloodless face ; his beard was torn, and twisted into knots ; his eyes shone with a terrible light; his unwashed flesh crackled with the fever that burned him up. Eight—nine— ten. If it was not a trick to frighten him, and those were the real hours treading on each other's heels, where would he be when they came round again! Eleven! Another struck, before the voice of the previous hour had ceased to vibrate. At eight, he would be the only mourner in his own funeral train ; at eleven—

Those dreadful walls of Newgate, which have hid den so much misery and such unspeakable anguish, not only from the eyes, but, too often, and too long, from the thoughts of men, never held so dread a

" HE BAT DOWN ON A STOA'E BENCH OPPOSITE THE DOOK."

mercy, but that he had never been able to consider more than the dim probability of dying so soon. He had spoken little to either of the two men who re lieved each other in their attendance upon him; and they, for their parts, made no effort to rouse his at tention. He had sat there, awake, but dreaming. Now, he started up every minute, and with gasping mouth and burning skin hurried to and fro, in such a paroxysm of fear and wrath that even they—used to such sights— recoiled from him with horror. He grew so terrible, at last, in all the tortures of his evil conscience, that one man could not bear to sit there, eying him, alone; and so the two kept watch together. He cowered down upon his stone bed, and thought of the past. He had been wounded with some mis siles from the crowd on the day of his capture, and

spectacle as that. The few who lingered as they passed, and wondered what the man was doing who was to be hanged to-morrow, would have slept but ill that night if they could have seen him.

From early in the evening until nearly midnight little groups of two and three presented themselves at the lodge-gate, and inquired, with anxious faces, whether any reprieve had been received. These be ing answered in the negative, communicated the wel come intelligence to clusters in the street, who point ed out to one another the door from which he must come out, and showed where the scaffold would be built, and, walking with unwilling steps away, turn ed back to conjure up the scene. By degrees they fell off, one by one; and for an hour, in the dead of r.ight, the street was left to solitude and darkness.

CLOSING IX.

The space before the prison was cleared, and a few strong barriers, painted black, had been already thrown across the road to break the pressure of the expected crowd, when Mr. Browulow and Oliver ap peared at the wicket, and presented an order of ad mission to the prisoner, signed by one of the sheriffs. They were immediately admitted into the lodge.

" Is the young gentleman to come too, sir ?" said the man whose duty it was to conduct them. " It's not a sight for children, sir."'

" It is not, indeed, my friend," rejoined Mr. Brown-low ; " but my business with this man is intimately connected with him; and as this child has seen him in the full career of his success and villainy, I think it as well—even at the cost of some pain and fear— that he should see him now."

These few words had been said apart, so as to be inaudible to Oliver. The man touched his hat, and glancing at Oliver with some curiosity, opened an other gate opposite to that by which they had en tered, and led them on through dark and winding ways toward the cells.

" This," said the man, stopping in a gloomy pas sage where a couple of workmen were making some preparations in profound silence—" this is the place he passes through. If you step this way, you can see the door he goes out at."

He led them into a stone kitchen, fitted with cop pers for dressing the prison food, and pointed to a door. There was an open grating above it through which came the sound of men's voices, mingled with the noise of hammering and the throwing down of boards. They were putting up the scaffold.

From this place they passed through several strong gates, opened by other turnkeys from the inner side, and, having entered an open yard, ascended a flight of narrow steps and came into a passage with a row of strong doors on the left hand. Motioning them to remain where they were, the turnkey knocked at one of these with his bunch of keys. The two attend ants, after a little whispering, came out into the pas sage, stretching themselves as if glad of the tempo rary relief, and motioned the visitors to follow the jailer into the cell. They did so.

The condemned criminal was seated on his bed, rocking himself from side to side, with a countenance more like that of a snared beast than the face of a man. His mind was evidently wandering to his old life, for he continued to mutter, without appearing conscious of their presence, otherwise than as a part of his vision:

"Good boy, Charley — well done," he mumbled. "Oliver too, ha! ha! ha! Oliver too — quite the gentleman now—quite the—take that boy away to bed!"

The jailer took the disengaged hand of Oliver, and, whispering him not to be alarmed, looked on with out speaking.

" Take him away to bed!" cried Fagin. " Do you hear me, some of you ? He has been the—the—some how the cause of all this. It's worth the money to bring him up to it— Bolter's throat, Bill; never mind the girl — Bolter's throat, as deep as you can cut. Saw his head off!"

" Fagin," said the jailer.

" That's me !" cried the Jew, falling instantly into

the attitude of listening he had assumed upon hi* trial. "An old man, my lord; a very old, old man!"

" Here," said the turnkey, laying his hand upon his breast to keep him down, "here's somebody wants to see you, to ask you some questions, I suppose. Fa-gin, Fagiu! Are you a man ?"

" I sha'n't be one long," he replied, looking up with a face retaining no human expression but rage and terror. " Strike them all dead! What right have they to butcher me ?"

As he spoke he caught sight of Oliver and Mr. Brownlow. Shrinking to the farthest corner of the seat, he demanded to know what they wanted there.

" Steady," said the turnkey, still holding him down. " Now, sir, tell him what you want. Quick, if you please, for he grows worse as the time gets on."

" You have some papers," said Mr. Brownlow, ad vancing, " which were placed in your hands, for bet ter security, by a man called Monks."

" It's all a lie together," replied Fagin. " I haven't one—not one."

" For the love of God," said Mr. Brownlow, solemn ly, " do not say that now, upon the very verge of death; but tell me where they are. You know that Sikes is dead, that Monks has confessed, that there is no hope of any further gain. Where are those papers f"

" Oliver," cried Fagin, beckoning to him. " Here, here! Let me whisper to you."

" I am not afraid," said Oliver, in a low voice, as he relinquished Mr. Brownlow's hand.

" The papers," said Fagin, drawing Oliver toward him, " are in a canvas bag, in a hole a little way up the chimney in the top front-room. I want to talk to you, my dear. I want to talk to you."

" Yes, yes," returned Oliver. " Let me say a prayer. Do! Let me say one prayer. Say only one upon your knees with me, and we will talk till morning."

"Outside, outside," replied Fagin, pushing the boy before him toward the door, and looking vacantly over his head. " Say I've gone to sleep—they'll be lieve you. You can get me out, if you take me so. Now then, now then !"

" Oh! God forgive this wretched man!" cried the boy, with a burst of tears.

" That's right, that's right," said Fagin. " That'll help us on. This door first. If I shake and tremble as we pass the gallows, don't you mind, but hurry on. Now, now, now!"

" Have you nothing else to ask him, sir ?" inquired the turnkey.

" No other question," replied Mr. Brownlow. " If I hoped we could recall him to a sense of his posi tion— ;

" Nothing will do that, sir," replied the man, shak ing his head. " You had better leave him."

The door of the cell opened, and the attendants returned.

" Press on, press on!" cried Fagin. " Softly, but not so slow. Faster, faster!"

The men laid hands upon him, and, disengaging Oliver from his grasp, held him back. He-struggled with the power of desperation for an instant; and then sent up cry upon cry that penetrated even those massive walls, and rang in their ears until they reached the open yard.

OLIVER TWIST.

It was some time before they left the prison. Ol iver nearly swooned after this frightful scene, and was so weak that for an hour or more he had not the strength to walk.

Day was dawning when they again emerged. A great multitude had already assembled; the win dows were filled with people, smoking and playing cards to beguile the time; the crowd were pushing, quarreling, joking. Every thing told of life and ani mation but one dark cluster of objects in the centre of all — the black stage, the cross -beam, the rope, aiid all the hideous apparatus of death.

CHAPTER LIII.

AND LAST.

THE fortunes of those who have figured in this tale are nearly closed. The little that remains to their historian to relate is told in few and simple words.

Before three months had passed Rose Fleming and Harry Maylie were married in the village chnrch Which was henceforth to be the scene of the young clergyman's labors ; on the same day they entered into possession of their new and happy home.

Mrs. Maylie took up her abode with her son and daughter-in-law, to enjoy, during the tranquil re mainder of her days, the greatest felicity that age and worth can know — the contemplation of the hap piness of those on whom the warmest affections and teuderest cares of a well-spent life have been unceas ingly bestowed.

It appeared, on full and careful investigation, that if the wreck of property remaining in the custody of Monks (which had never prospered either in his hands or in those of his mother) were equally di vided between himself and Oliver, it would yield to each little more than three thousand pounds. By the provisions of his father's will Oliver would have been entitled to the whole; but Mr. Brownlow, un willing to deprive the eldest son of the opportunity of retrieving his former vices and pursuing an honest career, proposed this mode of distribution, to which his young charge joyfully acceded.

Monks, still bearing that assumed name, retired with his portion to a distant part of the New World, where, having quickly squandered it, he once more fell into his old courses, and, after undergoing a long confinement for some fresh act of fraud and knavery, at length sunk under an attack of his old disorder, and died in prison. As far from home died the chief remaining members of his friend Fagin's gang.

Mr. Brownlow adopted Oliver as his son. Remov ing with him and the old housekeeper to within a mile of the parsonage-house, where his dear friends resided, he gratified the only remaining wish of Oli ver's warm and earnest heart, and thus linked to gether a little society whose condition approached as nearly to one of perfect happiness as can ever be known in this changing world.

Soon after the marriage of the young people the worthy doctor returned to Chertsey, where, bereft of the presence of his old friends, he would have been

discontented, if his temperament had admitted of such a feeling, and would have turned quite peevish, if he had known how. For two or three months he contented himself with hinting that he feared the air began to disagree with him; then, finding that the place really no longer was, to him, what it had been, he settled his business on his assistant, took a bachelor's cottage outside the village of which his young friend was pastor, and instantaneously recov ered. Here he took to gardening, planting, fishing, carpentering, and various other pursuits of a similar kind — all undertaken with his characteristic im petuosity. In each and all he has since become fa mous throughout the neighborhood as a most pro found authority.

Before his removal he had managed to contract a strong friendship for Mr. Grimwig, which that eccen tric gentleman cordially reciprocated. He is accord ingly visited by Mr. Grimwig a great many times in the course of the year. On all such occasions Mr. Grimwig plants, fishes, and carpenters with great ardor; doing every thing in a very singular and un precedented manner, but always maintaining, with his favorite asseveration, that his mode is the right one. On Sundays he never fails to criticise the ser mon to the young clergyman's face, always inform ing Mr. Losberne, in strict confidence, afterward, that he considers it an excellent performance, but deems it as well not to say so. It is a standing and very favorite joke for Mr. Browulow to rally him on his old prophecy concerning Oliver, and to remind him of the night on which they sat with the watch be tween them, waiting his return; but Mr. Grimwig contends that he was right in the main, and, in proof thereof, remarks that Oliver did not come back after all; which always calls forth a laugh on his side, and increases his good-humor.

Mr. Noah Claypole, receiving a free pardon from the Crown in consequence of being admitted ap prover against Fagin, and considering his profession not altogether as safe an one as he could wish, was, for some little time, at a loss for the means of a liveli hood not burdened with too much work. After some consideration, he went into business as an Informer, in which calling he realizes a genteel subsistence. His plan is, to walk out once a Aveek during church-time, attended by Charlotte, in respectable attire. The lady faints away at the doors of charitable pub licans, and the gentleman being accommodated with threepenny-worth of brandy to restore her, lays an information next day, and pockets half the penalty. Sometimes Mr. Claypole faints himself, but the result is the same.

Mr. and Mrs. Bumble, deprived of their situations, were gradually reduced to great indigence and mis ery, and finally became paupers in that very same work-house in which they had once lorded it over others. Mr. Bumble has been heard to say that, in this reverse and degradation, he has not even spir its to be thankful for being separated from his wife.

As to Mr. Giles and Brittles, they still remain in their old posts, although the former is bald and the last-named boy quite gray. They sleep at the par-sonage, but divide their attentions so equally among its inmates, and Oliver and Mr. Browulow, and Mr.

SUPPLEMEXTARY.

Losberne, that to this day the villagers have never beeu able to discover to which establishment they properly belong.

Master Charles Bates, appalled by Sikes's crime, fell into a train of reflection whether an honest life was not, after all, the best. Arriving at the conclu sion that it certainly was, he turned his back upon the scenes of the past, resolved to amend it in some new sphere of action. He struggled hard, and suf fered much, for some time, but, having a contented disposition and a good purpose, succeeded in the end; and, from being a farmer's drudge, and a car rier's lad, he is now the merriest young grazier in all Northamptonshire.

And now the hand that traces these words falters, as it approaches the conclusion of its task, and would weave, for a little longer space, the thread of these adventures.

I vrould fain liuger yet with a few of those among whom I have so long moved, and share their hap piness by endeavoring to depict it. I would show fiose Maylie in all the bloom and grace of early womanhood, shedding on her secluded path in life soft and gentle light, that fell on all who trod it with her, and shone into their hearts. I would paiut her the life and joy of the fireside circle and the lively summer group; I would follow her through the sultry fields at noon, and hear the low tones of her sweet voice in the moonlit evening walk; I would watch her iu all her goodness and charity abroad, and the smiling, untiring discharge of do mestic duties at home; I would paint her and her dead sister's child happy in their love for one anoth er, and passing whole hours together in picturing the friends whom they had so sadly lost; I would

summon before me, once again, those joyous little faces that clustered round her knee, and listen to their merry prattle; I would recall the tones of that clear laugh, and conjure up the sympathizing tear that glistened in the soft blue eye. These, and a thousand looks and smiles, and turns of thought and speech—I would fain recall them every one.

How Mr. Browulow \veut on, from day to day, fill ing the mind of his adopted child with stores of knowledge, and becoming attached to him more and more as his nature developed itself and showed the thriving seeds of all he wished him to become—how he traced in him new traits of his early friend, that awakened in his own bosom old remembrances, mel ancholy and yet sweet and soothing—how the two orphans, tried by adversity, remembered its lessens in mercy to others, and mutual love, and fervent thanks to Him who had protected and preserved them—these are all matters which need not to be told. I have said that they were truly happy; and without strong aifection and humanity of heart, and gratitude to that Being whose code is Mercy, and whose great attribute is Benevolence to all things that breathe, happiness can never be attained.

Within the altar of the old village church there stands a white marble tablet, which bears as yet but one word—" AGNES." There is no coffin in that tomb; and may it be many, many years, before an other name is placed above it! But if the spirits of the Dead ever come back to earth to visit spots hal lowed by the love—the love beyond the grave—of those whom they knew in life, I believe that the shade of Agnes sometimes hovers round that solemn nook. I believe it none the less because that nook is in a church, and she was weak and erring.

THE END.

Made in the USA
Columbia, SC
13 October 2023

24377073R00150